LEW WALLACE

BEN-HUR

David McKay Company, Inc. New York

Library of Congress Cataloging in Publication Data

Wallace, Lewis, 1827–1905.
  Ben-Hur.

  SUMMARY: A wealthy young jew and his family
experiencing changing fortunes under Roman tyranny
are affected by the life and teachings of a
Nazarene named Jesus Christ.
    1. Jesus Christ—Juvenile fiction. [1. Jesus
Christ—Fiction] I. King, Harold, 1945–
II. Title.
PZ7.W1584Be7   [Fic]   76-44198
ISBN 0-679-20392-3

Printed in Great Britain

Illustrations by Harold King. Based on a concept by René Simmen. Historical Consultant: Professor D. E. Strong, M.A.,
D. Phil., F. S. A., Department of the Archaeology of the Roman Provinces, University of London.

CONTENTS

LIST OF ILLUSTRATIONS

63 Studded iron chest for storing valuable objects or money

65 Roman tripod table, used as a sidetable during banquets

66 Advertisement for A GLADIATORIAL CONTEST. It reads: "The Aedile Ausus Suettius Cerius' gladiator troop will fight in Pompeii on the day before the Kalends of June (31 May). There will be beast baiting and the *vela* (canopies) will be stretched."

69 Strigils and oil flask. Strigils were used by the Romans to scrape the sweat off their skin after their baths. The edge of the strigil was anointed with oil to soften its effect on the skin. People with delicate skins used sponges rather than strigils.

70 Roman drinking cup, decorated with skeletons

74 Scourge or *flagrum*. This vicious instrument of punishment had thongs of ox-hide which were knotted with bones or heavy discs of bronze. Apart from its use on slaves and criminals, it was sometimes the chosen weapon in gladiatorial contests.

77 Pottery vessels for wine and corn of the 1st century

78 1st century Roman army altar from Jerusalem

80 Herod's Temple in Jerusalem – a tentative reconstruction

85 Holy water dispenser used in some Roman temples

86 Centurion's sword, with decorated silver-gilt, gilt-bronze and wooden scabbard (25 ins)

87 Legionary's dagger and scabbard (17 ins). The scabbard is of iron with leather infilling.

88 Terracotta camel, with two figures in a howdah

92 Roman and Palestinian carpenter's tools

96 Jewish costumes of the 1st century AD. Jews usually wore a prayer shawl with tassels at its ends which distinguished them from the rest of the population.

97 Tallith – a scarf worn by Jews, especially at prayer

99 Toilet accessories of silver, bronze and ivory

100 Roman soldier's boot (*caliga*). This was worn by common soldiers and officers up to the rank of centurion. The sole was heavily studded with hobnails.

103 Tear glasses

105 Instructions for making arrows, from 1st century patterns

107 Synagogue at Capernaum (1st century AD). Jesus preached here. Women sat in the gallery round the central hall (*atrium*); men on seats on the ground floor.

109 Roman scent bottles

110 Mirror

112 Plan of typical catacomb; the remains of the bodies were placed in the semi-circular niches in the walls. In the early days of the Roman Empire corpses were almost universally burnt and their bones and ashes would have been deposited in the catacombs. But by the 4th century the general practice was burial without burning.

CHARTS (numbers indicate the page next to the charts)

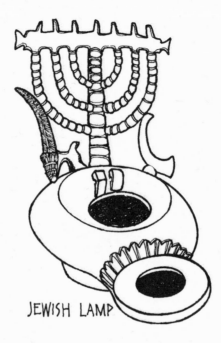

JEWISH LAMP

BOOK ONE

THE RIDER ON THE DROMEDARY

The Jebel es Zubleh is a mountain fifty miles and more in length, and so narrow that its tracery on the map gives it a likeness to a caterpillar crawling from the south to the north. Standing on its red-and-white cliffs, and looking off under the path of the rising sun, one sees only the Desert of Arabia, where the east winds, so hateful to the vine-growers of Jericho, have kept their playgrounds since the beginning. Its feet are well covered by sands tossed from the Euphrates, there to lie; for the mountain is a wall to the pasture-lands of Moab and Ammon on the west – lands which else had been of the desert a part.

The Arab has impressed his language upon everything south and east of Judea; so, in his tongue, the old Jebel is the parent of numberless wadies, which, intersecting the Roman road, run their furrows, deepening as they go, to pass the torrents of the rainy season into the Jordan, or their last receptacle, the Dead Sea. Out of one of these wadies a traveller passed, going to the table-lands of the desert.

Judged by his appearance, he was quite forty-five years old. His beard, once of the deepest black, flowing broadly over his breast, was streaked with white. His face was brown as a parched coffee-berry, and so hidden by a red kufiyeh (as the kerchief of the head is at this day called by the children of the desert) as to be but in part visible. Now and then he raised his eyes, and they were large and dark. He was clad in the flowing garments so universal in the East; but their style may not be described more particularly, for he sat under a miniature tent, and rode a great white dromedary.

For two hours the dromedary swung forward, keeping the trot steadily and the line due east. In that time the traveller never changed his position, nor looked to the right or left. On the desert distance is not measured by miles or leagues, but by the saat, or hour, and the manzil, or halt: three and a half leagues fill the former, fifteen or twenty-five the latter; but they are the rates for the common camel. A carrier of the genuine Syrian stock can make three leagues easily. At full speed he overtakes the ordinary winds. As one of the results of the rapid advance, the face of the landscape underwent a change. The Jebel stretched along the western horizon like a pale-blue ribbon. A tell, or hummock of clay and cemented sand, arose here and there. Now and then basaltic stones lifted their round crowns, outposts of the mountain against the forces of the plain; all else, however, was sand, sometimes smooth as the beaten beach, then heaped in rolling ridges; here chopped waves, there long swells. So, too, the condition of the atmosphere changed. The sun, high risen, had drunk his fill of dew and mist, and warmed the breeze that kissed the wanderer under the awning; far and near he was tinting the earth with faint milk-whiteness, and shimmering all the sky.

Two hours more passed without rest or deviation from the course. Vegetation entirely ceased. The sand, so crusted on the surface that it broke into rattling flakes at every step, held undisputed sway.

Exactly at noon the dromedary, of its own will, stopped, and uttered the cry or moan, peculiarly piteous, by which its kind always protest against an overload, and sometimes crave attention and rest. The master thereupon bestirred himself, waking, as it were, from sleep. He threw the curtains of the houdah up, looked at the sun, surveyed the country on every side long and carefully, as if to identify an appointed place. Satisfied with the inspection, he drew a deep breath and nodded, much as to say "At last, at last!" A moment after, he crossed his hands upon his breast, bowed his head, and prayed silently. The pious duty done, he prepared to dismount. From his throat proceeded the sound heard doubtless by the favourite camels of Job – *Ikh! ikh!* – the signal to kneel. Slowly the animal obeyed, grunting the while. The rider then put his foot upon the slender neck and stepped upon the sand.

9

THE MEETING OF
THE THREE WISE MEN

The man, as now revealed, was of admirable proportions, not so tall as powerful. Loosening the silken rope which held the kufiyeh on his head, he brushed the fringed folds back until his face was bare – a strong face, almost negro in colour; yet the low, broad forehead, aquiline nose, the outer corners of the eyes turned slightly upward, the hair profuse, straight, harsh, of metallic lustre, and falling to the shoulder in many plaits, were signs of origin impossible to disguise. So looked the Pharaohs and the later Ptolemies; so looked Mizraim, father of the Egyptian race. He wore the kamis, a white cotton shirt, tight-sleeved, open in front, extending to the ankles and embroidered down the collar and breast, over which was thrown a brown woollen cloak, now, as in all probability it was then, called the aba, an outer garment with long skirt and short sleeves, lined inside with stuff of mixed cotton and silk, edged all round with a margin of clouded yellow. His feet were protected by sandals, attached by thongs of soft leather. A sash held the kamis to his waist.

The traveller's limbs were numb, for the ride had been long and wearisome; so he rubbed his hands and stamped his feet, and walked round the faithful servant, whose lustrous eyes were closing in calm content with the cud he had already found. Often, while making the circuit, he paused, and, shading his eyes with his hands, examined the desert to the extremest verge of vision; and always, when the survey was ended, his face clouded with disappointment, slight, but enough to advise a shrewd spectator that he was expecting company.

However disappointed, there could be little doubt of the stranger's confidence in the coming of the expected company. In token thereof, he went first to the litter, and, from the cot or box opposite the one he had occupied in coming, produced a sponge and a small gurglet of water, with which he washed the eyes, face, and nostrils of the camel; that done, from the same depository he drew a circular cloth, red-and-white-striped, a bundle of rods, and a stout cane. The latter, after some manipulation, proved to be a cunning device of lesser joints, one within another, which, when united together, formed a centre pole higher than his head. When the pole was planted, and the rods set around it, he spread the cloth over them, and was literally at home.

All was now ready. He stepped out: lo! in the east a dark speck on the face of the desert. He stood as if rooted to the ground; his eyes dilated; his flesh crept chilly, as if touched by something supernatural. The speck grew; became large as a hand; at length assumed defined proportions. A little later, full into view swung a duplication of his own dromedary, tall and white, and bearing a houdah, the travelling litter of Hindustan. Then the Egyptian crossed his hands upon his breast, and looked to heaven.

"God only is great!" he exclaimed, his eyes full of tears, his soul in awe.

The stranger drew nigh – at last stopped. He beheld the kneeling camel, the tent, and the man standing prayerfully at the door. He crossed his hands, bent his head, and prayed silently; after which, in a little while, he stepped from his camel's neck to the sand, and advanced towards the Egyptian, as did the Egyptian towards him. A moment they looked at each other; then they embraced.

"Peace be with thee, O servant of the true God!" the stranger said.

"And to thee, O brother of the true faith! – to thee peace and welcome," the Egyptian replied, with fervour.

The new-comer was tall and gaunt, with lean face, sunken eyes, white hair and beard, and a complexion between the hue of cinnamon and bronze. The air of the man was high, stately, severe. Only in his eyes was there proof of humanity; when he lifted his face from the Egyptian's breast, they were glistening with tears.

They looked to the north, where, already plain to view, a third camel, of the whiteness of the others, came careening like a ship. They waited, standing together – waited until the new-comer arrived, dismounted, and advanced towards them.

"Peace to you, O my brother!" he said, while embracing the Hindu.

And the Hindu answered, "God's will be done!"

The last comer was all unlike his friends; his frame was slighter; his complexion white; a mass of waving light hair was a perfect crown for his small but beautiful head; the warmth of his dark-blue eyes certified a delicate mind, and a cordial, brave nature. He was bare-headed and unarmed. Under the folds of the Tyrian blanket which he wore with unconscious grace appeared a tunic, short-sleeved and low-necked, gathered to the waist by a band, and reaching nearly to the knee; leaving the neck, arms, and legs bare. No need to tell the student from what kindred he was sprung; if he came not himself from the groves of Athene, his ancestry did.

When his arms fell from the Egyptian, the latter said, with a tremulous voice, "The Spirit brought me first, wherefore I know myself chosen to be the servant of my brethren. The tent is set, and the bread is ready for the breaking. Let me perform my office."

Taking each by the hand, he led them within, and removed their sandals and washed their feet, and he poured water upon their hands, and he dried them with napkins.

He took them to the repast, and seated them so that they faced each other. Simultaneously their heads bent forward, their hands crossed upon their breasts, and, speaking together, they said aloud this simple grace:

"Father of all – God! – what we have here is of Thee. Take our thanks and bless us, that we may continue to do Thy will."

With the last word they raised their eyes, and looked at each other in wonder. Each had spoken in a language never before heard by the others; yet each understood perfectly what was said. Their souls filled with divine emotion; for by the miracle they recognized the Divine Presence.

GASPAR THE GREEK

To speak in the style of the period, the meeting just described took place in the year of Rome 747. The month was December, and winter reigned over all the regions east of the Mediterranean.

"To a wayfarer in a strange land nothing is so sweet as to hear his name on the tongue of a friend," said the Egyptian, who assumed to be president of the repast. "Before us lie many days of companionship. It is time we knew each other. So, if it be agreeable, he who came last shall be first to speak."

Then, slowly at first, like one watchful of himself, the Greek began:

"What I have to tell, my brethren, is so strange that I hardly know where to begin or what I may with propriety speak. Far to the west of this there is a land which may never be forgotten; if only because the world is too much its debtor, and because the indebtedness is for things that bring to men their purest pleasures. The land I speak of is Greece. I am Gaspar, son of Cleanthes the Athenian.

"My people," he continued, "were given wholly to study, and from them I derived the same passion. It happens that two of our philosophers, the very greatest of the many, teach, one the doctrine of a Soul in every man, and its Immortality; the other the doctrine of One God, infinitely just. From the multitude of subjects about which the schools were disputing, I separated them, as alone worth the labour of solution; for I thought there was a relation between God and the soul as yet unknown. On this theme the mind can reason to a point, a dead, impassable wall; arrived there, all that remains is to stand and cry aloud for help. So I did; but no voice came to me over the wall. In despair, I tore myself from the cities and the schools."

At these words a grave smile of approval lighted the gaunt face of the Hindu.

"In the northern part of my country – in Thessaly," the Greek proceeded to say, "there is a mountain famous as the home of the gods, where Theus, whom my countrymen believe supreme, has his abode: Olympus is its name. Thither I betook myself. I found a cave in a hill where the mountain, coming from the west, bends to the south-east; there I dwelt, giving myself up to meditation – no, I gave myself up to waiting for what every breath was a prayer – for revelation. One day I saw a man flung overboard from a ship sailing by. He swam ashore. I received and took care of him. He was a Jew, learned in the history and laws of his people; and from him I came to know that the God of my prayers did indeed exist, and had been for ages their law-maker, ruler, and king. What was that but the Revelation I dreamed of? The man so sent to me told me more. He said the prophets who, in the ages which followed the first revelation, walked and talked with God, declared He would come again. He gave me the names of the prophets, and from the sacred books quoted their very language. He told me, further, that the second coming was at hand – was looked for momentarily in Jerusalem.

"When the Jew was gone, and I was alone again, I chastened my soul with a new prayer – that I might be permitted to see the King when He was come, and worship Him. One night I sat by the door of my cave trying to get nearer the mysteries of my existence, knowing which is to know God; suddenly, on the sea below me, or rather in the darkness that covered its face, I saw a star begin to burn; slowly it arose and drew nigh, and stood over the hill and above my door, so that its light shone full upon me. I fell down, and slept, and in my dream I heard a voice say.

"'O Gaspar! Thy faith hath conquered! Blessed art thou! With two others, come from the uttermost parts of the earth, thou shalt see Him that is promised, and be a witness for Him, and the occasion of testimony in His behalf. In the morning arise, and go meet them, and keep trust in the Spirit that shall guide thee.'

"And in the morning I awoke with the Spirit as a light within me surpassing that of the sun. I put off my hermit's garb, and dressed myself as of old. From a hiding-place I took the treasure which I had brought from the city. A ship went sailing past. I hailed it, was taken aboard, and landed at Antioch. There I bought the camel and his furniture. Through the gardens and orchards that enamel the banks of the Orontes, I journeyed to Emesa, Damascus, Bostra, and Philadelphia; thence hither. And so, O brethren, you have my story. Let me now listen to you."

MELCHIOR THE HINDU

The Egyptian and the Hindu looked at each other; the former waved his hand; the latter bowed, and began:

"Our brother has spoken well. May my words be as wise."

He broke off, reflected a moment, then resumed:

"You may know me, brethren, by the name of Melchior. I speak to you in a language which, if not the oldest in the world, was at least the soonest to be reduced to letters – I mean the Sanskrit of India. I am a Hindu by birth.

"Brahma is said to have been the author of our race; which, in course of creation, he divided into four castes. First, he peopled the worlds below and the heavens above; next, he made the earth ready for terrestrial spirits; then from his mouth proceeded the Brahman caste, nearest in likeness to himself, highest and noblest, sole teachers of the Vedas, which at the same time flowed from his lips in finished state, perfect in all useful knowledge. From his arms next issued the Kshatriya, or warriors; from his breast, the seat of life, came the Vaisya, or producers – shepherds, farmers, merchants; from his foot, in sign of degradation, sprang the Sudra, or serviles, doomed to menial duties for the other classes – serfs, domestics, labourers, artisans.

SHIVA

11

"I was born a Brahman. My life, consequently, was ordered down to its last act, its last hour. My first draught of nourishment; the giving me my compound name; taking me out the first time to see the sun; investing me with the triple thread by which I became one of the twice-born; my induction into the first order – were all celebrated with sacred texts and rigid ceremonies.

"The part of a Brahman's life called the first order is his student life. When I was ready to enter the second order – that is to say, when I was ready to marry and become a householder – I questioned everything, even Brahm; I was a heretic.

"In my extremity I looked for a solitude in which to hide from all but God. I followed the Ganges to its source, far up in the Himalayas. Through gorges, over cliffs, across glaciers, by peaks that seemed star high, I made my way to the Lang Tso, a lake of marvellous beauty, asleep at the feet of the Tise Gangri, the Gurla, and the Kailas Parbot, giants which flaunt their crowns of snow everlastingly in the face of the sun. There, in the centre of the earth; where the Indus, Ganges, and Brahmapootra rise to run their different courses; I went to abide alone with God, praying, fasting, waiting for death."

Again the voice fell, and the bony hands met in a fervent clasp.

"One night I walked by the shores of the lake, and spoke to the listening silence, 'When will God come and claim His own? Is there to be no redemption?' Suddenly a light began to glow tremulously out on the water; soon a star arose, and moved towards me, and stood overoverhead. The brightness stunned me. While I lay upon the ground, I heard a voice of infinite sweetness say, 'Thy love hath conquered. Blessed art thou, O son of India! The redemption is at hand. With two others, from far quarters of the earth, thou shalt see the Redeemer, and be a witness that He hath come. In the morning arise, and go meet them; and put all they trust in the Spirit which shall guide thee.'

"And from that time the light has stayed with me; so I knew it was the visible presence of the Spirit. Alone I travelled, fearless, for the Spirit was with me, and is with me yet. What glory is ours, O brethren! We are to see the Redeemer – to speak to Him – to worship Him! I am done."

BALTHASAR THE EGYPTIAN

The Greek broke forth in expressions of joy and congratulations; after which the Egyptian said, with characteristic gravity:

"I salute you, my brother. You have suffered much, and I rejoice in your triumph. If you are both pleased to hear me, I will now tell you who I am, and how I came to be called.

"You each spoke particularly of your countries; in that there was a great object which I will explain; but to make the interpretation complete, let me first speak of myself and my people. I am Balthasar the Egyptian."

The last words were spoken quietly, but with so much dignity that both listeners bowed to the speaker.

"There are many distinctions I might claim for my race," he continued; "but I will content myself with one. History began with us. We were the first to perpetuate events by records kept. So we have no traditions; and instead of poetry, we offer you certainty."

From a gurglet of water near by the Egyptian took a draught, and proceeded:

"I was born at Alexandria, a prince and a priest, and had the education usual to my class. But very early I became discontented. Part of the faith imposed was that after death, upon the destruction of the body, the soul at once began its former progression from the lowest up to humanity, the highest and last existence; and that without reference to conduct in the mortal life. When I heard of the Persian's Realm of Light, his Paradise across the bridge Chinevat, where only the good go, the thought haunted me; insomuch that in the day, as in the night, I brooded over the comparative ideas Eternal Transmigration and Eternal Life in Heaven. If, as my teacher taught, God was just, why was there no distinction between the good and the bad? At length it became clear to me, a certainty, a corollary of the law to which I reduced pure religion, that death was only the point of separation at which the wicked are left or lost, and the faithful rise to a higher life; not the nirvana of Buddha, or the negative rest of Brahma, O Melchior; nor the better condition in hell, which is

all of Heaven allowed by the Olympic faith, O Gaspar; but life – life active, joyous, everlasting – *Life with God!* The discovery led to another inquiry. Why should the Truth be longer kept a secret for the selfish solace of the priesthood? The reason for the suppression was gone. Philosophy had at least brought us toleration. In Egypt we had Rome instead of Rameses. One day, in the Brucheium, the most splendid and crowded quarter of Alexandria, I arose and preached. The East and West contributed to my audience. Students going to the Library, priests from the Serapeion, idlers from the Museum, patrons of the racecourse, countrymen from the Rhacotis – a multitude – stopped to hear me. I preached God, the Soul, Right and Wrong, and Heaven, the reward of a virtuous life. You, O Melchior, were stoned. My auditors first wondered, then laughed. I tried again; they pelted me with epigrams, covered my God with ridicule, and darkened my Heaven with mockery. Not to linger needlessly, I fell before them."

The Hindu here drew a long sigh, as he said, "The enemy of man is man, my brother."

Balthasar lapsed into silence.

"I gave much thought to finding the cause of my failure, and at last succeeded," he said, upon beginning again. "Up the river, a day's journey from the city, there is a village of herdsmen and gardeners. I took a boat and went there. In the evening I called the people together, men and women, the poorest of the poor. I preached to them exactly as I had preached in the Brucheium. They did not laugh. Next evening I spoke again, and they believed and rejoiced, and carried the news abroad. From that day, O brethren, I travelled up and down the Nile, in the villages, and to all the tribes, preaching One God, a righteous life, and reward in Heaven. I have done good – it does not become me to say how much. I also know that part of the world to be ripe for the reception of Him we go to find."

A flush suffused the swarthy cheek of the speaker; but he overcame the feeling, and continued:

"Brethren, the world is now in the condition that, the reformer must have a more than human sanction; he must not merely come in God's name, he must have the proofs subject to his word; he must demonstrate all he says, even God. And who in this age can marry the faith of men to such a point but God Himself? To redeem the race – I do not mean to destroy it – to *redeem* the race, He must make Himself once more manifest; *He must come in person.*"

Intense emotion seized the three.

"Are we not going to find Him?" exclaimed the Greek.

"You understand why I failed in the attempt to organize," said the Egyptian, when the spell was passed. "I had not the sanction. To know that my work must be lost made me intolerably wretched. For a year and more the mountain gave me a home. The fruit of the palm fed my body, prayer my spirit. One night I walked in the orchard close by the little sea. 'The world is dying. When wilt Thou come? Why may I not see the redemption, O God?' So I prayed. The glassy water was sparkling with stars. One of them seemed to leave its place, and rise to the surface, where it became a brilliancy burning to the eyes. Then it moved towards me, and stood over my head, apparently in hand's reach. I fell down and hid my face. A voice, not of the earth, said, 'Thy good works have conquered. Blessed art thou, O son of Mizraim! The redemption cometh. With two others, from the remotenesses of the world, thou shalt see the Saviour, and testify for Him. In the morning arise, and go meet them. And when ye have all come to the holy city of Jerusalem, ask of the people, Where is He that is born King of the Jews? for we have seen His star in the East, and are sent to worship Him. Put all thy trust in the Spirit, which will guide thee.' "

A little while after, the tent was struck, and the friends mounted, and set out single file, led by the Egyptian.

By-and-by the moon came up. And as the three tall, white figures sped, with soundless tread, through the opalescent light, they appeared like spectres flying from hateful shadows. Suddenly, in the air before them, not farther up than a low hill-top, flared a lambent-flame; as they looked at it, the apparition contracted into a focus of dazzling lustre. Their hearts beat fast; their souls thrilled; and they shouted as with one voice, "The Star! the Star! God is with us!"

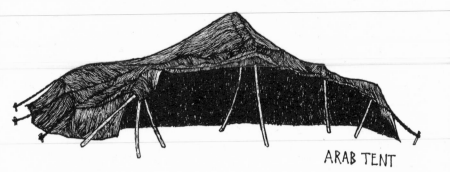

ARAB TENT

THE JOPPA GATE

In an aperture of the western wall of Jerusalem hang the "oaken valves" called the Bethlehem or Joppa Gate. The area outside of them is one of the notable places of the city. In Solomon's day there was great traffic at the locality, shared in by traders from Egypt, and the rich dealers from Tyre and Sidon. Nearly three thousand years have passed, and yet a kind of commerce clings to the spot. A pilgrim wanting a pin or a pistol, a cucumber or a camel, a house or a horse, a loan or a lentil, a date or a dragoman, a melon or a man, a dove or a donkey, has only to inquire for the article at the Joppa Gate. Sometimes the scene is quite animated, and then it suggests, What a place the old market must have been in the days of Herod the Builder! And to that period and that market the reader is now to be transferred.

The scene is at first one of utter confusion – confusion of action, sounds, colours, and things. It is especially so in the lane and court. The ground there is paved with broad unshaped flags, from which each cry and jar and hoof-stamp arises to swell the medley that rings and roars up between the solid impending walls. A little mixing with the throng, however, a little familiarity with the business going on, will make analysis possible.

Here stands a donkey, dozing under panniers full of lentils, beans, onions, and cucumbers, brought fresh from the gardens and terraces of Galilee. When not engaged in serving customers, the master, in a voice which only the initiated can understand, cries his stock. Nothing can be simpler than his costume – sandals, and an unbleached, undyed blanket, crossed over one shoulder and girt round the waist. Nearby, and far more imposing and grotesque, though scarcely as patient as the donkey, kneels a camel, raw-boned, rough, and grey, with long shaggy tufts of fox-coloured hair under its throat, neck, and body, and a load of boxes and baskets curiously arranged upon an enormous saddle. The owner is an Egyptian, small, lithe, and of a complexion which has borrowed a good deal from the dust of the roads and the sands of the desert. He wears a faded tarbooshe, a loose gown, sleeveless, unbelted, and dropping from the neck to the knee. His feet are bare. The camel, restless under the load, groans and occasionally shows his teeth; but the man paces indifferently to and fro, holding the driving-strap, and all the time advertising his fruits fresh from the orchards of the Kedron – grapes, dates, figs, apples, and pomegranates.

At the corner where the lane opens out into the court, some women sit with their backs against the grey stones of the wall. Their dress is that common to the humbler classes of the country – a linen frock extending the full length of the person, loosely gathered at the waist; and a veil or wimple, broad enough, after covering the head, to wrap the shoulders. Their merchandise is contained in a number of earthen jars, such as are still used in the East for bringing water from the wells, and some leathern bottles. Among the jars and bottles, rolling upon the stony floor, regardless of the crowd and cold, often in danger but never hurt, play half a dozen half-naked children; their brown bodies, jetty eyes, and thick black hair attesting the blood of Israel. Sometimes, from under the wimples, the mothers look up, and in the vernacular modestly bespeak their trade: in the bottles "honey of grapes," in the jars "strong drink." Their entreaties are usually lost in the general uproar, and they fare illy against the many competitors: brawny fellows with bare legs, dirty tunics, and long beards, going about with bottles lashed to their backs, and shouting, "Honey of wine! Grapes of En-Gedi!" When a customer halts one of them, round comes the bottle, and, upon lifting the thumb from the nozzle, out into the ready cup gushes the deep-red blood of the luscious berry.

Scarcely less blatant are the dealers in birds – doves, ducks, and frequently the singing bulbul, or nightingale, most frequently pigeons; and buyers, receiving them from the nets, seldom fail to think of the perilous life of the catchers, bold climbers of the cliffs – now hanging with hand and foot to the face of the crag, now swinging in a basket far down the mountain fissure.

Blent with pedlars of jewellery – sharp men cloaked in scarlet and blue, top-heavy under prodigious white turbans, and fully conscious of the power there is in the lustre of a ribbon and the incisive gleam of gold, whether in bracelet or necklace, or in rings for the finger or the nose – and with pedlars of household utensils, and with dealers in wearing apparel, and with retailers of unguents for anointing the person, and with hucksters of all articles, fanciful as well as of need, hither and thither, tugging at halters and ropes, now screaming, now coaxing, toil the vendors of animals – donkeys, horses, calves, sheep, bleating kids, and awkward camels – animals of every kind except the outlawed swine. All these are there; not singly, as described, but many times repeated; not in one place, but everywhere in the market.

Turning from this scene in the lane and court, this glance at the sellers and their commodities, the reader has need to give attention, in the next place, to visitors and buyers, for which the best studies will be found outside the gates, where the spectacle is quite as varied and animated; indeed, it may be more so, for there are superadded the effects of tent, booth, and sook, greater space, larger crowd, more unqualified freedom, and the glory of the Eastern sunshine.

ENTERING JERUSALEM

It was the third hour of the day, and many of the people had gone away, yet the press continued without apparent abatement. Of the new-comers, there was a group over by the south wall, consisting of a man, a woman, and a donkey, which requires extended notice.

The man stood by the animal's head, holding a leading-strap, and leaning upon a stick which seemed to have been chosen for the double purpose of goad and staff. His dress was like that of the ordinary Jews around him, except that it had an appearance of newness. He looked around him with the half-curious, half-vacant stare of a stranger and provincial.

The donkey ate leisurely from an armful of green grass, of which there was an abundance in the market. In its sleepy content, the brute did not admit of disturbance from the bustle and clamour about; no more was it mindful of the woman sitting upon its back in a cushioned pillion. An outer robe of dull woollen stuff completely covered her person, while a white wimple veiled her head and neck.

At length the man was accosted.

"Are you not Joseph of Nazareth?"

The speaker was standing close by.

"I am so called," answered Joseph, turning gravely around. "And you – ah, peace be unto you! my friend, Rabbi Samuel!"

"The same I give back to you." The Rabbi paused, looking at the woman, then added, "To you and unto your house, and all your helpers, be peace."

At this point the wimple was drawn aside, and for an instant the whole face of the woman was exposed. The eyes of the Rabbi wandered that way, and he had time to see a countenance of rare beauty, kindled by a look of intense interest; then a blush overspread her cheeks and brow, and the veil was returned to its place.

"Your daughter is comely," he said, speaking lower.

"She is not my daughter," Joseph answered.

The curiosity of the Rabbi was aroused; seeing which, the Nazarene hastened to say further, "She is the child of Joachim and Anna of Bethlehem, of whom you have at least heard, for they were of great repute——"

"Yes," remarked the Rabbi, deferentially, "I know them. They were lineally descended from David. I knew them well."

"Well, they are dead now," the Nazarene proceeded. "They died in Nazareth. Joachim was not rich, yet he left a house and garden to be divided between his daughters Marian and Mary. This is one of them; and to save her portion of the property, the law required her to marry her next of kin. She is now my wife."

"And you were——

"Her uncle."

"Yes, yes! And as you were both born in Bethlehem, the Roman compels you to take her there with you to be also counted."

The Rabbi clasped his hands, and looked indignantly to heaven, exclaiming, "The God of Israel still lives! The vengeance is His!"

With that he turned and abruptly departed. A stranger near by, observing Joseph's amazement, said quietly, "Rabbi Samuel is a zealot. Judas himself is not more fierce."

In another hour the party passed out the gate, and, turning to the left, took the road to Bethlehem. The descent into the valley of Hinnom was quite broken, garnished here and there with straggling wild olive-trees. Carefully, tenderly, the Nazarene walked by the woman's side, leading-strap in hand.

She was not more than fifteen. Her form, voice, and manner belonged to the period of transition from girlhood. Her face was perfectly oval, her complexion more pale than fair. The nose was faultless; the lips slightly parted, were full and ripe, giving to the lines of the mouth warmth, tenderness, and trust; the eyes were blue and large, and shaded by drooping lids and long lashes; and, in harmony with all, a flood of golden hair, in the style permitted to Jewish brides, fell unconfined down her back to the pillion on which she sat. The throat and neck had the downy softness sometimes seen, which leaves the artist in doubt whether it is an effect of contour or colour. To these charms of feature and person were added others more indefinable – an air of purity which only the soul can impart, and of abstraction natural to such as think much of things impalpable. Often, with trembling lips, she raised her eyes to heaven, itself not more deeply blue; often she crossed her hands upon her breast, as in adoration and prayer; often she raised her head like one listening eagerly for a calling voice.

So they skirted the great plain, and at length reached the elevation Mar Elias; from which, across a valley, they beheld Bethlehem, the old, old House of Bread, its white walls crowning a ridge, and shining above the brown scumbling of leafless orchards. They paused there and rested, while Joseph pointed out the places of sacred renown; then they went down into the valley to the well which was the scene of one of the marvellous exploits of David's strong men. The narrow space was crowded with people and animals. A fear came upon Joseph – a fear lest, if the town were so thronged, there might not be house-room for the gentle Mary. Without delay, he hurried on, past the pillar of stone marking the tomb of Rachel, up the gardened slope, saluting none of the many persons he met on the way, until he stopped before the portal of the khan that then stood outside the village gates, near a junction of roads.

ASS WITH PANNIERS

THE SEARCH FOR A LODGING

To understand thoroughly what happened to the Nazarene at the khan, the reader must be reminded that Eastern inns were different from the inns of the Western world. They were called khans, from the Persian, and, in simplest form, were fenced enclosures, without house or shed, often without a gate or entrance. Their sites were chosen with reference to shade, defence, or water. Such were the inns that sheltered Jacob when he went to seek a wife in Padan-Aram.

The singular management of these hostelries was the feature likely to strike a Western mind with most force. There was no host or hostess; no clerk, cook, or kitchen; a steward at the gate was all the assertion of government or proprietorship anywhere visible. Strangers arriving stayed at will without rendering account. A consequence of the system was that whoever came had to bring his food and culinary outfit with him, or buy them of dealers in the khan. The same rule held good as to his bed and bedding, and forage for his beasts. Water, rest, shelter, and protection were all he looked for from the proprietor, and they were gratuities. The peace of synagogues was sometimes broken by brawling disputants, but that of the khans never.

The khan at Bethlehem, before which Joseph and his wife stopped, was a good specimen of its class, being neither very primitive nor very princely. The building was purely Oriental; that is to say, a quadrangular block of rough stones, one storey high, flat-roofed, externally unbroken by a window, and with but one principal entrance – a doorway, which was also a gateway, on the eastern side or front. The road ran by the door so near that the chalk dust half covered the lintel. A fence of flat rocks, beginning at the north-eastern corner of the pile, extended many yards down the slope to a point from whence it swept westwardly to a limestone bluff; making what was in the highest degree essential to a respectable khan – a safe enclosure for animals.

In a village like Bethlehem, as there was but one sheik, there could not well be more than one khan; and, though born in the place, the Nazarene, from

long residence elsewhere, had no claim to hospitality in the town. So, before he drew nigh the great house, while he was yet climbing the slope, in the steep places toiling to hasten the donkey, the fear that he might not find accommodations in the khan became a painful anxiety; for he found the road thronged with men and boys, who, with great ado, were taking their cattle, horses, and camels to and from the valley, some to water, some to the neighbouring caves. And when he was come close by, his alarm was not allayed by the discovery of a crowd investing the door of the establishment, while the enclosure adjoining, broad as it was, seemed already full.

"We cannot reach the door," Joseph said, in his slow way "Let us stop here, and learn, if we can, what has happened."

The keeper sat on a great cedar block outside the gate. Against the wall behind him leaned a javelin. A dog squatted on the block by his side.

"The peace of Jehovah be with you," said Joseph, at last confronting the keeper.

"What you give, may you find again; and when found, be it many times multiplied to you and yours," returned the watchman, gravely, though without moving.

"I am a Bethlehemite," said Joseph, in his most deliberate way. "Is there not room for——"

"There is not."

"You may have heard of me – Joseph of Nazareth. This is the house of my fathers. I am of the line of David."

These words held the Nazarene's hope. If they failed him, further appeal was idle, even that of .the offer of many shekels.

The appeal was not without effect. The keeper of the gate slid down from the cedar block, and, laying his hand upon his beard, said respectfully: "Rabbi, I cannot tell you when this door first opened in welcome to the traveller, but it was more than a thousand years ago; and in all that time there is no known instance of a good man turned away, save when there was no room to rest him in. If it has been so with the stranger, just cause must the steward have who says no to one of the line of David. Wherefore, I salute you again; and, if you care to go with me, I will show you that there is not a lodging-place left in the house; neither in the chambers, nor in the lewens, nor in the court – not even on the roof.''

Still Joseph persisted.

"The court is large," he said.

"Yes, but it is heaped with cargoes – with bales of silk, and pockets of spices, and goods of every kind."

Then for a moment the face of the applicant lost its stolidity; the lustreless, staring eyes dropped. With some warmth he next said, "I do not care for myself, but I have with me my wife, and the night is cold – colder on these nights than in Nazareth. She cannot live in the open air. Is there not room in the town?"

"These people" – the keeper waved his hand to the throng before the door – "have all besought the town, and they report its accommodations all engaged."

Again Joseph studied the ground, saying, half to himself, "She is so young; if I make her bed on the hill the frosts will kill her."

Then he spoke to the keeper again:

"It may be you knew her parents, Joachim and Anna, once of Bethlehem, and, like myself, of the line of David."

"Yes, I knew them. They were good people. That was in my youth."

This time the keeper's eyes sought the ground in thought. Suddenly he raised his head.

"If I cannot make room for you," he said, "I cannot turn you away. Rabbi, I will do the best I can for you. How many are of your party?"

Joseph reflected, then replied, "My wife and a friend with his family, from Beth-Dagon, a little town over by Joppa; in all, six of us."

"Very well. You shall not lie out on the ridge. Bring your people, and hasten; for, when the sun goes down behind the mountain, you know the night comes quickly, and it is nearly there now."

"I give you the blessing of the houseless traveller; that of the sojourner will follow."

So saying, the Nazarene went back joyfully to Mary and the Beth-Dagonite. In a little while the latter brought up his family, the women mounted on donkeys. The wife was matronly, the daughters were images of what she must have been in youth; and as they drew nigh the door, the keeper knew them to be of the humble class.

"This is she of whom I spoke," said the Nazarene; "and these are our friends."

Mary's veil was raised.

"Blue eyes and hair of gold," muttered the steward to himself, seeing but her. "So looked the young king when he went to sing before Saul."

Then he took the leading-strap from Joseph, and said to Mary, "Peace to you, O daughter of David!" Then to the others, "Peace to you all!" Then to Joseph, "Rabbi, follow me."

The party were conducted into a wide passage paved with stone, from which they entered the court of the khan. To a stranger the scene would have been curious; but they noticed the lewens that yawned darkly upon them from all sides, and the court itself, only to remark how crowded they were. By a lane reserved in the stowage of the cargoes and thence by a passage similar to the one at the

CAMEL WITH WINE JARS

entrance, they emerged into the enclosure adjoining the house, and came upon camels, horses, and donkeys, tethered and dozing in close groups; among them were the keepers, men of many lands; and they, too, slept or kept silent watch. They went down the slope of the crowded yard slowly, for the dull carriers of the women had wills of their own. At length they turned into a path running towards the grey limestone bluff overlooking the khan on the west.

"We are going to the cave," said Joseph, laconically.

The guide lingered till Mary came to his side.

"The cave to which we are going," he said to her, "must have been a resort of

your ancestor David. From the field below us, and from the well down in the valley, he used to drive his flocks to it for safety; and afterwards, when he was king, he came back to the old house here for rest and health, bringing great trains of animals. The mangers yet remain as they were in his day. Better a bed upon the floor where he has slept than one in the courtyard or out by the roadside. Ah, here is the house before the cave!"

The building was low and narrow, projecting but a little from the rock to which it was joined at the rear, and wholly without a window. In its blank front there was a door, swung on enormous hinges and thickly daubed with ochreous clay. The wooden bolt of the lock was pushed back. Upon the opening of the door, the keeper called out:

"Come in!"

The guests entered, and stared about them. It became apparent immediately that the house was but a mask or covering for the mouth of a natural cave or grotto, probably forty feet long, nine or ten high, and twelve or fifteen in width. The light streamed through the doorway, over an uneven floor, falling upon piles of grain and fodder, and earthenware and household property, occupying the centre of the chamber. Along the sides were mangers, low enough for sheep, and built of stones laid in cement. There were no stalls or partitions of any kind. Dust and chaff yellowed the floor, filled all the crevices and hollows, and thickened the spider-webs, which dropped from the ceiling like bits of dirty linen; otherwise the place was cleanly, and, to appearance, as comfortable as any of the arched lewens of the khan proper. In fact, a cave was the model and first suggestion of the lewen.

"Come in," said the guide. "These piles upon the floor are for travellers like yourselves. Take what of them you need."

Then he spoke to Mary.

"Can you rest here?"

"The place is sanctified," she answered.

"I leave you then. Peace be with you!"

When he was gone, they busied themselves making the cave habitable.

A LIGHT AT MIDNIGHT

A mile and a half, it may be two miles, south-east of Bethlehem, there is a plain separated from the town by an intervening swell of the mountain. Besides being well sheltered from the north winds, the vale was covered with a growth of sycamore, dwarf-oak, and pine-trees, while in the glens and ravines adjoining there were thickets of olive and mulberry; all at this season of the year invaluable for the support of sheep, goats, and cattle, of which the wandering flocks consisted.

At the side farthest from the town, close under a bluff, there was an extensive mârâh, or sheepcote, ages old.

The day of the occurrences which occupy the preceding chapters, a number of shepherds, seeking fresh walks for their flocks, led them up to this plain; and from early morning the groves had been made ring with calls, and the blows of axes, the bleating of sheep and goats, the tinkling of bells, the lowing of cattle, and the barking of dogs. When the sun went down, they led the way to the mârâh, and by nightfall had everything safe in the field; then they kindled a fire down by the gate, partook of their humble supper, and sat down to rest and talk, leaving one on watch.

There were six of these men, omitting the watchman; and afterwhile they assembled in a group near the fire, some sitting, some lying prone. As they went bare-headed habitually, their hair stood out in thick, coarse, sunburnt shocks; their beard covered their throats, and fell in mats down the breast; mantles of the skin of kids and lambs, with the fleece on, wrapped them from neck to knee, leaving the arms exposed; broad belts girthed the rude garments to their waists; their sandals were of the coarsest quality; from their right shoulders hung scrips containing food and selected stones for slings, with which they were armed; on the ground near each one lay his crook, a symbol of his calling and a weapon of offence.

Such were the shepherds of Judea! In appearance, rough and savage as the gaunt dogs sitting with them around the blaze; in fact, simple-minded, tender-hearted; effects due, in part, to the primitive life they led, but chiefly to their constant care of things lovable and help-less.

While they talked, and before the first watch was over, one by one the shepherds went to sleep, each lying where he had sat.

The night, like most nights of the winter season in the hill country, was clear, crisp, and sparkling with stars. There was no wind. The atmosphere seemed never so pure, and the stillness was more than silence; it was a holy hush, a warning that heaven was stooping low to whisper some good thing to the listening earth.

By the gate, hugging his mantle close, the watchman walked; at times he stopped, attracted by a stir among the sleeping herds, or by a jackal's cry off on the mountain-side. The midnight was slow coming to him; but at last it came. His task was done; now for the dreamless sleep with which labour blesses its wearied children! He moved towards the fire, but paused; a light was breaking around him, soft and white, like the moon's. He waited breathlessly. The light deepened; things before invisible came to view; he saw the whole field, and all it sheltered. A chill sharper than that of the frosty air – a chill of fear – smote him. He looked up; the stars were gone; the light was dropping as from a window in the sky; as he looked, it became a splendour; then, in terror, he cried:

"Awake, awake!"

Up sprang the dogs, and, howling, ran away.

The herds rushed together bewildered.

The men clambered to their feet, weapons in hand.

"What is it?" they asked, in one voice.

"See!" cried the watchman, "the sky is on fire!"

Suddenly the light became intolerably bright, and they covered their eyes, and dropped upon their knees; then, as their souls shrank with fear, they fell upon their faces blind and fainting, and would have died had not a voice said to them:

"Fear not!"

And they listened.

"Fear not: for behold, I bring you good tidings of great joy, which shall be to all people."

The voice, in sweetness and soothing more than human, and low and clear, penetrated all their being, and filled them with assurance. They rose upon their knees, and, looking worshipfully, beheld in the centre of a great glory the appearance of a man, clad in a robe intensely white; above its shoulders towered the tops of wings shining and folded; a star over its forehead glowed with steady lustre, brilliant as Hesperus; its hands were stretched towards them in blessing; its face was serene and divinely beautiful.

Directly the angel continued:

"For unto you is born this day, in the city of David, a Saviour, which is Christ the Lord!"

Again there was a rest, while the words sank into their minds.

"And this shall be a sign unto you," the annunciator said next. "Ye shall find the babe, wrapped in swaddling-clothes, lying in a manger."

SLING

The herald spoke not again; his good tidings were told; yet he stayed awhile. Suddenly the light, of which he seemed the centre, turned roseate and began to tremble; then up, far as the men could see, there was flashing of white wings, and coming and going of radiant forms, and voices as of a multitude chanting in unison:

"Glory to God in the highest, and on earth, peace, goodwill towards men!"

Not once the praise, but many times.

Then the herald raised his eyes as seeking approval of one far off; his wings stirred, and spread slowly and majestically, on their upper side white as snow, in the shadow vari-tinted, like mother-of-pearl; when they were expanded many cubits beyond his stature, he rose lightly, and, without effort, floated out of view, taking the light up with him. Long after he was gone, down from the sky fell the refrain in measure mellowed by distance, "Glory to God in the highest, and on earth peace, goodwill towards men."

When the shepherds came fully to their senses, they stared at each other stupidly, until one of them said, "It was Gabriel, the Lord's messenger unto men."

None answered

"Christ the Lord is born; said he not so?"

Then another recovered his voice, and replied, "That is what he said."

"And did he not also say, in the city of David, which is our Bethlehem yonder.

ARAB DRESS

And that we should find Him a babe in swaddling-clothes?"

"And lying in a manger."

The first speaker gazed into the fire thoughtfully, but at length said, like one possessed of a sudden resolve, "There is but one place in Bethlehem where there are mangers; but one, and that is in the cave near the old khan. Brethren, let us go see this thing which has come to pass. The priests and doctors have been a long time looking for the Christ. Now He is born, and the Lord has given us a sign by which to know Him. Let us go up and worship Him."

"But the flocks!"

"The Lord will take care of them. Let us make haste."

Then they all rose and left the mârâh.

Around the mountain and through the town they passed, and came to the gate of the khan.

The door of the cavern was open. A lantern was burning within, and they entered unceremoniously.

"I give you peace," the watchman said to Joseph. "Here are people looking for a child born this night, whom they are to know by finding him in swaddling-clothes, and lying in a manger."

For a moment the face of the stolid Nazarene was moved; turning away, he said, "The child is here."

They were led to one of the mangers, and there the child was. The lantern was brought, and the shepherds stood by mute. The little one made no sign; it was as others just born.

"Where is the mother?" asked the watchman.

One of the women took the baby and went to Mary, lying near, and put it in her arms. Then the bystanders collected about the two.

"It is the Christ!" said a shepherd, at last.

"The Christ!" they all repeated, falling upon their knees in worship. One of them repeated several time over:

"It is the Lord, and His glory is above the earth and heaven."

And the simple men, never doubting, kissed the hem of the mother's robe, and with joyful faces departed. In the khan, to all people aroused and pressing about them, they told their story; and through the town, and all the way back to the mârâh, they chanted the refrain of the angels, "Glory to God in the highest, and on earth peace, goodwill towards men."

The story went abroad, confirmed by the light so generally seen; and the next day, and for days thereafter, the cave was visited by curious crowds, of whom some believed, though the greater part laughed and mocked.

THE THREE WISE MEN IN JERUSALEM

The eleventh day after the birth of the child in the cave, about mid-afternoon, the three wise men approached Jerusalem by the road from Shechem. After crossing Brook Cedron, they met many people, of whom none failed to stop and look after them curiously.

The approach to Jerusalem from the north is across a plain which dips southward, leaving the Damascus Gate in a vale or hollow. The road is narrow, but deeply cut by long use, and in places difficult on account of the cobbles left loose and dry by the washing of the rains.

"Good people," said Balthasar, stroking his plaited beard, and bending from his cot, "is not Jerusalem close by?"

"Yes," answered the woman into whose arms the child had shrunk. "If the trees on yon swell were a little lower, you could see the towers on the market-place."

Balthasar gave the Greek and the Hindu a look, then asked:

"Where is He that is born King of the Jews?"

The women gazed at each other without reply.

"You have not heard of Him?"

"No."

"Well, tell everybody that we have seen His star in the east, and are come to worship Him."

Thereupon the friends rode on. Of others they asked the same question, with like result. A large company whom they met going to the Grotto of Jeremiah were so astonished by the inquiry and the appearance of the travellers that they turned about and followed them into the city.

They came, at length, to a tower of great height and strength, overlooking the gate which, at that time, answered to the present Damascus Gate, and marked the meeting-place of the three roads from Shechem, Jericho, and Gibeon. A Roman guard kept the passage-way. By this time the people following the camels formed a train sufficient to draw the idlers hanging about the portal; so that when Balthasar stopped to speak to the sentinel, the three became instantly the centre of a close circle eager to hear all that passed.

"I give you peace," the Egyptian said, in a clear voice.

The sentinel made no reply.

"We have come great distances in search of one who is born King of the Jews. Can you tell us where He is?"

The soldier raised the visor of his helmet, and called loudly. From an apartment at the right of the passage an officer appeared.

"Give way," he cried, to the crowd which now pressed closer in; and as they seemed slow to obey, he advanced twirling his javelin vigorously, now right, now left; and so he gained room.

"What would you?" he asked of Balthasar, speaking in the idiom of the city.

And Balthasar answered in the same:

"Where is He that is born King of the Jews?"

"Herod?" asked the officer, confounded.

"Herod's kingship is from Caesar; not Herod."

"There is no other King of the Jews."

"But we have seen the star of Him we seek, and come to worship Him."

The Roman was perplexed.

"Go farther," he said, at last. "Go farther. I am not a Jew. Carry the question to the doctors in the Temples, or to Hannas the priest, or, better still, to Herod himself. If there be another King of the Jews, he will find him."

Thereupon he made way for the strangers, and they passed the gate. But, before entering the narrow street, Balthasar lingered to say to his friends, "We are sufficiently proclaimed. By midnight the whole city will have heard of us and of our mission. Let us to the khan now."

AN INTERVIEW WITH HEROD

Later in the evening the wise men were lying in a lewen of the khan awake.

While they were in this condition, a man stepped in under the arch, darkening the lewen.

"Awake!" he said to them. "I bring you a message which will not be put off. My master, the king, has sent me to invite you to the palace, where he would have speech with you privately."

"The king's will is our will," said Balthasar to the messenger. "We will follow you."

Following their guide the brethren proceeded without a word. At last they came to a portal reared across the way. Then by passages and arched halls; through courts, and under colonnades not always lighted; up long flights of stairs, past innumerable cloisters and chambers, they were conducted into a tower of great height. Suddenly the guide halted, and, pointing through an open door, said to them:

"Enter. The king is there."

The air of the chamber was heavy with the perfume of sandal-wood, and all the appointments within were effeminately rich. Upon the floor, covering the central space, a tufted rug was spread, and upon that a throne was set.

At the edge of the rug, to which they advanced uninvited, they prostrated themselves. The king touched a bell. An attendant came in, and placed three stools before the throne.

"Seat yourselves," said the monarch, graciously.

"From the North Gate," he continued, when they were at rest, "I had this afternoon report of the arrival of three strangers, curiously mounted, and appearing as if from far countries. Are you the men?"

The Egyptian took the sign from the Greek and the Hindu, and answered, with the profoundest salaam, "Were we other than we are, the mighty Herod, whose fame is as incense to the whole world, would not have sent for us. We may not doubt that we are the strangers."

Herod acknowledged the speech with a wave of the hand.

"Who are you? Whence do you come?"

he asked; adding, significantly, "Let each speak for himself."

In turn they gave him account, referring simply to the cities and lands of their birth, and the routes by which they came to Jerusalem. Somewhat disappointed, Herod plied them more directly.

"Is there another King of the Jews?"

The Egyptian did not blanch.

"There is one newly born."

An expression of pain knit the dark face of the monarch, as if his mind were swept by a harrowing recollection.

"Not to me, not to me!" he exclaimed.

Possibly the accusing images of his murdered children flitted before him; recovering from the emotion, whatever it was, he asked, steadily, "Where is the new King?"

"That, O king, is what we would ask."

"You bring me a wonder – a riddle surpassing any of Solomon's," the inquisitor said next. "As you see, I am in the time of life when curiosity is as ungovernable as it was in childhood, when to trifle with it is cruelty. Tell me further, and I will honour you as kings honour each other. Give me all you know about the newly born, and I will join you in the search for him; and when we have found him, I will do what you wish; I will bring him to Jerusalem, and train him in kingcraft; I will use my grace with Caesar for his promotion and glory. Jealousy shall not come between us, so I swear. But tell me first how, so widely separated by seas and deserts, you all came to hear of him."

"I will tell you truly, O king."

"Speak on," said Herod.

Balthasar raised himself erect, and said, solemnly:

"There is an Almighty God."

Herod was visibly startled.

"He bade us come hither, promising that we should find the Redeemer of the World; that we should see and worship Him, and bear witness that He was come; and, as a sign, we were each given to see a star. His Spirit stayed with us. O king, His Spirit is with us now."

An overpowering feeling seized the three. The Greek with difficulty restrained an outcry. Herod's gaze darted quickly from one to the other; he was more suspicious and dissatisfied than before.

"You are mocking me," he said. "If not, tell me more. What is to follow the coming of the new king?"

"The salvation of men."

"From what?"

"Their wickedness."

"How?"

"By the divine agencies – Faith, Love, and Good Works."

"Then——" Herod paused, and from his look no man could have said with what feeling he continued: "You are the heralds of the Christ. Is that all?"

Balthasar bowed low.

"We are your servants, O king."

The monarch touched a bell, and the attendant appeared.

"Bring the gifts," the master said.

The attendant went out, but in a little while returned, and, kneeling before the guests, gave each one an outer robe or mantle of scarlet and blue, and a girdle of gold. They acknowledged the honours with Eastern prostrations.

"A word further," said Herod, when the ceremony was ended. "To the officer of the gate, and but now to me, you spoke of seeing a star in the east."

"Yes," said Balthasar, "His star, the star of the newly born."

"What time did it appear?"

"When we were bidden come hither."

Herod arose, signifying the audience was over. Stepping from the throne towards them, he said, with all graciousness:

"If, as I believe, O illustrious men, you are indeed the heralds of the Christ just born, know that I have this night consulted those wisest in things Jewish, and they say with one voice He should be born in Bethlehem of Judea. I say to you, go thither; go and search diligently for the young child; and when you have found Him bring me word again, that I may come and worship Him. To your going there shall be no let or hindrance. Peace be with you."

And, folding his robe about him, he left the chamber.

Directly the guide came, and led them back to the street, and thence to the khan, at the portal of which the Greek said impulsively, "Let us to Bethlehem, O brethren, as the king has advised."

"Yes," cried the Hindu. "The Spirit burns within me."

"Be it so," said Balthasar, with equal warmth. "The camels are ready."

They gave gifts to the steward, mounted into their saddles, received directions to the Joppa Gate, and departed. At their approach the great valves were un-

barred, and they passed out into the open country, taking the road so lately travelled by Joseph and Mary. As they came up out of Hinnom, on the plain of Rephaim, a light appeared, at first widespread and faint. Their pulses fluttered fast. The light intensified rapidly; they closed their eyes against its burning brilliance: when they dared look again, lo! the star, perfect as any in the heavens,

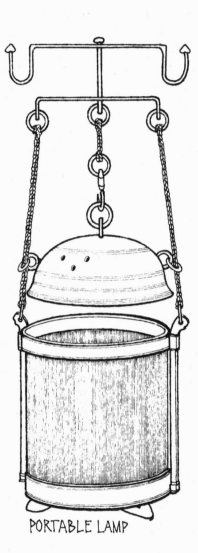

PORTABLE LAMP

but low down and moving slowly before them. And they folded their hands, and shouted, and rejoiced with exceeding great joy.

"God is with us! God is with us!" they repeated, in frequent cheer, all the way, until the star, rising out of the valley beyond Mar Elias, stood still over a house up on the slope of the hill near the town.

A CHILD NEWLY BORN

It was now the beginning of the third watch, and at Bethlehem the morning was breaking over the mountains in the east, but so feebly that it was yet night in the valley. The watchman on the roof of the old khan, shivering in the chilly air, was listening for the first distinguishable sounds with which life, awakening, greets the dawn, when a light came moving up the hill towards the house. He thought it a torch in someone's hand; next moment he thought it a meteor; the brilliance grew, however, until it became a star. Sore afraid, he cried out, and brought everybody within the walls to the roof. The phenomenon, in eccentric motion, continued to approach; the rocks, trees, and roadway about it shone as in a glare of lightning; directly its brightness became blinding. The more timid of the beholders fell upon their knees, and prayed, with their faces hidden; the boldest, covering their eyes, crouched, and now and then snatched glances fearfully. Afterwhile the khan and everything thereabout lay under the intolerable radiance. Such as dared look beheld the star standing still directly over the house in front of the cave where the Child had been born.

In the height of this scene, the wise men came up, and at the gate dismounted from their camels, and shouted for admission. When the steward so far mastered his terror as to give them heed, he drew the bars and opened to them. The camels looked spectral in the unnatural light, and, besides their outlandishness, there were in the faces and manner of the three visitors an eagerness and exaltation which still further excited the keeper's fears and fancy; he fell back, and for a time could not answer the question they put to him.

"Is not this Bethlehem of Judea?"

But others came, and by their presence gave him assurance.

"No, this is but the khan; the town lies father on."

"Is there not here a child newly born?"

The bystanders turned to each other marvelling, though some of them answered, "Yes, yes."

"Show us to Him!" said the Greek, impatiently.

"Show us to Him!" cried Balthasar, breaking through his gravity; "for we have seen His star, even that which ye behold over the house, and are come to worship Him."

The Hindu clasped his hands, exclaiming, "God indeed lives! Make haste, make haste! The Saviour is found. Blessed, blessed are we above men!"

The people from the roof came down and followed the strangers as they were taken through the court and out into the enclosure; at sight of the star yet above the cave, though less candescent than before, some turned back afraid; the greater part went on. As the strangers neared the house, the orb arose; when they were at the door, it was high up overhead vanishing; when they entered it went out lost to sight. And to the witnesses of what then took place came a conviction that there was a divine relation between the star and the strangers, which extended also to at least some of the occupants of the cave. When the door was opened, they crowded in.

The apartment was lighted by a lantern enough to enable the strangers to find the mother, and the child awake in her lap.

"Is the child thine?" asked Balthasar of Mary.

And she who had kept all the things in the least affecting the little one; and pondered them in her heart, held it up in the light, saying:

"He is my son."

And they fell down and worshipped Him.

BOOK TWO

HOW JUDEA BECAME A ROMAN PROVINCE

It is necessary now to carry the reader forward twenty-one years, to the beginning of the administration of Valerius Gratus, the fourth imperial governor of Judea – a period which will be remembered as rent by political agitations in Jerusalem, if, indeed, it be not the precise time of the opening of the final quarrel between the Jew and the Roman.

In the interval Judea had been subjected to changes affecting her in many ways, but in nothing so much as her political status. Herod the Great died within one year after the birth of the Child – died so miserably that the Christian world had reason to believe him overtaken by the Divine wrath. Like all great rulers who spend their lives in perfecting the power they create, he dreamed of transmitting his throne and crown – of being the founder of a dynasty. With that intent, he left a will dividing his territories between his three sons, Antipas, Philip, and Archelaus, of whom the last was appointed to succeed to the title. The testament was necessarily referred to Augustus, the emperor, who ratified all its provisions with one exception; he withheld from Archelaus the title of king until he proved his capacity and loyalty; in lieu thereof, he created him ethnarch, and as such permitted him to govern nine years, when, for misconduct and inability to stay the turbulent elements that grew and strengthened around him, he was sent into Gaul as an exile.

Caesar was not content with deposing Archelaus; he struck the people of Jerusalem in a manner that touched their pride, and keenly wounded the sensibilities of the haughty habitués of the Temple. He reduced Judea to a Roman province, and annexed it to the prefecture of Syria. So, instead of a king ruling royally from the palace left by Herod on Mount Zion, the city fell into the hands of an officer of the second grade, an appointee called procurator, who communicated with the court in Rome through the Legate of Syria, residing in Antioch. To make the hurt more painful, the procurator was not permitted to

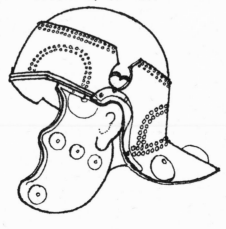

LEGIONARY HELMET

establish himself in Jerusalem; Caesarea was his seat of government. Most humiliating, however, most exasperating, most studied, Samaria, of all the world the most despised – Samaria was joined to Judea as a part of the same province.

Judea had been a Roman province eighty years and more – ample time for the Caesars to study the idiosyncrasies of the people – time enough, at least, to learn that the Jew, with all his pride, could be quietly governed if his religion were respected. Proceeding upon that policy, the predecessors of Gratus had carefully abstained from interfering with any of the sacred observances of their subjects. But he chose a different course: almost his first official act was to expel Hannas from the high-priesthood, and give the place to Ishmael, son of Fabus.

Hannas, the idol of his party, had used his power faithfully in the interest of his imperial patron. A Roman garrison held the Tower of Antonia; a Roman guard kept the gates of the palace; a Roman judge dispensed justice, civil and criminal; a Roman system of taxation, mercilessly executed, crushed both city and country; daily, hourly, and in a thousand ways, the people were bruised and galled, and taught the difference between a life of independence and a life of subjection; yet Hannas kept them in comparative quiet. Rome had no truer friend; and he made his loss instantly felt. Delivering his vestments to Ishmael, the new appointee, he walked from the courts of the Temple into the councils of the Separatists, and became the head of a new combination.

Gratus, the procurator, saw the fires which, in the fifteen years, had sunk into sodden smoke, begin to glow with returning life. A month after Ishmael took the office, the Roman found it necessary to visit him in Jerusalem. When from the walls, hooting and hissing him, the Jews beheld his guard enter the north gate of the city and march to the Tower of Antonia, they understood the real purpose of the visit – a full cohort of legionaries was added to the former garrison, and the keys of their yoke could now be tightened with impunity. If the procurator deemed it important to make an example, alas for the first offender!

THE PARTING OF FRIENDS

With the foregoing explanation in mind, the reader is invited to look into one of the gardens of the palace on Mount Zion. The time was noonday in the middle of July, when the heat of summer was at its highest.

The garden was bounded on every side by buildings, which in places arose two stories, with verandas shading the doors and windows of the lower story, while retreating galleries, guarded by strong balustrades, adorned and protected the upper. Here and there, moreover, the structures fell into what appeared low colonnades, permitting the passage of such winds as chanced to blow, and allowing other parts of the house to be seen, the better to realize its magnitude and beauty. The arrangement of the ground was equally pleasant to the eye. There were walks, and patches of grass and shrubbery, and a few large trees, rare specimens of the palm, grouped with the carob, apricot, and walnut. In all directions the grade sloped gently from the centre, where there was a reservoir, or deep marble basin, broken at intervals by little gates which, when raised, emptied the water into sluices bordering the walks – a cunning device for the rescue of the place from the aridity too prevalent elsewhere in the region.

Not far from the fountain, there was a small pool of clear water nourishing a clump of cane and oleander, such as grow on the Jordan and down by the Dead Sea. Between the clump and the pool, unmindful of the sun shining full

upon them in the breathless air, two boys, one about nineteen, the other seventeen, sat engaged in earnest conversation.

They were both handsome, and, at first glance, would have been pronounced brothers. Both had hair and eyes black; their faces were deeply browned; and sitting, they seemed of a size proper for the difference in their ages.

The elder was bareheaded. A loose tunic, dropping to the knees, was his attire complete, except sandals and a light-blue mantle spread under him on the seat. The costume left his arms and legs exposed, and they were brown as the face; nevertheless, a certain grace of manner, refinement of features, and culture of voice decided his rank. The tunic, of softest woollen, grey-tinted, at the neck, sleeves, and edge of the skirt bordered with red, and bound to the waist by a tasselled silken cord, certified him the Roman he was. And if in speech he now and then gazed haughtily at his companion and addressed him as an inferior, he might almost be excused, for he was of a family noble even in Rome – a circumstance which in that age justified any assumption. In the terrible wars between the first Caesar and his great enemies, a Messala had been the friend of Brutus. After Philippi, without sacrifice of his honour, he and the conqueror became reconciled. Yet later, when Octavius disputed for the empire, Messala supported him. Octavius, as the Emperor Augustus, remembered the service, and showered the family with honours. Among other things, Judea being reduced to a province, he sent the son of his old client or retainer to Jerusalem, charged with the receipt and management of the taxes levied in that region; and in that

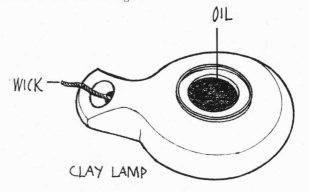

OIL

WICK

CLAY LAMP

service the son had since remained, sharing the palace with the High Priest. The youth just described was his son, whose habit it was to carry about with him all too faithfully a remembrance of the relation between his grandfather and the great Romans of his day.

The associate of the Messala was slighter in form, and his garments were of fine white linen and of the prevalent style in Jerusalem; a cloth covered his head, held by a yellow cord, and arranged so as to fall away from the forehead down low over the back of the neck. An observer skilled in the distinctions of race, and studying his features more than his costume, would have soon discovered him to be of Jewish descent. The forehead of the Roman was high and narrow, his nose sharp and aquiline, while his lips were thin and straight, and his eyes cold and close under the brows. The front of the Israelite, on the other hand, was low and broad; his nose long, with expanded nostrils; his upper lip, slightly shading the lower one, short and curving to the dimpled corners, like a Cupid's bow; points which in connection with the round chin, full eyes, and oval cheeks reddened with a wine-like glow, gave his face the softness, strength, and beauty peculiar to his race. The comeliness of the Roman was severe and chaste, that of the Jew rich and voluptuous.

"Did you not say the new procurator is to arrive tomorrow?"

"Yes, tomorrow," Messala answered.

"Who told you?"

"I heard Ishmael, the new governor in the palace – you call him High Priest – tell my father so last night."

The young Messala, educated in Rome, but lately returned, had caught the habit and manner; the scarce perceptible movement of the outer corner of the lower eyelid, the decided curl of the corresponding nostril, and a languid utterance affected as the best vehicle to convey the idea of general indifference, but more particularly because of the opportunities it afforded for certain rhetorical pauses thought to be of prime importance to enable the listener to take the happy conceit or receive the virus of the stinging epigram. The colour in the Jewish lad's cheeks deepened, and he may not have heard the rest of the speech, for he remained silent, looking absently into the depths of the pool.

"Our farewell took place in this garden. 'The peace of the Lord go with you!' – your last words. 'The gods keep you!' I said. Do you remember? How many years have passed since then?"

"Five," answered the Jew, gazing into the water. "I remember the parting; you went to Rome; I saw you start, and cried, for I loved you. The years are gone, and you have come back to me accomplished and princely – I do not jest; and yet – yet – I wish you were the Messala you went away."

The fine nostril of the satirist stirred, and he put on a longer drawl as he said, "Seriously, O my friend, in what am I not the Messala I went away? Let me understand you. Wherein have I hurt you?"

The other drew a long breath, and said, pulling at the cord about his waist, "In the five years, I, too, have learned somewhat. I know the space that lies between an independent kingdom and the petty province Judea is. I were meaner, viler, than a Samaritan not to resent the degradation of my country. Ishmael is not lawfully High Priest, and he cannot be while the noble Hannas lives; yet he is a Levite; one of the devoted who for thousands of years have acceptably served the Lord God of our faith and worship His——"

Messala broke in upon him with a biting laugh.

"Oh, I understand you now. Ishmael, you say, is a usurper, yet to believe an Idumaean sooner than Ishmael is to sting like an adder. By the drunken son of Semele, what it is to be a Jew! All men and things, even heaven and earth, change; but a Jew never. To him there is no backward, no forward; he is what his ancestor was in the beginning. Now tell me what more a Jew's life is?

"I am to be a soldier; and you, O my Judah, I pity you; what can you be?"

The Jew moved nearer the pool; Messala's drawl deepened.

"Yes, I pity you, my fine Judah. From the college to the synagogue; then to the Temple; then – oh, a crowning glory! – the seat in the Sanhedrim. A life without opportunities; the gods help you! But I——"

Judah looked at him in time to see the flush of pride that kindled in his haughty face as he went on.

"But I – ah, the world is not all conquered. The sea has islands unseen. In the north there are nations yet unvisited. The glory of completing Alexander's march to the Far East remains to someone. See what possibilities lie before a Roman. When I am perfect, with India to enrich me, I – will make you High Priest."

The Jew turned off angrily.

"Do not leave me," said Messala.

The other stopped irresolute.

"Gods, Judah, how hot the sun shines!" cried the patrician, observing his perplexity. "Let us seek a shade."

Judah answered coldly:

"We had better part. I wish I had not come. I sought a friend and find a——"

"Roman," said Messala, quickly.

The hands of the Jew clenched, but controlling himself again, he started off. Messala arose, and taking the mantle from the bench, flung it over his shoulder, and followed after. When he gained his side, he put his hand upon his shoulder and walked with him.

"This is the way – my hand thus – we used to walk when we were children. Let us keep it as far as the gate."

Apparently Messala was trying to be serious and kind, though he could not rid his countenance of the habitual satirical expression. Judah permitted the familiarity.

"You are a boy. I am a man; let me talk like one."

The complacency of the Roman was superb.

They were now at the gate. Judah stopped, and took the hand gently from his shoulder, and confronted Messala, tears trembling in his eyes.

"I understand you, because you are a Roman; you cannot understand me – I am an Israelite. You have given me suffering today by convincing me that we can never be the friends we have been – never! Here we part. The peace of the God of my father abide with you."

Messala offered him his hand; the Jew walked on through the gateway. When he was gone, the Roman was silent awhile; then he, too, passed through, saying to himself, with a toss of the head:

"Be it so. Eros is dead, Mars reigns."

RETURNING HOME

Not long after the young Jew parted from the Roman at the palace upon the market-place, he stopped before the western gate of the house described, and knocked. The wicket (a door hung in one of the valves of the gate) was opened to admit him. He stepped in hastily, and failed to acknowledge the low salaam of the porter.

To get an idea of the interior arrangement of the structure, as well as to see what more befell the youth, we will follow him.

The passage into which he was admitted appeared not unlike a narrow tunnel with panelled walls and pitted ceiling. There were benches of stone on both sides, stained and polished by long use. Twelve or fifteen steps carried him

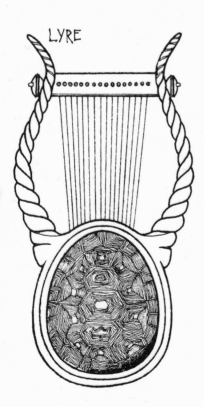

LYRE

into a courtyard, oblong north and south, and in every quarter, except the east, bounded by what seemed the fronts of two-story houses; of which the lower floor was divided into lewens, while the upper was terraced and defended by strong balustrading. The servants coming and going along the terraces; the noise of millstones grinding; the garments fluttering from ropes stretched from point to point; the chickens and pigeons in full enjoyment of the place; the goats, cows, donkeys, and horses stabled in the lewens; a massive trough of water, apparently for the common use, declared this court appurtenant to the domestic management of the owner. Eastwardly there was a division wall broken by another passage-way in all respects like the first one.

Clearing the second passage, the young man entered a second court, spacious, square, and set with shrubbery and vines, kept fresh and beautiful by water from a basin erected near a porch on the north side. The lewens here were high, airy, and shaded by curtains striped alternate white and red. The arches of the lewens rested on clustered columns. A flight of steps on the south ascended to the terraces of the upper story, over which great awnings were stretched as a defence against the sun. Another stairway reached from the terraces to the roof, the edge of which, all around the square, was defined by a sculptured cornice, and a parapet of burned-clay tiling, sexangular and bright-red. In this quarter, moreover, there was everywhere observable a scrupulous neatness, which, allowing no dust in the angles, not even a yellow leaf upon a shrub, contributed quite as much as anything else to the delightful general effect; insomuch that a visitor, breathing the sweet air, knew, in advance of introduction, the refinement of the family he was about calling upon.

A few steps within the second court, the lad turned to the right, and, choosing a walk through the shrubbery, part of which was in flower, passed to the stairway, and ascended to the terrace – a broad pavement of white and brown flags closely laid, and much worn. Making way under the awning to a doorway on the north side, he entered an apartment which the dropping of the screen behind him returned to darkness. Nevertheless, he proceeded, moving over a tiled floor to a divan, upon which he flung himself,

face downwards, and lay at rest, his forehead upon his crossed arms.

About nightfall a woman came to the door and called; he answered, and she went in.

"Supper is over, and it is night. Is not my son hungry?" she asked.

"No," he replied.

"Are you sick?"

"I am sleepy."

"Your mother has asked for you."

"Where is she?"

"In the summer-house on the roof."

He stirred himself, and sat up.

"Very well. Bring me something to eat."

"What do you want?"

"What you please, Amrah. I am not sick, but indifferent."

After a while she returned, bearing on a wooden platter a bowl of milk, some thin cakes of white bread broken, a bird broiled, and honey and salt. On one end of the platter there was a silver goblet full of wine, on the other a brazen hand-lamp lighted.

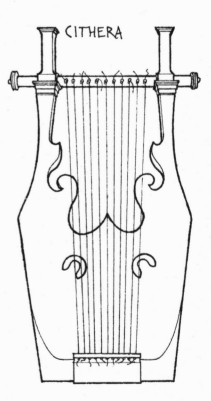

CITHERA

Drawing a stool to the divan, she placed the platter upon it, then knelt close by ready to serve him. Her face was that of a woman of fifty, dark-skinned, dark-eyed, and at the moment softened by a look of tenderness almost maternal. She was a slave, of Egyptian origin, to whom not even the sacred fiftieth year could have brought freedom; nor would she have accepted it, for the boy she was attending was her life. She had nursed him through babyhood, tended him as a child, and could not break the service. To her love he could never be a man.

He spoke but once during the meal.

"You remember, O my Amrah," he said, "the Messala who used to visit me here days at a time."

"I remember him."

"He went to Rome some years ago, and is now back. I called upon him today."

A shudder of disgust seized the lad.

"I knew something had happened," she said, deeply interested. "I never liked the Messala. Tell me all."

But he fell into musing, and to her repeated inquiries only said: "He is much changed, and I shall have nothing more to do with him."

When Amrah took the platter away, he also went out, and up from the terrace across the house-top to a tower built over the north-west corner of the palace. Had he been a stranger, he might have bestowed a glance upon the structure as he drew nigh it, and seen all the dimness permitted – a darkened mass, low, latticed, pillared, and domed. He entered, passing under a half-raised curtain. The interior was all darkness, except that on four sides there were arched openings like doorways, through which the sky, lighted with stars, was visible. In one of the openings, reclining against a cushion from a divan, he saw the figure of a woman, indistinct even in white floating drapery. At the sound of his steps upon the floor, the fan in her hand stopped, glistening where the starlight struck the jewels with which it was sprinkled, and she sat up, and called his name.

"Judah, my son!"

"It is I, mother," he answered, quickening his approach.

Going to her, he knelt, and she put her arms around him, and with kisses pressed him to her bosom.

JUDAH, THE SON OF HUR

The mother resumed her easy position against the cushion, while the son took place on the divan his head in her lap. The city was still. Only the winds stirred.

"Amrah tells me something has happened to you," she said, caressing his cheek. "When my Judah was a child, I allowed small things to trouble him, but he is now a man. He must not forget" – her voice became very soft – "that one day he is to be my hero."

She spoke in the language almost lost in the land, the language in which the loved Rebekah and Rachel sang to Benjamin.

The words appeared to set him thinking anew; after awhile, however, he caught the hand with which she fanned him, and said: "I have been up on the market-place. I visited the young Messala."

A certain change in his voice attracted the mother's attention. A presentiment quickened the beating of her heart; the fan became motionless again.

"The Messala!" she said. "What could he say to so trouble you."

"What Messala said, my mother, was sharp enough in itself; but taken with the manner, some of the sayings were intolerable.

"For the first time, in conversation with me today, he trifled with our customs and God. As you would have had me do, I parted with him finally. And now, O my dear mother, I would know with more certainty if there be just ground for the Roman's contempt. In what am I his inferior? Tell me, O my mother – and this is the sum of my trouble – why may not a son of Israel do all a Roman may?" The young Israelite proceeded then, and rehearsed his conversation with Messala, dwelling with particularity upon the latter's speeches in contempt of the Jews, their customs, and much pent round of life.

Afraid to speak the while, the mother listened, discerning the matter plainly. Judah had gone to the palace on the market-place, allured by love of a playmate whom he thought to find exactly as he had been at the parting years before; a man met him, and, in place of laughter

and references to the sports of the past, the man had been full of the future, and talked of glory to be won, and of riches, and power.

"There never has been a people," she began, "who did not think themselves at least equal to any other; never a great nation, my son, that did not believe itself the very superior. When the Roman looks down upon Israel and laughs, he merely repeats the folly of the Egyptian, the Assyrian, and the Macedonian; and as the laugh is against God, the result will be the same."

Her voice became firmer.

"As for what you shall do, my boy – serve the Lord, the Lord God of Israel, not Rome. For a child of Abraham there is no glory except in the Lord's ways, and in them there is much glory."

"I may be a soldier then?" Judah asked.

"Why not? Did not Moses call God a man of war?"

There was then a long silence in the summer chamber.

"You have my permission," she said, finally; "if only you serve the Lord instead of Caesar."

He was content with the condition, and by-and-by fell asleep. She arose then, and put the cushion under his head, and, throwing a shawl over him and kissing him tenderly, went away.

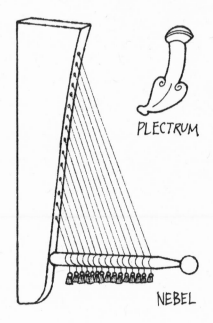

PLECTRUM

NEBEL

AN ACCIDENT AND AN ARREST

When Judah awoke, the sun was up over the mountains; the pigeons were abroad in flocks, filling the air with the gleams of their white wings; and off south-east he beheld the Temple, an apparition of gold in the blue of the sky. These, however, were familiar objects, and they received but a glance. Upon the edge of the divan, close by him, a girl scarcely fifteen sat singing to the accompaniment of a nebel, which she rested upon her knee, and touched gracefully.

Tirzah was her name, and, as the two looked at each other, their resemblance was plain. Her features had the regularity of his, and were of the same Jewish type; they had also the charm of childish innocency of expression. Altogether it would have been impossible to deny her grace, refinement, and beauty.

"Very pretty, my Tirzah, very pretty!" he said, with animation.

"The song?" she asked.

"Yes – and the singer, too. Have you another as good?"

"Very many. But let them go now. Amrah sent me to tell you she will bring you your breakfast, and that you need not come down. She should be here by this time. She thinks you sick – that a dreadful accident happened you yesterday."

"What do you think, Tirzah? I am going away."

"Going away! When? Where? For what?"

He laughed.

"Three questions, all in a breath! What a body you are!" Next instant he became serious. "You know the law requires me to follow some occupation. Our good father set me an example. Even you would despise me if I spent in idleness the results of his industry and knowledge. I am going to Rome."

"Oh, I will go with you."

"You must stay with mother. If both of us leave her, she will die."

The brightness faded from her face.

"Ah, yes, yes! But – must you go? Here in Jerusalem you can learn all that is needed to be a merchant – if that is what you are thinking of."

"But that is not what I am thinking of. The law does not require the son to be what the father was."

"What else can you be?"

"A soldier," he replied, with a certain pride of voice.

Tears came into her eyes.

"You will be killed."

"If God's will, be it so. But, Tirzah, the soldiers are not all killed."

She threw her arms around his neck, as if to hold him back.

"We are so happy! Stay at home, my brother."

"Home cannot always be what it is. You yourself will be going away before long."

"Never."

He smiled at her earnestness.

"A prince of Judah, or some other of one of the tribes, will come soon and claim my Tirzah, and ride away with her to be the light of another house. What will then become of me?"

She answered with sobs.

"War is a trade," he continued, more soberly. "To learn it thoroughly one must go to school, and there is no school like a Roman camp."

"You would not fight for Rome?" she asked, holding her breath.

"And you – even you hate her. The whole world hates her. In that, O Tirzah, find the reason of the answer I give you – Yes, I will fight for her, if, in return, she will teach me how one day to fight against her."

"When will you go?"

Amrah's steps were then heard.

"Hist!" he said. "Do not let her know of what I am thinking."

The faithful slave came in with breakfast, and placed the waiter holding it upon a stool before them; then, with white napkins upon her arm, she remained to serve them. They dipped their fingers in a bowl of water, and were rinsing them, when a noise arrested their attention. They listened, and distinguished martial music in the street on the north side of the house.

"Soldiers from the Praetorium! I must see them," he cried, springing from the divan, and running out.

In a moment more he was leaning over the parapet of tiles which guarded the roof at the extreme north-east corner, so absorbed that he did not notice Tirzah by his side, resting one hand upon his shoulder.

Their position – the roof being the highest one in the locality – commanded the house-tops eastward as far as the huge irregular Tower of Antonia, which has been already mentioned as a citadel for the garrison and military headquarters for the governor. The street, not more than ten feet wide, was spanned here and there by bridges, open and covered, which, like the roofs along the way, were beginning to be occupied by men, women, and children, called out by the music. The word is used, though it is hardly fitting; what the people heard when they came forth was rather an uproar of trumpets and the shriller litui so delightful to the soldiers.

The array after awhile came into view of the two upon the house of the Hurs. First, a vanguard of the light-armed – mostly slingers and bowmen – marching with wide intervals between their ranks and files; next a body of heavy-armed infantry, bearing large shields, and hastae longae, or spears identical with those used in the duels before Ilium; then the musicians; and then an officer riding alone, but followed closely by a guard of cavalry; after them again, a column of infantry, also heavy-armed, which, moving in close order, crowded the street from wall to wall, and appeared to be without end.

The brawny limbs of the men; the cadenced motion from right to left of the shields; the sparkle of scales, buckles, and breast-plates and helms, all perfectly burnished; the plumes nodding above the tall crests; the sway of ensigns and iron-shod spears; the bold, confident step, exactly timed and measured; the demeanour, so grave, yet so watchful; the machine-like unity of the whole moving mass – made an impression upon Judah, but as something felt rather than seen. Two objects fixed his attention – the eagle of the legion first – a gilded effigy perched on a tall shaft, with wings outspread until they met above its head. He knew that, when brought from its chamber in the Tower, it had been received with divine honours.

The officer riding alone in the midst of the column was the other attraction. His head was bare; otherwise he was in full armour. At his left hip he wore a short sword; in his hand, however, he carried a truncheon, which looked like a roll of white paper. He sat upon a purple cloth instead of a saddle, and that, and a bridle with a forestall of gold and reins of yellow silk broadly fringed at the lower edge, completed the housings of the horse.

While the man was yet in the distance, Judah observed that his presence was sufficient to throw the people looking at him into angry excitement. They would lean over the parapets or stand boldly out, and shake their fists at him; they followed him with loud cries, and spat at him as he passed under the bridges; the women even flung their sandals, sometimes with such good effect as to hit him. When he was nearer, the yells became distinguishable – "Robber, tyrant, dog of a Roman! Away with Ishmael! Give us back our Hannas!"

When quite near, Judah could see that, as was but natural, the man did not share the indifference so superbly shown by the soldiers. His face was dark and sullen, and the glances he occasionally cast at his persecutors were full of menace; the very timid shrank from them.

Now the lad heard of the custom, borrowed from a habit of the first Caesar, by which chief commanders, to indicate their rank, appeared in public with only a laurel vine upon their heads. By that sign he knew this officer – *Valerius Gratus, the New Procurator of Judea*!

To say truth now, the Roman under the unprovoked storm had the young Jew's sympathy; so that when he reached the corner of the house, the latter leaned yet farther over the parapet to see him go by, and in the act rested a hand upon a tile which had been a long time cracked and allowed to go unnoticed. The pressure was strong enough to displace the outerpiece, which started to fall. A thrill of horror shot through the youth. He reached out to catch the missile. In appearance the motion was exactly that of one pitching something from him. The effort failed – nay, it served to push the descending fragment farther out over the wall. He shouted with all his might. The soldiers of the guard looked up; so did the great man, and that moment the missile struck him, and he fell from his seat as dead.

The cohort halted; the guards leaped from their horses, and hastened to cover the chief with their shields. On the other hand, the people who witnessed the affair, never doubting that the blow had been purposely dealt, cheered the lad as he yet stooped in full view over the parapet, transfixed by what he beheld, and by

anticipation of the consequences, flashed all too plainly upon him.

He arose from the parapet, his face very pale.

"O Tirzah, Tirzah! What will become of us?"

"What has happened? What does it all mean?" she asked in sudden alarm.

"I have killed the Roman governor. The tile fell upon him. I did not do it purposely, Tirzah – it was an accident," he said, more calmly.

"What will they do?" she asked.

He looked off over the tumult momentarily deepening in the street and on the roofs, and thought of the sullen countenance of Gratus. If he were not dead, where would his vengeance stop? And if he were dead, to what height of fury would not the violence of the people lash the legionaries? To evade an answer, he peered over the parapet again, just as the guard were assisting the Roman to remount his horse.

"He lives, he lives, Tirzah! Blessed be the Lord God of our fathers!"

"Be not afraid, Tirzah. I will explain how it happened, and they will remember our father and his services, and not hurt us."

He was leading her to the summerhouse, when the roof jarred under their feet, and a crash of strong timbers being burst away, followed by a cry of surprise and agony, arose apparently from the courtyard below. He stopped and listened. The cry was repeated; then came a rush of many feet, and voices lifted in rage blent with voices in prayer; and then the screams of women in mortal terror. The soldiers had beaten in the north gate, and were in possession of the house. The terrible sense of being hunted smote him. His first impulse was to fly; but where? Nothing but wings would serve him. Tirzah, her eyes wild with fear, caught his arm.

"O Judah, what does it mean?"

The servants were being butchered – and his mother! Was not one of the voices he heard hers? With all the will left him, he said, "Stay here, and wait for me, Tirzah. I will go down and see what is the matter, and come back."

His voice was not steady as he wished. She clung closer to him.

Clearer, shriller, no longer a fancy, his mother's cry arose. He hesitated no longer.

"Come, then, let us go."

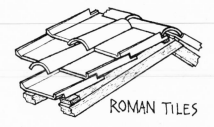

ROMAN TILES

The terrace or gallery at the foot of the steps was crowded with soldiers. Other soldiers with drawn swords ran in and out of the chambers. At one place a number of women on their knees clung to each other or prayed for mercy. Apart from them, one with torn garments, and long hair streaming over her face, struggled to tear loose from a man all whose strength was tasked to keep his hold. Her cries were shrillest of all; cutting through the clamour, they had risen distinguishably to the roof. To her Judah sprang – his steps were long and swift, almost a winged flight – "Mother, mother!" he shouted. She stretched her hands towards him, but when almost touching them he was seized and forced aside. Then he heard someone say, speaking loudly:

"That is he!"

Judah looked, and saw – Messala!

"What, the assassin – that?" said a tall man, in legionary armour of beautiful finish. "Why, he is but a boy."

"Gods!" replied Messala, not forgetting his drawl. "A new philosophy! What would Seneca say to the proposition that a man must be old before he can hate enough to kill? You have him; and that is his mother; yonder his sister. You have the whole family."

For love of them, Judah forgot his quarrel.

"Help them, O my Messala! Remember our childhood and help them. I – Judah – pray you."

Messala affected not to hear.

SUSPENDED CEILING

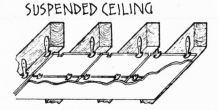

"I cannot be of further use to you," he said to the officer. "There is richer entertainment in the street. Down Eros, up Mars!"

With the last words he disappeared. Judah understood him, and, in the bitterness of his soul, prayed to heaven.

"In the hour of Thy vengeance, O Lord," he said, "be mine the hand to put it upon him!"

By great exertion he drew nearer the officer.

"O sir, the woman you hear is my mother. Spare her, spare my sister yonder. God is just, He will give you mercy for mercy."

The man appeared to be moved.

"To the Tower with the women!" he shouted, "but do them no harm. I will demand them of you." Then to those holding Judah, he said, "Get cords, and bind his hands, and take him to the street. His punishment is reserved."

The mother was carried away. The little Tirzah, in her home attire, stupefied with fear, went passively with her keepers. Judah gave each of them a last look, and covered his face with his hands, as if to possess himself of the scene fadelessly. He may have shed tears, though no one saw them.

There took place in him then what may be justly called the wonder of life. Yet there was no sign, nothing to indicate that he had undergone a change, except that when he raised his head, and held his arms out to be bound, the bend of the Cupid's bow had vanished from his lips. In that instant he had put off childhood and become a man.

The officer waited outside while a detail of men temporarily restored the gate.

In the street the fighting had almost ceased. Borne past the point of care for himself, Judah had heart for nothing in view but the prisoners, among whom he looked in vain for his mother and Tirzah.

Suddenly, from the earth where she had been lying, a woman arose and started swiftly back to the gate. She ran to Judah, and, dropping down, clasped his knees, the coarse black hair powdered with dust veiling her eyes.

"O Amrah, good Amrah," he said to her, "God help you; I cannot."

She could not speak.

He bent down, and whispered, "Live, Amrah, for Tirzah and my mother. They will come back, and——"

A soldier drew her away; whereupon she sprang up and rushed through the gateway and passage into the vacant courtyard.

"Let her go," the officer shouted. "We will seal the house, and she will starve."

The men resumed their work, and, when it was finished there, passed round to the west side. That gate was also secured, after which the palace of the Hurs was lost to use.

ARABS BY THE WELL

Next day a detachment of legionaries went to the desolated palace, and, closing the gates permanently, plastered the corners with wax, and at the sides nailed a notice in Latin:

THIS IS THE PROPERTY OF THE EMPEROR

In the haughty Roman idea, the sententious announcement was thought sufficient for the purpose – and it was.

The day after that again, about noon, a decurion with his command of ten

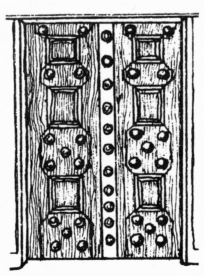

WOODEN GATE
IN JERUSALEM

horsemen approached Nazareth from the south – that is, from the direction of Jerusalem.

A prisoner whom the horsemen were guarding was the object of curiosity. He was afoot, bareheaded, half naked, his hands bound behind him. A thong fixed to his wrists was looped over the neck of a horse. The dust went with the party when in movement, wrapping him in yellow fog, sometimes in a dense cloud. He drooped forward, footsore and faint. The villagers could see he was young.

At the well the decurion halted, and, with most of the men, dismounted. The prisoner sank down in the dust of the road, stupefied, and asking nothing: apparently he was in the last stage of exhaustion. Seeing, when they came near, that he was but a boy, the villagers would have helped him had they dared.

In the midst of their perplexity, and while the pitchers were passing among the soldiers, a man was descried coming down the road from Sepphoris. At sight of him a woman cried out, "Look! Yonder comes the carpenter. Now we will hear something."

The person spoken of was quite venerable in appearance. Thin white locks fell below the edge of his full turban, and a mass of still whiter beard flowed down the front of his coarse grey gown. He came slowly, for, in addition to his age, he carried some tools – an axe, a saw, and a drawing-knife, all very rude and heavy – and had evidently travelled some distance without rest.

He stopped close by to survey the assemblage.

"O Rabbi, good Rabbi Joseph!" cried a woman, running to him. "Here is a prisoner; come ask the soldiers about him, that we may know who he is, and what he has done, and what they are going to do with him."

The rabbi's face remained stolid; he glanced at the prisoner, however, and presently went to the officer.

"The peace of the Lord be with you!" he said, with unbending gravity.

"And that of the gods with you," the decurion replied.

"Are you from Jerusalem?"

"Yes."

"Your prisoner is young."

"In years, yes."

"May I ask what he has done?"

"He is an assassin."

The people repeated the word in astonishment, but Rabbi Joseph pursued his inquest.

"Is he a son of Israel?"

"He is a Jew," said the Roman, dryly.

The wavering pity of the bystanders came back.

"I know nothing of your tribes, but can speak of his family," the speaker continued. "You may have heard of a prince of Jerusalem named Hur – Ben-Hur they called him. He lived in Herod's day."

"I have seen him." Joseph said.

"Well, this is his son."

Exclamations became general, and the decurion hastened to stop them.

"In the streets of Jerusalem, day before yesterday, he nearly killed the noble Gratus by flinging a tile upon his head from the roof of a palace – his father's, I believe."

There was a pause in the conversation, during which the Nazarenes gazed at the young Ben-Hur as at a wild beast.

"Did he kill him?" asked the rabbi.

"No."

"He is under sentence?"

"Yes – the galleys for life."

"The Lord help him!" said Joseph, for once moved out of his stolidity.

Thereupon a youth who came up with Joseph, but had stood behind him unobserved, laid down an axe he had been carrying, and, going to the great stone standing by the well, took from it a pitcher of water. The action was so quiet that before the guard could interfere, had they been disposed to do so, he was stooping over the prisoner, and offering him drink.

The hand laid kindly upon his shoulder awoke the unfortunate Judah, and, looking up, he saw a face he never forgot – the face of a boy about his own age, shaded by locks of yellowish bright chestnut hair; a face lighted by dark-blue eyes, at the time so soft, so appealing, so full of love and holy purpose, that they had all the power of command and will. The spirit of the Jew, hardened though it was by days and nights of suffering, and so embittered by wrong that its dreams of revenge took in all the world, melted under the stranger's look, and became as a child's. He put his lips to the pitcher, and drank long and deep. Not a word was said to him nor did he say a word.

And so, for the first time, Judah and the Son of Mary met and parted.

BOOK THREE

QUINTUS ARRIUS SETS SAIL

The city of Misenum gave name to the promontory which it crowned, a few miles south-west of Naples. An account of ruins is all that remains of it now; yet in the year of our Lord 24 – to which it is desirable to advance the reader – the place was one of the most important on the western coast of Italy.

In the year mentioned, a traveller coming to the promontory to regale himself with the view there offered, would have mounted a wall, and, with the city at his back, looked over the bay of Neapolis, as charming then as now; and then, as now, he would have seen the matchless shore, the smoking cone, the sky and waves so softly, deeply blue, Ischia here and Capri yonder; from one to the other and back again, through the purpled air, his gaze would have sported; at last – for the eyes do weary of the beautiful as the palate with sweets – at last it would have dropped upon a spectacle which the modern tourist cannot see – half the reserve navy of Rome astir or at anchor below him. Thus regarded, Misenum was a very proper place for three masters to meet, and at leisure parcel the world among them.

The watchman on the wall above the gateway was disturbed, one cool September morning, by a party coming down the street in noisy conversation. He gave one look, then settled into his drowse again.

There were twenty or thirty persons in the party, of whom the greater number were slaves with torches which flamed little and smoked much, leaving on the air the perfume of the Indian nard. The masters walked in advance arm-in-arm. One of them, apparently fifty years old, slightly bald, and wearing over his scant locks a crown of laurel, seemed, from the attentions paid him, the central object of some affectionate ceremony. They all sported ample togas of white wool broadly bordered with purple. A glance had sufficed the watchman. He knew, without question, they were of high rank, and escorting a friend to ship after a night of festivity. Further explanation will be found in the conversation they carried on.

"No, my Quintus," said one, speaking to him with the crown; "it is ill of Fortune to take thee from us so soon. Only yesterday thou didst return from the seas beyond the Pillars. Why, thou hast not even got back thy land legs."

"By Castor! if a man may swear a woman's oath." said another, somewhat worse of wine, "let us not lament. Our Quintus is but going to find what he lost last night. Dice on a rolling ship is not dice on shore – eh, Quintus?"

"Abuse not Fortune!" exclaimed a third. "She is not blind or fickle. At Antium, where our Arrius questions her, she answers him with nods, and at sea she abides with him holding the rudder. She takes him from us, but does she not always give him back with a new victory?"

"The Greeks are taking him away," another broke in. "Let us abuse them, not the gods. In learning to trade, they forgot how to fight."

With these words the party passed the gateway, and came upon the mole, with the bay before them, beautiful in the morning light. To the veteran sailor the plash of the waves was like a greeting. He drew a long breath, as if the perfume of the water were sweeter than that of the nard, and held his hand aloft.

"My gifts were at Praeneste, not Antium – and see! Wind from the west. Thanks, O Fortune, my mother," he said, earnestly.

The friends all repeated the exclamation, and the slaves waved their torches.

"She comes – yonder!" he continued, pointing to a galley outside the mole. "What need has a sailor for other mistress?"

He gazed at the coming ship, and justified his pride. A white sail was bent to the low mast, and the oars dipped, arose, poised a moment, then dipped again, with wing-like action, and in perfect time.

The sailor's eyes were full of his ship.

"What grace, what freedom! A bird hath not less care for the fretting of the waves. See!" he said, but almost immediately added: "Thy pardon, my Lentulus. I am going to the Aegean; and as my departure is so near, I will tell the occasion – only keep it under the rose. The trade between Greece and Alexandria, as ye may have heard, is hardly inferior to that between Alexandria and Rome. Ye may also have heard of the

Chersonesan pirates, nested up in the Euxine; none bolder, by the Bacchae! Yesterday word came to Rome that, with a fleet, they had rowed down the Bosphorus, sunk the galleys off Byzantium and Chalcedon, swept the Propontis, and, still unsated, burst through into the Aegean. The corn merchants who have ships in the East Mediterranean are frightened. They had audience with the Emperor himself, and from Ravenna there go today a hundred galleys, and from Misenum" – he paused as if to pique the curiosity of his friends, and ended with an emphatic – "one."

"Happy Quintus Arrius! We congratulate thee."

As the ship drew more plainly out of the perspective, she became more and more an attraction to him. The look with which he watched her was that of an enthusiast. At length he tossed the loosened folds of his toga in the air; in reply to the signal, over the aplustre, or fan-like fixture at the stern of the vessel, a scarlet flag was displayed, while several sailors appeared upon the bulwarks, and swung themselves hand over hand up the ropes to the antenna, or yard, and furled the sail. The bow was put round, and the time of the oars increased one-half; so that at racing speed she bore down directly towards him and his friends. He observed the manoeuvring with a perceptible brightening of the eyes. Her instant answer to the rudder, and the steadiness with which she kept her course, were especially noticeable as virtues to be relied upon in action.

"By the Nymphae!" said one of the friends, giving back the roll, "we may not longer say our friend will be great; he is already great. Our love will now have famous things to feed upon. What more hast thou for us?"

"Nothing more," Arrius replied. "What ye have of the affair is by this time old news in Rome, especially between the palace and the Forum. The duumvir is discreet; what I am to do, where go to find my fleet, he will tell on the ship, where a sealed package is waiting me. If, however, ye have offerings for any of the altars today, pray the gods for a friend plying oar and sail somewhere in the direction of Sicily. But she is here, and will come to," he said, reverting to the vessel. "I have interest in her masters, they will sail and fight with me. It is not an easy thing to lay ship side on a shore

like this, so let us judge their training and skill."

"What, is she new to thee?"

"I never saw her before; and, as yet, I know not if she will bring me one acquaintance."

"Is that well?"

"It matters but little. We of the sea come to know each other quickly; our loves, like our hates, are born of sudden dangers."

The vessel was of the class called naves liburnicae – long, narrow, low in the water, and modelled for speed and quick manoeuvre. The bow was beautiful. A jet of water spun from its foot as she came on, sprinkling all the prow, which rose in graceful curvature twice a man's stature above the plane of the deck. Upon the bending of the sides were figures of Triton blowing shells. Below the bow, fixed to the keel, and projecting forward under the water-line, was the rostrum, or beak, a device of solid wood, reinforced and armed with iron, in action used as a ram. A stout moulding extended from the bow the full length of the ship's sides, defining the bulwarks, which were taste-fully crenellated; below the moulding, in three rows, each covered with a cap or shield of bull-hide, were the holes in which the oars were worked – sixty on the right, sixty on the left. In further ornamentation, caducei leaned against the lofty prow. Two immense ropes passing across the bow marked the number of anchors stowed on the fore-deck.

The simplicity of the upper works declared the oars the chief dependence of the crew. A mast, set a little forward of midship, was held by fore and back stays and shrouds fixed to rings on the inner side of the bulwarks. The tackle was that required for the management of one great square sail and the yard to which it was hung. Above the bulwark the deck was visible.

Save the sailors who had reefed the sail, and yet lingered on the yard, but one man was to be seen by the party on the mole, and he stood by the prow helmeted and with a shield.

The hundred and twenty oaken blades, kept white and shining by pumice and the constant wash of the waves, rose and fell as if operated by the same hand, and drove the galley forward with a speed rivalling that of a modern steamer.

So rapidly, and apparently so rashly,

did she come that the landsmen of the tribune's party were alarmed. Suddenly the man by the prow raised his hand with a peculiar gesture; whereupon all the oars flew up, poised a moment in air then fell straight down. The water boiled and bubbled about them; the galley shook in every timber, and stopped as if scared. Another gesture of the hand, and again the oars arose, feathered, and fell; but this time those on the right, dropping towards the stern, pushed forward; while those on the left, dropping towards the bow, pulled backward. Three times the oars thus pushed and pulled against each other. Round to the right the ship swung as upon a pivot; then, caught by the wind, she settled gently broadside to the mole.

When the oars touched the mole, a bridge was sent out from the helmsman's deck. Then the tribune turned to his party, and said, with a gravity he had not shown:

"Duty now, O my friends."

To the company he opened his arms, and they came one by one and received his parting embrace.

"The gods go with thee, O Quintus!" they said.

"Farewell," he replied.

A GALLEY SLAVE WITH SPIRIT

At noon that day the galley was skimming the sea off Paestum. The wind was yet from the west, filling the sail to the master's content. The watches had been established. On the foredeck the altar had been set and sprinkled with salt and barley, and before it the tribune had offered solemn prayers to Jove and to Neptune and all the Oceanidae, and, with vows, poured the wine and burned the incense. And now, the better to study his men, he was seated in the great cabin, a very martial figure.

Thus at ease, lounging in the great chair, swaying with the motion of the vessel, the military cloak half draping his tunic, sword in belt, Arrius kept watchful eye over his command, and was as closely watched by them. He saw

critically everything in view, but dwelt longest upon the rowers. The reader would doubtless have done the same: only he would have looked with much sympathy, while, as is the habit with masters, the tribune's mind ran forward of what he saw, inquiring for results.

The spectacle was simple enough of itself. Along the sides of the cabin, fixed to the ship's timbers, were what at first appeared to be three rows of benches; a closer view, however, showed them a succession of rising banks, in each of which the second bench was behind and above the first one, and the third above and behind the second. To accommodate the sixty rowers on a side, the space devoted to them permitted nineteen banks separated by intervals of one yard, with a twentieth bank divided so that what would have been its upper seat or bench was directly above the lower seat of the first bank. The arrangement gave each rower when at work ample room, if he timed his movements with those of his associates, the principle being that of soldiers marching with cadenced step in close order. The arrangement also allowed a multiplication of banks, limited only by the length of the galley.

As to the rowers, those upon the first and second benches sat, while those upon the third, having longer oars to work, were suffered to stand. The oars were loaded with lead in the handles, and near the point of balance hung to pliable thongs, making possible the delicate touch called feathering, but, at the same time, increasing the need of skill, since an eccentric wave might at any moment catch a heedless fellow and hurl him from his seat. Each oar-hole was a vent through which the labourer opposite it had his plenty of sweet air. Light streamed down upon him from the grating which formed the floor of the passage between the deck and the bulwark over his head. In some respects, therefore, the condition of the men might have been much worse. Still, it must not be imagined that there was any pleasantness in their lives. Communication between them was not allowed. Day after day they filled their places without speech; in hours of labour they could not see each other's faces; their short respites were given to sleep and the snatching of food. They never laughed; no one ever heard one of them sing. What is the use of tongues when a sigh or a groan will tell all men feel,

while, perforce, they think in silence? Existence with the poor wretches was like a stream under ground sweeping slowly, laboriously on to its outlet, wherever that might chance to be.

From right to left, hour after hour, the tribune, swaying in his easy chair, turned with thought of everything rather than the wretchedness of the slaves upon the benches. Their motions, precise, and exactly the same on both sides of the vessel, after awhile became monotonous; and then he amused himself singling out individuals. With his stylus he made note of objections, thinking, if all went well, he would find among the pirates of whom he was in search better men for the places.

There was no need of keeping the proper names of the slaves brought to the galleys as to their graves; so, for convenience, they were usually identified by numerals painted upon the benches to which they were assigned. As the sharp eyes of the great man moved from seat to seat on either hand, they came at last to number sixty.

The bench of number sixty was slightly above the level of the platform, and but a few feet away. The light glinting through the grating over his head gave the rower fairly to the tribune's view – erect, and, like all his fellows, naked, except a cincture about the loins. There were, however, some points in his favour. He was very young, not more than twenty. Furthermore, Arrius was a connoisseur of men physically, and when ashore indulged a habit of visiting the gymnasia to see and admire the most famous athletae.

In course of the study, Arrius observed that the youth seemed of good height, and that his limbs, upper and nether, were singularly perfect. The arms, perhaps, were too long, but the objection was well hidden under a mass of muscle which, in some movements, swelled and knotted like kinking cords. Every rib in the round body was discernible. Yet the leanness was the healthful reduction so strained after in the palaestrae. And altogether there was in the rower's action a certain harmony which, besides addressing itself to the tribune's theory, stimulated both his curiosity and general interest.

"By the gods," he said to himself, "the fellow impresses me. He promises well. I will know more of him."

Directly the tribune caught the view he wished – the rower turned and looked at him.

"A Jew! and a boy!"

Under the gaze then fixed steadily upon him, the large eyes of the slave grew larger – the blood surged to his very brows – the blade lingered in his hands. But instantly, with an angry crash, down fell the gavel of the hortator. The rower started, withdrew his face from the inquisitor, and, as if personally chidden, dropped the oar half feathered. When he glanced again at the tribune, he was vastly more astonished – he was met with a kindly smile.

Meantime the galley entered the Straits of Messina, and, skimming past the city of that name, was after awhile turned eastward, leaving the cloud over Aetna in the sky astern.

Often as Arrius returned to his platform in the cabin he returned to study the rower, and he kept saying to himself, "The fellow hath a spirit. A Jew is not a barbarian. I will know more of him."

THE TRIBUNE AND THE SLAVE

The fourth day out, and the *Astraea* – so the galley was named – speeding through the Ionian Sea. The sky was clear, and the wind blew as if bearing the goodwill of all the gods.

Arrius, somewhat impatient, spent much time on deck. He took note diligently of matters pertaining to his ship, and, as a rule, was well pleased. In the cabin, swinging in the great chair, his thought continually reverted to the rower on number sixty.

"Knowest thou the man just come from yon bench?" he at length asked of the hortator.

"From number sixty?" returned the chief.

"Yes."

The chief looked sharply at the rower then going forward.

"As thou knowest," he replied, "the ship is but a month from the maker's hand, and the men are as new to me as the ship."

"He is a Jew," Arrius remarked thoughtfully.

"The noble Quintus is shrewd,"

"He is very young," Arrius continued.

"But our best rower," said the other. "I have seen his oar bend almost to breaking."

"Of what disposition is he?"

"He is obedient; further I know not. Once he made request of me."

"For what?"

"He wished me to change him alternately from the right to the left."

"Did he give a reason?"

"He had observed that the men who are confined to one side become misshapen. He also said that some day of storm or battle there might be sudden need to change him, and he might then be unserviceable."

"Perpol! The idea is new. What else hast thou observed of him?"

"He is cleanly above his companions."

"In that he is Roman," said Arrius, approvingly. "Have you nothing of his history?"

"Not a word."

The tribune reflected awhile, and turned to go to his own seat.

"If I should be on deck when his time is up," he paused to say, "send him to me. Let him come alone."

About two hours later Arrius stood under the aplustre of the galley, in the mood of one who, seeing himself carried swiftly towards an event of mighty import, has nothing to do but wait. Arrius beheld the rower approaching.

"The chief called thee the noble Arrius, and said it was thy will that I should see thee here. I am come."

There was in the voice a suggestion of life at least partly spent under refining influences; the eyes were clear and open, and more curious than defiant. In tacit acknowledgment of the effect, the Roman spoke as an older man to a younger, not as a master to a slave.

"The hortator tells me thou art his best rower."

"The hortator is very kind," the rower answered.

"Hast thou seen much service?"

"About three years."

"At the oars?"

"I cannot recall a day of rest from them."

"The labour is hard; few men bear it a year without breaking, and thou – thou art but a boy."

"The noble Arrius forgets that the spirit hath much to do with endurance. By its help the weak sometimes thrive, when the strong perish."

"From thy speech, thou art a Jew."

"My ancestors further back than the first Roman were Hebrews. My father was a prince of Jerusalem, and, as a merchant, he sailed the seas. He was known and honoured in the guest-chamber of the great Augustus."

"His name?"

"Ithamar, of the house of Hur."

The tribune raise his hand in astonishment.

"A son of Hur – thou?"

After a silence, he asked:

"What brought thee here?"

Judah lowered his head, and his breast laboured hard. When his feelings were sufficiently mastered, he looked the tribune in the face, and answered:

"I was accused of attempting to assassinate Valerius Gratus, the procurator.

"Thou!" cried Arrius, yet more amazed, and retreating a step. "Thou that assassin! All Rome rang with the story. It came to my ship in the river by Lodinum."

The two regarded each other silently.

"I thought the family of Hur blotted from the earth," said Arrius, speaking first.

A flood of tender recollections carried the young man's pride away; tears shone upon his cheeks.

"Mother – mother! And my little Tirzah! Where are they? O tribune, noble tribune, if thou knowest anything of them" – he clasped his hands in appeal – "tell me all thou knowest. Tell me if they are living – if living, where are they, and in what condition? Oh, I pray thee, tell me."

"Dost thou admit thy guilt?" asked Arrius, sternly.

The change that came upon the youth was wonderful to see, it was so instant and extreme. The voice sharpened; the hands arose tight-clenched; every fibre thrilled; his eyes flamed.

"Thou hast heard of the God of my fathers," he said; "of the infinite Jehovah. By His truth and almightiness, and by the love with which He hath followed Israel from the beginning, I swear I am innocent."

The tribune was much moved.

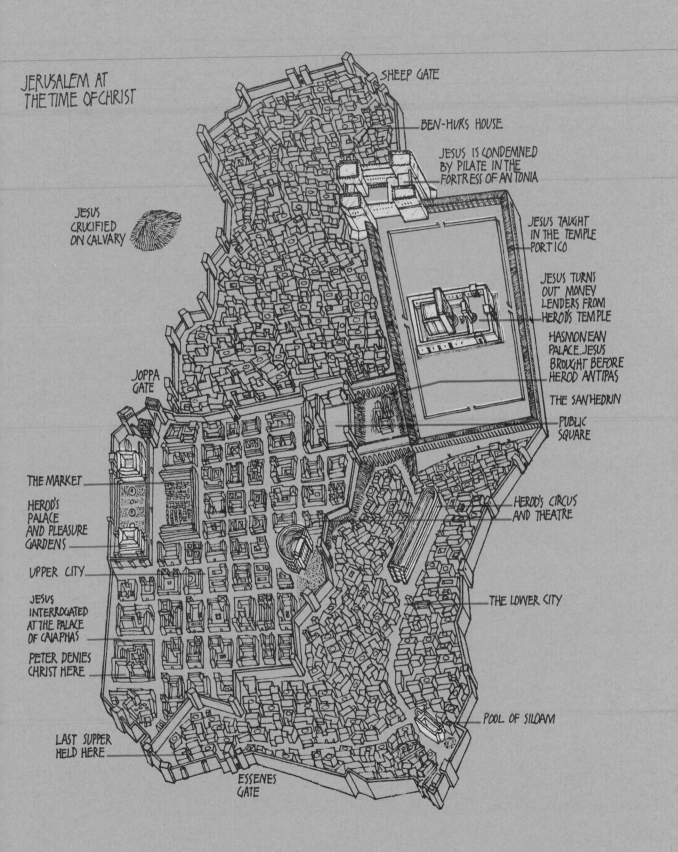

JERUSALEM AT
THE TIME OF CHRIST

SHEEP GATE

BEN-HUR'S HOUSE

JESUS IS CONDEMNED
BY PILATE IN THE
FORTRESS OF ANTONIA

JESUS
CRUCIFIED
ON CALVARY

JESUS TAUGHT
IN THE TEMPLE
PORTICO

JESUS TURNS
OUT MONEY
LENDERS FROM
HEROD'S TEMPLE

HASMONEAN
PALACE. JESUS
BROUGHT BEFORE
HEROD ANTIPAS

JOPPA
GATE

THE SANHEDRIN

PUBLIC
SQUARE

THE MARKET

HEROD'S
PALACE
AND PLEASURE
GARDENS

HEROD'S CIRCUS
AND THEATRE

UPPER CITY

JESUS
INTERROGATED
AT THE PALACE
OF CAIAPHAS

THE LOWER CITY

PETER DENIES
CHRIST HERE

POOL OF SILOAM

LAST SUPPER
HELD HERE

ESSENES
GATE

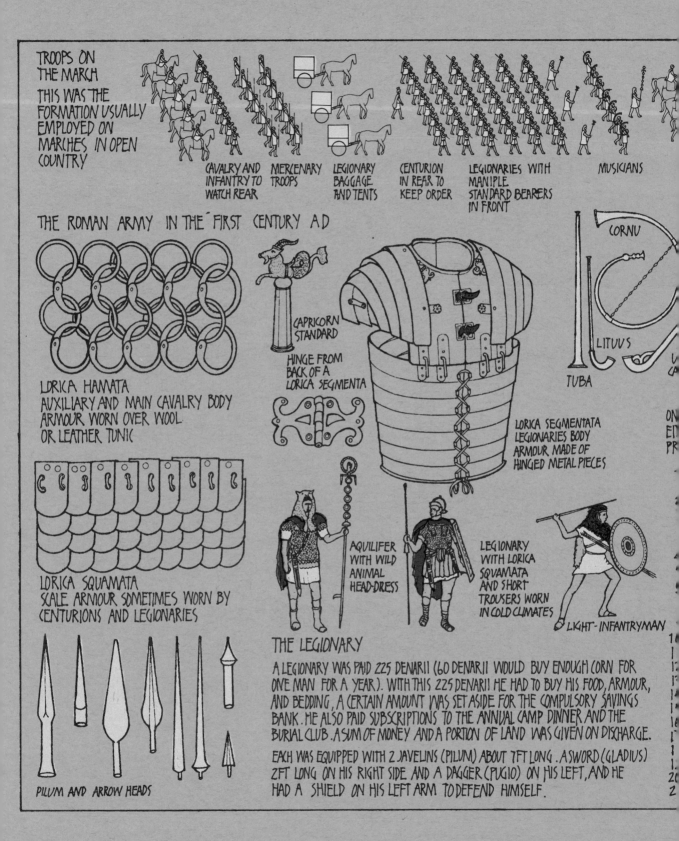

TROOPS ON THE MARCH

THIS WAS THE FORMATION USUALLY EMPLOYED ON MARCHES IN OPEN COUNTRY

CAVALRY AND INFANTRY TO WATCH REAR

MERCENARY TROOPS

LEGIONARY BAGGAGE AND TENTS

CENTURION IN REAR TO KEEP ORDER

LEGIONARIES WITH MANIPLE STANDARD BEARERS IN FRONT

MUSICIANS

THE ROMAN ARMY IN THE FIRST CENTURY A.D.

CAPRICORN STANDARD

HINGE FROM BACK OF A LORICA SEGMENTA

CORNU

LITUUS

TUBA

LORICA HAMATA
AUXILIARY AND MAIN CAVALRY BODY ARMOUR WORN OVER WOOL OR LEATHER TUNIC

LORICA SEGMENTATA LEGIONARIES BODY ARMOUR MADE OF HINGED METAL PIECES

LORICA SQUAMATA
SCALE ARMOUR SOMETIMES WORN BY CENTURIONS AND LEGIONARIES

AQUILIFER WITH WILD ANIMAL HEAD-DRESS

LEGIONARY WITH LORICA SQUAMATA AND SHORT TROUSERS WORN IN COLD CLIMATES

LIGHT-INFANTRYMAN

PILUM AND ARROW HEADS

THE LEGIONARY

A LEGIONARY WAS PAID 225 DENARII (60 DENARII WOULD BUY ENOUGH CORN FOR ONE MAN FOR A YEAR). WITH THIS 225 DENARII HE HAD TO BUY HIS FOOD, ARMOUR, AND BEDDING, A CERTAIN AMOUNT WAS SET ASIDE FOR THE COMPULSORY SAVINGS BANK. HE ALSO PAID SUBSCRIPTIONS TO THE ANNUAL CAMP DINNER AND THE BURIAL CLUB. A SUM OF MONEY AND A PORTION OF LAND WAS GIVEN ON DISCHARGE.

EACH WAS EQUIPPED WITH 2 JAVELINS (PILUM) ABOUT 7FT LONG. A SWORD (GLADIUS) 2FT LONG ON HIS RIGHT SIDE AND A DAGGER (PUGIO) ON HIS LEFT, AND HE HAD A SHIELD ON HIS LEFT ARM TO DEFEND HIMSELF.

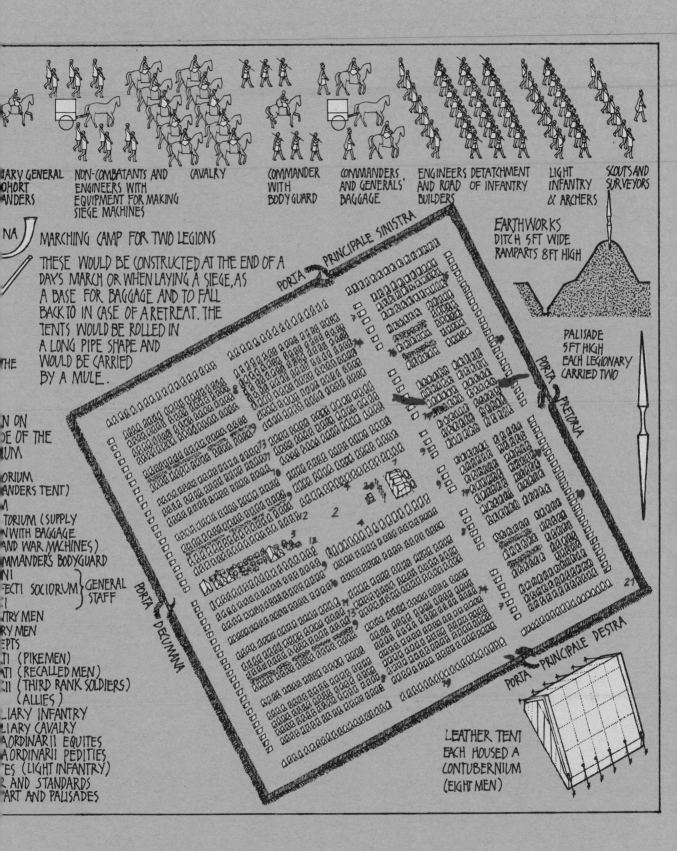

NA

...ARY GENERAL
...OHORT
...ANDERS

NON-COMBATANTS AND ENGINEERS WITH EQUIPMENT FOR MAKING SIEGE MACHINES

CAVALRY

COMMANDER WITH BODYGUARD

COMMANDERS AND GENERALS' BAGGAGE

ENGINEERS AND ROAD BUILDERS

DETACHMENT OF INFANTRY

LIGHT INFANTRY & ARCHERS

SCOUTS AND SURVEYORS

MARCHING CAMP FOR TWO LEGIONS

THESE WOULD BE CONSTRUCTED AT THE END OF A DAY'S MARCH OR WHEN LAYING A SIEGE, AS A BASE FOR BAGGAGE AND TO FALL BACK TO IN CASE OF A RETREAT. THE TENTS WOULD BE ROLLED IN A LONG PIPE SHAPE AND WOULD BE CARRIED BY A MULE.

N ON
...E OF THE
...UM

...ORIUM (...ANDERS TENT)
A
...TORIUM (SUPPLY ...N WITH BAGGAGE ...AND WAR MACHINES)
...MMANDER'S BODYGUARD
...NI
...FECTI SOCIORUM } GENERAL STAFF

...TRY MEN
...RY MEN
...EPTS
...TI (PIKEMEN)
...ATI (RECALLED MEN)
...II (THIRD RANK SOLDIERS)
(ALLIES)
...LIARY INFANTRY
...LIARY CAVALRY
...AORDINARII EQUITES
...AORDINARII PEDITES
...ES (LIGHT INFANTRY)
...R AND STANDARDS
...ART AND PALISADES

PORTA PRINCIPALE SINISTRA

PORTA PRETORIA

PORTA PRINCIPALE DESTRA

PORTA DECUMANA

EARTHWORKS DITCH 5FT WIDE RAMPARTS 8FT HIGH

PALISADE 5FT HIGH EACH LEGIONARY CARRIED TWO

LEATHER TENT EACH HOUSED A CONTUBERNIUM (EIGHT MEN)

THE ROMAN LEGION AND ITS COMPOSITION   1ST CENTURY AD

ONLY ROMAN CITIZENS COULD SERVE AS LEGIONARIES.
THERE WAS A FORM OF CONSCRIPTION BUT QUITE A NUMBER
VOLUNTEERED
THE STANDING ARMY WAS ESTABLISHED IN 13 BC BY AUGUSTUS.
UNTIL THEN THE ARMY WAS RECRUITED ONLY IN TIMES OF
TROUBLE AND THEN DISBANDED WHEN IT CEASED.

THERE WERE NEVER MORE THAN 30 LEGIONS THE USUAL
NUMBER BEING 28 SPREAD THROUGHOUT THE EMPIRE.
THE DIAGRAM ON THE RIGHT, REPRESENTS THE UNITS OF MEN
IN A LEGION. THE DIAGRAM UNDER, THE OFFICERS AND
SPECIALIST STAFF.

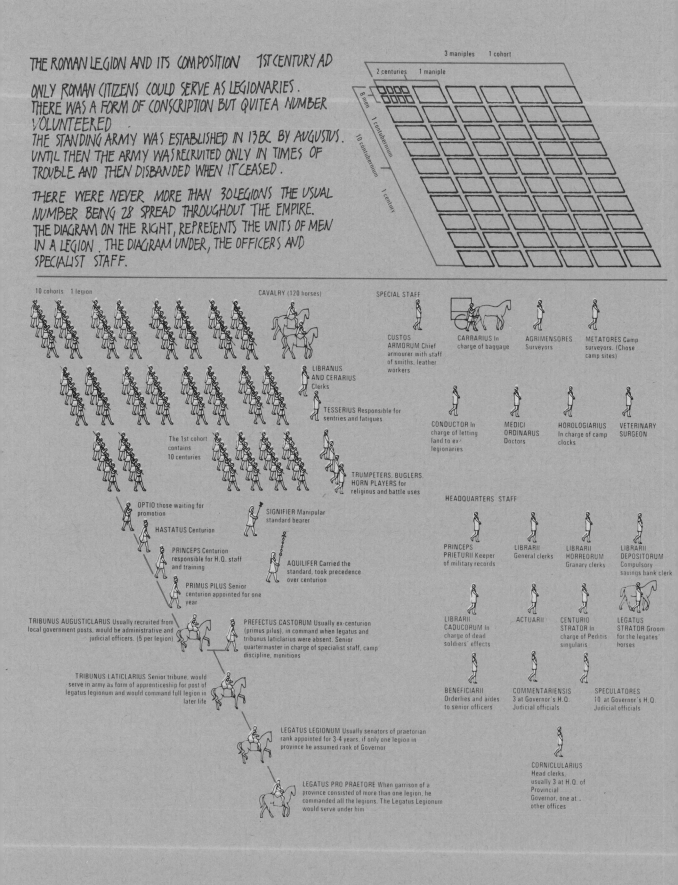

3 maniples   1 cohort
2 centuries   1 maniple
8 men
1 contubernium
10 contubernium
1 century

10 cohorts   1 legion

CAVALRY (120 horses)

SPECIAL STAFF

CUSTOS ARMORUM Chief armourer with staff of smiths, leather workers

CARRARIUS In charge of baggage

AGRIMENSORES Surveyors

METATORES Camp surveyors. (Chose camp sites)

LIBRANUS AND CERARIUS Clerks

TESSERIUS Responsible for sentries and fatigues

The 1st cohort contains 10 centuries

CONDUCTOR In charge of letting land to ex- legionaries

MEDICI ORDINARUS Doctors

HOROLOGIARIUS In charge of camp clocks

VETERINARY SURGEON

TRUMPETERS, BUGLERS, HORN PLAYERS for religious and battle uses

HEADQUARTERS STAFF

OPTIO those waiting for promotion

HASTATUS Centurion

SIGNIFIER Manipular standard bearer

PRINCEPS Centurion responsible for H.Q. staff and training

PRIMUS PILUS Senior centurion appointed for one year

AQUILIFER Carried the standard, took precedence over centurion

PRINCEPS PRIETURII Keeper of military records

LIBRARII General clerks

LIBRARII HORREORUM Granary clerks

LIBRARII DEPOSITORUM Compulsory savings bank clerk

TRIBUNUS AUGUSTICLARUS Usually recruited from local government posts, would be administrative and judicial officers. (5 per legion)

PREFECTUS CASTORUM Usually ex-centurion (primus pilus), in command when legatus and tribunus laticlarius were absent. Senior quartermaster in charge of specialist staff, camp discipline, munitions

LIBRARII CADUCORUM In charge of dead soldiers' effects

ACTUARII

CENTURIO STRATOR In charge of Peditis singularis

LEGATUS STRATOR Groom for the legates' horses

TRIBUNUS LATICLARIUS Senior tribune, would serve in army as form of apprenticeship for post of legatus legionum and would command full legion in later life

BENEFICIARII Orderlies and aides to senior officers

COMMENTARIENSIS 3 at Governor's H.Q. Judicial officials

SPECULATORES 10 at Governor's H.Q. Judicial officials

LEGATUS LEGIONUM Usually senators of praetorian rank appointed for 3-4 years, if only one legion in province he assumed rank of Governor

LEGATUS PRO PRAETORE When garrison of a province consisted of more than one legion, he commanded all the legions. The Legatus Legionum would serve under him

CORNICULARIUS Head clerks, usually 3 at H.Q. of Provincial Governor, one at other offices

"Didst thou not have a trial?" he asked, stopping suddenly.

"No."

The Roman raised his head, surprised.

"No trial – no witnesses! Who passed judgment upon thee?"

Romans, it should be remembered, were at no time such lovers of the law and its forms as in the ages of their decay.

"They bound me with cords, and dragged me to a vault in the Tower. I saw no one. No one spoke to me. Next day soldiers took me to the sea. I have been a galley-slave ever since."

"What couldst thou have proven?"

"I was a boy, too young to be a conspirator. Gratus was a stranger to me. If I had meant to kill him that was not the time or the place. He was riding in the midst of a legion, and it was broad day. I could not have escaped. I was of a class most friendly to Rome. My father had been distinguished for his services to the emperor. We had a great estate to lose. Ruin was certain to myself, my mother, my sister. I had no cause for malice, while every consideration – property, family, life, conscience, the law – to a son of Israel as the breath of his nostrils – would have stayed my hand, though the foul intent had been ever so strong. I was not mad. Death was preferable to shame; and, believe me, I pray, it is so yet."

"Who was with thee when the blow was struck?"

"I was on the house-top – my father's house. Tirzah was with me – at my side – the soul of gentleness. Together we leaned over the parapet to see the legion pass. A tile gave way under my hand, and fell upon Gratus. I thought I had killed him. Ah, what horror I felt!"

"Where was thy mother?"

"In her chamber below."

"What became of her?"

Ben-Hur clenched his hands, and drew a breath like a gasp.

"I do not know. I saw them drag her away – that is all I know. Out of the house they drove every living thing even the dumb cattle, and they sealed the gates. The purpose was that she should not return. I, too, ask for her. Oh, for one word! She, at least, was innocent. I can forgive – but I pray thy pardon, noble tribune. A slave like me should not talk of forgiveness or of revenge. I am bound to an oar for life."

Arrius listened intently. He brought all his experience with slaves to his aid. If the feeling shown in this instance were assumed, the acting was perfect; on the other hand, if it were real, the Jew's innocence might not be doubted; and if he were innocent, with what blind fury the power had been exercised. A whole family blotted out to atone an accident. The thought shocked him.

For once the tribune was at loss, and hesitated. His power was ample. He was monarch of the ship. His prepossessions all moved him to mercy. His faith was won. Yet, he said to himself, there was no haste – or, rather, there was haste to Cythera; the best rower could not then be spared; he would wait; he would learn more; he would at least be sure this was the prince Ben-Hur [son of Hur], and that he was of a right disposition. Ordinarily, slaves were liars.

"It is enough," he said aloud. "Go back to thy place."

A CONFRONTATION

In the Bay of Antemona, east of Cythera the island, the hundred galleys assembled. There the tribune gave one day to inspection. He sailed then to Naxos, the largest of the Cyclades, midway the coasts of Greece and Asia, like a great stone planted in the centre of a highway, from which he could challenge everything that passed; at the same time, he would be in position to go after the pirates instantly, whether they were in the Aegean or out on the Mediterranean.

As the fleet, in order, rowed in towards the mountain shores of the island, a galley was descried coming from the north. Arrius went to meet it. She proved to be a transport just from Byzantium, and from her commander he learned the particular of which he stood in most need.

The pirates were from all the farther shores of the Euxine. Even Tanais, at the mouth of the river which was supposed to feed Palus Maeotis, was represented among them. Their preparations had been with the greatest secrecy. There were quite sixty galleys in the squadron, all well manned and supplied. A few were biremes, the rest stout triremes. A Greek was in command, and the pilots, said to be familiar with all the Eastern Seas, were Greek. The plunder had been incalculable. The panic, consequently, was not on the sea alone; cities, with closed gates, sent their people nightly to the walls. Traffic had almost ceased.

Where were the pirates now?

To this question, of most interest to Arrius, he received answer.

After sacking Hephaestia, on the island of Lemnos, the enemy had coursed across to the Thessalian group, and, by last account, disappeared in the gulfs between Euboea and Hellas.

Such were the tidings.

If the reader will take a map of Greece and the Aegean, he will notice the island of Euboea lying along the classic coast like a rampart against Asia, leaving a channel between it and the continent quite a hundred and twenty miles in length, and scarcely an average of eighty in width. The inlet on the north had admitted the fleet of Xerxes, and now it received the bold raiders from the Euxine. The towns along the Pelasgic and Meliac gulfs were rich and their plunder seductive. All things considered, therefore, Arrius judged that the robbers might be found somewhere below Thermopylae. Welcoming the chance, he resolved to enclose them north and south, to do which not an hour could be lost; even the fruits and wines and women of Naxos must be left behind. So he sailed away without stop or tack until, a little before nightfall, Mount Ocha was seen upreared against the sky, and the pilot reported the Euboean coast.

At a signal the fleet rested upon its oars. When the movement was resumed, Arrius led a division of fifty of the galleys, intending to take them up the channel, while another division, equally strong, turned their prows to the outer or seaward side of the island, with orders to make all haste to the upper inlet, and descend, sweeping the waters.

To be sure, neither division was equal in number to the pirates; but each had advantages in compensation, among them, by no means least, a discipline impossible to a lawless horde, however brave. Besides, it was a shrewd count on the tribune's side, if peradventure, one should be defeated, the other would find the enemy shattered by his victory, and in condition to be easily overwhelmed.

Meantime Ben-Hur kept his bench, relieved every six hours. The rest in the Bay of Antemona had freshened him, so that the oar was not troublesome, and the chief on the platform found no fault.

When the sun, going down, withdrew his last ray from the cabin, the galley still held northward. About that time the smell of incense floated down the gangways from the deck.

"The tribune is at the altar," he thought. "Can it be we are going into battle?"

And when, finally, Ben-Hur saw the tribune mount his platform and don his armour, and get his helmet and shield out, the meaning of the preparations might not be any longer doubted, and he made ready for the last ignominy of his service.

To every bench, as a fixture, there was a chain with heavy anklets. These the hortator proceeded to lock upon the oarsmen, going from number to number, leaving no choice but to obey, and, in event of disaster, no possibility of escape.

Every man upon the benches felt the shame, Ben-Hur more keenly than his companions. Soon the clanking of the fetters notified him of the progress the chief was making in his round. He would come to him in turn, but would not the tribune interpose for him?

Ben-Hur waited anxiously.

The hortator approached. Now he was at number one – the rattle of the iron links sounded horribly. At last number sixty! Calm from despair, Ben-Hur held his oar at poise, and gave his foot to the officer. Then the tribune stirred – sat up – beckoned to the chief.

The chief went to the tribune, and, smiling, pointed to number sixty.

"What strength!" he said.

"And what spirit!" the tribune answered. "Perpol! He is better without the irons. Put them on him no more."

So saying he stretched himself upon the couch again.

The ship sailed on hour after hour under the oars in water scarcely rippled by the wind. And the people not on duty slept, Arrius in his place, the marines on the floor.

The deeper darkness before the dawn was upon the waters, and all things going well with the *Astraea*, when a man, descending from the deck, walked swiftly to the platform where the tribune slept, and awoke him. Arrius arose, put on his helmet, sword, and shield, and went to the commander of the marines.

"The pirates are close by. Up and ready!" he said and passed to the stairs, calm, confident.

PIRATES

Every soul aboard, even the ship, awoke. Officers went to their quarters. The marines took arms, and were led out, looking in all respects like legionaries. Sheaves of arrows and armfuls of javelins were carried on deck. By the central stairs the oil-tanks and fire-balls were set ready for use. Additional lanterns were lighted. Buckets were filled with water. The rowers in relief assembled under guard in front of the chief. As Providence would have it, Ben-Hur was one of the latter.

At a signal passed down from the deck, and communicated to the hortator by a petty officer stationed on the stairs, all at once the oars stopped.

What did it mean?

Of the hundred and twenty slaves chained to the benches, not one but asked himself the question. There was little time, however, for such thought with them. A sound like the rowing of galleys astern attracted Ben-Hur, and the *Astraea* rocked as if in the midst of countering waves. The idea of a fleet at hand broke upon him – a fleet in manoeuvre – forming probably for attack. His blood started with the fancy.

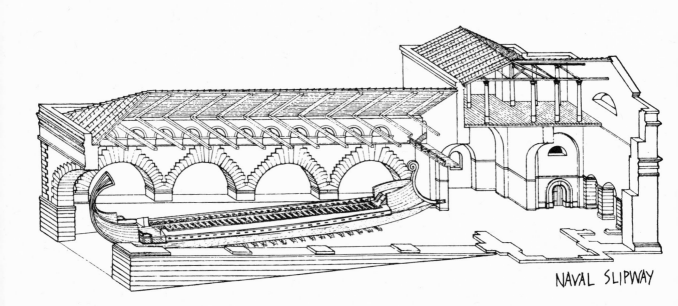

NAVAL SLIPWAY

Another signal came down from the deck. The oars dipped, and the galley started imperceptibly. No sound from without, none from within, yet each man in the cabin instinctively poised himself for a shock; the very ship seemed to catch the sense, and hold its breath, and go crouched tiger-like.

In such a situation time is inappreciable; so that Ben-Hur could form no judgment of distance gone. At last there was a sound of trumpets on deck, full, clear, long blown. The chief beat the sounding-board until it rang; the rowers reached forward full length, and, deepening the dip of their oars, pulled suddenly with all their united force. The galley, quivering in every timber, answered with a leap. Other trumpets joined in the clamour – all from the rear, none forward – from the latter quarter only a rising sound of voices in tumult heard briefly. There was a mighty blow; the rowers in front of the chief's platform reeled, some of them fell; the ship bounded back, recovered, and rushed on more irresistibly than before. Shrill and high arose the shrieks of men in terror; over the blare of trumpets, and the grind and crash of the collision, they arose; then under his feet, under the keel, pounding, rumbling, breaking to pieces, drowning, Ben-Hur felt something overridden. The men about him looked at each other afraid. A shout of triumph from the deck – the beak of the Roman had won! But who were they whom the sea had drunk? Of what tongue, from what land were they?

No pause, no stay! Forward rushed the *Astraea*; and, as it went, some sailors ran down, and plunging the cotton balls into the oil-tanks, tossed them dripping to comrades at the head of the stairs; fire was to be added to other horrors of the combat.

Directly the galley heeled over so far that the oarsmen on the uppermost side with difficulty kept their benches. Again the hearty Roman cheer, and with it despairing shrieks. An opposing vessel, caught by the grappling-hooks of the great crane swinging from the prow, was being lifted into the air that it might be dropped and sunk.

The shouting increased on the right hand and on the left; before, behind, swelled an indescribable clamour. Occasionally there was a crash, followed by sudden peals of fright, telling of other ships ridden down, and their crews drowned in the vortexes.

Nor was the fight all on one side. Now and then a Roman in armour was borne down the hatchway, and laid bleeding, sometimes dying, on the floor.

Sometimes, also, puffs of smoke, blended with steam, and foul with the scent of roasting human flesh, poured into the cabin, turning the dimming light into yellow murk. Gasping for breath the while, Ben-Hur knew they were passing through the cloud of a ship on fire, and burning up with the rowers chained to the benches.

The *Astraea* all this time was in motion. Suddenly she stopped. The oars forward were dashed from the hands of rowers, and the rowers from their benches. On deck, then, a furious trampling, and on the sides a grinding of ships afoul of each other. For the first time the beating of the gavel was lost in the uproar. Men sank on the floor in fear or looked about seeking a hiding-place. In the midst of the panic a body plunged or was pitched headlong down the hatchway, falling near Ben-Hur. He beheld the half-naked carcass, a mass of hair blackening the face, and under it a shield of bull-hide and wicker-work — a barbarian from the white-skinned nations of the North whom death had robbed of plunder and revenge. How came he there? An iron hand had snatched him from the opposing deck – no, the *Astraea* had been boarded! The Romans were fighting on their own deck. A chill smote the young Jew; Arrius was hard pressed – he might be defending his own life. If he should be slain! God of Abraham forfend! The hopes and dreams so lately come, were they only hopes and dreams? Mother and sister – house – home – Holy Land – was he not to see them, after all? The tumult thundered above him; he looked around; in the cabin all was confusion – the rowers on the benches paralyzed; men running blindly hither and thither.

A very short space lay between him and the stairs of the hatchway aft. He took it with a leap, and was half-way up the steps – up far enough to catch a glimpse of the sky blood-red with fire, of the ships alongside, of the sea covered with ships and wrecks, of the fight closed in about the pilot's quarter, the assailants many, the defenders few – when suddenly his foothold was knocked away, and he pitched backward. The floor, when he reached it, seemed to be lifting itself and breaking to pieces; then, in a twinkling, the whole after-part of the hull broke asunder, and, as if it had all the time been lying in wait, the sea, hissing and foaming, leaped in, and all became darkness and surging water to Ben-Hur.

The influx of the flood tossed him like a log forward into the cabin, where he would have drowned but for the refluence of the sinking motion. As it was, fathoms under the surface the hollow mass vomited him forth, and he arose along with the loosed débris. In the act of rising, he clutched something, and held to it. The time he was under seemed an age, longer than it really was; at last he gained the top; with a great gasp he filled his lungs afresh, and, tossing the water from his hair and eyes, climbed higher upon the plank he held, and looked about him.

Death had pursued him closely under the waves; he found it waiting for him when he was risen – waiting multiform.

Smoke lay upon the sea like a semi-transparent fog, through which here and there shone cores of intense brilliance. A quick intelligence told him that they were ships on fire. The battle was yet on; nor could he say who was victor. Within the radius of his vision now and then ships passed, shooting shadows athwart lights. Out of the dun clouds farther on he caught the crash of other ships colliding.

About that time he heard oars in quickest movement, and beheld a galley coming down upon him. The tall prow seemed doubly tall, and the red light playing upon its gilt and carving gave it an appearance of snaky life. Under its foot the water churned to flying foam.

He struck out, pushing the plank, which was very broad and unmanageable. Seconds were precious – half a second might save or lose him. In the crisis of the effort, up from the sea, within arm's reach, a helmet shot like a gleam of gold. Next came two hands with fingers extended – large hands were they, and strong – their hold once fixed, might not be loosed. Ben-Hur swerved from them appalled. Up rose the helmet and the head it encased – then two arms, which began to beat the water wildly – the head turned back, and gave the face to the light. The mouth gaping wide; the eyes open, but sightless, and the bloodless pallor of a drowning man –

never anything more ghastly! Yet he gave a cry of joy at the sight, and as the face was going under again, he caught the sufferer by the chain which passed from the helmet beneath the chin, and drew him to the plank.

The man was Arrius, the tribune.

For awhile the water foamed and eddied violently about Ben-Hur, taxing all his strength to hold to the support and at the same time keep the Roman's head above the surface. The galley had passed, leaving the two barely outside the stroke of its oars. Right through the floating men, over heads helmeted as well as heads bare, she drove, in her wake nothing but the sea sparkling with fire. A muffled crash, succeeded by a great outcry, made the rescuer look again from his charge. A certain savage pleasure touched his heart – the *Astraea* was avenged.

After that the battle moved on. Resistance turned to flight. But who were the victors? Ben-Hur was sensible how much his freedom and the life of the tribune depended upon that event. He pushed the plank under the latter until it floated him, after which all his care was to keep him there. The dawn came slowly. He watched its growing hopefully, yet sometimes afraid. Would it bring the Romans or the pirates? If the pirates, his charge was lost.

At last morning broke in full, the air without a breath. Off to the left he saw the land, too far to think of attempting to make it. Here and there men were adrift like himself. In spots the sea was blackened by charred and sometimes smoking fragments. A galley up a long way was laying-to with a torn sail hanging from the tilted yard, and the oars all idle. Still farther away he could discern moving specks, which he thought might be ships in flight or pursuit, or they might be white birds awing.

An hour passed thus. His anxiety increased. If relief came not speedily, Arrius would die. Sometimes he seemed already dead, he lay so still. He took the helmet off, and then, with greater difficulty, the cuirass; the heart he found fluttering. He took hope at the sign, and held on. There was nothing to do but wait, and, after the manner of his people, pray.

THE RESCUE

The throes of recovery from drowning are more painful than the drowning. These Arrius passed through, and, at length, to Ben-Hur's delight, reached the point of speech.

Gradually, from incoherent questions as to where he was, and by whom and how he had been saved, he reverted to the battle. The doubt of the victory stimulated his faculties to full return, a result aided not a little by a long rest – such as could be had on their frail support. After awhile he became talkative.

"Our rescue, I see, depends upon the result of the fight. I see also what thou hast done for me. To speak fairly, thou hast saved my life at the risk of thy own. I make the acknowledgment broadly; and, whatever cometh, thou hast my thanks. More than that, if fortune doth but serve me kindly, and we get well out of this peril, I will do thee such favour as becometh a Roman who hath power and opportunity to prove his gratitude."

"If I live I will make thee free, and restore thee to thy home and people; or thou mayst give thyself to the pursuit that pleaseth thee most. Dost thou hear?"

"I could not choose but hear. Yonder cometh a ship."

"In what direction?"

"From the north."

"Canst thou tell her nationality by outward signs?"

"No. My service hath been at the oars."

"Hath she a flag?"

"I cannot see one."

Arrius remained quiet some time, apparently in deep reflection.

"Does the ship hold this way yet?" he at length asked.

"Still this way."

"Look for the flag now."

"She hath none."

"Nor any other sign?"

SHIPS RAM

"She hath a sail set, and is of three banks, and cometh swiftly – that is all I can say of her."

"A Roman in triumph would have out many flags. She must be an enemy."

Ben-Hur looked often at the coming ship. Arrius rested with closed eyes, indifferent.

"Art thou sure she is an enemy?" Ben-Hur asked.

"I think so," was the reply.

"She stops, and puts a boat over the side."

"Dost thou see her flag?"

"Is there no other sign by which she may be known if Roman?"

"If Roman, she hath a helmet over the mast's top."

"Then be of cheer. I see the helmet."

Still Arrius was not assured.

"The men in the small boat are taking in the people afloat. Pirates are not humane."

"They may need rowers," Arrius replied, recurring, possibly, to times when he had made rescues for the purpose.

Ben-Hur was very watchful of the actions of the strangers.

"The ship moves off," he said.

"Whither?"

"Over on our right there is a galley which I take to be deserted. The newcomer heads towards it. Now she is alongside. Now she is sending men aboard."

Then Arrius opened his eyes and threw off his calm.

"Thank thou thy God," he said to Ben-Hur, after a look at the galleys; "thank thou thy God, as I do my many gods. A pirate would, sink, not save, yon ship. By the act and the helmet on the mast I know a Roman. The victory is mine. Fortune hath not deserted me. We are saved. Wave thy hand – call to them – bring them quickly. I shall be duumvir, and thou! I knew thy father, and loved him. He was a prince indeed. He taught me a Jew was not a barbarian. I will take thee with me. I will make thee my son. Give thy God thanks, and call the sailors. Haste! The pursuit must be kept. Not a robber shall escape. Hasten them!"

Judah raised himself upon the plank, and waved his hand, and called with all his might; at last he drew the attention of the sailors in the small boat, and they were speedily taken up.

Arrius was received on the galley with

all the honours due a hero so the favourite of Fortune. Upon a couch on the deck he heard the particulars of the conclusion of the fight. When the survivors afloat upon the water were all saved and the prize secured, he spread his flag of commandant anew, and hurried northward to rejoin the fleet and perfect the victory. In due time the fifty vessels coming down the channel closed in upon the fugitive pirates, and crushed them utterly; not one escaped. To swell the tribune's glory, twenty galleys of the enemy were captured.

Upon his return from the cruise, Arrius had warm welcome on the mole at Misenum. The young man attending him very early attracted the attention of his friends there; and to their questions as to who he was, the tribune proceeded in the most affectionate manner to tell the story of his rescue and introduce the stranger, omitting carefully all that pertained to the latter's previous history. At the end of the narrative, he called Ben-Hur to him, and said, with a hand resting affectionately upon his shoulder:

"Good friends, this is my son and heir, who, as he is to take my property – if it be the will of the gods that I leave any – shall be known to you by my name. I pray you all to love him as you love me."

Speedily as opportunity permitted, the adoption was formally perfected. And in such manner the brave Roman kept his faith with Ben-Hur, giving him happy introduction into the imperial world. The month succeeding Arrius's return, the armilustrium was celebrated with the utmost magnificence in the theatre of Scaurus. One side of the structure was taken up with military trophies, among which by far the most conspicuous and most admired were twenty prows, complemented by their corresponding aplustra, cut bodily from as many galleys, and over them, so as to be legible to the eighty thousand spectators in the seats, was this inscription:

TAKEN FROM THE PIRATES IN THE GULF
OF EURIPUS,
BY
QUINTUS ARRIUS,
DUUMVIR.

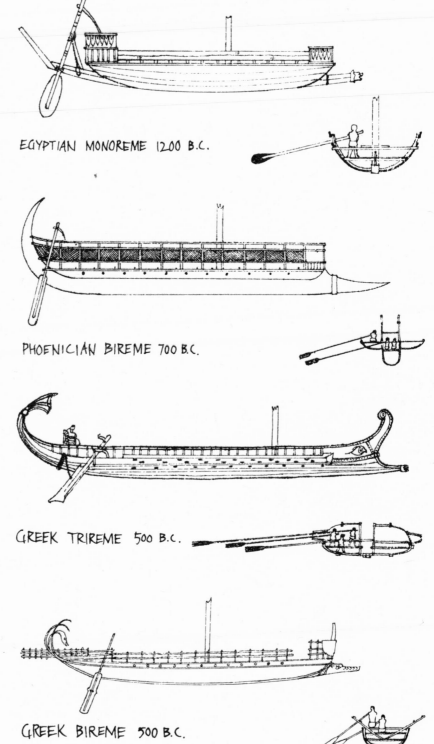

EGYPTIAN MONOREME 1200 B.C.

PHOENICIAN BIREME 700 B.C.

GREEK TRIREME 500 B.C.

GREEK BIREME 500 B.C.

BOOK FOUR

RETURN TO THE EAST

The month to which we now come is July, the year that of our Lord 29, and the place Antioch, then Queen of the East, and next to Rome the strongest, if not the most populous, city in the world.

A transport galley entered the mouth of the river Orontes from the blue waters of the sea. It was in the forenoon. The heat was great, yet all on board who could avail themselves of the privilege were on deck, Ben-Hur among others.

The five years had brought the young Jew to perfect manhood. Though the robe of white linen in which he was attired somewhat masked his form, his appearance was unusually attractive. For an hour and more he had occupied a seat in the shade of the sail, and in that time several fellow-passengers of his own nationality had tried to engage him in conversation, but without avail. His replies to their questions had been brief, though gravely courteous, and in the Latin tongue. The purity of his speech, his cultivated manners, his reticence, served to stimulate their curiosity the more.

The galley, in coming, had stopped at one of the ports of Cyprus, and picked up a Hebrew of most respectable appearance, quiet, reserved, paternal. Ben-Hur ventured to ask him some questions; the replies won his confidence, and resulted finally in an extended conversation.

It chanced also that as the galley from Cyprus entered the receiving bay of the Orontes, two other vessels which had been sighted out in the sea met it and passed into the river at the same time; and as they did so both the strangers threw out small flags of brightest yellow. There was much conjecture as to the meaning of the signals. At length a passenger addressed himself to the respectable Hebrew for information upon the subject.

"Yes, I know the meaning of the flags," he replied; "they do not signify nationality – they are merely marks of ownership."

"Has the owner many ships?"

"He has."

"You know him?"

"I have dealt with him."

The passengers looked at the speaker as if requesting him to go on.

"He lives in Antioch," the Hebrew continued, in his quiet way. "That he is vastly rich has brought him into notice, and the talk about him is not always kind. There used to be in Jerusalem a prince of very ancient family named Hur."

Judah strove to be composed, yet his heart beat quicker.

"The prince was a merchant, with a genius for business. He set on foot many enterprises, some reaching far East, others West. In the great cities he had branch houses. The one in Antioch was in charge of a man said by some to have been a family servant called Simonides, Greek in name, yet an Israelite. The master was drowned at sea. His business, however, went on, and was scarcely less prosperous. After awhile misfortune overtook the family. The prince's only son, nearly grown, tried to kill the procurator, Gratus, in one of the streets of Jerusalem. He failed by a narrow chance, and has not since been heard of. In fact, the Roman's rage took in the whole house – not one of the name was left alive. Their palace was sealed up, and is now a rookery for pigeons; the estate was confiscated; everything that could be traced to the ownership of the Hurs was confiscated. The procurator cured his hurt with a golden salve."

The passengers laughed.

"You mean he kept the property," said one of them.

"They say so," the Hebrew replied; "I am only telling a story as I received it. And, to go on, Simonides, who had been the prince's agent here in Antioch, opened trade in a short time on his own account, and in a space incredibly brief became the master merchant of the city. In imitation of his master, he sent caravans to India; and on the sea at present he has galleys enough to make a royal fleet. They say nothing goes amiss with him. His camels do not die, except of old age; his ships never founder; if he throw a chip into the river, it will come back to him gold."

"How long has he been going on thus?"

"Not ten years."

"He must have had a good start."

"Yes, they say the procurator took only the prince's property ready at hand – his horses, cattle, houses, land, vessels, goods. The money could not be found, though

DATE PALM

there must have been vast sums of it. What became of it has been an unsolved mystery."

"Not to me," said a passenger, with a sneer.

"I understand you," the Hebrew answered. "Others have had your idea. That it furnished old Simonides his start is a common belief. The procurator is of that opinion – or he has been – for twice in five years he has caught the merchant, and put him to torture."

Judah gripped the rope he was holding with crushing force.

"It is said," the narrator continued, "that there is not a sound bone in the man's body. The last time I saw him he sat in a chair, a shapeless cripple."

"So tortured!" exclaimed several listeners in a breath.

"Disease could not have produced such a deformity. Still the suffering made no impression upon him. All he had was his lawfully, and he was making lawful use of it – that was the most they wrung from him. Now, however, he is past persecution. He has a license to trade signed by Tiberius himself."

When the city came into view, the passengers were on deck, eager that nothing of the scene might escape them.

Finally, the lines were thrown, the oars shipped, and the voyage was done. Then Ben-Hur sought the respectable Hebrew.

"Let me trouble you a moment before saying farewell."

The man bowed assent.

"Your story of the merchant has made me curious to see him. You called him Simonides?"

"Yes. He is a Jew with a Greek name."

"Where is he to be found?"

The acquaintance gave a sharp look before he answered:

"One would think," he then replied, "that the richest merchant in Antioch would have a house for business corresponding to his wealth, but if you would find him in the day, follow the river to yon bridge, under which he quarters in a building that looks like a buttress of the wall. Before the door there is an immense landing, always covered with cargoes come and to go. The fleet that lies moored there is his. You cannot fail to find him."

"I give you thanks."

"The peace of our fathers go with you."

"And with you."

With that they separated.

THE FIRST MEETING WITH SIMONIDES

Next day early, to the neglect of the city, Ben-Hur sought the house of Simonides. Through an embattled gateway he passed to a continuity of wharves; thence up the river midst a busy press, to the Seleucian Bridge, under which he paused to take in the scene.

There, directly under the bridge, was the merchant's house, a mass of grey stone, unhewn, referable to no style, looking like a buttress of the wall against which it leaned. Two immense doors in front communicated with the wharf. Some holes near the top, heavily barred, served as windows. Weeds waved from the crevices, and in places black moss splotched the otherwise bald stones.

The doors were open. Through one of them business went in, through the other it came out, and there was hurry, hurry in all its movements.

He passed boldly into the house.

The interior was that of a vast depot where, in ordered spaces, and under careful arrangement, goods of every kind were heaped and pent. Though the light was murky and the air stifling, men moved about briskly; and in places he saw workmen with saws and hammers making packages for shipments.

At length a man approached and spoke to him.

"What would you have?"

"I would see Simonides, the merchant."

"Will you come this way?"

By a number of paths left in the stowage, they finally came to a flight of steps; ascending which, he found himself on the roof of the depot, and in front of a structure which cannot be better described than as a lesser stone house built upon another, invisible from the landing below, and out west of the bridge under the open sky. The roof, hemmed in by a low wall, seemed like a terrace, which, to his astonishment, was brilliant with flowers; in the rich surrounding, the house sat squat, a plain square block, unbroken except by a doorway in front. A dustless path led to the door, through a bordering of shrubs of Persian rose in perfect bloom. Breathing a sweet attar-perfume, he followed the guide.

At the end of a darkened passage within, they stopped before a curtain half parted. The man called out:

"A stranger to see the master."

A clear voice replied, "In God's name, let him enter."

In the midlight of the room were two persons – a man resting in a chair high-backed, broad-armed, and lined with pliant cushions; and at his left, leaning against the back of the chair, a girl well forward into womanhood. At sight of them Ben-Hur felt the blood redden his forehead; bowing, as much to recover himself as in respect, he lost the lifting of the hands, and the shiver and shrink with which the sitter caught sight of him – an emotion as swift to go as it had been to come. When he raised his eyes the two were in the same position, except the girl's hand had fallen and was resting lightly upon the elder's shoulder; both of them were regarding him fixedly.

"If you are Simonides, the merchant, and a Jew" – Ben-Hur stopped an instant – "then the peace of the God of our father Abraham upon you and – yours."

The last word was addressed to the girl.

"I am the Simonides of whom you speak, by birthright a Jew," the man made answer, in a voice singularly clear. "I am Simonides, and a Jew; and I return you your salutation, with prayer to know who calls upon me."

Ben-Hur looked as he listened, and where the figure of the man should have been in healthful roundness, there was only a formless heap sunk in the depths of the cushions, and covered by a quilted robe of sombre silk. Over the heap shone a head royally proportioned – the ideal head of a statesman and conqueror – a head broad of base and dome-like in front, such as Angelo would have modelled for Caesar. White hair dropped in thin locks over the white brows, deepening the blackness of the eyes shining through them like sullen lights. The face was bloodless, and much puffed with folds, especially under the chin. In other words, the head and face were those of a man who might move the world more readily than the world could move him – a man to be twice twelve times tortured into the shapeless cripple he was, without a groan, much less a confession; a man to yield his life, but never a purpose or a point; a man born in armour, and assailable only through his loves. To him Ben-Hur stretched his hands, open and palm up, as he would offer peace at the same time he asked it.

"I am Judah, son of Ithamar, late head of the house of Hur, and a prince of Jerusalem."

The merchant's right hand lay outside the robe – a long, thin hand, articulate to deformity with suffering. It closed tightly; otherwise there was not the slightest expression of feeling of any kind on his part; nothing to warrant an inference of surprise or interest; nothing but this calm answer:

"The princes of Jerusalem, of the pure blood, are always welcome in my house; you are welcome. Give the young man a seat, Esther."

The girl took an ottoman near by, and carried it to Ben-Hur. As she arose from placing the seat, their eyes met.

"The peace of our Lord with you," she said, modestly. "Be seated and at rest."

Ben-Hur did not take the offered seat, but said, deferentially: "I pray the good master Simonides that he will not hold

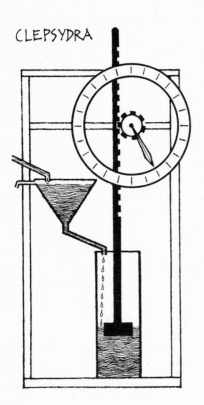

CLEPSYDRA

me an intruder. Coming up the river yesterday, I heard he knew my father."

"I knew the Prince Hur. We were associated in some enterprises lawful to merchants who find profit in lands beyond the sea and the desert. But sit, I pray you – and, Esther, some wine for the young man. Nehemiah speaks of a son of Hur who once ruled the half part of Jerusalem; an old house, very old, by the faith! In the days of Moses and Joshua even some of them found favour in the sight of the Lord, and divided honours with those princes among men. It can hardly be that their descendant, lineally come to us, will refuse a cup of wine-fat of the genuine vine of Sorek, grown on the south hillsides of Hebron."

By the time of the conclusion of this speech, Esther was before Ben-Hur with a silver cup filled from a vase upon a table a little removed from the chair. She offered the drink with downcast face. He touched her hand gently to put it away. Again their eyes met; whereat he noticed that she was small, not nearly to his shoulder in height; but very graceful, and fair and sweet of face, with eyes black and inexpressibly soft. She is kind and pretty, he thought, and looks as Tirzah would were she living. Poor Tirzah! Then he said aloud:

"No, thy father – if he is thy father?" – he paused.

"I am Esther, the daughter of Simonides," she said, with dignity.

"Then, fair Esther, thy father, when he has heard my further speech, will not think worse of me if yet I am slow to take his wine of famous extract; not less I hope not to lose grace in thy sight. Stand thou here with me a moment."

Both of them, as in common cause, turned to the merchant. "Simonides," he said, firmly, "my father, at his death, had a trusted servant of thy name, and it has been told me that thou art the man."

There was a sudden start of the wrenched limbs under the robe, and the thin hand clenched.

"Because I am that I am, before I make return to thy demand touching my relations to the Prince Hur, and as something which of right should come first, do thou show me proofs of who thou art. Is thy witness in writing? Or cometh it in person?"

The demand was plain, and the right of it indisputable. Ben-Hur blushed,

clasped his hands, stammered, and turned away at loss. Simonides pressed him.

"The proofs, the proofs, I say! Set them before me – lay them in my hands!"

Yet Ben-Hur had no answer. He had not anticipated the requirement; and, now that it was made, to him as never before came the awful fact that the three years in the galley had carried away all the proofs of his identity; mother and sister gone, he did not live in the knowledge of any human being.

"Master Simonides," he said, at length, "I can only tell my story; and I will not that unless you stay judgment so long, and with goodwill deign to hear me."

"Speak," said Simonides, now, indeed, master of the situation – "speak, and I will listen the more willingly that I have not denied you to be the very person you claim yourself."

Ben-Hur proceeded then, and told his life hurriedly.

"O good Simonides!" Ben-Hur then said, advancing a step, his whole soul seeking expression, "I see thou art not convinced, and that yet I stand in the shadow of thy distrust."

The merchant held his features fixed as marble, and his tongue as still.

"And not less clearly I see the difficulties of my position," Ben-Hur continued. "All my Roman connections I can prove; I have only to call upon the consul, now the guest of the governor of the city; but I cannot prove the particulars of thy demand upon me. I cannot prove I am my father's son. They who could serve me in that – alas! they are dead or lost."

He covered his face with his hands; whereupon Esther arose, and, taking the rejected cup to him, said, "The wine is of the country we all so love. Drink, I pray thee!"

The voice was sweet as that of Rebekah offering drink at the well near Nahor the city; he saw there were tears in her eyes, and he drank, saying: "Daughter of Simonides, thy heart is full of goodness; and merciful art thou to let the stranger share it with thy father. Be thou blessed of our God! I thank thee."

Then he addressed himself to the merchant again:

"As I have no proof that I am my father's son, I will withdraw that I demanded of thee, O Simonides, and go hence to trouble you no more; only let me say I did not seek thy return to servitude nor account of thy fortune; in any event, I would have said, as now I say, that all which is product of thy labour and genius is thine; keep it in welcome. I have no need of any part thereof. When the good Quintus, my second father, sailed on the voyage which was his last, he left me his heir, princely rich. If, therefore, thou dost think of me again, be it with remembrance of this question, which, as I do swear by the prophets and Jehovah, thy God and mine, was the chief purpose of my coming here: What dost thou know – what canst thou tell me – of my mother and Tirzah, my sister – she who should be in beauty and grace even as this one, thy sweetness of life, if not thy very life? Oh! what canst thou tell me of them?"

The tears ran down Esther's cheeks; but the man was wilful: in a clear voice, he replied:

"I have said I knew the Prince Ben-Hur. I remember hearing of the misfortune which overtook his family. I remember the bitterness with which I heard it. He who wrought such misery to the widow of my friend is the same who, in the same spirit, hath since wrought upon me. I will go further, and say to you, I have made diligent quest concerning the family, but – I have nothing to tell you of them. They are lost."

Ben-Hur uttered a great groan.

"Then – then it is another hope broken!" he said, struggling with his feelings. "I am used to disappointments. I pray you pardon my intrusion; and, if I have occasioned you annoyance, forgive it because of my sorrow. I have nothing to live for but vengeance. Farewell!"

At the curtain he turned, and said, simply: "I thank you both."

"Peace go with you," the merchant said.

Esther could not speak for sobbing.

And so he departed.

SIMONIDES TELLS HIS STORY

Scarcely was Ben-Hur gone, when Simonides seemed to wake as from sleep: his countenance flushed; the sullen light of his eyes changed to brightness; and he said, cheerily:

"Esther, ring – quick!"

She went to the table, and rang a service-bell.

One of the panels in the wall swung back, exposing a doorway, which gave admittance to a man, who passed round to the merchant's front, and saluted him with a half-salaam.

"Malluch, here – nearer – to the chair," the master said, imperiously. "I have a mission which shall not fail though the sun should. Harken! A young man is now descending to the store-room – tall, comely, and in the garb of Israel; follow him, his shadow not more faithful; and every night send me report of where he is, what he does, and the company he keeps; and if, without discovery, you overhear his conversations, report them word for word, together with whatever will serve to expose him, his habits, motives, life. Understand you? Go quickly! Stay, Malluch: if he leave the city, go after him – and, mark you, Malluch, be as a friend. If he bespeak you, tell him what you will to the occasion most suited, except that you are in my service – of that not a word. Haste – make haste!"

The man saluted as before, and was gone.

Then Simonides rubbed his wan hands together, and laughed.

"What is the day, daughter?" he said, in the midst of the mood. "What is the day? I wish to remember it for happiness come. See, and look for it laughing, and laughing tell me, Esther."

The merriment seemed unnatural to her; and, as if to entreat him from it, she answered, sorrowfully: "Woe's me, father, that I should ever forget this day!"

His hands fell down the instant, and his chin, dropping upon his breast, lost itself in the muffling folds of flesh composing his lower face.

"When the young man was speaking, Esther, I observed thee, and thought thou wert won by him."

Her eyes fell as she replied:

"Speak you of faith, father, I believed him."

"In thy eyes, then, he is the lost son of the Prince Hur?"

"If he is not——" She hesitated.

"And if he is not, Esther?"

"I have been thy handmaiden, father, since my mother answered the call of the Lord God; by thy side I have heard and seen thee deal in wise ways with all manner of men seeking profit, holy and unholy; and now I say, if indeed the young man be not the prince he claims to be, then before me falsehood never played so well the part of righteous truth."

"By the glory of Solomon, daughter, thou speakest earnestly. Dost thou believe thy father his father's servant?"

"I understood him to ask of that as something he had but heard."

For a time Simonides' gaze swam among his swimming ships, though they had no place in his mind.

"Well, thou art a good child, Esther, of genuine Jewish shrewdness, and of years and strength to hear a sorrowful tale. Wherefore give me heed, and I will tell you of myself, and of thy mother, and of many things pertaining to the past not in thy knowledge or thy dreams – things withheld from the persecuting Roman for a hope's sake, and from thee that thy nature should grow towards the Lord straight as the reed to the sun. . . . I was born in a tomb in the valley of Hinnom, on the south side of Zion. My father and mother were Hebrew bond-servants, tenders of the fig and olive trees growing, with many vines, in the king's garden hard by Siloam; and in my boyhood I helped them. They were of the class bound to serve for ever. They sold me to the Prince Hur, then, next to Herod the King, the richest man in Jerusalem. From the garden he transferred me to his storehouse in Alexandria of Egypt, where I came of age. I served him six years, and in the seventh, by the law of Moses, I went free."

Esther clapped her hands lightly.

"O, then, thou art not his father's servant!"

"Nay, daughter, hear. Now, in those days there were lawyers in the cloisters of the Temple who disputed vehemently, saying the children of servants bound for ever took the condition of their parents; but the Prince Hur was a man righteous in all things, and an interpreter of the law after the straitest sect, though not of them. He said I was a Hebrew servant bought, in the true meaning of the great lawgiver, and by sealed writings, which I yet have, he set me free."

"And my mother?" Esther asked.

"Thou shalt hear all, Esther; be patient. Before I am through thou shalt see it were easier for me to forget myself than thy mother. . . . At the end of my service, I came up to Jerusalem to the Passover. My master entertained me. I was in love with him already, and I prayed to be continued in his service. . . . One day I was a guest in his house in Jerusalem. A servant entered with some bread on a platter. She came to me first. It was then I saw thy mother, and loved her, and took her away in my secret heart. After awhile a time came when I sought the prince to make her my wife. He told me she was bond-servant for ever; but if she wished, he would set her free that I might be gratified. She gave me love for love, but was happy where she was, and refused her freedom. I prayed and besought, going again and again after long intervals. She would be my wife, she all the time said, if I would become her fellow in servitude. Our father Jacob served yet other seven years for his Rachel. Could I not as much for mine? But thy mother said I must become as she, to serve for ever. I came away, but went back. Look, Esther, look here!"

He pulled out the lobe of his left ear.

"See you not the scar of the awl?"

"I see it," she said; "and, oh, I see how thou didst love my mother!"

"Love her, Esther! She was to me more than the Shulamite to the singing king, fairer, more spotless; a fountain of gardens, a well of living waters, and streams from Lebanon. The master, even as I required him, took me to the judges, and back to his door, and thrust the awl through my ear into the door, and I was his servant for ever. So I won my Rachel. And was ever love like mine?"

Esther stooped and kissed him, and they were silent, thinking of the dead.

"My master was drowned at sea, the first sorrow that ever fell upon me," the merchant continued. "There was mourning in his house, and in mine here in Antioch, my abiding-place at the time. Now, Esther, mark you! When the good prince was lost, I had risen to be his chief steward, with everything of property belonging to him in my management and control. Judge you how much he loved and trusted me. I hastened to Jerusalem to render account to the widow. She continued me in the stewardship. I applied myself with greater diligence. The business prospered, and grew year by year. Ten years passed; then came the blow which you heard the young man tell about – the accident, as he called it, to the procurator Gratus. The Roman gave it out an attempt to assassinate him. Under that pretext, by leave from Rome, he confiscated to his own use the immense fortune of the widow and children. Nor stopped he there. That there might be no reversal of the judgment, he removed all the parties interested. From that dreadful day to this the family of Hur have been lost. The son, whom I had seen as a child, was sentenced to the galleys. The widow and daughter are supposed to have been buried in some of the many dungeons of Judea, which, once closed upon the doomed, are like sepulchres sealed and locked. They passed from the knowledge of men as utterly as if the sea had swallowed them unseen. We could not hear how they died – nay, not even that they were dead."

Esther's eyes were dewy with tears.

"Thy heart is good, Esther, good as thy mother's was; and I pray it have not the fate of most good hearts – to be trampled upon by the unmerciful and blind. But hearken further. I went up to Jerusalem to give help to my benefactress, and was seized at the gate of the city and carried to the sunken cells of the Tower of Antonia; why, I knew not, until Gratus himself came and demanded of me the moneys of the house of Hur, which he knew, after our Jewish custom of exchange, were subject to my draft in the different marts of the world. He required me to sign to his order. I refused. He had the houses, lands, goods, ships, and movable property of those I served; he had not their moneys. I saw, if I kept favour in the sight of the Lord, I could rebuild their broken fortunes. I refused the tyrant's demands. He put me to torture; my will held good, and he set me free, nothing gained. I came home and began again, in the name of Simonides of Antioch, instead of the Prince Hur of Jerusalem. Thou knowest, Esther, how I have prospered; that the increase of the millions of the prince in my hands was miraculous; thou knowest how, at the end of three years, while going up to Caesarea, I was taken and a second time tortured by Gratus to compel a confession that my goods and moneys were subject to his order of confiscation; thou knowest he failed as before. Broken in body, I came home and found my Rachel dead of fear and grief for me. The Lord our God reigned, and I lived. From the emperor himself I bought immunity and license to trade throughout the world. Today – praised be He who maketh the clouds His chariot and walketh upon the winds! – today, Esther, that which was in my hands for stewardship is multiplied into talents sufficient to enrich a Caesar."

He lifted his head proudly. Their eyes met; each read the other's thought. "What shall I with the treasure, Esther?" he asked, without lowering his gaze.

"My father," she answered, in a low voice, "did not the rightful owner call for it but now?"

Still his look did not fail.

"And thou, my child; shall I leave thee a beggar?"

"Nay, father, am not I, because I am thy child, his bond-servant? And of whom was it written, 'Strength and honour are her clothing, and she shall rejoice in time to come?'"

A gleam of ineffable love lighted his face as he said, "The Lord hath been good to me in many ways; but thou, Esther, art the sovereign excellence of His favour."

He drew her to his breast and kissed her many times.

Esther caressed the faded hands, and said, as if her spirit with his were running forward to results: "He is gone. Will he come again?"

"Ay, Malluch the faithful goes with him, and will bring him back when I am ready."

"And when will that be, father?"

"Not long, not long. He thinks all his witnesses dead. There is one living who will not fail to know him, if he be indeed my master's son."

"His mother?"

"Nay, daughter, I will set the witness before him; till then let us rest the business with the Lord. I am tired. Call Abimelech."

Esther called the servant, and they returned into the house.

When Ben-Hur sallied from the great warehouse, it was with the thought that another failure was to be added to the many he had already met in the quest for his people; and the idea was depressing exactly in proportion as the objects of his quest were dear to him; it curtained him round about with a sense of utter loneliness on earth, which, more than anything else, serves to eke from a soul cast down its remaining interest in life.

MALLUCH THE FRIEND

In front of Ben-Hur there was a forest of cypress-trees, each a column tall and straight as a mast. Venturing into the shady precinct, he heard a trumpet gaily blown, and an instant after a man arose, and came to him.

"I give you peace," he said, pleasantly.

"Thank you," Ben-Hur replied; then asked, "Go you my way?"

"I am for the stadium, if that is your way."

"The stadium?"

"Yes. The trumpet you heard but now was a call for the competitors."

"That will delight me. Hark! I hear the wheels of the chariots. They are taking the track."

Ben-Hur listened a moment, then completed the introduction by laying his hand upon the man's arm, and saying: "I am the son of Arrius, the duumvir, and thou?"

"I am Malluch, a merchant of Antioch."

"Well, good Malluch, the trumpet and the gride of wheels, and the prospect of diversion excite me. I have some skill in the exercises. In the palaestrae of Rome I am not unknown. Let us to the course."

Malluch lingered to say, quickly: "The duumvir was a Roman, yet I see his son in the garments of a Jew."

"The noble Arrius was my father by adoption," Ben-Hur answered.

"Ah! I see and beg pardon."

Passing through the belt of forest, they came to a field with a track laid out upon it, in shape and extent exactly like those of the stadia.

Ben-Hur counted the chariots as they went by – nine in all.

"I commend the fellows," he said, with goodwill. "Here, in the East, I thought they aspired to nothing better than the two; but they are ambitious, and play with royal fours. Let us study their performance."

Eight of the fours passed the stand, some walking, others on the trot, and all unexceptionally handled; then the ninth one came on the gallop. Ben-Hur burst into exclamation.

"I have been in the stables of the emperor, Malluch, but, by our father Abraham of blessed memory, I never saw the like of these."

The last four was then sweeping past. All at once they fell into confusion. Some one on the stand uttered a sharp cry. Ben-Hur turned, and saw an old man half risen from an upper seat, his hands clenched and raised, his eyes fiercely bright, his long white beard fairly quivering. Some of the spectators nearest him began to laugh.

"They should respect his beard at least. Who is he?" asked Ben-Hur.

"A mighty man from the Desert, somewhere beyond Moab, and owner of camels in herds, and horses descended, they say, from the racers of the first Pharoah – Sheik Ilderim by name and title."

Thus Malluch replied.

The driver meanwhile exerted himself to quiet the four, but without avail. Each ineffectual effort excited the sheik the more.

"Abaddon seize him!" yelled the patriarch, shrilly. "Run! fly! Do you hear, my children?" The question was to his

ASSARION OF TIBERIUS

GREEK DIDRACHMA

VALERIUS GRATUS
15 – 26 A.D.

PROCURATOR
COPONIUS
6 – 9 A.D.

ASHKELON MINT
1st CENT. A.D.

DENARIUS OF AUGUSTUS

DENARIUS OF TIBERIUS

attendants, apparently of the tribe. "Do you hear? They are Desert-born, like yourselves. Catch them – quick!"

The plunging of the animals increased.

"Accursed Roman!" and the sheik shook his fist at the driver. "Did he not swear he could drive them – swear it by all his brood of bastard Latin gods? Nay, hands off me – off, I say! They should run swift as eagles, and with the temper of handbred lambs, he swore. Cursed be he – cursed the mother of liars who calls

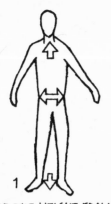

1

MEASURE THE HEIGHT FROM NECK TO FLOOR (A UNIT). MEASURE THE WAIST.

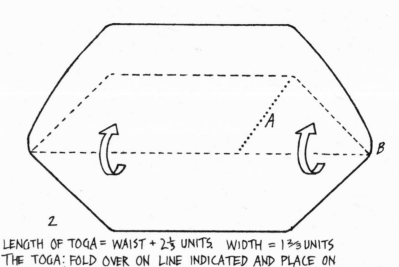

2

LENGTH OF TOGA = WAIST + 2⅓ UNITS. WIDTH = 1⅔ UNITS THE TOGA: FOLD OVER ON LINE INDICATED AND PLACE ON THE BODY, (SEE FIG. 3.)

him son! See them, the priceless. Let him touch one of them with a lash and——" The rest of the sentence was lost in a furious grinding of teeth. "To their heads, some of you, and speak them – a word, one is enough, from the tent-song your mothers sang you. Oh, fool, fool that I was to put trust in a Roman!"

Some of the shrewder of the old man's friends planted themselves between him and the horses. An opportune failure of breath on his part helped the stratagem.

Ben-Hur, thinking he comprehended the sheik, sympathized with him.

Before the patriarch was done with his expletives, a dozen hands were at the bits of the horses, and their quiet assured. About that time another chariot appeared upon the track; and, unlike the others, driver, vehicle, and racers were precisely as they would be presented in the circus the day of final trial.

The other contestants had been received in silence; the last comer was more fortunate. While moving towards the stand from which we are viewing the scene, his progress was signalized by loud demonstrations, by clapping of hands and cheers, the effect of which was to centre attention upon him exclusively.

The coming of the beautiful horses and resplendent chariot drew Ben-Hur to look at the driver with increased interest.

Who was he?

And directly the whole person of the driver was in view. A companion rode

with him, in classic description a Myrtilus, permitted men of high estate indulging their passion for the racecourse. Ben-Hur could see only the driver, standing erect in the chariot, with the reins passed several times round his body – a handsome figure, scantily covered by a tunic of light-red cloth; in the right hand a whip; in the other, the arm raised and lightly extended, the four lines. Ben-Hur stood transfixed – his instinct and memory had served him faithfully – *the driver was Messala!*

AN ENCOUNTER WITH MESSALA

As Ben-Ḥur descended the steps of the stand, an Arab arose upon the last one at the foot, and cried out:

"Men of the East and West – hearken! The good Sheik Ilderim giveth greeting. With four horses, sons of the favourites of Solomon the Wise, he hath come up against the best. Needs he most a mighty man to drive them. Whoso will take them to his satisfaction, to him he promiseth enrichment for ever. So saith

my master, Sheik Ilderim the Generous."

The proclamation awakened a great buzz among the people under the awning. By night it would be repeated and discussed in all the sporting circles of Antioch. Ben-Hur, hearing it, stopped and looked hesitatingly from the herald to the sheik. Malluch thought he was about to accept the offer, but was relieved when he presently turned to him, and asked, "Good Malluch, where to now?"

"Castalia."

"Oh! it has repute throughout the world. Let us thither."

Malluch kept watch on his companion as they went, and saw that for the moment at least his good spirits were out. To the people passing he gave no attention; over the wonders they came upon there were no exclamations; silently, even sullenly, he kept a slow pace.

The truth was, the sight of Messala had set Ben-Hur to thinking. It seemed scarce an hour ago that the strong hands had torn him from his mother, scarce an hour ago that the Roman had put seal upon the gates of his father's house. He recounted how, in the hopeless misery of the life – if such it might be called – in the galleys, he had little else to do, aside from labour, than dream dreams of vengeance, in all of which Messala was the principal. There might be, he used to say to himself, escape for Gratus, but for Messala – never! And to strengthen and

3 DRAPE FROM ANKLE OVER LEFT SHOULDER, ROUND THE BACK, AND SLIGHTLY OVER RIGHT SHOULDER.

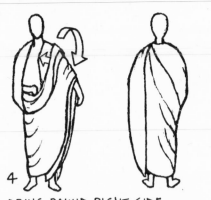

4 BRING ROUND RIGHT SIDE, DIAGONALLY OVER FRONT AND DRAPE OVER LEFT SHOULDER TO REACH ANKLE AT BACK.

harden his resolution, he was accustomed to repeat over and over, Who pointed us out to the persecutors? And when I begged him for help – not for myself – who mocked me, and went away laughing? And always the dream had the same ending. The day I meet him, help me, thou good God of my people! – help me to some fitting special vengeance.

And now the meeting was at hand.

Perhaps, if he had found Messala poor and suffering, Ben-Hur's feeling had been different; but it was not so. He found him more than prosperous; in the prosperity there was a dash and glitter – gleam of sun on gilt of gold.

So it happened that what Malluch accounted a passing loss of spirit was pondering when the meeting should be, and in what manner he could make it most memorable.

They turned after awhile into an avenue of oaks, where the people were going and coming in groups; footmen here, and horsemen; there women in litters borne by slaves; and now and then chariots rolled by thunderously.

At the end of the avenue the road, by an easy grade, descended into a lowland, where, on the right hand, there was a precipitous facing of grey rock, and on the left an open meadow. Then they came in view of the famous Fountain of Castalia.

Edging through a company assembled at the point, Ben-Hur beheld a jet of sweet water pouring from the crest of a stone into a basin of black marble, where, after much boiling and foaming, it disappeared as if through a funnel.

Before Ben-Hur could test the oracle, some other visitors were seen approaching across the meadow, and their appearance piqued the curiosity of the company, his not less than theirs.

He saw first a camel, very tall and very white, in leading of a driver on horseback. A houdah on the animal, besides being unusually large, was of crimson and gold. Two other horsemen followed the camel with tall spears in hand.

But who were the man and woman under the houdah?

Every eye saluted them with the inquiry.

The woman was seated in the manner of the East, amidst veils and laces of surpassing fineness.

It was a fair face to see; quite youthful; in form, oval; complexion not white, like the Greek; nor brunette, like the Roman; nor blonde, like the Gaul; but rather the tinting of the sun of the Upper Nile upon a skin of such transparency that the blood shone through it on cheek and brow with nigh the ruddiness of lamplight. The eyes, naturally large, were touched along the lids with the black paint immemorial throughout the East. The lips were slightly parted, disclosing, through their scarlet lake, teeth of glistening whiteness.

As if satisfied with the survey of people and locality, the fair creature spoke to the driver – an Ethiopian of vast brawn, naked to the waist – who led the camel nearer the fountain, and caused it to kneel; after which he received from her hand a cup, and proceeded to fill it at the basin. That instant the sound of wheels and the trampling of horses in rapid motion broke the silence her beauty had imposed, and, with a great outcry, the bystanders parted in every direction, hurrying to get away.

"The Roman has a mind to ride us down. Look out!" Malluch shouted to Ben-Hur.

The latter faced to the direction the sounds came from, and beheld Messala in his chariot pushing the four straight at the crowd. This time the view was near and distinct.

The parting of the company uncovered the camel, which might have been more agile than his kind generally; yet the hoofs were almost upon him, and he resting with closed eyes, chewing the endless cud with such sense of security as long favouritism may be supposed to have bred in him. The Ethiopian wrung his hands afraid. In the houdah, the old man moved to escape; but he was hampered with age, and could not, even in the face of danger, forget the dignity which was plainly his habit. It was too late for the woman to save herself. Ben-Hur stood nearest them, and he called to Messala:

"Hold! Look where thou goest! Back, back!"

The patrician was laughing in hearty good-humour; and, seeing there was but one chance of rescue, Ben-Hur stepped in, and caught the bits of the left yoke-steed and his mate. "Dog of a Roman! Carest thou so little for life?" he cried, putting forth all his strength. The two horses reared, and drew the others round; the tilting of the pole tilted the chariot; Messala barely escaped a fall, while his complacent Myrtilus rolled back like a clod to the ground. Seeing the peril past, all the bystanders burst into derisive laughter.

The matchless audacity of the Roman then manifested itself. Loosing the lines from his body, he tossed them to one side, dismounted, walked round the camel, looked at Ben-Hur, and spoke partly to the old man and partly to the woman.

"Pardon, I pray you – I pray you both. I am Messala," he said; "and, by the old

45

Mother of the earth, I swear I did not see you or your camel. As to these good people – perhaps I trusted too much to my skill. I sought a laugh at them – the laugh is theirs. Good may it do them."

The good-natured, careless look and gesture he threw the bystanders accorded well with the speech. To hear what more he had to say, they became quiet. Assured of victory over the body of the offended, he signed his companion to take the chariot to a safer distance, and addressed himself boldly to the woman.

"Thou hast interest in the good man here, whose pardon, if not granted now, I shall seek with the greater diligence hereafter; his daughter, I should say."

At this point she broke in upon him.

"Wilt thou come here?" she asked, smiling, and with gracious bend of the head to Ben-Hur.

"Take the cup and fill it, I pray thee," she said to the latter. "My father is thirsty."

"I am thy most willing servant."

Ben-Hur turned about to do the favour, and was face to face with Messala. Their glances met; the Jew's defiant; the Roman's sparkling with humour.

"O stranger, beautiful as cruel!" Messala said, waving his hand to her. "If Apollo get thee not, thou shalt see me again. Not knowing thy country, I cannot name a god to commend thee to; so, by all the gods, I will commend thee to – myself."

Seeing the Myrtilus had the four composed and ready, he returned to the chariot. The woman looked after him as he moved away, and, whatever else there was in her look, there was no displeasure. Presently she received the water; her father drank, then she raised the cup to her lips, and, leaning down, gave it to Ben-Hur, never action more graceful and gracious.

"Keep it, we pray of thee! It is full of blessings – all thine!"

Immediately the camel was aroused, and on his feet, and about to go, when the old man called:

"Stand thou there."

Ben-Hur went to him respectfully.

"Thou has served the stranger well to-day. There is but one God. In His holy name I thank thee. I am Balthasar, the Egyptian. In the great orchard of palms, beyond the village of Daphne, in the shade of the palms, Sheik Ilderim the Generous abideth in his tents, and we are his guests. Seek us there. Thou shalt have

welcome sweet with the savour of the grateful."

Ben-Hur was left in wonder at the old man's clear voice and reverend manner. As he gazed after the two departing, he caught sight of Messala going as he had come, joyous, indifferent, and with a mocking laugh.

A SCHEME, BEN HUR CONFIDES IN MALLUCH

As a rule, there is no surer way to the dislike of men than to behave well where they have behaved badly. In this instance, happily, Malluch was an exception to the rule. The affair he had just witnessed raised Ben-Hur in his estimation, since he could not deny him courage and address; could he now get some insight into the young man's history, the results of the day would not be all unprofitable to good master Simonides.

On the latter point, referring to what he had as yet learned, two facts comprehended it all – the subject of his investigation was a Jew, and the adopted son of a famous Roman. Another conclusion which might be of importance was beginning to formulate itself in the shrewd mind of the emissary; between Messala and the son of the duumvir there was a connection of some kind. But what was it? – and how could it be reduced to assurance? With all his sounding, the ways and means of solution were not at call. In the heat of the perplexity, Ben-Hur himself came to his help. He laid his hand on Malluch's arm and drew him out of the crowd.

"Good Malluch," he said, stopping, "may a man forget his mother?"

"One day an accident happened to a Roman in authority as he was riding past our house at the head of a cohort; the legionaries burst the gate and rushed in and seized us. I have not seen my mother or sister since. I cannot say they are dead or living. I do not know what became of them. But, Malluch, the man in the chariot yonder was present at the separation; he gave us over to the captors; he

heard my mother's prayer for her children, and he laughed when they dragged her away. Hardly may one say which graves deepest in memory, love or hate. Today I knew him afar – and, Malluch——"

He caught the listener's arm again.

"And, Malluch, he knows and takes with him now the secret I would give my life for: he could tell if she lives, and where she is, and her condition; if she – no, *they* – much sorrow has made the two as one – if they are dead, he could tell where they died, and of what, and where their bones await my finding."

"And will he not?"

"No."

"Why?"

"I am a Jew and he is a Roman."

"But Romans have tongues, and Jews, though ever so despised, have methods to beguile them."

"For such as he? No; and, besides, the secret is one of State. All my father's property was confiscated and divided."

Malluch nodded his head slowly, much as to admit the argument; then he asked anew, "Did he not recognize you?"

"He could not. I was sent to death in life, and have been long since accounted of the dead."

"I wonder you did not strike him," said Malluch, yielding to a touch of passion.

"That would have been to put him past serving me for ever. I would have had to kill him, and Death, you know, keeps secrets better even than a guilty Roman. I would not take his life, good Malluch; against that extreme the possession of the secret is for the present, at least, his safeguard; yet I may punish him, and so you give me help, I will try."

"He is a Roman," said Malluch, without hesitation; "and I am of the tribe of Judah. I will help you. If you choose, put me under oath – under the most solemn oath."

"Give me your hand, that will suffice."

As their hands fell apart, Ben-Hur said, with lightened feeling: "That I would charge you with is not difficult, good friend; neither is it dreadful to conscience. Let us move on."

They took the road which led to the right across the meadow spoken of in the description of the coming to the fountain. Ben-Hur was first to break the silence.

"Do you know the Sheik Ilderim the Generous?"

"Yes."

"Where is his Orchard of Palms? or, rather, Malluch, how far is it beyond the village of Daphne?"

Malluch was touched by a doubt; he recalled the prettiness of the favour shown him by the woman at the fountain, and wondered if he who had the sorrows of a mother in mind was about to forget them for a lure of love; yet he replied, "The Orchard of Palms lies beyond the village two hours by horse, and one by a swift camel."

"Thank you; and to your knowledge once more. Have the games of which you told me been widely published, and when will they take place?"

The questions were suggestive; and if they did not restore Malluch his confidence, they at least stimulated his curiosity.

"Oh yes, they will be of ample splendour. The prefect is rich, and could afford to lose his place; yet, as is the way with successful men, his love of riches is nowise diminished; and to gain a friend at Court, if nothing more, he must make ado for the Consul Maxentius, who is coming hither to make final preparations for a campaign against the Parthians."

"One thing more now, O Malluch. When will the celebration be?"

"Ah! your pardon," the other answered. "Tomorrow – and the next day," he said, counting aloud, "then, to speak in the Roman style, if the sea-gods be propitious, the consul arrives. Yes, the sixth day from this we have the games."

"The time is short, Malluch, but it is enough." The last words were spoken decisively. "By the prophets of our old Israel! I will take the reins again. Stay! a condition; is their assurance that Messala will be a competitor?"

"The Messala will drive," he said, directly. "He is committed to the race in many ways – by publication in the streets, and in the baths and theatres, the palace and barracks; and, to fix him past retreat, his name is on the tablets of every young spendthrift in Antioch."

"In wager, Malluch?"

"Yes, in wager; and every day he comes ostentatiously to practise, as you saw him."

"Ah! and that is the chariot, and those the horses, with which he will make the race? Thank you, thank you, Malluch. You have served me well already. I am satisfied. Now be my guide to the Orchard of Palms, and give me introduction to Sheik Ilderim the Generous."

"When?"

"Today. His horses may be engaged tomorrow."

Malluch took a moment for reflection.

"It is best we go straight to the village, which is fortunately near by; if two swift camels are to be had for hire there, we will be on the road but an hour."

"Let us about it, then."

The village was an assemblage of palaces in beautiful gardens, interspersed with khans of princely sort. Dromedaries were happily secured, and upon them the journey to the famous Orchard of Palms was begun.

THE ORCHARD OF PALMS

Beyond the village the country was undulating and cultivated; in fact, it was the garden-land of Antioch, with not a foot lost to labour. The steep faces of the hills were terraced; even the hedges were brighter of the trailing vines which, besides the lure of shade, offered passers-by sweet promise of wine to come, and grapes in clustered purple ripeness.

In course of their journey the friends came to the river, which they followed with the windings of the road, now over bold bluffs, and then into vales, all alike allotted for country-seats; and if the land was in full foliage of oak and sycamore and myrtle, and bay and arbutus, and perfuming jasmine, the river was bright with slanted sunlight, which would have slept where it fell but for ships in endless procession, gliding with the current, tacking for the wind, or bounding under the impulse of oars – some coming, some going, and all suggestive of the sea, and distant peoples, and famous places, and things coveted on account of their rarity. And down the shore the friends went continuously till they came to a lake fed by backwater from the river, clear, deep, and without current. An old palm-tree dominated the angle of the inlet; turning to the left at the foot of the tree, Malluch clapped his hands and shouted:

"Look, look! The Orchard of Palms!"

The road wound in close parellelism with the shore of the lake; and when it carried the travellers down to the water's edge, there was always on that side a shining expanse limited not far off by the opposite shore, on which, as on this one, no tree but the palm was permitted.

"See that," said Malluch, pointing to a giant of the place. "Each ring upon its trunk marks a year of its life. Count them from root to branch, and if the sheik tells you the grove was planted before the Seleucidae were heard of in Antioch, do not doubt him."

One may not look at a perfect palm-tree but that, with a subtlety all its own, it assumes a presence for itself, and makes a poet of the beholder. This is the explanation of the honours it has received, beginning with the artists of the first kings, who could find no form in all the earth to serve them so well as a model for the pillars of their palaces and temples; and for the same reason Ben-Hur was moved to say:

"As I saw him at the stand today, good Malluch, Sheik Ilderim appeared to be a very common man. The rabbis in Jerusalem would look down upon him, I fear, as a son of a dog of Edom. How came he in possession of the Orchard? And how has he been able to hold it against the greed of Roman governors?"

SLAVE BADGE

HOLD ME-LEST
I ESCAPE-AND TAKE
ME BACK TO MY MASTER
VIVENTIUS ON THE
ESTATE OF CALLISTUS

"If blood derives excellence from time, son of Arrius, then is old Ilderim a man, though he be an uncircumcised Edomite."

Malluch spoke warmly.

"All his fathers before him were sheiks. One of them – I shall not say when he lived or did the good deed – once helped a king who was being hunted with swords. The story says he loaned him a thousand horsemen, who knew the paths of the wilderness and its hiding-places as shepherds know the scant hills they inhabit with their flocks; and they carried him here and there until the opportunity came, and then with their spears they slew the enemy, and set him upon his throne again. And the king, it is said, remembered the service, and brought the son of the Desert to this place, and bade him set up his tent and bring his family and his herds, for the lake and trees, and all the land from the river to the nearest mountains, were his and his children's for ever. And they have never been disturbed in the possession. The rulers succeeding have found it policy to keep good terms with the tribe, to whom the Lord has given increase of men and horses, and camels and riches, making them masters of many highways between cities; so that it is with them any time they please to say to commerce, 'Go in peace,' or 'Stop,' and what they say shall be done. Even the prefect in the citadel overlooking Antioch thinks it happy day with him when Ilderim, surnamed the Generous on account of good deeds done unto all manner of men, with his wives and children, and his trains of camels and horses, and his belongings of sheik, moving as our fathers Abraham and Jacob moved, comes up to exchange briefly his bitter wells for the pleasantness you see about us."

"How is it, then?" said Ben-Hur. "I saw the sheik tear his beard while he cursed himself that he had put trust in a Roman. Caesar, had he heard him, might have said, 'I like not such a friend as this; put him away.'"

"It would be but shrewd judgment," Malluch replied, smiling. "Ilderim is not a lover of Rome; he has a grievance. Three years ago the Parthians rode across the road from Bozra to Damascus, and fell upon a caravan laden, among other things, with the incoming tax-returns of a district over that way. They slew every creature taken, which the censors in

Rome could have forgiven if the imperial treasure had been spared and forwarded. The farmers of the taxes, being chargeable with the loss, complained to Caesar, and Caesar held Herod to payment, and Herod, on his part, seized property of Ilderim, whom he charged with treasonable neglect of duty. The sheik appealed to Caesar, and Caesar has made him such answer as might be looked for from the unwinking sphinx. The old man's heart has been aching sore ever since, and he nurses his wrath, and takes pleasure in its daily growth."

"He can do nothing, Malluch."

"Well," said Malluch, "that involves another explanation, which I will give you, if we can draw nearer.

"You must know," Malluch continued, "that the merchant Simonides gives me his confidence, and sometimes flatters me by taking me into council; and as I attend him at his house, I have made acquaintance with many of his friends, who, knowing my footing with the host, talk to him freely in my presence. In that way I became somewhat intimate with Sheik Ilderim."

For a moment Ben-Hur's attention wandered. Before his mind's eye there arose the image, pure, gentle, and appealing, of Esther, the merchant's daughter.

"A few weeks ago," said Malluch, continuing, "the old Arab called on Simonides, and found me present. I observed he seemed much moved about something, and, in deference, offered to withdraw, but he himself forbade me. 'As you are an Israelite,' he said, 'stay for I have a strange story to tell.' A good many years ago, three men called at Ilderim's tent out in the wilderness. They were all foreigners – a Hindu, a Greek, and an Egyptian; and they had come on camels, the largest he had ever seen, and all white. He welcomed them, and gave them rest. Next morning they arose and prayed a prayer new to the sheik – a prayer addressed to God and His Son – this with much mystery besides. After breaking fast with him, the Egyptian told who they were, and whence they had come. Each had seen a star, out of which a voice had bidden them go to Jerusalem and ask, 'Where is He that is born King of the Jews?' They obeyed. From Jerusalem they were led by a star to Bethlehem, where, in a cave, they found a child newly born, which they fell down and worshipped; and after worshipping

it, and giving it costly presents, and bearing witness of what it was, they took their camels, and fled without pause to the sheik, because if Herod – meaning him surnamed the Great – could lay hands upon them, he would certainly kill them. And, faithful to his habit, the sheik took care of them, and kept them concealed for a year, when they departed, leaving with him gifts of great value, and each going a separate way."

"It is, indeed, a most wonderful story," Ben-Hur exclaimed, at its conclusion. "Has Ilderim nothing more of the three men? What became of them?"

"Ah, yes, that was the cause of his coming to Simonides the day of which I was speaking. Only the night before that day the Egyptian reappeared to him. Balthasar, the Egyptian."

"Balthasar, you said?"

"Yes. Balthasar, the Egyptian."

"That was the name the old man gave us at the fountain today."

Then, at the reminder, Malluch became excited.

"It is true," he said; "and the camel was the same – and you saved the man's life. But hark! Someone comes overtaking us.

The noise grew louder, until presently they heard the rumble of wheels mixed with the beating of horse-hoofs – a moment later Sheik Ilderim himself appeared on horseback, followed by a train, among which were the four wine-red Arabs drawing the chariot. The sheik's chin, in its muffling of long white beard, was drooped upon his breast. Our friends had out-travelled him; but at sight of them, he raised his head, and spoke kindly.

"Peace to you! Ah, my friend Malluch! Welcome! And tell me you are not going, but just come; that you have something for me from the good Simonides – may the Lord of his fathers keep him in life for many years to come. Ay, take up the straps, both of you, and follow me. I have bread and leben, or, if you prefer it, arrack, and the flesh of young kid."

They followed after him to the door of the tent, in which, when they were dismounted, he stood to receive them, holding a platter with three cups filled with creamy liquor drawn from a great smoke-stained skin bottle, pendent from the central post.

"Drink," he said, heartily, "drink, for this is the fearnaught of the tentmen."

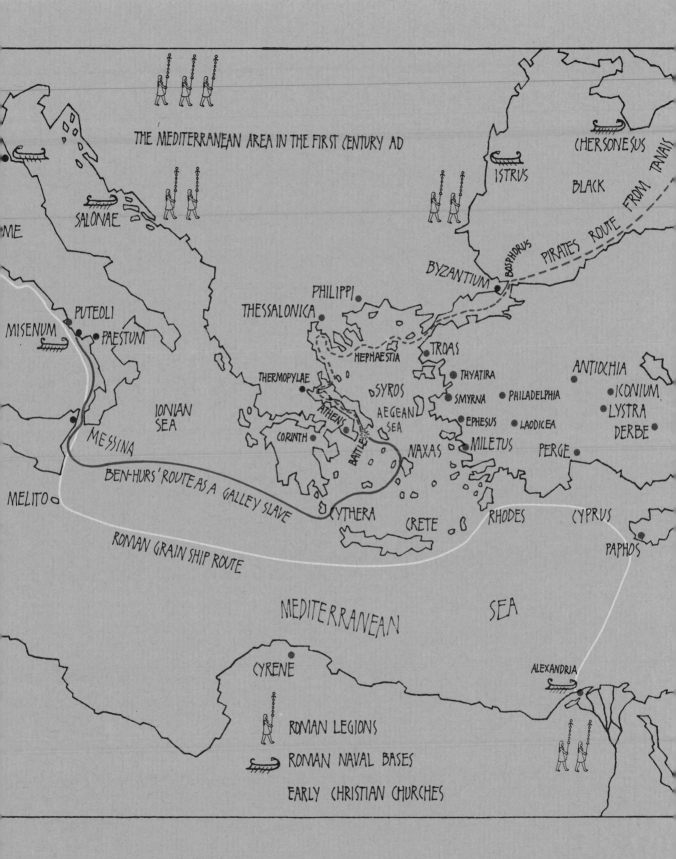

THE MEDITERRANEAN AREA IN THE FIRST CENTURY AD

CHERSONESUS

BLACK

PIRATES' ROUTE FROM TANAIS

ISTRUS

BOSPHORUS

BYZANTIUM

ME

SALONAE

PHILIPPI

THESSALONICA

TROAS

ANTIOCHIA

PUTEOLI

THYATIRA

ICONIUM

MISENUM

PAESTUM

HEPHAESTIA

SYROS

SMYRNA

PHILADELPHIA

LYSTRA

THERMOPYLAE

DERBE

IONIAN
SEA

AEGEAN
SEA

EPHESUS

LAODICEA

ATHENS

MESSINA

CORINTH

MILETUS

PERGE

NAXAS

BEN-HURS' ROUTE AS A GALLEY SLAVE

CYTHERA

CRETE

RHODES

CYPRUS

MELITO

ROMAN GRAIN SHIP ROUTE

PAPHOS

MEDITERRANEAN

SEA

CYRENE

ALEXANDRIA

ROMAN LEGIONS

ROMAN NAVAL BASES

EARLY CHRISTIAN CHURCHES

POSITIONS OF OARSMEN

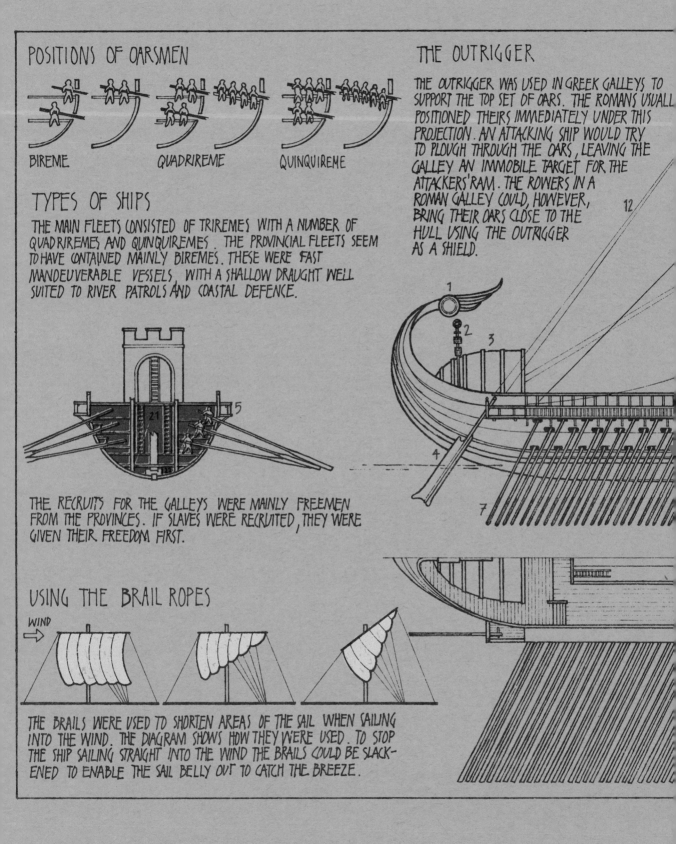

BIREME   QUADRIREME   QUINQUIREME

TYPES OF SHIPS

THE MAIN FLEETS CONSISTED OF TRIREMES WITH A NUMBER OF
QUADRIREMES AND QUINQUIREMES. THE PROVINCIAL FLEETS SEEM
TO HAVE CONTAINED MAINLY BIREMES. THESE WERE FAST
MANOEUVERABLE VESSELS, WITH A SHALLOW DRAUGHT WELL
SUITED TO RIVER PATROLS AND COASTAL DEFENCE.

THE RECRUITS FOR THE GALLEYS WERE MAINLY FREEMEN
FROM THE PROVINCES. IF SLAVES WERE RECRUITED, THEY WERE
GIVEN THEIR FREEDOM FIRST.

THE OUTRIGGER

THE OUTRIGGER WAS USED IN GREEK GALLEYS TO
SUPPORT THE TOP SET OF OARS. THE ROMANS USUALL
POSITIONED THEIRS IMMEDIATELY UNDER THIS
PROJECTION. AN ATTACKING SHIP WOULD TRY
TO PLOUGH THROUGH THE OARS, LEAVING THE
GALLEY AN IMMOBILE TARGET FOR THE
ATTACKERS'RAM. THE ROWERS IN A
ROMAN GALLEY COULD, HOWEVER,
BRING THEIR OARS CLOSE TO THE
HULL USING THE OUTRIGGER
AS A SHIELD.

USING THE BRAIL ROPES

WIND ⇒

THE BRAILS WERE USED TO SHORTEN AREAS OF THE SAIL WHEN SAILING
INTO THE WIND. THE DIAGRAM SHOWS HOW THEY WERE USED. TO STOP
THE SHIP SAILING STRAIGHT INTO THE WIND THE BRAILS COULD BE SLACK-
ENED TO ENABLE THE SAIL BELLY OUT TO CATCH THE BREEZE.

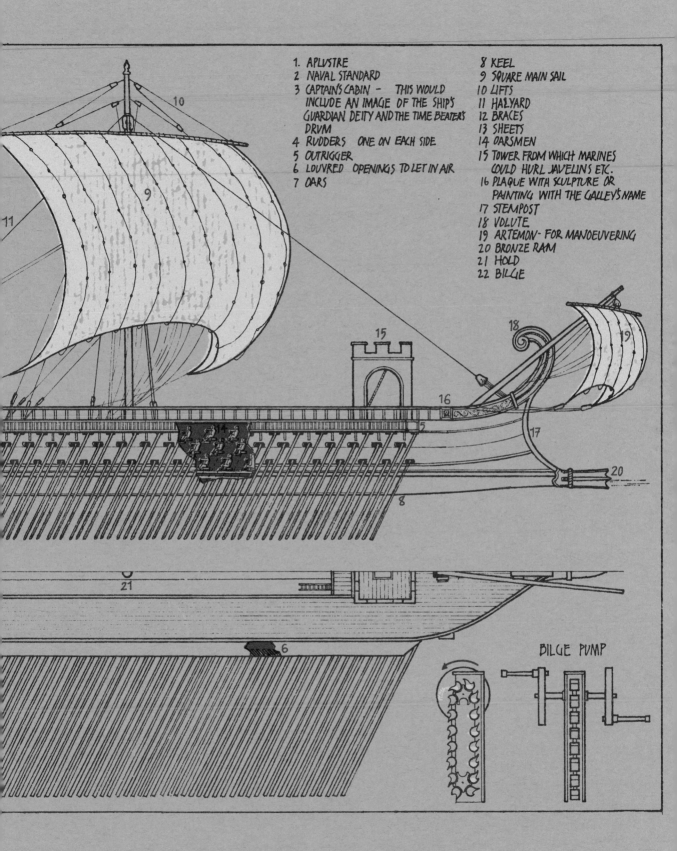

1. APLUSTRE
2. NAVAL STANDARD
3. CAPTAIN'S CABIN - THIS WOULD INCLUDE AN IMAGE OF THE SHIP'S GUARDIAN DEITY AND THE TIME BEATER'S DRUM
4. RUDDERS ONE ON EACH SIDE
5. OUTRIGGER
6. LOUVRED OPENINGS TO LET IN AIR
7. OARS
8. KEEL
9. SQUARE MAIN SAIL
10. LIFTS
11. HALYARD
12. BRACES
13. SHEETS
14. OARSMEN
15. TOWER FROM WHICH MARINES COULD HURL JAVELINS ETC.
16. PLAQUE WITH SCULPTURE OR PAINTING WITH THE GALLEY'S NAME
17. STEMPOST
18. VOLUTE
19. ARTEMON - FOR MANOEUVERING
20. BRONZE RAM
21. HOLD
22. BILGE

BILGE PUMP

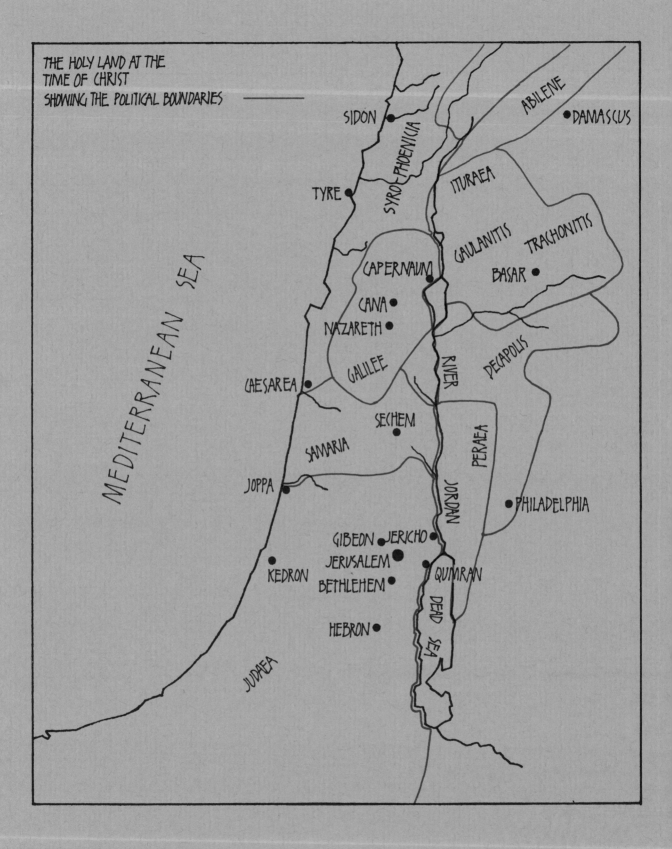

THE HOLY LAND AT THE
TIME OF CHRIST
SHOWING THE POLITICAL BOUNDARIES ———

SIDON

ABILENE

●DAMASCUS

SYROE-PHOENICIA

TYRE

ITURAEA

GAULANITIS

TRACHONITIS

CAPERNAUM

BASAR

CANA

NAZARETH

MEDITERRANEAN SEA

GALILEE

RIVER

DECAPOLIS

CAESAREA

SECHEM

PERAEA

SAMARIA

JOPPA

JORDAN

PHILADELPHIA

GIBEON   JERICHO

JERUSALEM

KEDRON   BETHLEHEM   QUMRAN

DEAD SEA

HEBRON

JUDAEA

They each took a cup, and drank till but the foam remained.

"Enter now, in God's name."

And when they were gone in, Malluch took the sheik aside, and spoke to him privately; after which he went to Ben-Hur and excused himself.

"I have told the sheik about you, and he will give you the trial of his horses in the morning. He is your friend. Having done for you all I can, you must do the rest, and let me return to Antioch. There is one there who has my promise to meet him tonight. I have no choice but to go. I will come back tomorrow prepared, if all goes well in the meantime, to stay with you until the games are over."

With blessings given and received, Malluch set out in return.

MALLUCH REPORTS

What time the lower horn of a new moon touched the castellated piles on Mount Sulpius, and two-thirds of the people of Antioch were out on their house-tops comforting themselves with the night breeze when it blew, and with fans when it failed, Simonides sat in the chair which had come to be a part of him, and from the terrace looked down over the river, and his ships a-swing at their moorings. The wall at his back cast its shadow broadly over the water to the opposite shore. Above him the endless tramp upon the bridge went on. Esther was holding a plate for him containing his frugal supper – some wheaten cakes light as wafers, some honey, and a bowl of milk, into which he now and then dipped the wafers after dipping them into the honey.

Malluch came to the chair.

"Peace to you, good master," he said, with a low obeisance, "and to you, Esther, most excellent of daughters."

He stood before them deferentially, and the attitude and the address left it difficult to define his relation to them; the one was that of a servant, the other indicated the familiar and friend. On the other side, Simonides, as was his habit in business, after answering the salutation, went straight to the subject.

"What of the young man, Malluch?"

The events of the day were told quietly and in the simplest words, and until he was through there was no interruption; nor did the listener in the chair so much as move a hand during the narration;

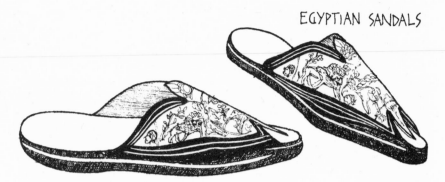

EGYPTIAN SANDALS

but for his eyes, wide open and bright, and an occasional long-drawn breath, he might have been accounted an effigy.

"Thank you, thank you, Malluch," he said, heartily, at the conclusion; "you have done well – no one could have done better. Now what say you of the young man's nationality?"

"He is an Israelite, good master, and of the tribe of Judah."

"You are positive?"

"Very positive."

"Did he display moneys – coin of Rome or Israel?"

"None, none, good master."

"Surely, Malluch, where there are so many inducements to folly – so much, I mean, to eat and drink – surely he made you generous offer of some sort. His age, if nothing more, would warrant that much."

"He neither ate nor drank in my company."

"In what he said or did, Malluch, could you in anywise detect his master-idea? You know they peep through cracks close enough to stop the wind."

"Give me to understand you," said Malluch, in doubt.

"Well, you know we nor speak nor act, much less decide grave questions concerning ourselves, except we be driven by a motive. In that respect, what made you of him?"

"As to that, Master Simonides, I can answer with much assurance. He is devoted to finding his mother and sister

– that first. Then he has a grievance against Rome; and as the Messala of whom I told you had something to do with the wrong, the great present object is to humiliate him. The meeting at the fountain furnished an opportunity, but it was put aside as not sufficiently public."

"The Messala is influential," said Simonides, thoughtfully.

"Yes; but the next meeting will be in the Circus."

"Well – and then?"

"The son of Arrius will win."

"How know you?"

Malluch smiled.

"I am judging by what he says."

"Is that all?"

"No; there is a much better sign – his spirit."

Simonides gazed for a time at the ships and their shadows slowly swinging together in the river; when he looked up, it was to end the interview.

"Enough, Malluch," he said. "Get you to eat, and make ready to return to the Orchard of Palms; you must help the young man in his coming trial. Come to me in the morning. I will send a letter to Ilderim." Then in an undertone, as if to himself, he added, "I may attend the Circus myself."

When Malluch, after the customary benediction given and received, was gone, Simonides took a deep draught of milk, and seemed refreshed and easy of mind.

"Put the meal down, Esther," he said; "it is over."

She obeyed.

"Here now."

She resumed her place upon the arm of the chair close to him.

"God is good to me, very good," he said,

49

fervently. "His habit is to move in mystery, yet sometimes He permits us to think we see and understand Him. I am old, dear, and must go; but now, in this eleventh hour, when my hope was beginning to die, He sends me this one with a promise, and I am lifted up. I see the way to a great part in a circumstance itself so great that it shall be as a new birth to the whole world. And I see a reason for the gift of my great riches, and the end for which they were designed. Verily, my child, I take hold on life anew."

Esther nestled closer to him, as if to bring his thoughts from their far-flying.

"The King has been born," he continued, imagining he was still speaking to her, "and He must be near the half of common life. Balthasar says He was a child on His mother's lap when he saw Him, and gave Him presents and worship; and Ilderim holds it was twenty-seven years ago last December when Balthasar and his companions came to his tent asking a hiding-place from Herod. Wherefore the coming cannot now be long delayed. Tonight – tomorrow it may be. Holy fathers of Israel, what happiness in the thought! I will put the thinking by for the present; only dear, when the King comes He will need money and men, for as He was a child born of woman He will be but a man after all, bound to human ways as you and I are. And for the money He will have need of getters and keepers, and for the men leaders. There, there! See you not a broad road for my walking, and the running of the youth our master – and at the end of it glory and revenge for us both – and – and——" He paused, struck with the selfishness of a scheme in which she had no part or good result; then added, kissing her, "And happiness for my mother's child."

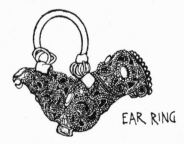

EAR RING

SHEIK ILDERIM'S HORSES

Sheik Ilderim was a man of too much importance to go about with a small establishment. He had a reputation to keep with his tribe, such as became a prince and patriarch of the greatest following in all the Desert east of Syria; with the people of the cities he had another reputation, which was that of one of the richest personages not a king in all the East; and, being rich in fact – in money as well as in servants, camels, horses, and flocks of all kinds – he took pleasure in a certain state, which, besides magnifying his dignity with strangers, contributed to his personal price and comfort. Wherefore the reader must not be misled by the frequent reference to his tent in the Orchard of Palms. He had there really a respectable dowar; that is to say, he had there three large tents – one for himself, one for visitors, one for his favourite wife and her women; and six or eight lesser ones, occupied by his servants and such tribal retainers as he had chosen to bring with him as a bodyguard – strong men of approved courage, and skilful with bow, spear, and horses.

To be sure, his property of whatever kind was in no danger at the Orchard; yet as the habits of a man go with him to town not less than the country, and as it is never wise to slip the bands of discipline, the interior of the dowar was devoted to his cows, camels, goats, and such property in general as might tempt a lion or a thief.

To do him full justice, Ilderim kept well all the customs of his people, abating none, not even the smallest; in consequence his life at the Orchard was a continuation of his life in the Desert; nor that alone, it was a fair reproduction of the old patriarchal modes – the genuine pastoral life of primitive Israel.

Recurring to the morning the caravan arrived at the Orchard, "Here, plant it here," he said, stopping his horse, and thrusting a spear into the ground. "Door to the south; the lake before it thus; and these, the children of the Desert, to sit under at the going down of the sun."

At the last words he went to a group of three great palm-trees, and patted one of them as he would have patted his horse's neck, or the cheek of the child of his love.

Who but the sheik could of right say to the caravan, Halt! or of the tent, Here be it pitched? The spear was wrested from the ground, and over the wound it had riven in the sod the base of the first pillar of the tent was planted, marking the centre of the front door. Then eight others were planted – in all, three rows of pillars, three in a row. Then, at call, the women and children came, and unfolded the canvas from its packing on the camels. Who might do this but the women? Had they not sheared the hair from the brown goats of the flock, and twisted it into thread, and woven the thread into cloth, and stitched the cloth together, making the perfect roof, dark brown in fact, though in the distance black as the tents of Kedar? And, finally, with what jests and laughter, and pulls all together, the united following of the sheik stretched the canvas from pillar to pillar, driving the stakes and fastening the cords as they went? And when the walls of open reed matting were put in place – the finishing-touch to the building after the style of the Desert – with what hush of anxiety they waited the good man's judgment? When he walked in and out, looking at the house in connection with the sun, the trees, and the lake, and said, rubbing his hands with might of heartiness, "Well done! Make the dowar now as ye well know, and to-night we will sweeten the bread with arrack, and the milk with honey, and at every fire there shall be a kid. God with ye! Want of sweet water there shall not be, for the lake is our well; neither shall the bearers of burden hunger, or the least of the flock, for here is green pasture also. God with you all, my children! Go."

And, shouting, the many happy went their ways then to pitch their own habitations. A few remained to arrange the interior for the sheik; and of these the men-servants hung a curtain to the central row of pillars, making two apartments; the one on the right sacred to Ilderim himself, the other sacred to his horses – his jewels of Solomon – which they led in, and with kisses and love-taps set at liberty. Against the middle pillar they then erected the arms-rack, and filled it with javelins and spears, and bows, arrows, and shields; outside of them hanging the master's sword, modelled after the new moon; and the glitter of its blade rivalled the glitter of the jewels bedded in its grip. Upon one end of the rack they hung the housings of the horses, gay some of them as the livery of a king's servant, while on the other end they displayed the great man's wearing-apparel – his robes woollen and robes linen, his tunics and trousers, and many coloured kerchiefs for the head. Nor did they give over the work until he pronounced it well.

Meantime the women drew out and set up the divan, more indispensable to him than the beard down-flowing over his breast, white as Aaron's. They put a frame together in shape of three sides of a square, the opening to the door, and covered it with cushions and base curtains, and the cushions with a changeable spread striped brown and yellow; at the corners they placed pillows and bolsters sacked in cloth blue and crimson; then around the divan they laid a margin of carpet, and the inner space they carpeted as well; and when the carpet was carried from the opening of the divan to the door of the tent, their work was done; whereupon they again waited until the master said it was good. Nothing remained then but to bring and fill the jars with water, and hang the skin bottles of arrack ready for the hand – tomorrow the leben. Nor might an Arab see why Ilderim should not be both happy and generous – in his tent by the lake of sweet waters, under the palms of the Orchard of Palms.

Such was the tent at the door of which we left Ben-Hur.

Servants were already waiting the master's direction. One of them took off his sandals; another unlatched Ben-Hur's Roman shoes; then the two exchanged their dusty outer garments for fresh ones of white linen.

"Enter – in God's name, enter, and take thy rest," said the host, heartily, in the dialect of the market-place of Jerusalem; forthwith he led the way to the divan.

"I will sit here," he said next, pointing; "and there the stranger."

A woman – in the old time she would have been called a hand-maid – answered, and dexterously piled the pillows and bolsters as rests for the back; after which they sat upon the side of the divan, while water was brought fresh from the lake, and their feet bathed and dried with napkins.

"We have a saying in the Desert," Ilderim began, gathering his beard and combing it with his slender fingers, "that a good appetite is the promise of a long life. Hast thou such?"

"By that rule, good sheik, I will live a hundred years. I am a hungry wolf at thy door," Ben-Hur replied.

"Well, thou shalt not be sent away like a wolf. I will give thee the best of the flocks."

Ilderim clapped his hands.

"Seek the stranger in the guest-tent, and say I, Ilderim, send him a prayer that his peace may be as incessant as the flowing of waters."

The man in waiting bowed.

"Say, also," Ilderim continued, "that I have returned with another for breaking of bread; and, if Balthasar the wise careth to share the loaf, three may partake of it, and the portion of the birds be none the less."

The second servant went away.

"Let us take our rest now."

Thereupon Ilderim settled himself upon the divan, as at this day merchants sit on their rugs in the bazaars of Damascus; and when fairly at rest, he stopped combing his beard, and said, gravely, "That thou art my guest, and hast drunk my leben, and art about to taste my salt, ought not to forbid a question: Who art thou?"

"Sheik Ilderim," said Ben-Hur, calmly enduring his gaze, "I pray thee not to think me trifling with thy just demand; but was there never a time in thy life when to answer such a question would have been a crime to thyself?"

"By the splendour of Solomon, yes!" Ilderim answered. "Betrayal of self is at times as base as the betrayal of a tribe."

"Thanks, thanks, good sheik!" Ben-Hur exclaimed. "Never answer became thee better. Now I know thou dost but seek assurance to justify the trust I have come to ask, and that such assurance is of more interest to thee than the affairs of my poor life."

The sheik in his turn bowed, and Ben-Hur hastened to pursue his advantage.

"So it please thee then," he said, "first, I am not a Roman, as the name given thee as mine implieth."

Ilderim clasped the beard overflowing his breast, and gazed at the speaker with eyes faintly twinkling through the shade of the heavy close-drawn brows.

"In the next place," Ben-Hur continued, "I am an Israelite of the tribe of Judah."

EGYPTIAN JEWELRY

RING

BROOCH

The sheik raised his brows a little.

"Nor that merely. Sheik, I am a Jew with a grievance against Rome compared with which thine is not more than a child's trouble."

The old man combed his beard with nervous haste, and let fall his brows until even the twinkle of the eyes went out.

"Still further: I swear to thee, Sheik Ilderim – I swear by the covenant the Lord made with my fathers – so thou but give me the revenge I seek, the money and the glory of the race shall be thine."

Ilderim's brows relaxed; his head arose; his face began to beam; and it was almost possible to see the satisfaction taking possession of him.

"Enough!" he said. "If at the roots of thy tongue there is a lie in coil, Solomon himself had not been safe against thee. That thou art not a Roman – that as a Jew thou hast a grievance against Rome, and revenge to compass, I believe; and on that score enough. But as to thy skill. What experience has thou in racing with chariots? And the horses – canst thou make them creatures of thy will? – to know thee? to come at call? to go, if thou sayest it, to the last extreme of breath and strength? and then, in the perishing moment, out of the depths of thy life thrill them to one exertion of the mightiest of all? The gift, my son, is not to every one. Ah, by the splendour of God!

51

I knew a king who governed millions of men, their perfect master, but could not win the respect of a horse. Ho, there!"

A servant came forward.

"Let my Arabs come!"

The man drew aside part of the division curtain of the tent, exposing to view a group of horses, who lingered a moment where they were as if to make certain of the invitation.

"Come!" Ilderim said to them. "Why stand ye there? What have I that is not yours? Come, I say!"

They stalked slowly in.

A head of exquisite turn – with large eyes, soft as a deer's, and half hidden by the dense forelock, and small ears, sharp-pointed and sloped well forward – approached then quite to his breast, the nostrils open, and the upper lip in motion. "Who are you?" it asked, plainly as ever man spoke. Ben-Hur recognized one of the four racers he had seen on the course, and gave his open hand to the beautiful brute.

At that moment there was a stir at the rear entrance to the tent.

"The supper – it is here! and yonder my friend Balthasar, whom thou shalt know. He hath a story to tell which an Israelite should never tire of hearing."

THE MEAL IN THE TENT

Three rugs were spread on the carpet within the space so nearly enclosed by the divan; a table not more than a foot in height was brought and set within the same place, and covered with a cloth. Off to one side a portable earthenware oven was established under the presidency of a woman whose duty it was to keep the company in bread, or, more precisely, in hot cakes of flour from the handmills grinding with constant sound in a neighbouring tent.

Meanwhile Balthasar was conducted to the divan, where Ilderim and Ben-Hur received him standing. A loose black gown covered his person: his step was

feeble, and his whole movement slow and cautious, apparently dependent upon a long staff and the arm of a servant.

"Peace to you, my friend," said Ilderim, respectfully. "Peace and welcome."

The Egyptian raised his head and re-plied: "And to thee, good sheik – to thee and thine, peace and the blessing of the One God – God, the true and loving."

"This is he, O Balthasar," said the sheik, laying his hand on Ben-Hur's arm, "who will break bread with us this evening."

The Egyptian glanced at the young man, and looked again surprised and doubting; seeing which the sheik con-tinued: "I have promised him my horses for trial tomorrow; and if all goes well, he will drive them in the Circus."

Balthasar continued his gaze.

"He came well recommended," Ilderim pursued, much puzzled. "You may know him as the son of Arrius, who was a noble Roman sailor, though" – the sheik hesi-tated, then resumed, with a laugh – "though he declares himself an Israelite of the tribe of Judah; and, by the splen-dour of God, I believe that he tells me!"

Balthasar could no longer withhold explanation.

"Today, O most generous sheik, my life was in peril, and would have been lost had not a youth, the counterpart of this one – if, indeed, he be not the very same – intervened when all others fled, and saved me." Then he addressed Ben-Hur directly, "Art thou not he?"

"I cannot answer so far," Ben-Hur replied, with modest deference. "I am he who stopped the horses of the insolent Roman when they were rushing upon thy camel at the Fountain of Castalia."

"What!" said the sheik to Ben-Hur. "Thou saidst nothing of this to me, when better recommendation thou couldst not have brought. Am I not an Arab, and sheik of my tribe of tens of thousands? And is not he my guest? And is it not in my guest-bond that the good or evil thou dost him is good or evil done to me? Whither shouldst thou go for reward but here? And whose the hand to give it but mine?"

His voice at the end of the speech rose to cutting shrillness.

"Good sheik, spare me, I pray. I came not for reward, great or small; and that I may be acquitted of the thought, I say the help I gave this excellent man would have been given as well to thy humblest servant."

"But he is my friend, my guest – not my servant; and seest thou not in the differ-ence the favour of Fortune?" Then to Balthasar the sheik subjoined, "Ah, by the splendour of God! I tell thee again he is not a Roman."

With that he turned away, and gave attention to the servants, whose prepara-tions for the supper were about com-plete.

"Come," he said to them, "the meal is ready."

Ben-Hur gave his arm to Balthasar, and conducted him to the table, where shortly they were all seated on their rugs Eastern fashion. The lavers were brought them, and they washed and dried their hands; then the sheik made a sign, the servants stopped, and the voice of the Egyptian arose tremulous with holy feeling.

"Father of All – God! What we have is of Thee; take our thanks, and bless us, that we may continue to do Thy will."

With such a company – an Arab, a Jew, and an Egyptian, all believers alike in one God – there could be at that age but one subject of conversation; and of the three, which should be speaker but he to whom the Deity had been so nearly a personal appearance, who had seen Him in a star, had heard His voice in direction, had been led so far and so miraculously by His Spirit? And of what should he talk but that of which he had been called to testify?

A MAN WHOM THE WORLD COULD NOT DO WITHOUT

The shadows cast over the Orchard of Palms by the mountains at set of sun left no sweet margin time of violet sky and drowsing earth between the day and night. The latter came early and swift; and against its glooming in the tent this evening the servants brought four candle-sticks of brass, and set them by the corners of the table.

The Egyptian told his story of the meeting of the three in the desert, and

CUP

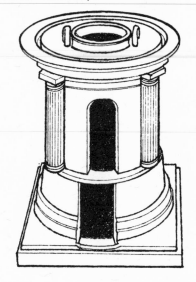

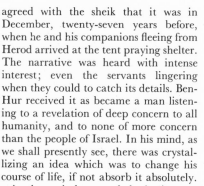

SILVER LIBATION BOWL
AND LADLE

agreed with the sheik that it was in December, twenty-seven years before, when he and his companions fleeing from Herod arrived at the tent praying shelter. The narrative was heard with intense interest; even the servants lingering when they could to catch its details. Ben-Hur received it as became a man listening to a revelation of deep concern to all humanity, and to none of more concern than the people of Israel. In his mind, as we shall presently see, there was crystallizing an idea which was to change his course of life, if not absorb it absolutely.

As the recital proceeded, the impression made by Balthasar upon the young Jew increased; at its conclusion, his feeling was too profound to permit a doubt of its truth; indeed, there was nothing left him desirable in the connection but assurances, if such were to be had, pertaining exclusively to the consequences of the amazing event.

To Sheik Ilderim the story was not new; yet, in the nature of things, its mighty central fact could not come home to him with the force and absorbing

effect it came to Ben-Hur. He was an Arab, whose interest in the consequences was but general; on the other hand, Ben-Hur was an Israelite and a Jew, with more than a special interest in – if the solecism can be pardoned – the truth of the fact. He laid hold of the circumstance with a purely Jewish mind.

From his cradle, let it be remembered, he had heard of the Messiah; at the colleges he had been made familiar with all that was known of that Being, at once the hope, the fear, and the peculiar glory of the chosen people; the prophets from the first to the last of the heroic line foretold Him; and the coming had been, and yet was, the theme of endless exposition with the rabbis – in the synagogues, in the schools, in the Temple, of fast-days and feast-days, in public and in private, the national teachers expounded and kept expounding until all the children of Abraham, wherever their lots were cast, bore the Messiah in expectation, and by it literally, and with iron severity, ruled and moulded their lives.

It remains to be said now that Ben-Hur

was in agreement with the mass of men of his time not Romans. The five years' residence in the capital served him with opportunity to see and study the miseries of the subjugated world; and in full belief that the evils which afflicted it were political, and to be cured only by the sword, he was going forth to fit himself for a part in the day of resort to the heroic remedy.

The feelings with which he listened to Balthasar can be now understood. The story touched two of the most sensitive points of his being so they rang within him. His heart beat fast – and faster still when, searching himself, he found not a doubt either that the recital was true in every particular, or that the Child so miraculously found was the Messiah. Marvelling much that Israel rested so dead to the revelation, and that he had never heard of it before that day, two questions presented themselves to him as centring all it was at that moment further desirable to know:

Where was the Child then?

And what was His mission?

"If I could answer you," Balthasar said, in his simple, earnest devout way – "oh, if I knew where He is, how quickly I would go to Him! The seas should not stay me, nor the mountains."

"You have tried to find Him, then?" asked Ben-Hur.

A smile flitted across the face of the Egyptian.

"The first task I charged myself with after leaving the shelter given me in the desert" – Balthasar cast a grateful look at Ilderim – "was to learn what became of the Child. But a year had passed, and I dared not go up to Judea in person, for Herod still held the throne bloody-minded as ever. In Egypt, upon my return, there were a few friends to believe the wonderful things I told them of what I had seen and heard – a few who rejoiced with me that a Redeemer was born – a few who never tired of the story. Some of them came up for me looking after the Child. They went first to Bethlehem, and found there the khan and the cave; but the steward – he who sat at the gate the night of the birth, and the night we came following the star – was gone. The king had taken him away, and he was no more seen."

"But they found some proofs, surely," said Ben-Hur, eagerly.

"Yes, proofs written in blood – a village in mourning; mothers yet crying for their little ones. You must know, when Herod heard of our flight, he sent down and slew the youngest-born of the children of Bethlehem. Not one escaped. The faith of my messengers was confirmed; but they came saying the Child was dead, slain with the other innocents."

"Dead!" exclaimed Ben-Hur, aghast. "Dead, sayest thou?"

"Nay, my son, I did not say so. I said they, my messengers, told me the Child was dead. I did not believe the report then. I do not believe it now."

"I see – thou hast some special knowledge."

"I have no special knowledge," Balthasar continued, observing the dejection which had fallen upon Ben-Hur; "but, my son, I have given the matter much thought – thought continuing through years, inspired by faith, which, I assure you, calling God for witness, is as strong in me now as in the hour I heard the voice of the Spirit calling me by the shore of the lake. If you will listen, I will tell you why I believe the Child is living."

Both Ilderim and Ben-Hur looked assent, and appeared to summon their faculties that they might understand as well as hear. The interest reached the servants, who drew near to the divan, and stood listening. Throughout the tent there was the profoundest silence.

"We three believe in God."

Balthasar bowed his head as he spoke.

"And He is the Truth," he resumed. "His word is God. The hills may turn to dust, and the seas be drunk dry by south winds; but His word shall stand, because it is the Truth."

The utterance was in a manner inexpressibly solemn.

"The voice, which was His, speaking to me by the lake, said, 'Blessed art thou, O son of Mizraim! The Redemption cometh. With two others from the remotenesses of the earth, thou shalt see the Saviour.' I have seen the Saviour – blessed be His name! – but the Redemption, which was the second part of the promise, is yet to come. Seest thou now? If the Child be dead, there is no agent to bring the Redemption about, and the word is naught, and God – nay, I dare not say it!"

He threw up both hands in horror.

"The Redemption was the work for which the Child was born; and so long as the promise abides, not even death can separate Him from His work until it is fulfilled, or at least in the way of fulfilment. Take you that now as one reason for my belief; then give me further attention."

The good man paused.

"Wilt thou not taste the wine? It is at thy hand – see," said Ilderim, respectfully.

Balthasar drank, and, seeming refreshed, continued:

"The Saviour I saw was born of woman, in nature like us, and subject to all our ills – even death. Let that stand as the first proposition. Consider next the work set apart to Him. Was it not a performance for which only a man is fitted? – a man wise, firm, discreet – a man, not a child? To become such He had to grow as we grow. Bethink you now of the dangers His life was subject to in the interval – the long interval between childhood and maturity. The existing powers were His enemies; Herod was His enemy; and what would Rome have been? And as for Israel – that He should not be accepted by Israel was the motive for cutting Him off. See you now. What better way was there to take care of His life in the helpless growing time than by passing Him into obscurity? Wherefore I say to myself, and to my listening faith, which is never moved except by yearning of love – I say He is not dead, but lost; and, His work remaining undone, He will come again."

A thrill of awe struck Ben-Hur – a thrill which was but the dying of his half-formed doubt.

"Where thinkest thou He is?" he asked in a low voice, and hesitating, like one who feels upon his lips the pressure of a sacred silence.

Balthasar looked at him kindly, and replied, his mind not entirely freed from its abstraction:

"In my house on the Nile, so close to the river than the passers-by in boats see it and its reflection in the water at the same time – in my house, a few weeks ago, I sat thinking. A man thirty years old, I said to myself, should have his fields of life all ploughed, and his planting well done; for after that it is summer-time, with space scarce enough to ripen his sowing. The Child, I said further, is now twenty-seven – His time to plant must be at hand. I asked myself, as you here asked me, my son, and answered by coming hither, as to a good resting-place close by the land thy fathers had from God. Where else should He appear, if not in Judea? In what city should He begin His work if not in Jerusalem? Who should be first to receive the blessings He

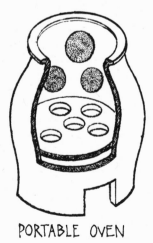

PORTABLE OVEN

54

is to bring, if not the children of Abraham, Isaac, and Jacob; in love, at least, the children of the Lord? If I were bidden go seek Him, I would search well the hamlets and villages on the slopes of the mountains of Judea and Galilee falling eastwardly into the valley of the Jordan. He is there now. Standing in a door on a hilltop, only this evening He saw the sun set one day nearer the time when He Himself shall become the light of the world."

Balthasar ceased, with his hand raised and finger pointing as if at Judea. All the listeners, even the dull servants outside the divan, affected by his fervour, were startled as if by a majestic presence suddenly apparent within the tent. Nor did the sensation die away at once: of those at the table, each sat awhile thinking. The spell was finally broken by Ben-Hur.

"I see, good Balthasar," he said, "that thou hast been much and strangely favoured. I see, also, that thou art a wise man indeed. It is not in my power to tell how grateful I am for the things thou hast told me. I am warned of the coming of great events, and borrow somewhat from thy faith. Complete the obligation, I pray thee, by telling further of the mission of Him for whom thou art waiting, and for whom from this night I too shall wait as becomes a believing son of Judah. He is to be a Saviour, thou saidst; is He not to be King of the Jews also?"

"My son," said Balthasar, in his benignant way, "the mission is yet a purpose in the bosom of God. All I think about it is wrung from the words of the Voice in connection with the prayer to which they were in answer. Shall we refer to them again?"

"Thou art the teacher."

"The cause of my disquiet," Balthasar began, calmly – "that which made me a preacher in Alexandria and in the villages of the Nile; that which drove me at last into the solitude where the Spirit found me – was the fallen condition of men, occasioned, as I believed, by loss of the knowledge of God. I sorrowed for the sorrows of my kind – not of one class, but all of them. So utterly were they fallen it seemed to me there could be no Redemption unless God Himself would make it His work; and I prayed Him to come, and that I might see Him. 'Thy good works have conquered. The Redemption cometh; thou shalt see the Saviour' –

thus the Voice spake; and with the answer I went up to Jerusalem rejoicing. Now, to whom is the Redemption? To all the world. And how shall it be? Strengthen thy faith, my son! Men say, I know, that there will be no happiness until Rome is razed from her hills. That is to say, the ills of the time are not, as I thought them, from ignorance of God, but from the misgovernment of rulers. Do we need to be told that human governments are never for the sake of religion? How many kings have you heard of who were better than their subjects? Oh no, no! The Redemption cannot be for a political purpose – to pull down rulers and powers, and vacate their places merely that others may take and enjoy them. If that were all of it, the wisdom of God would cease to be surpassing. I tell you, though it be but the saying of blind to blind. He that comes is to be a Saviour of souls; and the Redemption means God once more on earth, and righteousness, that His stay here may be tolerable to Himself."

Disappointment showed plainly on Ben-Hur's face – his head drooped; and if he was not convinced, he yet felt himself incapable that moment of disputing the opinion of the Egyptian. Not so Ilderim.

"By the splendour of God!" he cried, impulsively, "the judgment does away with all custom. The ways of the world are fixed, and cannot be changed. There must be a leader in every community clothed with power, else there is no reform."

Balthasar received the burst gravely.

"Thy wisdom, good sheik, is of the world; and thou dost forget that it is from the ways of the world we are to be redeemed. Man as a subject is the ambition of a king; the soul of a man for its salvation is the desire of a God."

Ilderim, though silenced, shook his head, unwilling to believe. Ben-Hur took up the argument for him.

"Father – I call thee such by permission," he said – "for whom wert thou required to ask at the gates of Jerusalem?"

The sheik threw him a grateful look.

"I was to ask of the people," said Balthasar, quietly, " 'Where is He that is born King of the Jews?' "

"And you saw Him in the cave by Bethlehem?"

"We saw and worshipped Him, and

gave Him presents – Melchior, gold; Gaspar, frankincense; and I, myrrh."

After that there was a long silence, which Balthasar accepted as the end of the conversation.

"Good sheik," he said, in his placid way, "tomorrow or the next day I will go up to the city for a time. My daughter wishes to see the preparations for the games. I will speak further about the time of our going. And, my son, I will see you again. To you both, peace and good-night."

They all arose from the table. The sheik and Ben-Hur remained looking after the Egyptian until he was conducted out of the tent.

"Sheik Ilderim," said Ben-Hur then, "I have heard strange things tonight. Give me leave, I pray, to walk by the lake that I may think of them."

"Go; and I will come after you."

They washed their hands again; after which, at a sign from the master, a servant brought Ben-Hur his shoes, and directly he went out.

BEN HUR REFLECTS

Up a little way from the dowar there was a cluster of palms, which threw its shade half in the water, half on the land. A bulbul sang from the branches a song of invitation. Ben-Hur stopped beneath to listen. His imagination was heated, his feelings aroused, his will all unsettled.

His scheme of life has been explained. In all reflection about it heretofore there had been one hiatus which he had not been able to bridge or fill up – one so broad he could see but vaguely to the other side of it. When, finally, he was graduated a captain as well as a soldier, to what object should he address his efforts?

The hours and days he had given this branch of his scheme were past calculation – all with the same conclusion – a dim, uncertain, general idea of national liberty. Was it sufficient? He could not say no, for that would have been the

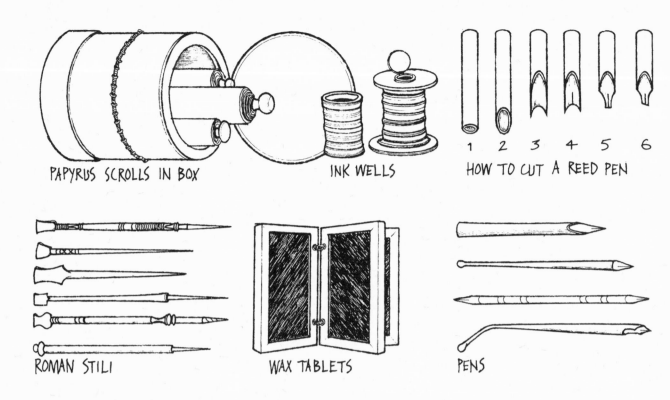

PAPYRUS SCROLLS IN BOX

INK WELLS

HOW TO CUT A REED PEN
1 2 3 4 5 6

ROMAN STILI

WAX TABLETS

PENS

death of his hope; he shrank from saying yes, because his judgment taught him better. He could not assure himself even that Israel was able single-handed to successfully combat Rome. He knew the resources of that great enemy; he knew her art was superior to her resources. A universal alliance might suffice, but alas! that was impossible, except – and upon the exception how long and earnestly he had dwelt – except a hero would come from one of the suffering nations, and by martial successes accomplish a renown to fill the whole earth. What glory to Judea could she prove the Macedonia of the new Alexander? Alas, again! Under the rabbis valour was possible, but not discipline. And then the taunt of Messala in the garden of Herod – "All you conquer in the six days, you lose on the seventh."

So it happened he never approached the chasm thinking to surmount it, but he was beaten back; and so incessantly had he failed in the object that he had about given it over, except as a thing of chance. The hero might be discovered in his day, or he might not. God only knew. Such his state of mind, there need be no

lingering upon the effect of Malluch's skeleton recital of the story of Balthasar. He heard it with a bewildering satisfaction — a feeling that here was the solution of the trouble – here was the requisite hero found at last; and he a son of the Lion tribe, and King of the Jews! Behind the hero, lo! the world in arms.

The king implied a kingdom; he was to be a warrior glorious as David, a ruler wise and magnificent as Solomon; the kingdom was to be a power against which Rome was to dash itself to pieces. There would be colossal war, and the agonies of death and birth – then peace, meaning, of course, Judean dominion for ever.

"What of this kingdom? And what is it to be?" Ben-Hur asked himself in thought.

In the midst of his reverie a hand was laid upon his shoulder.

"I have a word to say, O son of Arrius," said Ilderim, stopping by his side – "A word, and then I must return, for the night is going."

"I give you welcome, sheik."

"As to the things you have heard but now," said Ilderim, almost without pause, "take in belief all save that re-

lating to the kind of kingdom the Child will set up when He comes; as to so much keep virgin mind until you hear Simonides the merchant – a good man here in Antioch, to whom I will make you known. The Egyptian gives you coinage of his dreams which are too good for the earth; Simonides is wiser; he will ring you the sayings of your prophets, giving book and page, so you cannot deny that the Child will be King of the Jews in fact – ay, by the splendour of God! a king as Herod was, only better and far more magnificent. And then, see you, we will taste the sweetness of vengeance. I have said. Peace to you!"

"Stay – sheik!"

If Ilderim heard his call, he did not stay.

"Simonides again!" said Ben-Hur, bitterly. "Simonides here, Simonides there; from this one now, then from that! I am like to be well ridden by my father's servant, who knows at least to hold fast that which is mine; wherefore he is richer, if indeed he be not wiser, than the Egyptian. By the covenant! it is not to the faithless a man should go to find a faith to keep – and I will not."

BOOK FIVE

MESSALA WRITES TO VALERIUS GRATUS

It is of great concern now that the reader should be fully informed of the contents of a letter, and it is accordingly given:

"MESSALA TO GRATUS.

"Antioch, XII. Kal. Jul.

"O my Midas!

"I have to relate to thee an astonishing event, which, though as yet somewhat in the field of conjecture, will, I doubt not, justify thy instant consideration.

"Allow me first to revive thy recollection. Remember, a good many years ago, a family of a prince in Jerusalem, incredibly ancient and vastly rich – by name Ben-Hur. If thy memory have a limp or ailment of any kind, there is, if I mistake not, a wound on thy head which may help thee to a revival of the circumstance.

"Next, to arouse thy interest. In punishment of the attempt upon thy life – for dear repose of conscience, may all the gods forbid it should ever prove to have been an accident! – the family were seized and summarily disposed of, and their property confiscated. And inasmuch, O my Midas! as the action had the approval of our Caesar, who was as just as he was wise – be there flowers upon his altars for ever! – there should be no shame in referring to the sums which were realized to us respectively from that source, for which it is not possible I can ever cease to be grateful to thee, certainly not while I continue, as at present, in the uninterrupted enjoyment of the part which fell to me.

"In vindication of thy wisdom I recall further that thou didst make disposition of the family of Hur, both of us at the time supposing the plan hit upon to be the most effective possible for the purposes in view, which were silence and delivery over to inevitable but natural death. Thou wilt remember what thou didst with the mother and sister of the malefactor; yet, if now I yield to a desire to learn whether they be living or dead, I know, from knowing the amiability of thy nature, O my Gratus, that thou wilt pardon me as one scarcely less amiable than thyself.

"As more immediately essential to the present business, however, I take the liberty of inviting to thy remembrance that the actual criminal was sent to the galleys a slave for life –

"Referring to the limit of life at the oar, the outlaw thus justly disposed of should be dead, or, better speaking, some one of the three thousand Oceanides should have taken him to husband at least five years ago. And if thou wilt excuse a momentary weakness, O most virtuous and tender of men, inasmuch as I loved him in childhood, and also because he was very handsome – I used in much admiration to call him my Ganymede – he ought in right to have fallen into the arms of the most beautiful daughter of the family. Of opinion, however, that he was certainly dead, I have lived quite five years in calm and innocent enjoyment of the fortune for which I am in a degree indebted to him. I make the admission of indebtedness without intending it to diminish my obligation to thee.

"Now I am at the very point of interest.

"Last night, while acting as master of the feast for a party just from Rome – their extreme youth and inexperience appealed to my compassion – I heard a singular story. Maxentius, the consul, as you know, comes today to conduct a campaign against the Parthians. Of the ambitious who are to accompany him there is one, a son of the late duumvir Quintus Arrius. I had occasion to inquire about him particularly. When Arrius set out in pursuit of the pirates, whose defeat gained him his final honours, he had no family; when he returned from the expedition, he brought back with him an heir. Now be thou composed as becomes the owner of so many talents in ready sestertia. The son and heir of whom I speak is he whom thou didst send to the galleys – the very Ben-Hur who should have died at his oar five years ago – returned now with fortune and rank, and possibly as a Roman citizen to—— Well, thou art too firmly seated to be alarmed, but I, O my Midas! I am in danger – no need to tell thee of what. Who should know, if thou dost not?

"When Arrius, the father, by adoption, joined battle with the pirates, his vessel was sunk, and but two of all her crew escaped drowning – Arrius himself and this one, his heir.

"The officers who took them from the plank on which they were floating say the associate of the fortunate tribune was a young man who, when lifted to the deck, was in the dress of a galley slave.

"This should be convincing, to say least; I tell thee, O my Midas! that yesterday, by good chance – I have a vow to Fortune in consequence – I met the mysterious son of Arrius, face to face; and I declare now that, though I did not recognize him, he is the very Ben-Hur who was for years my playmate; the very Ben-Hur who, if he be a man, though of the commonest grade, must this very moment of my writing be

57

thinking of vengeance – for so would I were I he – vengeance not to be satisfied short of life; vengeance for country, mother, sister, self, and – I say it last, though thou mayst think it should be first – for fortune lost.

"The sun is now fairly risen. An hour hence two messengers will depart from my door, each with a sealed copy hereof; one of them will go by land, the other by sea, so important do I regard it that thou shouldst be early and particularly informed of the appearance of our enemy in this part of our Roman world.

"I will await thy answer here.

"Ben-Hur's going and coming will of course be regulated by his master, the consul, who, though he exert himself without rest day and night, cannot get away under a month. Thou knowest what work it is to assemble and provide for an army destined to operate in a desolate, townless country.

"I saw the Jew yesterday in the Grove of Daphne; and if he be not there now, he is certainly in the neighbourhood, making it easy for me to keep him in eye. Indeed, wert thou to ask me where he is now, I should say, with the most positive assurance, he is to be found at the old Orchard of Palms, under the tent of the traitor Sheik Ilderim, who cannot long escape our strong hand. Be not surprised if Maxentius, as his first measure, places the Arab on ship for forwarding to Rome.

"I am so particular about the whereabouts of the Jew because it will be important to thee, O illustrious! when thou comest to consider what is to be done; for already I know, and by the knowledge I flatter myself I am growing in wisdom, that in every scheme involving human action there are three elements always to be taken into account – time, place, and agency.

"If thou sayest this is the place, have thou then no hesitancy in trusting the business to thy most loving friend, who would be thy aptest scholar as well.

"Messala."

BEN HUR TESTS ILDERIM'S HORSES

About the time the couriers departed from Messala's door with the letter (it being yet the early morning hour), Ben-Hur entered Ilderim's tent. He had taken a plunge into the lake, and breakfasted, and appeared now in an under-tunic,

sleeveless, and with skirt scarcely reaching to the knee.

The sheik saluted him from the divan.

"I give thee peace, son of Arrius," he said, with admiration, for, in truth, he had never seen a more perfect illustration of glowing, powerful, confident manhood. "I give thee peace and goodwill. The horses are ready, I am ready. And thou?"

"The peace thou givest me, good sheik, I give thee in return. I thank thee for so much goodwill. I am ready."

Ilderim clapped his hands.

"I will have the horses brought. Be seated."

"Are they yoked?"

"No."

"Then suffer me to serve myself," said Ben-Hur. "It is needful that I make the acquaintance of thy Arabs. I must know them by name, O sheik, that I may speak to them singly; nor less must I know their temper, for they are like men: if bold, the better of scolding; if timid, the better of praise and flattery. Let the servants bring me the harness."

"And the chariot?" asked the sheik.

"I will let the chariot alone today. In its place, let them bring me a fifth horse, if thou hast it; he should be barebacked, and fleet as the others."

Ilderim's wonder was aroused, and he summoned a servant immediately.

"Bid them bring the harness for the four," he said; "the harness for the four, and the bridle for Sirius."

The harness was brought. With his own hands Ben-Hur equipped ·the horses; with his own hands he led them out of the tent, and there attached the reins.

"Bring me Sirius," he said.

An Arab could not have better sprung to seat on the courser's back.

"And now the reins."

They were given him, and carefully separated.

"Good sheik," he said, "I am ready. Let a guide go before me to the field, and send some of thy men with water."

There was no trouble at starting. The horses were not afraid. Already there seemed a tacit understanding between them and the new driver, who had performed his part calmly, and with the confidence which always begets confidence. The order of going was precisely that of driving, except that Ben-Hur sat upon Sirius instead of standing in the chariot. Ilderim's spirit arose. He combed

his beard, and smiled with satisfaction as he muttered, "He is not a Roman, no, by the splendour of God!" He followed on foot, the entire tenantry of the dowar – men, women, and children – pouring after him, participants all in his solicitude, if not in his confidence.

The field, when reached, proved ample and well fitted for the training, which Ben-Hur began immediately by driving the four at first slowly, and in perpendicular lines, and then in wide circles. Advancing a step in the course, he put them next into a trot; again progressing, he pushed into a gallop; at length he contracted the circles, and yet later drove eccentrically here and there, right, left and without a break. An hour was thus occupied. Slowing the gait to a walk, he drove up to Ilderim.

"The work is done, nothing now but practice," he said. "I give you joy, Sheik Ilderim, that you have such servants as these. See," he continued, dismounting and going to the horses, "see, the gloss of their red coats is without spot; they breathe lightly as when I began. I give thee great joy, and it will go hard if" – he turned his flashing eyes upon the old man's face – "if we have not the victory and our——"

He stopped, coloured, bowed. At the sheik's side he observed for the first time, Balthasar, leaning upon his staff, and two women closely veiled. At one of the latter he looked a second time saying to himself, with a flutter about his heart, "'Tis she – 'tis the Egyptian!" Ilderim picked up his broken sentence:

"The victory, and our revenge!" Then he said aloud: "I am not afraid; I am glad. Son of Arrius, thou art the man. Be the end like the beginning, and thou shalt see of what stuff is the lining of the hand of an Arab who is able to give."

"I thank thee, good sheik," Ben-Hur returned, modestly. "Let the servants bring drink for the horses."

With his own hands he gave the water. Remounting Sirius, he renewed the training, going as before from walk to trot, from trot to gallop; finally, he pushed the steady racers into the run, gradually quickening it to full speed. The performance then became exciting; and there were applause for the dainty handling of the reins, and admiration for the four, which were the same, whether they flew forward or wheeled in varying curvature. In their action there were unity, power, grace, pleasure, all without effort or sign of labour. The admiration was unmixed with pity or reproach, which would have been as well bestowed upon swallows in their evening flight.

In the midst of the exercises, and the attention they received from the by-standers, Malluch came upon the ground, seeking the sheik.

"I have a message for you, O sheik," he said, availing himself of a moment he supposed favourable for the speech – "a message from Simonides, the merchant."

"Simonides!" ejaculated the Arab. "Ah! 'tis well. May Abaddon take all his enemies!"

"He bade me give thee first the holy peace of God," Malluch continued; "and then this despatch, with prayer that thou read it the instant of receipt."

Ilderim, standing in his place, broke the sealing of the package delivered to him, and from a wrapping of fine linen took two letters, which he proceeded to read.

[No. 1.]
"Simonides to Sheik Ilderim.
"O friend!
"Assure thyself first of a place in my inner heart.
"Then –
"There is in thy dowar a youth of fair presence, calling himself the son of Arrius; and such he is by adoption.
"He is very dear to me.
"He hath a wonderful history, which I will tell thee; come thou today or tomorrow, that I may tell the history, and have thy counsel.

"Meantime, favour all his requests, so they be not against honour. Should there be need of reparation, I am bound to thee for it.
"That I have interest in this youth, keep thou private.
"Remember me to thy other guests. He, his daughter, thyself, and all whom thou mayst choose to be of thy company, must depend upon me at the Circus the day of the games. I have seats already engaged.
"To thee and all thine, peace.
"What should I be, O my friend, but thy friend?
"Simonides."

[No. 2.]
"Simonides to Sheik Ilderim.
"O friend!
"Out of the abundance of my experience, I send you a word.
"There is a sign which all persons not Romans, and who have moneys or goods subject to despoilment, accept as warning – that is, the arrival at a seat or power of some high Roman official charged with authority.
"Today comes the Consul Maxentius.
"Be thou warned.
"Another word of advice.
"A conspiracy, to be of effect against thee, O friend, must include the Herods as parties; thou hast great properties in their dominions.
"Wherefore keep thou watch.
"Send this morning to thy trusty keepers of the roads leading south from Antioch, and bid them search every courier going and coming; if they find private despatches relating to thee or thy affairs, thou shouldst see them.
"You should have received this yesterday, though it is not too late, if you act promptly.

"If couriers left Antioch this morning, your messengers know the byways and can get before them with your orders.
"Do not hesitate.
"Burn this after reading.
"O my friend! thy friend!
"Simonides."

Ilderim read the letters a second time, and refolded them in the linen wrap, and put the package under his girdle.

The exercises in the field continued but a little longer – in all about two hours. At their conclusion, Ben-Hur brought the four to a walk, and drove to Ilderim.

"With leave, O sheik," he said, "I will return thy Arabs to the tent, and bring them out again this afternoon."

Ilderim walked to him as he sat on Sirius, and said: "I give them to you, son of Arrius, to do with as you will until after the games. You have done with them in two hours what the Roman – may jackals gnaw his bones fleshless! – could not in as many weeks. We will win – by the splendour of God, we will win!"

At the tent Ben-Hur remained with the horses while they were being cared for; then, after a plunge in the lake and a cup of arrack with the sheik, whose flow of spirits was royally exuberant, he dressed himself in his Jewish garb again, and walked with Malluch on into the Orchard.

There was much conversation between the two, not all of it important. One part, however, must not be overlooked. Ben-Hur was speaking.

"I will give you," he said, "an order for

RACING CHARIOT

my property stored in the khan this side the river by the Seleucian Bridge. Bring it to me today, if you can. And, good Malluch – if I do not overtask you——"

Malluch protested heartily his willingness to be of service.

"Thank you, Malluch, thank you," said Ben-Hur. "I will take you at your word, remembering that we are brethren of the old tribe, and that the enemy is a Roman. First, then – as you are a man of business, which I much fear Sheik Ilderim is not——"

"Arabs seldom are," said Malluch, gravely.

"Nay, I do not impeach their shrewdness, Malluch. It is well, however, to look after them. To save all forfeit or hindrance in connection with the race, you would put me perfectly at rest by going to the office of the Circus, and seeing that he has complied with every preliminary rule; and if you can get a copy of the rules, the service may be of great avail to me. I would like to know the colours I am to wear, and particularly the number of the crypt I am to occupy at the starting; if it be next Messala's on the right or left, it is well; if not, and you can have it changed so as to bring me next the Roman, do so. Have you good memory, Malluch?"

"It has failed me, but never, son of Arrius, where the heart helped it as now."

"I will venture, then, to charge you with one further service. I saw yesterday that Messala was proud of his chariot, as he might be, for the best of Caesar's scarcely surpass it. Can you not make its display an excuse which will enable you to find if it be light or heavy? I would like to have its exact weight and measurements – and, Malluch, though you fail in all else, bring me exactly the height his axle stands above the ground. You understand, Malluch? I do not wish him to have any actual advantage of me. I do not care for his splendour; if I beat him, it will make his fall the harder, and my triumph the more complete. If there are advantages really important, I want them."

"I see, I see!" said Malluch. "A line dropped from the centre of the axle is what you want."

"Thou hast it; and be glad, Malluch – it is the last of my commissions."

Shortly afterwards Malluch returned to the city.

During their absence, a messenger well mounted had been despatched with orders as suggested by Simonides. He was an Arab, and carried nothing written.

MESSALA'S SPIES

Ilderim returned to the dowar next day about the third hour. As he dismounted, a stranger made his appearance, coming, apparently, from the city.

"I am looking for Sheik Ilderim, surnamed the Generous," the stranger said.

His language and attire bespoke him a Roman.

What he could not read, he yet could speak; so the old Arab answered, with dignity, "I am Sheik Ilderim."

The man's eyes fell; he raised them again, and said, with forced composure, "I heard you had need of a driver for the games."

Ilderim's lip under the white moustache curled contemptuously.

"Go thy way," he said. "I have a driver."

And every day thereafter, down to the great day of the games, a man – sometimes two or three men – came to the sheik at the Orchard, pretending to seek an engagement as driver.

In such a manner Messala kept watch over Ben-Hur.

SHEIK ILDERIM'S RAGE

The sheik waited, well satisfied, until Ben-Hur drew his horses off the field for the forenoon – well satisfied, for he had seen them, after being put through all the other paces, run full speed in such manner that it did not seem there were one the slowest and another the fastest – run, in other words, as the four were one.

Ilderim drew forth a package, and opened it slowly, while they walked to the divan and seated themselves – "Son of Arrius, see thou here, and help me with thy Latin."

He passed the despatched to Ben-Hur.

"There; read – and read aloud, rendering what thou findest into the tongue of thy fathers. Latin is an abomination."

Ben-Hur was in good spirits, and began the reading carelessly. " 'Messala to Gratus!' " He paused. A premonition drove the blood to his heart. Ilderim observed his agitation.

"Well; I am waiting."

Ben-Hur prayed pardon, and recommenced the paper, which, it is sufficient to say, was one of the duplicates of the letter despatched so carefully to Gratus by Messala the morning after the revel in the palace.

The paragraphs in the beginning were remarkable only as proof that the writer had not outgrown his habit of mockery; when they were passed, and the reader came to the parts intended to refresh the memory of Gratus, his voice trembled, and twice he stopped to regain his self-control.

The paper fell from his hands, and he covered his face.

"They are dead – dead. I alone am left."

The sheik had been a silent, but not unsympathetic, witness of the young man's suffering; now he arose and said, "Son of Arrius, it is for me to beg thy pardon. Read the paper by thyself. When thou art strong enough to give the rest of it to me, send word, and I will return."

He went out of the tent, and nothing in all his life became him better.

Ben-Hur flung himself on the divan and gave way to his feelings. When somewhat recovered, he recollected that a portion of the letter remained unread, and, taking it up, he resumed the reading. "Thou wilt remember," the missive ran, "what thou didst with the mother and sister of the malefactor; yet, if now I yield to a desire to learn if they be living or dead" – Ben-Hur started, and read again, and then again, at last broke into exclamation.

"They are not dead," he said; "they are not dead, or he would have heard of it."

A second reading, more careful than the first, confirmed him in the opinion. Then he sent for the sheik.

"In coming to your hospitable tent, O sheik," he said, calmly, when the Arab was seated and they were alone, "it was not in my mind to speak of myself further than to assure you I had sufficient training to be intrusted with your horses. I declined to tell you my history. But the chances which have sent this paper to my hand and given it to me to be read are so strange that I feel bidden to trust you with everything. And I am the more inclined to do so by knowledge here conveyed that we are both of us threatened by the same enemy, against whom it is needful that we make common cause. I will read the letter and give you explanation; after which you will not wonder I was so moved. If you thought me weak or childish, you will then excuse me."

The sheik held his peace, listening closely, until Ben-Hur came to the paragraph in which he was particularly mentioned: "'he is to be found at the old Orchard of Palms under the tent of the traitor sheik Ilderim, who cannot long escape our strong hand. Be not surprised if Maxentius, as his first measure, places the Arab on ship for forwarding - to Rome.'"

"To Rome! Me – Ilderim – sheik of ten thousand horsemen with spears – me to Rome!"

He leaped rather than rose to his feet, his arms outstretched, his eyes glittering like a serpent's.

"O God! – nay, by all the gods except of Rome! – when shall this insolence end? A freeman am I; free are my people. Must we die slaves? Or, worse, must I live a dog, crawling to a master's feet? Must I lick his hand lest he lash me? What is mine is not mine; I am not my own; for breath of body I must be beholden to a Roman. Oh, if I were young again! Oh, could I shake off twenty years – or ten – or five!"

He ground his teeth and shook his hands overhead; then, under the impulse of another idea, he walked away and back again to Ben-Hur swiftly, and caught his shoulder with a strong grasp.

"If I were as thou, son of Arrius – as young, as strong, as practised in arms; if I had a motive hissing me to revenge – a motive, like thine, great enough to make hate holy— Away with disguise on thy part and on mine! Son of Hur, son of Hur I say—"

At that name all the currents of Ben-Hur's blood stopped; surprised, bewildered, he gazed into the Arab's eyes, now close to his, and fiercely bright.

"Son of Hur, I say, were I as thou, with half thy wrongs, bearing about with me memories like thine, I would not, I could not, rest." Never pausing, his words following each other torrent-like, the old man swept on. "To all my grievances, I would add those of the world, and devote myself to vengeance. From land to land I would go firing all mankind. Of nights I would pray the gods, the good and the bad alike, to lend me their special terrors – tempests, drought, heat, cold, and all the nameless poisons they let loose in air, all the thousand things of which men die on sea and on land. Oh, I could not sleep. I – I—"

The sheik stopped for want of breath, panting, wringing his hands. And, sooth to say, of all the passionate burst Ben-Hur retained but a vague impression wrought by fiery eyes, a piercing voice, and a rage too intense for coherent expression.

For the first time in years, the desolate youth heard himself addressed by his proper name.

"Good sheik, tell me how you came by this letter."

"My people keep the roads between cities," Ilderim answered, bluntly. "They took it from a courier."

"Are they known to be thy people?"

"No. To the world they are robbers, whom it is mine to catch and slay."

"Again, sheik. You call me son of Hur – my father's name. I did not think myself known to a person on earth. How came you by the knowledge?"

Ilderim hesitated; but, rallying, he answered, "I know you, yet I am not free to tell you more."

"What sayest thou?" he asked, while waiting for his horse and retinue. "I told what I would do, were I thou, and thou hast made no answer."

"I intended to answer, sheik, and I will." Ben-Hur's countenance and voice changed with the feeling invoked. "All thou hast said, I will do – all at least in the power of a man. I devoted myself to vengeance long ago. Every hour of the five years past, I have lived with no other thought. I have taken no respite. I have had no pleasures of youth. O sheik, I am a soldier; but the things of which I dream require me to be a captain. With that thought, I have taken part in the campaign against the Parthians; when it is over, then, if the Lord spare my life and strength – then" – he raised his clenched hands, and spoke vehemently –

"then I will be an enemy Roman-taught in all things; then Rome shall account to me in Roman lives for her ills. You have my answer, sheik."

Ilderim put an arm over his shoulder, and kissed him, saying, passionately, "If thy God favour thee not, son of Hur, it is because He is dead. Take thou this from me – sworn to, if so thy preference run: thou shalt have my hands, and their fulness – men, horses, camels, and the desert for preparation. I swear it! For the present, enough. Thou shalt see or hear from me before night."

Turning abruptly off, the sheik was speedily on the road to the city.

DANGER

The intercepted letter was conclusive upon a number of points of great interest to Ben-Hur. So when Ilderim left the tent, Ben-Hur had much to think about, requiring immediate action. His enemies were as adroit and powerful as any in the East. If they were afraid of him, he had greater reason to be afraid of them. He strove earnestly to reflect upon the situation, but could not; his feelings constantly overwhelmed him.

Occasionally, referring to the words of Ilderim, he wondered whence the Arab derived his information about him; not from Malluch certainly; nor from Simonides, whose interests, all adverse, would hold him dumb. Could Messala have been the informant? No, no: disclosure might be dangerous in that quarter.

After nightfall, Ben-Hur sat by the door of the tent waiting for Ilderim, not yet returned from the city. At last there was a sound of horse's feet coming rapidly, and Malluch rode up.

"Son of Arrius," he said, cheerily, after salutation, "I salute you for Sheik Ilderim, who requests you to mount and go to the city. He is waiting for you."

Ben-Hur asked no questions, but went in where the horses were feeding. Very shortly the two were on the road, going swiftly and in silence.

Some distance below the Seleucian Bridge, they crossed the river by a ferry, and, riding far round on the right bank, and recrossing by another ferry, entered the city from the west. The detour was long, but Ben-Hur accepted it as a precaution for which there was good reason.

Down to Simonides' landing they rode, and in front of the great warehouse, under the bridge, Malluch drew rein.

"We are come," he said. "Dismount."

Ben-Hur recognized the place.

"Where is the sheik?" he asked.

"Come with me. I will show you."

A watchman took the horses, and almost before he realized it Ben-Hur stood once more at the door of the house up on the greater one, listening to the response from within – "In God's name, enter."

SIMONIDES' ACCOUNTS

Malluch stopped at the door; Ben-Hur entered alone.

Three persons were present, looking at him – Simonides, Ilderim, and Esther.

He glanced hurriedly from one to another, as if to find answer to the question half formed in his mind. What business can these have with me? He became calm, with every sense on the alert, for the question was succeeded by another. Are they friends or enemies?

At length his eyes rested upon Esther.

The men returned his look kindly; in her face there was something more than kindness – something too *spirituel* for definition, which yet went to his inner consciousness without definition.

Shall it be said, good reader? Back of his gaze there was a comparison in which the Egyptian arose and set herself over against the gentle Jewess; but it lived an instant, and, as is the habit of such comparisons, passed away without a conclusion.

"Son of Hur——"

The guest turned to the speaker.

"Son of Hur," said Simonides, repeating the address slowly, and with distinct emphasis, as if to impress all its meaning upon him most interested in understand-

ing it, "take thou the peace of the Lord God of our fathers – take it from me." He paused, then added, "From me and mine."

The speaker sat in his chair; there were the royal head, the bloodless face, the masterful air, under the influence of which visitors forgot the broken limbs and distorted body of the man. The full black eyes gazed out under the white brows steadily, but not sternly. A moment thus, then he crossed his hands upon his breast.

"Simonides," Ben-Hur answered, much moved, "the holy peace you tender is

HEROD THE GREAT
37 – 4 B.C.

PONTIUS PILATE
26 – 36 A.D.

HEROD ARCHELAUS 4 B.C.

accepted. A son to father, I return it to you. Only let there be perfect understanding between us."

Thus delicately he sought to put aside the submission of the merchant, and, in place of the relation of master and servant, substitute one higher and holier.

Simonides bowed his acknowledgment.

"Esther, child, bring me the paper," he said, with a breath of relief.

She went to a panel in the wall, opened it, took out a roll of papyri, and brought and gave it to him.

"Here, Esther, stand by me and receive the sheets, lest they fall into confusion."

She took place by his chair, letting her right arm fall lightly across his shoulder, so, when he spoke, the account seemed to have rendition from both of them jointly.

"This," said Simonides, drawing out the first leaf, "shows the money I had of

thy father's, being the amount saved from the Romans; there was no property saved, only money, and that the robbers would have secured but for our Jewish custom of bills of exchange. The amount saved, being sums I drew from Rome, Alexandria, Damascus, Carthage, Valentia, and elsewhere within the circle of trade, was one hundred and twenty talents Jewish money."

He gave the sheet to Esther, and took the next one.

"With that amount – one hundred and twenty talents – I charged myself. Hear now my credits. I use the word, as thou wilt see, with reference rather to the proceeds gained from the use of the money."

From separate sheets he then read footings, which, fractions omitted, were as follows:

By ships	..	..	..	60 talents
,, goods in store	..	..	110	,,
,, cargoes in transit	..	75	,,
,, camels, horses, etc.	..	20	,,
,, warehouses	..	..	10	,,
,, bills due ..	..	..	54	,,
,, money on hand and subject to draft	..	..	224	,,
Total	..	..	..	553	,,

"To these now, to the five hundred and fifty-three talents gained, add the original capital I had from thy father, and thou hast *Six hundred and seventy-three talents!* – and all thine – making thee, O son of Hur, the richest subject in the world."

He took the papyri from Esther, and, reserving one, rolled them and offered them to Ben-Hur. The pride perceptible in his manner was not offensive: it might have been from a sense of duty well done; it might have been for Ben-Hur without reference to himself.

"And there is nothing," he added, dropping his voice, but not his eyes – "there is nothing now thou mayst not do."

Taking the roll, Ben-Hur arose, struggling with emotion.

"O Simonides, thy faithfulness outweighs the cruelty of others, and redeems our human nature. 'There is nothing I cannot do:' be it so. Shall any man in this my hour of such mighty privilege be more generous than I? Serve me as a witness now, Sheik Ilderim. Hear thou my words as I shall speak them – hear and remember. And thou, Esther, good angel of this good man! hear thou also."

He stretched his hand with the roll to Simonides.

"The things these papers take into account – all of them: ships, houses, goods, camels, horses, money; the least as well as the greatest – give I back to thee, O Simonides, making them all thine, and sealing them to thee and thine for ever."

Esther smiled through her tears; Ilderim pulled his beard with rapid motion, he eyes glistening like beads of jet. Simonides alone was calm.

"Sealing them to thee and thine for ever," Ben-Hur continued, with better control of himself, "with one exception, and upon one condition."

The breath of the listeners waited upon his words.

"The hundred and twenty talents which were my father's thou shalt return to me."

Ilderim's countenance brightened.

"And thou shalt join me in search of my mother and sister, holding all thine subject to the expense of discovery, even as I will hold mine."

Simonides was much affected. Stretching out his hand, he said: "I see thy spirit, son of Hur, and I am grateful to the Lord that He hath sent thee to me such as thou art. If I served well thy father in life, and his memory afterwards, be not afraid of default to thee; yet must I say the exception cannot stand."

Exhibiting, then, the reserved sheet, he continued:
"Take this and read – read aloud."

Ben-Hur took the supplement, and read it.

"Statement of the servants of Hur, rendered by Simonides, steward of the estate.
1. *Amrah, Egyptian, keeping the palace in Jerusalem.*
2. *Simonides, the steward, in Antioch.*
3. *Esther, daughter of Simonides."*

Now, in all his thoughts of Simonides, not once had it entered Ben-Hur's mind that, by the law, a daughter followed the parent's condition. In all his visions of her, the sweet-faced Esther had figured as the rival of the Egyptian, and an object of possible love. He shrank from the revelation so suddenly brought him, and looked at her, blushing; and, blushing, she dropped her eyes before him. Then he said, while the papyrus rolled itself together:

"A man with six hundred talents is indeed rich, and may do what he pleases; but rarer than the money, more priceless than the property, is the mind which amassed the wealth, and the heart it could not corrupt when amassed. O Simonides – and thou, fair Esther – fear not. Sheik Ilderim here shall be witness that in the same moment ye were declared my servants, that moment I declared ye free; and what I declare, that will I put in writing. Is it not enough? Can I do more?"

"Son of Hur," said Simonides, "verily thou dost make servitude lightsome. I was wrong; there are some things thou canst not do; thou canst not make us free in law. I am thy servant for ever, because I went to the door with thy father one day, and in my ear the awl-marks yet abide."

"Did my father that?"

"Judge him not," cried Simonides, quickly. "He accepted me a servant of that class because I prayed him to do so.

I never repented the step. It was the price I paid for Rachel, the mother of my child here; for Rachel, who would not be my wife unless I became what she was."

"Was she a servant for ever?"

"Even so."

Ben-Hur walked the floor in pain of impotent wish.

"I was rich before," he said, stopping suddenly. "I was rich with the gifts of the generous Arrius; now comes this greater fortune, and the mind which achieved it. Is there not a purpose of God in it all? Counsel me, O Simonides! Help me to see the right and do it. Help me to be worthy my name, and what thou art in law to me, that will I be to thee in fact and deed. I will be thy servant for ever."

Simonides' face actually glowed.

"O son of my dead master! I will do better than help; I will serve thee with all my might of mind and heart. Body, I have not; it perished in thy cause; but with mind and heart I will serve thee. I

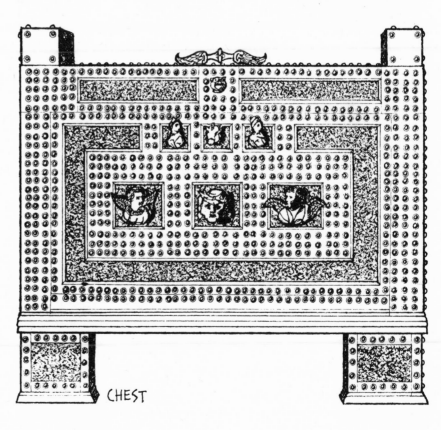

CHEST

swear it, by the altar of our God, and the gifts upon the altar! Only make me formally what I have assumed to be."

"Name it," said Ben-Hur, eagerly.

"As steward the care of the property will be mine."

"Count thyself steward now; or wilt thou have it in writing?"

"Thy word simply is enough; it was so with the father, and I will not more from the son. And now, if the understanding be perfect——" Simonides paused.

"It is with me," said Ben-Hur.

"And thou, daughter of Rachel, speak!" said Simonides, lifting her arm from his shoulder.

Esther, left thus alone, stood a moment abashed, her colour coming and going; then she went to Ben-Hur, and said, with a womanliness singularly sweet: "I am not better than my mother was; and, as she is gone, I pray you, O my master, let me care for my father."

Ben-Hur took her hand, and led her back to the chair, saying, "Thou art a good child. Have thy will."

Simonides replaced her arm upon his neck, and there was silence for a time in the room.

AN OATH OF REVENGE

Simonides looked up, none the less a master.

"Esther," he said, quietly, "the night is going fast; and, lest we become too weary for that which is before us, let the refreshments be brought."

She rang a bell. A servant answered with wine and bread, which she bore round.

"The understanding, good my master," continued Simonides, when all were served, "is not perfect in my sight. Henceforth our lives will run on together like rivers which have met and joined their waters. I think their flowing will be better if every cloud is blown from the sky above them. You left my door the other day with what seemed a denial of the claims which I have just allowed in the broadest terms; but it was not so, indeed it was not. Esther is witness that I recognized

you; and that I did not abandon you, let Malluch say."

"Malluch!" exclaimed Ben-Hur.

"One bound to a chair, like me, must have many hands far-reaching, if he would move the world from which he is so cruelly barred. I have many such, and Malluch is one of the best of them. And, sometimes" – he cast a grateful glance at the sheik – "sometimes I borrow from others good of heart, like Ilderim the Generous – good and brave. Let him say if I either denied or forgot you."

Ben-Hur looked at the Arab.

"This is he, good Ilderim, this is he who told you of me?"

Ilderim's eyes twinkled as he nodded his answer.

"How, O my master," said Simonides, "may we without trial tell what a man is? I knew you; I saw your father in you; but the kind of man you were I did not know. There are people to whom fortune is a curse in disguise. Were you of them? I sent Malluch to find out for me, and in the service he was my eyes and ears. Do not blame him. He brought me report of you which was all good."

"I do not," said Ben-Hur, heartily. "There was wisdom in your goodness."

"The words are very pleasant to me," said the merchant, with feeling, "very pleasant. My fear of misunderstanding is laid. Let the rivers run on now as God may give them direction."

After an interval he continued:

"I am compelled now by truth. You have seen Balthasar?"

"And heard him tell his story," said Ben-Hur.

"A miracle! – a very miracle!" cried Simonides. "As he told it to me, good my master, I seemed to hear the answer I had so long waited; God's purpose burst upon me. Poor will the King be when He comes – poor and friendless; without following, without armies, without cities or castles; a kingdom to be set up, and Rome reduced and blotted out. See, see, O my master! thou flushed with strength, thou trained to arms, thou burdened with riches; behold the opportunity the Lord hath sent thee! Shall not His purpose be thine? Could a man be born to a more perfect glory?"

Simonides put his whole force in the appeal.

"But the kingdom, the kingdom!" Ben-Hur answered, eagerly. "Balthasar says it is to be of souls."

The pride of the Jew was strong in Simonides, and therefore the slightly contemptuous curl of the lip with which he began his reply:

"Balthasar has been a witness of wonderful things – of miracles, O my master; and when he speaks of them, I bow with belief, for they are of sight and sound personal to him. But he is a son of Mizraim, and not even a proselyte. May the testimony of a whole people be slighted, my master? Though you travel from Tyre, which is by the sea in the north, to the capital of Edom, which is in the desert south, you will not find a lisper of the Shema, an alms-giver in the Temple, or any one who has ever eaten of the lamb of the Passover, to tell you the kingdom the King is coming to build for us, the children of the covenant, is other than of this world, like out father David's. Now where got they the faith, ask you?"

Simonides sat a moment thinking.

"The question of power should not trouble you." he next said.

Ben-Hur looked at him inquiringly.

"You were seeing the lowly King in the act of coming to His own," Simonides answered – "seeing Him on the right hand, as it were, and on the left the brassy legions of Caesar, and you were asking, 'What can He do?'"

"It was my very thought,"

"O my master!" Simonides continued. "You do not know how strong our Israel is. You think of him as a sorrowful old man weeping by the rivers of Babylon. But go up to Jerusalem next Passover, and stand on the Xystus or in the Street of Barter, and see him as he is. The promise of the Lord to father Jacob coming out of Padan-Aram was a law under which our people have not ceased multiplying – not even in captivity; they grew under foot of the Egyptian; the clench of the Roman has been but wholesome nurture to them; now they are indeed 'a nation, and a company of nations.' Nor that only, my master; in fact, to measure the strength of Israel – which is, in fact, measuring what the King can do – you shall not bide solely by the rule of natural increase, but add thereto the other – I mean the spread of the faith, which will carry you to the far and near of the whole known earth. Further, the habit is, I know, to think and speak of Jerusalem as Israel, which may be likened to our finding an embroidered shred, and hold-

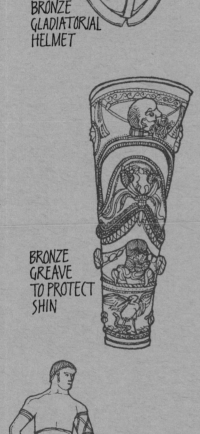

BRONZE
GLADIATORIAL
HELMET

BRONZE
GREAVE
TO PROTECT
SHIN

BRONZE
SCULPTURE
OF A
RETIARIUS

THE GLADIATORS

The origin of the gladiators goes back to the ancient Etruscan religious practice of men fighting to the death outside their chief's burial place. (This was to give his soul strength to cross to the "other world").

Gladiators were usually condemned criminals, prisoners of war, slaves sold to the gladiatorial schools or sometimes free citizens who signed on voluntarily.

They were all trained in special gladiatorial schools and were attended by doctors, masseurs and armourers. The novice took an oath of obedience, "I undertake to be burnt by fire, to be bound in chains, to be beaten, to die by the sword." The novices trained with wooden weapons and dummies made of wood and straw.

CLASSES OF GLADIATORS

SAMNITES Originally war captives (3rd c. B.C.) from southern Italy. Heavy armour, oblong shield, leather or metal greave on left leg, sleeve on right arm, visored helmet with large crest or plume, sword or lance for defence.

THRACIANS Small shield, bands of leather around legs and thighs, greaves on both legs, carried sickle for defence.

SECUTORS (The chasers) Rectangular or round shield, body bare except for large belt of metal or leather round waist and thighs, leather bands on right arm, greave on left leg, round visored helmet, dagger for defence.

MYRMILLO (After sea-fish emblem on helmet.) Armed with curved sword. Usually fought against secutors but sometimes with thracians or retiarii.

RETIARII Head band, large belt, bands of leather round legs or ankles, left shoulder protected by leather shoulder piece. For defence a trident, dagger and net with cord for retrieval if the opponent was not snared.

ANDABATAE Chain mail shirt, helmet which covered the face. The opponents charged at each other blindly, on horseback, unable to see as their helmets lacked eye-holes.

EQUITES Fought on horseback, with round shield, wore short tunic.

VELITES Armed with spears (with leather strap attached).

ESSEDARII Fought from chariots with drivers by their sides. (Introduced from Britain.)

DIMACHAERI Bare headed, fought with two daggers.

SAGITTARII Wild animal fighters, used bows and arrows.

BESTIARII Short tunics with long sleeves, fought wild animals with long spears.

LAQUEARII Armed with noose to strangle opponent.

THE PRELIMINARIES

Special sign writers were employed to paint advertisements for the games on walls and even on tombstones in the town where the games were to be held. Handbills were produced and programmes sold. People were hired to call out the list of events in the streets. The night before the show a magnificent feast was given by the patron for the gladiators who were to fight the next day.

THE SPORT

The games opened with wild beast fights and at mid-day condemned criminals or war criminals were executed. After this the pagniarii (these could be gladiators too old for the main rounds) fought with sticks and whips; or perhaps the lusorii (or mock gladiators) fought with wooden weapons using gladiatorial techniques. At the end of these bouts the main contestants were chosen by lot in the arena. The weapons were tested for sharpness in a special ceremony presided over by the patron. Then the main bouts started, music was played and the gladiators warmed up with shadow boxing and mock fights. They shouted abuse at each other to make themselves "fighting mad"! The trumpet sounded and the bouts started between the heavily armed gladiators (myrmillos, samnites or secutors) and the lightly armed thracians.

When one of the gladiators was wounded and fell to the ground, begging for mercy, he raised one finger of his left hand as a plea to the sponsor. The "thumbs" up sign or a handkerchief waved by the sponsor meant that the gladiator would be saved to fight another day. The "thumbs down" sign meant that he should be killed.

This was usually done by the Charons (named after the ferryman to the underworld). The gladiator was taken out of the arena, but not before a hot iron was placed on his body to make sure that he was dead. This was done by men in masks representing the god Mercury (the guide to the underworld).

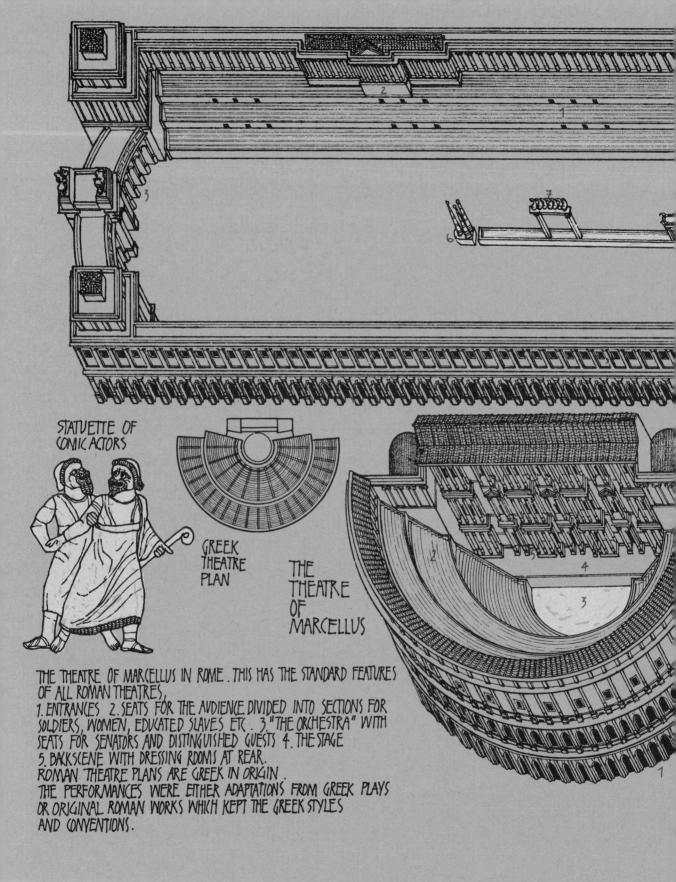

STATUETTE OF
COMIC ACTORS

GREEK
THEATRE
PLAN

THE
THEATRE
OF
MARCELLUS

THE THEATRE OF MARCELLUS IN ROME. THIS HAS THE STANDARD FEATURES
OF ALL ROMAN THEATRES,
1. ENTRANCES 2. SEATS FOR THE AUDIENCE DIVIDED INTO SECTIONS FOR
SOLDIERS, WOMEN, EDUCATED SLAVES ETC. 3. "THE ORCHESTRA" WITH
SEATS FOR SENATORS AND DISTINGUISHED GUESTS 4. THE STAGE
5. BACKSCENE WITH DRESSING ROOMS AT REAR.
ROMAN THEATRE PLANS ARE GREEK IN ORIGIN.
THE PERFORMANCES WERE EITHER ADAPTATIONS FROM GREEK PLAYS
OR ORIGINAL ROMAN WORKS WHICH KEPT THE GREEK STYLES
AND CONVENTIONS.

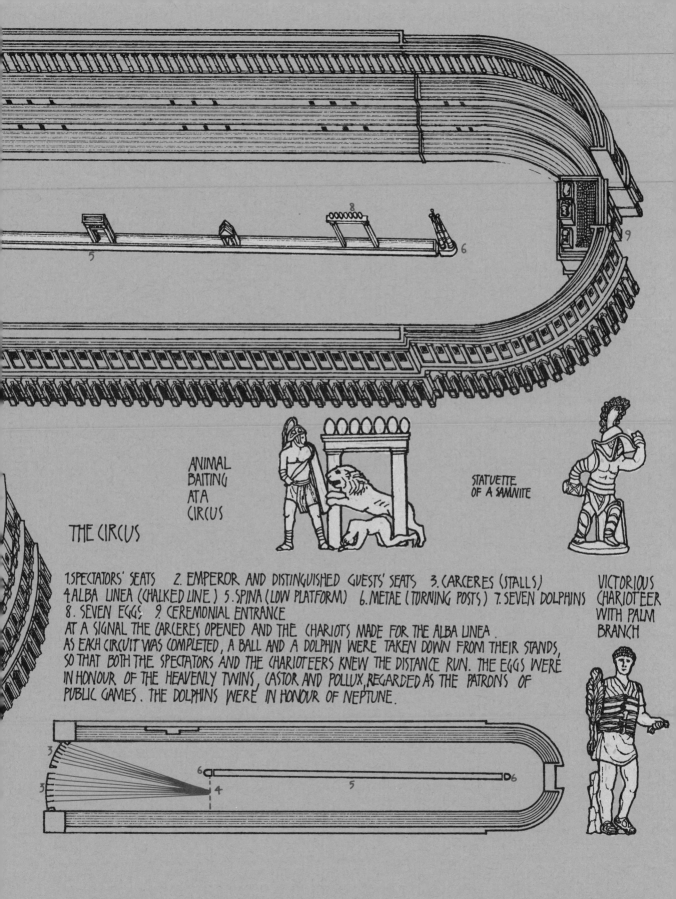

ANIMAL
BAITING
AT A
CIRCUS

STATUETTE
OF A SAMNITE

THE CIRCUS

VICTORIOUS
CHARIOTEER
WITH PALM
BRANCH

1. SPECTATORS' SEATS   2. EMPEROR AND DISTINGUISHED GUESTS' SEATS   3. CARCERES (STALLS)
4. ALBA LINEA (CHALKED LINE.) 5. SPINA (LOW PLATFORM) 6. METAE (TURNING POSTS) 7. SEVEN DOLPHINS
8. SEVEN EGGS. 9. CEREMONIAL ENTRANCE
AT A SIGNAL THE CARCERES OPENED AND THE CHARIOTS MADE FOR THE ALBA LINEA.
AS EACH CIRCUIT WAS COMPLETED, A BALL AND A DOLPHIN WERE TAKEN DOWN FROM THEIR STANDS,
SO THAT BOTH THE SPECTATORS AND THE CHARIOTEERS KNEW THE DISTANCE RUN. THE EGGS WERE
IN HONOUR OF THE HEAVENLY TWINS, CASTOR AND POLLUX, REGARDED AS THE PATRONS OF
PUBLIC GAMES. THE DOLPHINS WERE IN HONOUR OF NEPTUNE.

THE FIRST AMPHITHEATRE WAS BUILT BETWEEN 70-65BC IN POMPEII. THE COLOSSEUM WAS BUILT BY VESPASIAN AND OPENED IN 80AD. IT WAS ENLARGED BY SUCCESSIVE EMPERORS OVER THE NEXT 200 YEARS.
SPECTATORS ENTERED THROUGH THE ARCHES (1) AND REACHED THEIR SEATS BY STAIRS (2) AND CORRIDORS (3) BLOCKS OF SEATS (4) WERE SET ASIDE FOR VARIOUS CLASSES OF CITIZENS. WOMEN WOULD OCCUPY THE WOODEN SEATS (5) ON THE TOP FLOOR, THE ROOF (6) WOULD BE USED BY THE VERY POOR. THE EMPEROR AND HIS GUESTS WOULD SIT ON THE PODIUM (7) A CANVAS AWNING WAS STRETCHED FROM POLES (8) TO PROTECT SPECTATORS FROM THE SUN. IN THE BASEMENT WERE THE CAGES FOR WILD ANIMALS (9) THEY WERE DRIVEN INTO LIFTS (10) AND UP RAMPS (11) INTO THE ARENA (12).

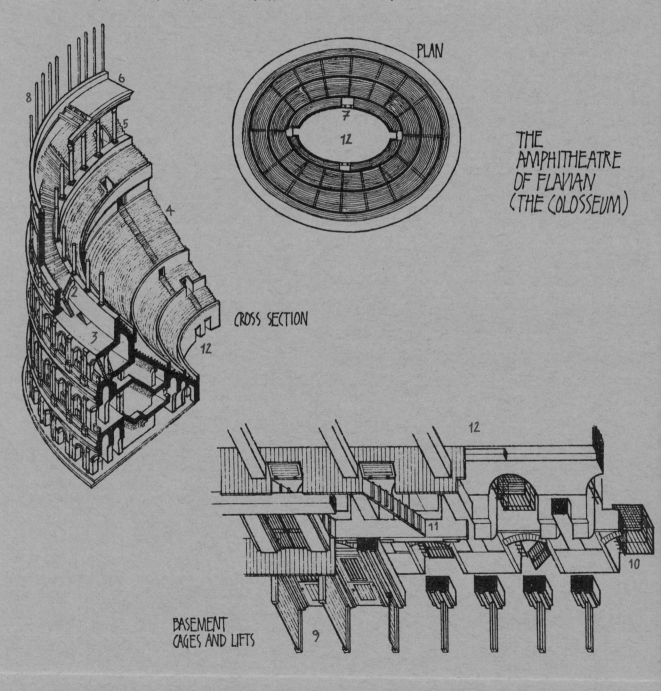

PLAN

THE
AMPHITHEATRE
OF FLAVIAN
(THE COLOSSEUM)

CROSS SECTION

BASEMENT
CAGES AND LIFTS

ing it up as a magisterial robe of Caesar's. Jerusalem is but a stone of the Temple, or the heart in the body. Turn from beholding the legions, strong though they be, and count the hosts of the faithful waiting the old alarm, 'To your tents, O Israel!' – count the many in Persia, children of those who chose not to return with the returning; count the brethren who swarm the marts of Egypt and Farther Africa; count the Hebrew colonists eking profit in the West – in Lodinum and the trade courts of Spain; count the pure of blood and the proselytes in Greece and in the isles of the sea, and over in Pontus, and here in Antioch, and, for that matter, those of that city lying accursed in the shadow of the unclean walls of Rome herself; count the worshippers of the Lord dwelling in tents along the desert next us, as well as in the deserts beyond the Nile: and in the regions across the Caspian, and up in the old lands of Gog and Magog even, separate those who annually send gifts to the Holy Temple in acknowledgement of God – separate them, that they may be counted also. And when you have done counting, lo! my master, a census of the sword hands that await you; lo! a kingdom ready fashioned for Him who is to do 'judgment and justice in the whole earth' – in Rome not less than in Zion. Have then the answer, what Israel can do, that can the King."

The picture was fervently given.

Upon Ilderim it operated like the blowing of a trumpet. "Oh that I had back my youth!" he cried, starting to his feet.

Ben-Hur sat still. The speech, he saw, was an invitation to devote his life and fortune to the mysterious Being who was palpably as the centre of a great hope with Simonides as with the devout Egyptian.

"Let us concede all you say, O Simonides," said Ben-Hur – "that the King will come, and His kingdom be as Solomon's; say also I am ready to give myself and all I have to Him and His cause; yet more, say that I should do as was God's purpose in the ordering of my life and in your quick amassment of astonishing fortune; then what? Shall we proceed like blind men building? Shall we wait till the King comes? Or until He sends for me? You have age and experience on your side. Answer."

Simonides answered at once.

"We have no choice; none. This letter" – he produced Messala's despatch as he spoke – "this letter is the signal for action. The alliance proposed between Messala and Gratus we are not strong enough to resist; we have not the influence at Rome nor the force here. They will kill you if we wait. How merciful they are, look at me and judge."

"What then, of revenge?"

The spark dropped upon the inflammable passion; the man's eyes gleamed; his hands shook; he answered, quickly: "Revenge is a Jew's of right; it is the law."

TABLE

"A camel, even a dog, will remember a wrong." cried Ilderim.

Directly Simonides picked up the broken thread of his thought.

"There is a work, a work for the King, which should be done in advance of His coming. We may not doubt that Israel is to be His right hand; but, alas! it is a hand of peace, without cunning in war. Of the millions, there is not one trained band, not a captain. The mercenaries of the Herods I do not count, for they are kept to crush us. The condition is as the Roman would have it; his policy has

fruited well for his tyranny; but the time of change is at hand, when the shepherd shall put on armour, and take to spear and sword, and the feeding flocks be turned to fighting lions. Someone, my son, must have place next the King at His right hand. Who shall it be if not he who does this work well?"

Ben-Hur's face flushed at the prospect, though he said: "I see, but speak plainly. A deed to be done is one thing; how to do it is another."

Simonides sipped the wine Esther brought him, and replied:

"The sheik, and thou, my master, shall be principals, each with a part. I will remain here, carrying on as now, and watchful that the spring go not dry. Thou shalt betake thee to Jerusalem, and thence to the wilderness, and begin numbering the fighting-men of Israel, and telling them into tens and hundreds, and choosing captains and training them, and in secret places hoarding arms, for which I shall keep thee supplied. Until the ripening time no one shall know what is here contracted. Mine is but a servant's part. I have spoken to Ilderim. What sayest thou?"

Ben-Hur looked at the sheik.

"It is as he says, son of Hur," the Arab responded. "I have given my word, and he is content with it; but thou shalt have my oath, binding me, and the ready hands of my tribe, and whatever serviceable thing I have."

The three – Simonides, Ilderim, Esther – gazed at Ben-Hur fixedly.

"Every man," he answered, at first sadly, "has a cup of pleasure poured for him, and soon or late it comes to his hand, and he tastes and drinks – every man but me. I see, Simonides, and thou, O generous sheik! – I see whither the proposal tends. If I accept, and enter upon the course, farewell peace, and the hopes which cluster around it. The doors I might enter and the gates of quiet life will shut behind me, never to open again, for Rome keeps them all; and her outlawry will follow me, and her hunters; and in the tombs near cities and the dismal caverns of remotest hills, I must eat my crust and take my rest."

The speech was broken by a sob. All turned to Esther, who hid her face upon her father's shoulder.

"I did not think of you, Esther," said Simonides, gently, for he was himself deeply moved.

"It is well enough, Simonides," said Ben-Hur. "A man bears a hard doom better, knowing there is pity for him. Let me go on."

They gave him ear again.

"I was about to say," he continued, "I have no choice, but take the part you assign me; and as remaining here is to meet an ignoble death, I will to the work at once."

"Shall we have writings?" asked Simonides, moved by his habit of business.

"I rest upon your word," said Ben-Hur.

"And I," Ilderim answered.

Thus simply was effected the treaty which was to alter Ben-Hur's life.

THE DAY BEFORE THE GAMES

The day before the games, in the afternoon, all Ilderim's racing property was taken to the city, and put in quarters adjoining the Circus.

Neither he nor Ben-Hur over-estimated the influence of Messala; it was their opinion, however, that he would not begin active measures against them until after the meeting in the Circus. If defeated there, especially if defeated by Ben-Hur, they might instantly look for the worst he could do; he might not even wait for advices from Gratus. With this view, they shaped their course, and were prepared to betake themselves out of harm's way. They rode together now in good spirits, calmly confident of success on the morrow.

On the way, they came upon Malluch in waiting for them. The faithful fellow gave no sign by which it was possible to infer any knowledge on his part of the relationship so recently admitted between Ben-Hur and Simonides, or of the treaty between them and Ilderim.

"There is nothing now to prevent your meeting Messala. Every condition preliminary to the race is complied with. I have the assurance from the editor himself."

"I thank you, Malluch," said Ben-Hur.

Malluch proceeded:

"Your colour is white, and Messala's mixed scarlet and gold. The good effects of the choice are visible already. Boys are now hawking white ribbons along the streets; tomorrow every Arab and Jew in the city will wear them. In the Circus you will see the white fairly divide the galleries with the red."

"The galleries – but not the tribunal over the Porta Pompae."

"No; the scarlet and gold will rule there. But if we win" – Malluch chuckled with the pleasure of the thought – "if we win, how the dignitaries will tremble! They will bet, of course, according to their scorn of everything not Roman – two, three, five to one on Messala, because he is Roman."

"Ay, Malluch; would you serve me perfectly, help me to fix the public eye upon our race – Messala's and mine."

Malluch spoke quickly: "It can be done."

"Then let it be done," said Ben-Hur.

"Enormous wagers offered will answer; if the offers are accepted, all the better."

Malluch turned his eyes watchfully upon Ben-Hur.

"Shall I not have back the equivalent of his robbery?" said Ben-Hur, partly to himself.

"Yes, it shall be. Hark, Malluch! Stop not in thy offer of sestertii. Advance them to talents, if any there be who dare so high. Five, ten, twenty talents; ay, fifty, so the wager be with Messala himself."

And Malluch, greatly delighted, gave him parting salutation, and started to ride away, but returned presently.

"Your pardon," he said to Ben-Hur.

"There was another matter. I could not get near Messala's chariot myself, but I had another measure it; and, from his report, its hub stands quite a palm higher from the ground than yours."

"A palm! So much?" cried Ben-Hur, joyfully.

Then he leaned over to Malluch.

"As thou art a son of Judah, Malluch, and faithful to thy kin, get thee a seat in the gallery over the Gate of Triumph, down close to the balcony in front of the pillars, and watch well when we make the turns there; watch well, for if I have favour at all, I will— Nay, Malluch, let it go unsaid!"

At that moment a cry burst from Ilderim.

"Ha! By the splendour of God! what is

ADVERTISEMENT FOR GLADIATORIAL CONTEST

ASSVETTII· CERII
AEDILIS·FAMILIA·GLADIATORIA·PVGNABIT
POMPEIS·PR· K·IVNIAS·VENATIO ·ET· VELA
ERVNT

He drew near Ben-Hur, with a finger pointing on the face of the notice.

"Read," said Ben-Hur.

"No; better thou."

Ben-Hur took the paper, which, signed by the prefect of the province as editor, performed the office of a modern programme, giving particularly the several divertisements provided for the occasion. It informed the public that there would be first a procession of extraordinary splendour; that the procession would be succeeded by the customary honours to the god Consus, whereupon the games would begin; running, leaping, wrestling, boxing, each in the order stated. The names of the competitors were given, with their several nationalities and schools of training, the trails in which they had been engaged, the prizes won, and the prizes now offered; under the latter head the sums of money were stated in illuminated letters, telling of the departure of the day when the simple chaplet of pine or laurel was fully enough for the victor, hungering for glory as something better than riches, and content with it.

Over these parts of the programme Ben-Hur sped with rapid eyes. At last he came to the announcement of the race. He read it slowly. The entries were six in all – fours only permitted; and, to further interest in the performance, the competitors would be turned into the course together. Each four then received description.

"I. A four of Lysippus the Corinthian – two greys, a bay, and a black; entered at Alexandria last year, and again at Corinth, where they were winners. Lysippus, driver. Colour, yellow.

"II. A four of Messala of Rome – two white, two black; victors of the Circensian as exhibited in the Circus Maximus last year. Messala, driver. Colours, scarlet and gold.

"III. A four of Cleanthes the Athenian – three grey, one bay; winners at the Isthmian last year. Cleanthes, driver. Colour green.

"IV. A four of Dicaeus the Byzantine – two black, one grey, one bay; winners this year at Byzantium. Dicaeus, driver. Colour, black.

"V. A four of Admetus the Sidonian – all greys; thrice entered at Caesarea, and thrice victors. Admetus, driver. Colour, blue.

"VI. A four of Ilderim, Sheik of the Desert – all bays; first race. Ben-Hur, a Jew, driver. Colour, white."

Ben-Hur, a Jew, driver! Why that name instead of Arrius?

Ben-Hur raised his eyes to Ilderim. He found the cause of the Arab's outcry. Both rushed to the same conclusion.

The hand was the hand of Messala!

A WAGER WITH MESSALA

Evening was hardly come upon Antioch, when the Omphalus, nearly in the centre of the city, became a troubled fountain, from which in every direction, but chiefly down to the Nymphaeum and east and west along the Colonnade of Herod, flowed currents of people, for the time given up to Bacchus and Apollo.

For such indulgence anything more fitting cannot be imagined than the great roofed streets, which were literally miles on miles of porticos wrought of marble, polished to the last degree of finish, and all gifts to the voluptuous city by princes careless of expenditure, where, as in this instance, they thought they were eternizing themselves. Darkness was not permitted anywhere; and the singing, the laughter, the shouting, were incessant, and in compound like the roar of waters dashing through hollow grots, confused by a multitude of echoes.

The many nationalities represented, though they might have amazed a stranger, were not peculiar to Antioch. Of the various missions of the great empire, one seems to have been the fusion of men and the introduction of strangers to each other: accordingly, whole peoples rose up and went at pleasure, taking with them their costumes, customs, speech, and gods; and where they chose, they stopped, engaged in business, built houses, erected altars, and were what they had been at home.

There was a peculiarity, however, which could not have failed the notice of a looker-on this night in Antioch. Nearly everybody wore the colours of one or other of the charioteers announced for the morrow's race. Sometimes it was in form of a scarf, sometimes a badge; often a ribbon or a feather. Whatever the form, it signified merely the wearer's partiality; thus, green published a friend of Cleanthes the Athenian, and black an adherent of the Byzantine. This was according to a custom, old probably as the day of the race of Orestes – a custom, by the way, worthy of study as a marvel of history, illustrative of the absurd yet appalling extremities to which men frequently suffer their follies to drag them.

The observer abroad on this occasion, once attracted to the wearing of colours, would have very shortly decided that there were three in predominance – green, white, and the mixed scarlet and gold.

But let us from the streets to the palace on the island.

The five great chandeliers in the saloon are freshly lighted. The assemblage is much the same as that already noticed in connection with the place. The divan has its corps of sleepers and burden of garments, and the tables yet resound with the rattle and clash of dice. Yet the greater part of the company are not doing anything. They walk about, or yawn tremendously, or pause as they pass each other to exchange idle nothings. Will the weather be fair tomorrow? Are the preparations for the games complete? Do the laws of the Circus in Antioch differ from the laws of the Circus in Rome? Truth is, the young fellows are suffering from ennui. Their heavy work is done; that is, we would find their tablets, could we look at them, covered with memoranda of wagers – wagers on every contest; on the running, the wrestling, the boxing; on everything but the chariot-race.

And why not on that?

Good reader, they cannot find anybody who will hazard so much as a denarius with them against Messala.

There are no colours in the saloon but his.

No one thinks of his defeat.

Why, they say, is he not perfect in his training? Did he not graduate from an imperial lanista? Were not his horses winners at the Circensian in the Circus Maximus? And then – ah, yes! he is a Roman!

In a corner, at ease on the divan, Messala himself may be seen. Around him, sitting or standing, are his courtierly admirers, plying him with questions. There is, of course, but one topic.

Enter Drusus and Cecilius.

"Ah!" cries the young prince, throwing himself on the divan at Messala's feet; "ah, by Bacchus, I am tired!"

"Whither away?" asked Messala.

"Up the street; up the Omphalus, and beyond – who shall say how far? Rivers of people; never so many in the city before. They say we will see the whole world at the Circus tomorrow."

Messala laughed scornfully.

"The idiots! Perpol! They never beheld a Circensian with Caesar for editor. But my Drusus, what found you?"

"Nothing."

"O – ah! You forget," said Cecilius.

"What?" asked Drusus.

"The procession of whites."

"Mirabile!" cried Drusus, half rising. "We met a faction of whites, and they had a banner. But – ha, ha, ha!"

He fell back indolently.

"Cruel Drusus – not to go on," said Messala.

"Scum of the desert were they, my Messala, and garbage-eaters from the Jacob's Temple in Jersusalem. What had I to do with them?"

"Nay," said Cecilius, "Drusus is afraid of a laugh, but I am not, my Messala."

"Speak thou, then,"

"Well, we stopped the faction, and——"

"Offered them a wager," said Drusus, relenting, and taking the word from the shadow's mouth. "And – ha, ha, ha! – one fellow, with not enough skin on his face to make a worm for a carp, stepped forth, and – ha, ha, ha! – said yes. I drew my tablets. 'Who is your man?' I asked. 'Ben-Hur, the Jew,' said he. Then I: 'What shall it be? How much?' He answered, 'A – a——' Excuse me, Messala. By Jove's thunder, I cannot go on for laughter! Ha, ha, ha!"

The listeners leaned forward.

Messala looked to Cecilius.

"A shekel," said the latter.

"A shekel! A shekel!"

A burst of scornful laughter ran fast upon the repetition.

"And what did Drusus?" asked Messala.

An outcry over about the door just then occasioned a rush to that quarter; and as the noise there continued, and grew louder, even Cecilius betook himself off, pausing only to say, "The noble Drusus, my Messala, put up his tablets and – lost the shekel."

"A white! A white!"

"Let him come!"

"This way, this way!"

These and like exclamations filled the saloon, to the stoppage of other speech. The dice-players quit their games: the sleepers awoke, rubbed their eyes, drew their tablets, and hurried to the common centre.

"I offer you——"

"And I——"

"I——"

The person so warmly received was the respectable Jew, Ben-Hur's fellow voyager from Cyprus. He entered grave, quiet, observant. His robe was spotlessly white; so was the cloth of his turban. Bowing and smiling at the welcome, he moved slowly towards the central table. Arrived there, he drew his robe about him in a stately manner, took seat, and waved his hand. The gleam of a jewel on a finger helped him not a little to the silence which ensued.

"Romans – most noble Romans – I salute you!" he said

"Easy, by Jupiter! Who is he?" asked Drusus.

"A dog of Israel – Sanballat by name – purveyor for the army; residence, Rome; vastly rich; grown so as a contractor of furnishings which he never furnishes. He spins mischiefs, nevertheless, finer than spiders spin their webs. Come – by the girdle of Venus! let us catch him!"

Messala arose as he spoke, and, with Drusus, joined the mass crowded about the purveyor.

"It came to me on the street," said that person, producing his tablets, and opening them on the table with an impressive air of business, "that there was great discomfort in the palace because offers on Messala were going without takers. The gods, you know, must have sacrifices; and here am I. You see my colour; let us to the matter. Odds first, amounts next. What will you give me?"

The audacity seemed to stun his hearers.

"Haste!" he said. "I have an engagement with the consul."

The spur was effective.

"Two to one," cried half a dozen in a voice.

"What!" exclaimed the purveyor, astonished. "Only two to one, and yours a Roman!"

"Take three, then."

"Three, say you – only three – and mine but a dog of a Jew! Give me four."

"Four it is," said a boy, stung by the taunt.

"Five – give me five," cried the purveyor, instantly.

A profound stillness fell upon the assemblage.

"The consul – your master and mine – is waiting for me."

The inaction became awkward to the many.

"Give me five – for the honour of Rome,"

"Five let it be," said one in answer.

There was a sharp cheer – a commotion – and Messala himself appeared.

"Five let it be," he said.

And Sanballat smiled, and made ready to write.

"If Caesar die tomorrow," he said, "Rome will not be all bereft. There is at least one other with spirit to take his place. Give me six."

"Six be it," answered Messala.

There was another shout louder than the first.

"Six be it," repeated Messala. "Six to one – the difference between a Roman and a Jew. And, having found it, now, O redemptor of the flesh of swine, let us on. The amount – and quickly. The consul may send for thee, and I will then be bereft."

Sanballat took the laugh against him coolly, and wrote, and offered the writing to Messala.

"Read, read!" everybody demanded.

And Messala read:

"Mem. – *Chariot-race. Messala of Rome, in wager with Sanballat, also of Rome, says he will beat Ben-Hur, the Jew. Amount of wager, twenty talents. Odds to Sanballat, six to one.*

"*Witnesses:*

"SANBALLAT."

There was no noise, no motion. Each person seemed held in the pose the reading found him. Messala stared at the memorandum, while the eyes which had him in view opened wide, and stared at him. He felt the gaze, and thought rapidly. So lately he stood in the same place, and in the same way hectored the countrymen around him. They would remember it. If he refused to sign, his heroship was lost. And sign he could not; he was not worth one hundred talents, not the fifth part of the sum. Suddenly his mind became a blank; he stood speechless; the colour fled his face. An idea at last came to his relief.

"Thou Jew!" he said, "where hast thou twenty talents? Show me."

Sanballat's provoking smile deepened.

"There," he replied, offering Messala a paper.

Again Messala read:

"At Antioch, Tammuz, 16th day.
"The bearer, Sanballat of Rome, hath now to his order with me fifty talents, coin of Caesar.

SIMONIDES."

"Fifty talents, fifty talents!" echoed the throng, in amazement.

Then Drusus came to the rescue.

"By Hercules!" he shouted, "the paper lies, and the Jew is a liar. Who but Caesar hath fifty talents at order? Down with the insolent white!"

The cry was angry, and it was angrily repeated; yet Sanballat kept his seat, and his smile grew more exasperating the longer he waited. At length Messala spoke.

"Hush! One to one, my countrymen – one to one, for love of our ancient Roman name."

The timely action recovered him his ascendency.

"O thou circumcised dog!" he continued, to Sanballat, "I gave thee six to one, did I not?"

"Yes," said the Jew quietly.

"Well, give me now the fixing of the amount."

"With reserve, if the amount be trifling, have thy will," answered Sanballat.

"Write, then, five in place of twenty."

"Hast thou so much?"

"By the mother of the gods, I will show you receipts."

"Nay, the word of so brave a Roman must pass. Only make the sum even – six make it, and I will write."

"Write it so."

And forthwith they exchanged writings.

Sanballat immediately arose and looked around him, a sneer in place of his smile. No man better than he knew those with whom he was dealing.

"Romans," he said, "another wager, if you dare! Five talents against five talents that the white will win. I challenge you collectively."

They were again surprised.

"What!" he cried louder. "Shall it be said in the Circus tomorrow that a dog of Israel went into the saloon of the palace full of Roman nobles – among them the scion of a Caesar – and laid five talents before them in challenge, and they had not the courage to take it up?"

The sting was unendurable.

"Have done, O insolent!" said Drusus,

"write the challenge, and leave it on the table; and tomorrow, if we find thou hast indeed so much money to put at such hopeless hazard, I, Drusus, promise it shall be taken."

Sanballat wrote again, and, rising, said, unmoved as ever, "See, Drusus, I leave the offer with you. When it is signed, send it to me any time before the race begins. I will be found with the consul in a seat over the Porta Pompae. Peace to you; peace to all."

He bowed, and departed, careless of the shout of derision with which they pursued him out of the door.

In the night the story of the prodigious wager flew along the streets and over the city; and Ben-Hur, lying with his four, was told of it and also that Messala's whole fortune was on the hazard.

And he slept never so soundly.

THE DAY OF THE CIRCUS

The Circus at Antioch stood on the south bank of the river, nearly opposite the island, differing in no respect from the plan of such buildings in general.

The better people, their seats secured, began moving towards the Circus about the first hour of the morning, the noble and very rich among them distinguished by litters and retinues of liveried servants.

By the second hour, the efflux from the city was a stream unbroken and innumerable.

At the third hour, the audience, if such it may be termed, was assembled; at last, a flourish of trumpets called for silence, and instantly the gaze of over a hundred thousand persons was directed towards a pile forming the eastern section of the building.

Out of the Porta Pompae over the east rises a sound mixed of voices and instruments harmonized. Presently, forth issues the chorus of the procession with which the celebration begins; the editor and civic authorities of the city, givers of the games, follow in robes and garlands; then the gods, some on platforms borne by men, other in great four-wheel

carriages gorgeously decorated; next them, again, the contestants of the day, each in costume exactly as he will run, wrestle, leap, box, or drive.

Slowly crossing the arena, the procession proceeds to make circuit of the course. The display is beautiful and imposing. Approval runs before it in a shout, as the water rises and swells in front of a boat in motion. If the dumb, figured gods make no sign of appreciation of the welcome, the editor and his associates are not so backward.

The reception of the athletes is even more demonstrative, for there is not a man in the assemblage who has not something in wager upon them, though but a mite or farthing. And it is noticeable, as the classes move by, that the favourites among them are speedily singled out: either their names are loudest in the uproar, or they are more profusely showered with wreaths and garlands tossed to them from the balcony.

If there is a question as to the popularity with the public of the several games, it is now put to rest. To the splendour of the chariots and the super-excellent beauty

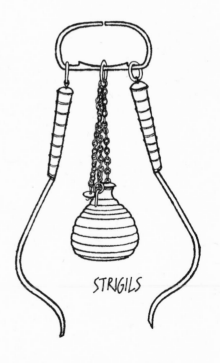

STRIGILS

SILVER DRINKING CUP

of the horses, the charioteers add the personality necessary to perfect the charm of their display. Their tunics, short, sleeveless, and of the finest woollen texture, are of the assigned colours. A horseman accompanies each one of them except Ben-Hur, who, for some reason – possibly distrust – has chosen to go alone; so, too, they are all helmeted but him. As they approach, the spectators stand upon the benches, and there is a sensible deepening of the clamour, in which a sharp listener may detect the shrill piping of women and children; at the same time, the things roseate flying from the balcony thicken into a storm, and, striking the men, drop into the chariot-beds, which are threatened with filling to the tops. Even the horses have a share in the ovation; nor may it be said they are less conscious than their masters of the honours they receive.

As the charioteers move on in the circuit, the excitement increases; at the second goal, where, especially in the galleries, the white is the ruling colour, the people exhaust their flowers and rive the air with screams.

"Messala! Messala!"

"Ben-Hur! Ben-Hur!"

Such are the cries.

Upon the passage of the procession, the factionists take their seats and resume conversation.

"Ah, by Bacchus! was he not handsome?" exclaims a woman, whose Romanism is betrayed by the colours flying in her hair.

"And how splendid his chariot!" replies a neighbour, of the same proclivities. "It is all ivory and gold. Jupiter grant he wins!"

The notes on the bench behind them were entirely different.

"A hundred shekels on the Jew!"

The voice is high and shrill.

"Nay, be thou not rash," whispers a moderating friend to the speaker. "The children of Jacob are not much given to Gentile sports, which are too often accursed in the sight of the Lord."

"True, but saw you ever one more cool and assured? And what an arm he has!"

"And what horses!" said a third.

"And for that," a fourth one adds, "they say he has all the tricks of the Romans."

A woman completes the eulogium.

"Yes, and he is even handsomer than the Roman."

Thus encouraged, the enthusiast shrieks again, "A hundred shekels on the Jew!"

"Thou fool!" answers an Antiochian, from a bench well forward on the balcony. "Knowest thou not there are fifty talents laid against him, six to one, on Messala? Put up thy shekels, lest Abraham rise and smite thee."

"Ha, ha! thou ass of Antioch! Cease thy bray. Knowest thou not it was Messala betting on himself?"

Such the reply.

And so ran the controversy, not always good-natured.

When at length the march was ended and the Porta Pompae received back the procession, Ben-Hur knew he had his prayer.

The eyes of the East were upon his contest with Messala.

THE RACE BEGINS

About three o'clock, speaking in modern style, the programme was concluded except the chariot-race.

Now, however, a third class of spectators, composed of citizens who desired only to witness the chariot-race, availed themselves of the recess to come in and take their reserved seats; by so doing they thought to attract the least attention and give the least offence. Among these were Simonides and his party, whose places were in the vicinity of the main entrance on the north side, opposite the consul.

Ilderim was also recognized and warmly greeted; but nobody knew Balthasar or the two women who followed him closely veiled.

The women were Iras and Esther.

Upon being seated, the latter cast a frightened look over the Circus, and drew the veil closer about her face; while the Egyptian, letting her veil fall upon her shoulders, gave herself to view, and gazed at the scene with the seeming unconsciousness of being stared at, which, in a woman, is usually the result of long social habitude.

The new-comers generally were yet making their first examination of the great spectacle, beginning with the consul and his attendants, when some workmen ran in and commenced to stretch a chalked rope across the arena from balcony to balcony in front of the pillars of the first goal.

About the same time, also, six men came in through the Porta Pompae and took post, one in front of each occupied stall; whereat there was a prolonged hum of voices in every quarter.

"See, see! The green goes to number four on the right; the Athenian is there."

"And Messala – yes, he is in number two."

"The Corinthian——"

"Watch the white! See, he crosses over, he stops; number one it is – number one on the left."

"No, the black stops there, and the white at number two."

"So it is."

These gate-keepers, it should be understood, were dressed in tunics coloured like those of the competing charioteers; so, when they took their stations, everybody knew the particular stall in which his favourite was that moment waiting.

"Did you ever see Messala?" the Egyptian asked Esther.

The Jewess shuddered as she answered no. If not her father's enemy, the Roman was Ben-Hur's.

"He is beautiful as Apollo."

As Iras spoke, her large eyes brightened

and she shook her jewelled fan. Esther looked at her with the thought, "Is he, then, so much handsomer than Ben-Hur?" Next moment she heard Ilderim say to her father, "Yes, his stall is number two on the left of the Porta Pompae;" and, thinking it was of Ben-Hur he spoke, her eyes turned that way. Taking but the briefest glance at the wattled face of the gate, she drew the veil close and muttered a little prayer.

At length the recess came to an end.

The trumpeters blew a call at which the absentees rushed back to their places. At the same time, some attendants appeared in the arena, and, climbing upon the division wall, went to an entablature near the second goal at the west end, and placed upon it seven wooden balls; then returning to the first goal, upon an entablature there they set up seven other pieces of wood hewn to represent dolphins.

"What shall they do with the balls and fishes, O shiek?" asked Balthasar.

"Hast thou never attended a race?"

"Never before; and hardly know I why I am here."

"Well, they are to keep the count. At the end of each round run thou shalt see one ball and one fish taken down."

The preparations were now complete, and presently a trumpeter in gaudy uniform arose by the editor, ready to blow the signal of commencement promptly at his order. Straightway the stir of the people and the hum of their conversation died away. Every face nearby, and every face in the lessening perspective, turned to the east, as all eyes settled upon the gates of the six stalls which shut in the competitors.

Again the trumpet blew, and simultaneously the gate-keepers threw the stalls open.

First appeared the mounted attendants of the charioteers, five in all, Ben-Hur having rejected the service. The chalked line was lowered to let them pass, then raised again. They were beautifully mounted, yet scarcely observed as they rode forward; for all the time the trampling of eager horses, and the voices of drivers scarcely less eager, were heard behind in the stalls, so that one might not look away an instant from the gaping doors.

The chalked line up again, the gate-keepers called their men; instantly the ushers on the balcony waved their hands, and shouted with all their strength, "Down! down!"

As well have whistled to stay a storm.

Forth from each stall, like missiles in a volley from so many great guns, rushed the six fours; and up the vast assemblage arose, electrified and irrepressible, and, leaping upon the benches, filled the Circus and the air above it with yells and screams. This was the time for which they had so patiently waited! – this the moment of supreme interest treasured up in talk and dreams since the proclamation of the games!

"He is come – there – look!" cried Iras, pointing to Messala.

"I see him," answered Esther, looking at Ben-Hur.

The competitors were now under view from nearly every part of the Circus, yet the race was not begun; they had first to make the chalked line successfully.

The line was stretched for the purpose of equalizing the start. If it were dashed upon, discomfiture of man and horses might be apprehended; on the other hand, to approach it timidly was to incur the hazard of being thrown behind in the beginning of the race; and that was certain forfeit of the great advantage always striven for – the position next the division wall on the inner line of the course.

The arena swam in a dazzle of light; yet each driver looked first thing for the rope, then for the coveted inner line. So, all six aiming at the same point and speeding furiously, a collision seemed inevitable; nor that merely. What if the editor, at the last moment, dissatisfied with the start, should withhold the signal to drop the rope? Or if he should not give it in time?

The crossing was about two hundred and fifty feet in width. Quick the eye, steady the hand, unerring the judgment required. If now one look away! or his mind wander! or a rein slip! And what attraction in the ensemble of the thousands over the spreading balcony! Calculating upon the natural impulse to give one glance – just one – in sooth of curiosity or vanity, malice might be there with an artifice; while friendship and love, did they serve the same result, might be as deadly as malice.

The competitors having started each on the shortest line for the position next the wall, yielding would be like giving up the race; and who dared yield? It is not in common nature to change a purpose in mid-career; and the cries of encouragement from the balcony were indistinguishable and indescribable; a roar which had the same effect upon all the drivers.

The fours neared the rope together. Then the trumpeter by the editor's side blew a signal vigorously. Twenty feet away it was not heard. Seeing the action, however, the judges dropped the rope, and not an instant too soon, for the hoof of one of Messala's horses struck it as it fell. Nothing daunted the Roman shook out his long lash, loosed the reins, leaned forward, and, with a triumphant shout, took the wall.

"Jove with us! Jove with us!" yelled all the Roman faction in a frenzy of delight.

As Messala turned in, the bronze lion's head at the end of his axle caught the fore leg of the Athenian's right-hand trace-mate, flinging the brute over against its yoke-fellow. Both staggered, struggled, and lost their headway. The ushers had their will at least in part. The thousands held their breath with horror; only up where the consul sat was there shouting.

"Jove with us!" screamed Drusus, frantically.

"He wins! Jove with us!" answered his associates, seeing Messala speed on.

Messala having passed, the Corinthian was the only contestant on the Athenian's right, and to that side the latter tried to turn his broken four; and then, as ill-fortune would have it, the wheel of the Byzantine, who was next on the left, struck the tail-piece of his chariot, knocking his feet from under him. There was a crash; a scream of rage and fear, and the unfortunate Cleanthes fell under the hoofs of his own steeds: a terrible sight, against which Esther covered her eyes. On swept the Corinthian, on the Byzantine, on the Sidonian.

When the Jewess ventured to look again, a party of workmen were removing the horses and broken car; another party were taking off the man himself; and every bench upon which there was a Greek was vocal with execrations and prayers for vengeance. Suddenly she dropped her hands; Ben-Hur, unhurt, was to the front, coursing freely forward along with the Roman! Behind them, in a group, followed the Sidonian, the Corinthian, and the Byzantine.

The race was on; the souls of the racers were in it; over them bent the myriads.

MESSALA'S FATE

When the dash for position began, Ben-Hur, as we have seen, was on the extreme left of the six. For a moment, like the others, he was half blinded by the light of the arena; yet he managed to catch sight of his antagonists and divine their purpose. At Messala, who was more than an antagonist to him, he gave one searching look. The air of passionless hauteur characteristic of the fine patrician face was there as of old, and so was the Italian beauty, which the helmet rather increased; but more – it may have been a jealous fancy, or the effect of the brassy shadow in which the features were at the moment cast, still the Israelite thought he saw the soul of the man as through a glass, darkly: cruel, cunning, desperate; not so excited as determined – a soul in a tension of watchfulness and fierce resolve.

In a time not longer than was required to turn to his four again, Ben-Hur felt his own resolution harden to a like temper. At whatever cost, at all hazards, he would humble this enemy! He had his plan, and, confiding in himself, he settled to the task, never more observant, never more capable. The air about him seemed aglow with a renewed and perfect transparency.

When not half-way across the arena, he saw that Messala's rush would, if there was no collision, and the rope fell, give him the wall; that the rope would fall, he ceased as soon to doubt; and, further, it came to him, a sudden flash-like insight, that Messala knew it was to be let drop at the last moment (pre-arrangement with the editor could safely reach that point in the contest); and it suggested, what more Roman-like than for the official to lend himself to a countryman who, besides being so popular, had also so much at stake? There could be no other accounting for the confidence with which Messala pushed his four forward the instant his competitors were prudentially checking their fours in front of the obstruction – no other except madness.

It is one thing to see a necessity and another to act upon it. Ben-Hur yielded the wall for the time.

The rope fell, and all the fours but his sprang into the course under urgency of voice and lash. He drew head to the right, and, with all the speed of his Arabs, darted across the trails of his opponents, the angle of movement being such as to lose the least time and gain the greatest possible advance. So, while the spectators were shivering at the Athenian's mishap, and the Sidonian, Byzantine, and Corinthian were striving, with such skill as they possessed, to avoid involvement in the ruin, Ben-Hur swept around and took the course neck and neck with Messala, though on the outside. The marvellous skill shown in making the change thus from the extreme left across to the right without appreciable loss did not fail the sharp eyes upon the benches; the Circus seemed to rock and rock again with prolonged applause. Then Esther clapped her hands in glad surprise; and then the Romans began to doubt, thinking Messala might have found an equal, if not a master, and that in an Israelite!

And now, racing together side by side, a narrow interval between them, the two neared the second goal.

The pedestal of the three pillars there, viewed from the west, was a stone wall in the form of a half-circle, around which the course and opposite balcony were bent in exact parallelism. Making this turn was considered in all respects the most telling test of a charioteer; it was, in fact, the very feat in which Orestes failed. As an involuntary admission of interest on the part of the spectators, a hush fell over all the Circus, so that for the first time in the race the rattle and clang of the cars plunging after the tugging steeds were distinctly heard. Then, it would seem, Messala observed Ben-Hur, and recognized him; and at once the audacity of the man flamed out in an astonishing manner.

"Down Eros, up Mars!" he shouted, whirling his lash with practised hand. "Down Eros, up Mars!" he repeated, and caught the well-doing Arabs of Ben-Hur a cut the like of which they had never known.

The blow was seen in every quarter, and the amazement was universal. The silence deepened; up on the benches behind the consul the boldest held his breath, waiting for the outcome. Only a moment thus: then, involuntarily, down from the balcony, as thunder falls, burst the indignant cry of the people.

The four sprang forward affrighted. No hand had ever been laid upon them except in love; they had been nurtured ever so tenderly; and as they grew, their confidence in man became a lesson to men beautiful to see. What should such dainty natures do under such indignity but leap as from death?

Forward they sprang as with one impulse, and forward leaped the car. Past question, every experience is serviceable to us. Where got Ben-Hur the large hand and mighty grip which helped him now so well? Where but from the oar with which so long he fought the sea? And what was this spring of the floor under his feet to the dizzy eccentric lurch with which in the old time the trembling ship yielded to the beat of staggering billows, drunk with their power? So he kept his place, and gave the four free rein, and called to them in soothing voice, trying merely to guide them round the dangerous turn; and before the fever of the people began to abate, he had back the mastery. Nor that only: on approaching the first goal, he was again side by side with Messala, bearing with him the sympathy and admiration of everyone not a Roman. So clearly was the feeling shown, so vigorous its manifestation, that Messala, with all his boldness, felt it unsafe to trifle further.

As the cars whirled round the goal, Esther caught sight of Ben-Hur's face – a little pale, a little higher raised, otherwise calm, even placid.

Immediately a man climbed on the entablature at the west end of the division wall, and took down one of the conical wooden balls. A dolphin on the east entablature was taken down at the same time.

In like manner, the second ball and second dolphin disappeared.

And then the third ball and third dolphin.

Three rounds concluded: still Messala held the inside position; still Ben-Hur moved with him side by side; still the other competitors followed as before. The contest began to have the appearance of one of the double races which became so popular in Rome during the later Caesarean period – Messala and Ben-Hur in the first, the Corinthian, Sidonian, and Byzantine in the second. Meantime the ushers succeeded in returning the multitude to their seats, though the clamour continued to run the rounds, keeping, as it were, even pace with the rivals in the course below.

In the fifth round the Sidonian succeeded in getting a place outside Ben-Hur but lost it directly.

The sixth round was entered upon without change of relative position.

Gradually the speed had been quickened – gradually the blood of the competitors warmed with the work. Men and beasts seemed to know alike that the final crisis was near, bringing the time for the winner to assert himself.

The interest which from the beginning had centred chiefly in the struggle between the Roman and the Jew, with an intense and general sympathy for the latter, was fast changing to anxiety on his account. On all the benches the spectators bent forward motionless, except as their faces turned following the contestants. Ilderim quitted combing his beard, and Esther forgot her fears.

"Messala hath reached his utmost speed. See him lean over his chariot-rim, the reins loose as flying ribbons. Look then at the Jew. If the gods help not our friend, he will be run away with by the Israelite. No, not yet. Look! Jove with us, Jove with us!"

The cry, swelled by every Latin tongue, shook the velaria over the consul's head.

If it were true that Messala had attained his utmost speed, the effort was with effect; slowly but certainly he was beginning to forge ahead. His horses were running with their heads low down; from the balcony their bodies appeared actually to skim the earth; their nostrils showed blood-red in expansion; their eyes seemed straining in their sockets. Certainly the good steeds were doing their best! How long could they keep the pace? It was but the commencement of the sixth round.

On they dashed. As they neared the second goal, Ben-Hur turned in behind the Roman's car.

The joy of the Messala faction reached its bound: they screamed and howled, and tossed their colours; and Sanballat filled his tablets with wagers of their tendering.

Malluch, in the lower gallery over the Gate of Triumph, found it hard to keep his cheer. He had cherished the vague hint dropped to him by Ben-Hur of something to happen in the turning of the western pillars. It was the fifth round, yet the something had not come; and he

had said to himself, the sixth will bring it; but lo! Ben-Hur was hardly holding a place at the tail of his enemy's car.

Over in the east end, Simonides' party held their peace. The merchant's head was bent low. Ilderim tugged at his beard, and dropped his brows till there was nothing of his eyes but an occasional sparkle of light. Esther scarcely breathed. Iras alone appeared glad.

Along the home-stretch – sixth round – Messala leading, next him Ben-Hur, and so close it was the old story.

Thus to the first goal, and round it. Messala, fearful of losing his place, hugged the stony wall with perilous clasp; a foot to the left, and he had been dashed to pieces; yet, when the turn was finished, no man, looking at the wheel-tracks of the two cars, could have said, here went Messala, there the Jew. They left but one trace behind them.

As they whirled by, Esther saw Ben-Hur's face again, and it was whiter than before.

Simonides, shrewder than Esther, said to Ilderim, the moment the rivals turned into the course: "I am no judge, good sheik, if Ben-Hur be not about to execute some design. His face hath that look."

To which Ilderim answered: "Saw you how clean they were and fresh? By the splendour of God, friend, they have not been running! But now watch!"

One ball and one dolphin remained on the entablatures; and all the people drew a long breath, for the beginning of the end was at hand.

First, the Sidonian gave the scourge to his four, and, smarting with fear and pain, they dashed desperately forward, promising for a brief time to go to the front. The effort ended in promise. Next, the Byzantine and Corinthian each made the trial with like result, after which they were practically out of the race. Thereupon, with a readiness perfectly explicable, all the factions except the Romans joined hope in Ben-Hur, and openly indulged their feeling.

"Ben-Hur! Ben-Hur!" they shouted, and the blent voices of the many rolled overwhelmingly against the consular stand.

From the benches above him as he passed, the favour descended in fierce injunctions.

"Speed thee, Jew!"
"Take the wall now!"

"On! loose the Arabs! Give them rein and scourge!"

"Let him not have the turn on thee again. Now or never!"

Over the balustrade they stooped low, stretching their hands imploringly to him.

Either he did not hear, or could not do better, for half-way round the course and he was still following; at the second goal even still no change!

And now, to make the turn, Messala began to draw in his left-hand steeds, an act which necessarily slackened their speed. His spirit was high; more than one altar was richer of his vows; the Roman genius was still president. On the three pillars only six hundred feet away were fame, increase of fortune, promotions, and a triumph ineffably sweetened by hate, all in store for him! That moment Malluch, in the gallery, saw Ben-Hur lean forward over his Arabs, and give them the reins. Out flew the many-folded lash in his hand; over the backs of the startled steeds it writhed and hissed, and hissed and writhed again and again; and though it fell not, there were both sting and menace in its quick report; and as the man passed thus from quiet to resistless action, his face suffused, his eyes gleaming, along the reins he seemed to flash his will; and instantly not one, but the four as one, answered with a leap that landed them alongside the Roman's car. Messala, on the perilous edge of the goal, heard, but dared not look to see what the awakening portended. From the people he received no sign. Above the noises of the race there was but one voice, and that was Ben-Hur's. In the old Aramaic, as the sheik himself, he called to the Arabs:

"On, Atair! On, Rigel! What, Antares! dost thou linger now? Good horse – oho, Aldebaran! I hear them singing in the tents. I hear the children singing and the women – singing of the stars, of Atair, Antares, Rigel, Aldebaran, victory! – and the song will never end. Well done! Home tomorrow, under the black tent – home! On, Antares! The tribe is waiting for us, and the master is waiting! 'Tis done! 'tis done! Ha ha! We have overthrown the proud. The hand that smote us is in the dust. Ours the glory! Ha, ha! – steady! The work is done – soho! Rest!"

There had never been anything of the kind more simple; seldom anything so instantaneous.

At the moment chosen for the dash, Messala was moving in a circle round the goal. To pass him, Ben-Hur had to cross the track, and good strategy required the movement to be in a forward direction; that is, on a like circle limited to the least possible increase. The thousands on the benches understood it all: they saw the signal given – the magnificent response; the four close outside Messala's outer wheel; Ben-Hur's inner wheel behind the other's car – all this they saw. Then they heard a crash loud enough to send a thrill through the Circus, and, quicker than thought, out over the course a spray of shining white and yellow flinders flew. Down on its right side toppled the bed of the Roman's chariot. There was a rebound as of the axle hitting the hard earth; another and another; then the car went to pieces; and Messala, entangled in the reins, pitched forward headlong.

To increase the horror of the sight by making death certain, the Sidonian, who had the wall next behind, could not stop or turn out. Into the wreck full speed he drove; then over the Roman, and into the latter's four, all mad with fear. Presently, out of the turmoil, the fighting of horses, the resound of blows, the murky cloud of dust and sand, he crawled, in time to see the Corinthian and Byzantine go on down the course after Ben-Hur, who had not been an instant delayed.

The people arose, and leaped upon the benches, and shouted and screamed. Those who looked that way caught glimpses of Messala, now under the trampling of the fours, now under the abandoned cars. He was still; they thought him dead; but far the greater number followed Ben-Hur in his career. They had not seen the cunning touch of the reins by which, turning a little to the left, he caught Messala's wheel with the iron-shod point of his axle, and crushed it; but they had seen the transformation of the man, and themselves felt the heat and glow of his spirit, the heroic resolution, the maddening energy of action with which, by look, word, and gesture, he so suddenly inspired his Arabs. And such running! It was rather the long leaping of lions in harness; but for the lumbering chariot, it seemed the four were flying. When the Byzantine and Corinthian were half-way down the course, Ben-Hur turned the first goal.

And the race was WON!

The consul arose; the people shouted themselves hoarse; the editor came down from his seat, and crowned the victors.

The fortunate man among the boxers was a low-browed, yellow-haired Saxon, of such brutalized face as to attract a second look from Ben-Hur, who recognized a teacher with whom he himself had been a favourite at Rome. From him the young Jew looked up and beheld Simonides and his party on the balcony. They waved their hands to him. Esther kept her seat; but Iras arose, and gave him a smile and a wave of her fan – favours not the less intoxicating to him because we know, O reader, they would have fallen to Messala had he been the victor.

The procession was then formed, and, midst the shouting of the multitude, which had had its will, passed out of the Gate of Triumph.

And the day was over.

A MESSAGE FROM IRAS

Ben-Hur tarried across the river with Ilderim; for at midnight, as previously determined, they would take the road which the caravan, then thirty hours out, had pursued.

The sheik was happy; his offers of gifts had been royal; but Ben-Hur had refused everything, insisting that he was satisfied with the humiliation of his enemy. The generous dispute was long continued.

In the midst of a controversy of the kind, two messengers arrived – Malluch and one unknown. The former was admitted first.

The good fellow did not attempt to hide his joy over the event of the day.

"But, coming to that with which I am charged," he said, "the master Simonides sends me to say that, upon the adjournment of the games, some of the Roman faction made haste to protest against payment of the money prize."

Ilderim started up, crying, in his shrillest tones:

"By the splendour of God! the East shall decide whether the race was fairly won."

"Nay, good sheik," said Malluch, "the editor has paid the money."

"'Tis well."

"When they said Ben-Hur struck Messala's wheel, the editor laughed, and reminded them of the blow the Arabs had at the turn of the goal."

"And what of the Athenian?"

"He is dead."

"Dead!" cried Ben-Hur.

"Dead!" echoed Ilderim. "What fortune these Roman monsters have! Messala escaped?"

"Escaped – yes, O sheik, with life; but it shall be a burden to him. The physicians say he will live, but never walk again."

Ben-Hur looked silently up to heaven. He had a vision of Messala, chair-

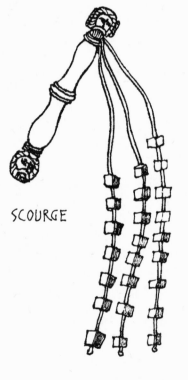

SCOURGE

bound like Simonides, and, like him, going abroad on the shoulders of servants. The good man had abode well; but what would this one with his pride and ambition?

"Simonides bade me say, further," Malluch continued, "Drusus, and those

74

who signed the wager, referred the question of paying the five talents they lost to the Consul Maxentius, and he has referred it to Caesar. Messala also refused his losses, and the matter is still in advisement. The better Romans say the protestants shall not be excused; and all the adverse factions join with them. The city rings with the scandal."

"What says Simonides?" asked Ben-Hur.

"The master laughs, and is well pleased. If the Roman pays, he is ruined; if he refuses to pay, he is dishonoured. The imperial policy will decide the matter. To offend the East would be a bad beginning with the Parthians; to offend Sheik Ilderim would be to antagonize the Desert, over which lie all Maxentius's lines of operation. Wherefore Simonides bade me tell you to have no disquiet; Messala will pay."

Ilderim was at once restored to his good-humour.

"Let us be off now," he said, rubbing his hands. "The business will do well with Simonides. The glory is ours. I will order the horses."

"Stay," said Malluch. "I left a messenger outside. Will you see him?"

"By the splendour of God! I forgot him."

Malluch retired, and was succeeded by a lad of gentle manners and delicate appearance, who knelt upon one knee, and said, winningly: "Iras, the daughter of Balthasar, well known to good Sheik Ilderim, hath intrusted me with a message to the sheik, who, she saith, will do her great favour so he receive her congratulations on account of the victory of his four."

"The daughter of my friend is kind," said Ilderim, with sparkling eyes. "Do thou give her this jewel, in sign of the pleasure I have from her message."

He took a ring from his finger as he spoke.

"I will as thou sayest, O sheik," the lad replied, and continued: "The daughter of the Egyptian charged me further. She prays the good Sheik Ilderim to send word to the youth Ben-Hur that her father hath taken residence for a time in the palace of Idernee, where she will receive the youth after the fourth hour tomorrow. And if, with her congratulations, Sheik Ilderim will accept her gratitude for this other favour done, she will be ever so pleased."

The sheik looked at Ben-Hur, whose face was suffused with pleasure.

"What will you?" he asked.

"By your leave, O sheik, I will see the fair Egyptian."

Ilderim laughed, and said: "Shall not a man enjoy his youth?"

Then Ben-Hur answered the messenger: "Say to her who sent you that I, Ben-Hur, will see her at the palace of Idernee, wherever that may be, tomorrow at noon."

The lad arose, and departed.

At midnight Ilderim took the road, having arranged to leave a horse and a guide for Ben-Hur, who was to follow him.

A TRAP AND MEETING WITH AN OLD ACQUAINTANCE

Going next day to fill his appointment with Iras, Ben-Hur turned from the Omphalus, which was in the heart of the city, into the Colonnade of Herod, and came shortly to the palace of Idernee.

Standing in the shade of the dull passage, and looking through the doorway, he beheld the atrium of a Roman house, roomy and rich to a fabulous degree of magnificence.

Still in his dreamful mood, Ben-Hur sauntered about, charmed by all he beheld, and waiting. He did not mind a little delay; when Iras was ready, she would come or send a servant. In every well-regulated Roman house the atrium was the reception chamber for visitors.

Twice, thrice, he made the round. As often he stood under the opening in the roof, and pondered the sky and its azure depth; then, leaning against a pillar, he studied the distribution of light and shade, and its effects; here a veil diminishing objects, there a brilliance exaggerating others; yet nobody came.

There might be a mistake. No, the messenger had come from the Egyptian, and this was the palace of Idernee. Then he remembered how mysteriously the door had opened, so soundlessly, so of itself. He would see!

He went to the same door. Though he walked ever so lightly, the sound of his stepping was loud and harsh, and he shrank from it. He was getting nervous. The cumbrous Roman lock resisted his first effort to raise it; and the second – the blood chilled in his cheeks – he wrenched with all his might: in vain – the door was not even shaken. A sense of danger seized him, and for a moment he stood irresolute.

Who in Antioch had the motive to do him harm?

Messala!

And this palace of Idernee? He had seen Egypt in the vestibule, Athens in the snowy portico; but here, in the atrium, was Rome; everything about him betrayed Roman ownership. The atrium underwent a change; with all its elegance and beauty, it was no more than a trap. Apprehension always paints in black.

The idea irritated Ben-Hur.

There were many doors on the right and left of the atrium, leading, doubtless, to sleeping-chambers; he tried them, but they were all firmly fastened. Knocking might bring response. Ashamed to make outcry, he betook himself to a couch, and, lying down, tried to reflect.

All too plainly he was a prisoner; but for what purpose? and by whom?

If the work were Messala's!

Half an hour passed – a much longer period to Ben-Hur – when the door which had admitted him opened and closed noiselessly as before, and without attracting his attention.

The moment of the occurrence he was sitting at the farther end of the room. A footstep startled him.

"At last she has come!" he thought, with a throb of relief and pleasure, and arose.

The step was heavy, and accompanied with the gride and clang of coarse sandals. The gilded pillars were between him and the door; he advanced quietly, and leaned against one of them. Presently he heard voices – the voices of men – one of them rough and guttural. What was said he could not understand, as the language was not of the East or South of Europe.

After a general survey of the room, the strangers crossed to their left, and were brought into Ben-Hur's view – two men, one very stout, both tall, and both in short tunics. They had not the air of masters of the house or domestics. They were vulgarians.

The mystery surrounding his own

presence in the palace tended, as we have seen, to make Ben-Hur nervous; so now, when in the tall stout stranger he recognized the Northman whom he had known in Rome, and seen crowned only the day before in the Circus as the winning pugilist; when he saw the man's face, scarred with the wounds of many battles, and imbruted by ferocious passions; when he surveyed the fellow's naked limbs, very marvels of exercise and training, and his shoulders of Herculean breadth, a thought of personal danger started a chill along every vein. A sure instinct warned him that the opportunity for murder was too perfect to have come by chance; and here now were the myrmidons, and their business was with him. He turned an anxious eye upon the Northman's comrade – young, black-eyed, black-haired, and altogether Jewish in appearance; he observed, also, that both the men were in costume exactly such as professionals of their class were in the habit of wearing in the arena. Putting the several circumstances together, Ben-Hur could not be longer in doubt: he had been lured into the palace with design. Out of reach of aid, in this splendid privacy, he was to die!

He undid the sash around his waist, and, baring his head and casting off his white Jewish gown, stood forth in an undertunic not unlike those of the enemy, and was ready, body and mind. Folding his arms, he placed his back against the pillar, and calmly waited.

Directly the Northman turned, and said something in the unknown tongue; then both looked at Ben-Hur. A few more words, and they advanced towards him.

"Who are you?" he asked in Latin.

The Northman fetched a smile which did not relieve his face of its brutalism, and answered:

"Barbarians."

"You are Thord the Northman."

The giant opened his blue eyes.

"I was your scholar."

"No," said Thord, shaking his head. "By the beard of Irmin, I had never a Jew to make a fighting-man of."

"But I will prove my saying."

"How?"

"You came here to kill me."

"That is true."

"Then let this man fight me singly, and I will make the proof on his body."

A gleam of humour shone in the North-man's face. He spoke to his companion, who made answer; then he replied, with the naïveté of a diverted child:

"Wait till I say begin."

By repeated touches of his foot, he pushed a couch out on the floor, and proceeded leisurely to stretch his burly form upon it; when perfectly at ease, he said, simply, "Now begin."

Without ado, Ben-Hur walked to his antagonist.

"Defend thyself," he said.

The man, nothing loth, put up his hands.

As the two thus confronted each other in approved position, there was no discernible inequality between them; on the contrary, they were as like as brothers. To the stranger's confident smile, Ben-Hur opposed an earnestness which, had his skill been known, would have been accepted fair warning of danger. Both knew the combat was to be mortal.

Ben-Hur feinted with his right hand. The stranger warded, slightly advancing his left arm. Ere he could return to guard, Ben-Hur caught him by the wrist in a grip which years at the oar had made terrible as a vice. The surprise was complete, and no time given. To throw himself forward; to push the arm across the man's throat and over his right shoulder, and turn him left side front; to strike surely with the ready left hand; to strike the bare neck under the ear – were but petty divisions of the same act. No need of a second blow. The myrmidon fell heavily, and without a cry, and lay still.

Ben-Hur turned to Thord.

"Ha! What! By the beard of Irmin!" the latter cried, in astonishment, rising to a sitting posture. Then he laughed. "Ha, ha, ha! I could not have done it better myself."

He viewed Ben-Hur coolly from head to foot, and, rising, faced him with undisguised admiration.

"It was my trick – the trick I have practised for ten years in the schools of Rome. You are not a Jew. Who are you?"

"You knew Arrius the duumvir."

"Quintus Arrius? Yes, he was my patron."

"He had a son."

"Yes," said Thord, his battered features lighting dully, "I knew the boy; he would have made a king gladiator. Caesar offered him his patronage. I taught him the very trick you played on this one here – a trick impossible except to a hand and arm like mine. It has won me many a crown."

"I am that son of Arrius."

Thord drew nearer, and viewed him carefully; then his eyes brightened with genuine pleasure, and, laughing, he held out his hand.

"Ha, ha, ha! He told me I would find a Jew here – a Jew – a dog of a Jew – killing whom was serving the gods."

"Who told you so?" asked Ben-Hur, taking the hand.

"He – Messala – ha, ha, ha!"

"When, Thord?"

"Last night."

"I thought he was hurt."

"He will never walk again. On his bed he told me between groans."

A very vivid portrayal of hate in a few words; and Ben-Hur saw that the Roman, if he lived, would still be capable and dangerous, and follow him unrelentingly. A light came to him, and he asked: "Thord, what was Messala to give you for killing me?"

"A thousand sestertii."

"You shall have them yet; and so you do now what I tell you, I will add three thousand more to the sum."

The giant reflected aloud:

"I won five thousand yesterday; from the Roman one – six. Give me four, good Arrius – four more – and I will stand firm for you, though old Thor, my namesake, strike me with his hammer. Make it four, and I will kill the lying patrician, if you say so. I have only to cover his mouth with my hand – thus."

"I will make it four thousand," Ben-Hur continued; "and in what you shall do for the money there will be no blood on your hands, Thord. Hear me now. Did not your friend here look like me?"

"I would have said he was an apple from the same tree."

"Well, if I put on his tunic, and dress him in these clothes of mine, and you and I go away together, leaving him here, can you not get your sestertii from Messala all the same? You have only to make him believe it me that is dead."

Thord laughed till the tears ran into his mouth.

"Ha, ha, ha! Ten thousand sestertii were never won so easily. And a wine-shop by the Great Circus! – all for a lie without blood in it! Ha, ha, ha!"

They shook hands after which the exchange of clothes was effected. It was arranged then that a messenger should go at night to Thord's lodging-place with the four thousand sestertii. When they were done, the giant knocked at the front door; it opened to him; and, passing out of the atrium, he led Ben-Hur into a room adjoining, where the latter completed his attired from the coarse garments of the dead pugilist. They separated directly in the Omphalus.

"Fail not, O son of Arrius, fail not the wine-shop near the Great Circus! Ha, ha, ha! By the beard of Irmin, there was never fortune gained so cheap. The gods keep you!"

Upon leaving the atrium, Ben-Hur gave a last look at the myrmidon as he lay in the Jewish vestments, and was satisfied. The likeness was striking. If Thord kept faith, the cheat was a secret to endure for ever.

At night, in the house of Simonides, Ben-Hur told the good man all that had taken place in the palace of Idernee; and it was agreed that, after a few days, public inquiry should be set afloat for the discovery of the whereabouts of the son of Arrius. Eventually the matter was to be carried boldly to Maxentius; then, if the mystery came not out, it was concluded that Messala and Gratus would be at rest and happy, and Ben-Hur free to betake himself to Jerusalem, to make search for his lost people.

At the leave-taking, Simonides sat in his chair out on the terrace overlooking the river, and gave his farewell and the peace of the Lord with the impressment of a father.

He crossed the river next to the late quarters of Ilderim, where he found the Arab who was to serve him as guide. The

horses were brought out.

"This one is thine," said the Arab.

Ben-Hur looked, and, lo! it was Aldebaran, the swiftest and brightest of the sons of Mira, and, next to Sirius, the beloved of the sheik; and he knew the old man's heart came to him along with the gift.

The corpse in the atrium was taken up and buried by night; and, as part of Messala's plan, a courier was sent off to Gratus to make him at rest by the announcement of Ben-Hur's death – this time past question.

Ere long a wine-shop was opened near the Circus Maximus, with inscription over the door:

THORD THE NORTHMAN

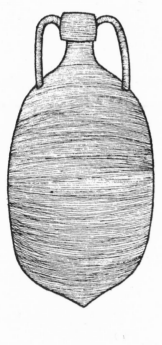

STORAGE VESSELS FOR WINE AND CORN

BOOK SIX

A NEW GOVERNOR FOR JERUSALEM

Our story moves forward now thirty days from the night Ben-Hur left Antioch to go out with Sheik Ilderim into the desert.

A great change has befallen – great at least as respects the fortunes of our hero. *Valerius Gratus has been succeeded by Pontius Pilate!*

Brief as the time was, already the Jews knew the change of rulers was not for the better.

The worst of men do once in a while vary their wickednesses by good acts; so with Pilate. He ordered an inspection of all the prisons in Judea, and a return of the names of the persons in custody, with a statement of the crimes for which they had been committed. Doubtless, the motive was the one so common with officials just installed – dread of entailed responsibility; the people however, in thought of the good which might come of the measure, gave him credit, and for a period were comforted. The revelations were astonishing. Hundreds of persons were released against whom there were no accusations; many others came to light who had long been accounted dead; yet more amazing, there was opening of dungeons not merely unknown at the time by the people, but actually forgotten by the prison authorities. With one instance of the latter kind we have now to deal; and, strange to say, it occurred in Jerusalem.

The Tower of Antonia was originally a castle built by the Macedonians. All through the administration of Gratus it had been a garrisoned citadel and underground prison terrible to revolutionists. Woe when the cohorts poured from its gates to suppress disorder! Woe not less when a Jew passed the same gates going in under arrest!

With this explanation, we hasten to our story.

* * *

The order of the new procurator requiring a report of the persons in custody was received at the Tower of Antonia, and promptly executed; and two days have gone since the last unfortunate was brought up for examination.

The tribune's office is spacious and cool, and furnished in a style suitable to the dignity of the commandant of a post in every respect so important. Looking in upon him about the seventh hour of the day, the officer appears weary and impatient; when the report is despatched, he will to the roof of the colonnade for air and exercise, and the amusement to be had watching the Jews over in the courts of the Temple. His subordinates and clerks share his impatience.

In the spell of waiting a man appeared in a doorway leading to an adjoining apartment. He rattled a bunch of keys, each heavy as a hammer, and at once attracted the chief's attention.

"Ah, Gesius! come in," the tribune said.

As the new-comer approached the table behind which the chief sat in an easy-chair, everybody present looked at him, and, observing a certain expression of alarm and mortification on his face, became silent that they might hear what he had to say.

"It is now about eight years since Valerius Gratus selected me to be keeper of prisoners here in the Tower," said the man, deliberately. "I remember the morning I entered upon the duties of my office. There had been a riot the day before, and fighting in the streets. We slew many Jews, and suffered on our side. The affair came, it was said, of an attempt to assassinate Gratus, who had been knocked from his horse by a tile thrown from a roof. I found him sitting where you now sit, O tribune, his head swathed in bandages. He told me of my selection, and gave me these keys, numbered to correspond with the numbers of the cells; they were the badges of my office, he said, and not to be parted with.

"I saluted him, and turned to go away; he called me back. 'Ah, I forgot,' he said. 'Give me the map of the third floor.' I gave it to him, and he spread it upon the table. 'Here, Gesius,' he said, 'see this cell.' He laid his finger on the one numbered V. 'There are three men confined in that cell, desperate characters, who by some means got hold of a state secret, and suffer for their curiosity, which' – he looked at me severely – 'in such matters is worse than a crime. Accordingly, they are blind and tongueless, and are placed there for life. They shall have nothing but food and drink, to be given them through a hole, which you will find in the wall covered by a slide. Do you hear, Gesius?' I made him answer. 'It is well,' he continued. 'One thing more

ROMAN ARMY ALTAR

which you shall not forget, or——' He looked at me threateningly. 'The door of their cell – cell number V. on the same floor – this one, Gesius' – he put his finger on the particular cell to impress my memory – 'shall never be opened for any purpose, neither to let one in nor out, not even yourself.' 'But if they die?' I asked. 'If they die,' he said, 'the cell shall be their tomb. They were put there to die, and be lost. The cell is leprous. Do you understand?' With that he let me go."

Gesius stopped, and from the breast of his tunic drew three parchments, all much yellowed by time and use; selecting one of them, he spread it upon the table before the tribune, saying simply, "This is the lower floor."

The whole company looked at –

THE MAP

PASSAGE				
V	IV	III	II	I

"This is exactly, O tribune, as I had it from Gratus. It shows but five cells upon that floor, while there are six."

"Six, sayest thou?"

"I will show you the floor as it is – or as I believe it to be."

Upon a page of his tablets, Gesius drew the following diagram, and gave it to the tribune:

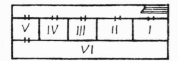

"Thou hast done well," said the tribune, examining the drawing, and thinking the narrative at an end. "I will have the map corrected, or, better, I will have a new one made, and given thee. Come for it in the morning."

So saying, he arose.

"But hear me further, O tribune."

"I will hurry," said the keeper, humbly. As required, I visited all the cells, beginning with those on the first floor, and ending with those on the lower. The order that the door of number V. should not be opened had been respected; through all the eight years food and drink

for three men had been passed through a hole in the wall. I went to the door yesterday, curious to see the wretches who, against all expectation, had lived so long. The locks refused the key. We pulled a little, and the door fell down, rusted from its hinges. Going in, I found but one man, old, blind, tongueless, and naked. His hair dropped in stiffened mats below his waist. His skin was like the parchment there. He held his hands out, and the finger-nails curled and twisted like the claws of a bird. I asked him where his companions were. He shook his head in denial. Thinking to find the others, we searched the cell. The floor was dry; so were the walls. If three men had been shut in there, and two of them had died, at least their bones would have endured."

"Wherefore thou thinkest——"

"You have but half the story, O tribune. When you have it all, you will agree with me. You know what I did with the man: that I sent him to the bath, and had him shorn and clothed, and then took him to the gate of the Tower, and bade him go free. I washed my hands of him. Today he came back, and was brought to me. By signs and tears, he at last made me understand he wished to return to his cell, and I so ordered. When we were in the cell again, and the prisoner knew it, he caught my hand eagerly, and led me to a hole like that through which we were accustomed to pass him his food. Though large enough to push your helmet through, it escaped me yesterday. Still holding my hand, he put his face to the hole and gave a beast-like cry. A sound came faintly back. I was astonished, and drew him away, and called out, 'Ho, here!' At first there was no answer. I called again, and received back these words, 'Be thou praised, O Lord!' Yet more astonishing, O tribune, the voice was a woman's. And I asked, 'Who are you?' and had reply, 'A woman of Israel, entombed here with her daughter. Help us quickly, or we die.' I told them to be of cheer, and hurried here to know your will."

The tribune arose hastily.

"Thou wert right, Gesius," he said, "and I see now. The map was a lie, and so was the tale of the three men. There have been better Romans than Valerius Gratus."

"Yes," said the keeper. "I gleaned from the prisoner that he had regularly given

the women of the food and drink he had received."

"It is accounted for," replied the tribune, and observing the countenances of his friends, and reflecting how well it would be to have witnesses, he added: "Let us rescue the women. Come all."

Gesius was pleased.

"We will have to pierce the wall," he said. "I found where a door had been, but it was filled solidly with stones and mortar."

The tribune stayed to say to a clerk: "Send workmen after me with tools. Make haste; but hold the report, for I see it will have to be corrected."

In a short time they were gone.

THE TOWER OF ANTONIA AND ITS SECRET

"A woman of Israel, entombed here with her daughter. Help us quickly, or we die."

Such was the reply Gesius, the keeper, had from the cell which appears on his amended map as VI. The reader, when he observed the answer, knew who the unfortunates were, and, doubtless, said to himself, "At last the mother of Ben-Hur, and Tirzah, his sister!"

And so it was.

The morning of their seizure, eight years before, they had been carried to the Tower, where Gratus proposed to put them out of the way. He had chosen the Tower for the purpose as more immediately in his own keeping, and cell VI. because, first, it could be better lost than any other; and, secondly, it was infected with leprosy; for these prisoners were not merely to be put in a safe place, but in a place to die.

As the last step in the scheme, Gratus summarily removed the old keeper of the prisons; not because he knew what had been done – for he did not – but because, knowing the underground floors as he did, it would be next to impossible to keep the transaction from him. Then, with masterly ingenuity, the procurator had new maps drawn for delivery to a new keeper, with the omission, as we have seen, of cell VI. The instructions given the latter, taken with the omission on the map, accomplished the design – the cell and its unhappy tenants were all alike lost.

The two women are grouped close by the aperture; one is seated, the other is half reclining against her; there is nothing between them and the bare rock.

Our recollections of them in former days enjoin us to be respectful; their sorrows clothe them with sanctity. Without going too near, across the dungeon, we see they have undergone a change of appearance not to be accounted for by time or long confinement. The mother was beautiful as a woman, the daughter beautiful as a child; not even love could say so much now. Their hair is long, unkempt, and strangely white; they make us shrink and shudder with an indefinable repulsion, though the effect may be from an illusory glozing of the light glimmering dismally through the unhealthy murk; or they may be enduring the tortures of hunger and thirst, not having had to eat or drink since their servant, the convict, was taken away – that is, since yesterday.

Tirzah, reclining against her mother in half-embrace, moans piteously.

"Patience, Tirzah: they are coming – they are almost here."

She thought she heard a sound over by the little trap in the partition-wall through which they held all their actual communication with the world. And she was not mistaken.

"Praised be the Lord for ever!" exclaimed the mother, with the fervour of restored faith and hope.

"Ho, there!" they heard next; and then, "Who are you?"

The voice was strange. What matter? Except from Tirzah, they were the first and only words the mother had heard in eight years. The revulsion was mighty – from death to life – and so instantly!

"A woman of Israel, entombed here with her daughter. Help us quickly, or we die."

"Be of cheer. I will return."

The women sobbed aloud. They were found; help was coming. From wish to wish hope flew as the twittering swallows fly. They were found; they would be released. And restoration would follow – restoration to all they had lost – home, society, property, son and brother! The

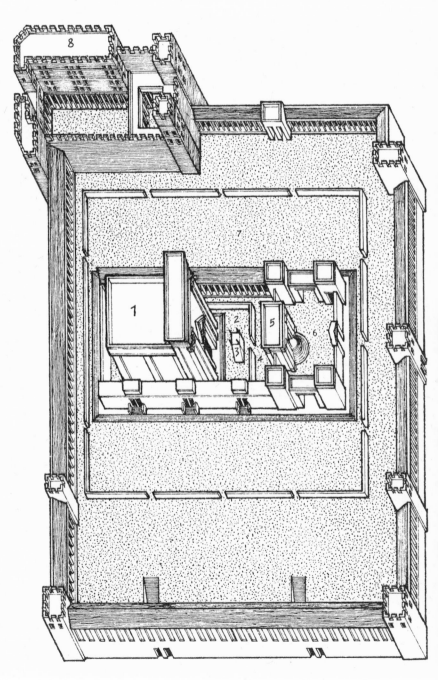

HEROD'S TEMPLE
AND THE FORTRESS
OF ANTONIA

1 THE TEMPLE
2 THE COURT OF THE PRIESTS

3 THE ALTAR
4 THE COURT OF THE ISRAELITES
5 THE GATE OF NICANOR
6 THE COURT OF THE WOMEN
7 THE COURT OF THE GENTILES
8 THE FORTRESS OF ANTONIA

SPOONS

SOME ROMAN RECIPES

EGG SPONGE WITH MILK
MIX TOGETHER 4 EGGS, ½ PINT OF MILK, 1oz OIL.
POUR A LITTLE OIL INTO A THIN FRYING-PAN,
BRING TO SIZZLING POINT, AND ADD THE
PREPARED MIXTURE. WHEN IT IS COOKED ON ONE
SIDE TURN OUT ON TO A ROUND DISH, POUR
HONEY OVER, SPRINKLE WITH PEPPER AND SERVE

ROSE WINE
THREAD TOGETHER ROSE-LEAVES FROM WHICH
THE WHITE PART HAS BEEN REMOVED, AND STEEP
AS MANY AS POSSIBLE IN WINE FOR SEVEN DAYS.
AFTER SEVEN DAYS TAKE THE ROSE-LEAVES OUT
OF THE WINE, AND IN THE SAME WAY PUT IN
OTHER FRESH ROSE-LEAVES THREADED
TOGETHER, TO REST SEVEN DAYS IN THE WINE
THEN TAKE THEM OUT. REPEAT A THIRD TIME,
TAKE OUT THE ROSE-LEAVES, STRAIN THE WINE,
AND, WHEN YOU WANT TO USE IT FOR
DRINKING, ADD HONEY TO MAKE ROSE WINE.

HOME-MADE SWEET
STONE DATES, AND STUFF WITH NUTS, PINE-
KERNELS, OR GROUND PEPPER. ROLL IN SALT,
FRY IN COOKED HONEY, AND SERVE.

ROMAN MEALS

The Romans usually had only one main meal a day. Dinner (coena) could last from 3 p.m. till after midnight. For breakfast (ientaculum) some had a bite of bread and cheese, many ate nothing at all, though schoolboys were always given something substantial. Lunch (prandium) was generally a light snack, meat or fish with fruit and wine, often taken standing up. The upper classes enjoyed some form of exercise in the early afternoon, followed by a bath, before the heavy meal of the day.

The dining-room (triclinium) was named after the 3 couches, each usually seating 3 guests, arranged round a square table. (During the Empire a single semicircular couch at a round table became fashionable.) The Romans enjoyed their food and the dining-room table was a most important piece of furniture; a wealthy citizen's table was made of maple or citron wood, decorated with ivory.

A Roman dined, leaning on his left elbow, using his left hand to hold his plate and his right to pick up his food, with cushions behind. The most distinguished guest, sitting next to the host, was usually given the place with most room for receiving messengers or carrying on his own business affairs. Romans often wrote or dictated their letters during meals.

The art of cooking was greatly respected by the Romans—the cook was the most expensive slave of the household, he could cost as much as a horse. The slaves waiting at table had their own hierarchy; the most important slave supervised the whole feast and usually carved. Those who served the wine and cut up the food were chosen for their skill and good looks. They were often brightly dressed with long curly hair. But those doing the more menial chores were simply clothed with their heads shaved. Before and after the meal slaves carried round bowls of water for the guests to wash their hands. This was more than a luxury as Romans ate with their hands, spoons being the only form of cutlery ever used. Each guest brought his own slave to a dinner party, and often his own napkin to take home titbits for his own household slaves.

Dinner (coena) was divided into 3 parts: the hors d'oeuvres, probably eggs and assorted vegetables; the main course, a variety of meat and fish dishes with elaborate sources and wine to drink (guests selected a few of these; and after, fruit and sweetmeats.

Guests were sometimes graded by their host. A minor acquaintance might be given inferior food on inferior tableware, whilst a distinguished guest at the same meal was given a sumptuous spread.

Most ordinary Romans could only afford the simplest diet of bread and soup (meal or millet), with turnips, olives, beans, cheese, and occasionally the luxury of some pork. Only those living near the sea or by a river had fish, which was otherwise very expensive. In contrast, the great feasts enjoyed by the wealthy Romans were sometimes very costly orgies of gluttony, drunkenness and dissipation, much criticized by satirists such as Seneca. Laws were passed unsuccessfully in order to try and restrict the numbers of guests and the sum of money spent on these feasts.

The only alcohol was wine and the Romans mixed theirs with hot or cold water. They only drank it neat on occasions of very heavy drinking. After the meal, guests were given garlands for their heads, before the drinking and toasting began. Romans originally believed the smell of some plants could counteract the effects of the wine. They used to anoint their faces and hair with perfume and sometimes mixed this with their wine and drank it.

The Romans enjoyed many different forms of entertainment during these lengthy meals. In more cultured homes there were readings (many households owned at least one "reader" among its slaves), humorous recitations or music. For others there were performances by buffoons, dancing girls (preferably from Cadiz or Syria), acrobats, gambling and even occasionally gladiatorial combats.

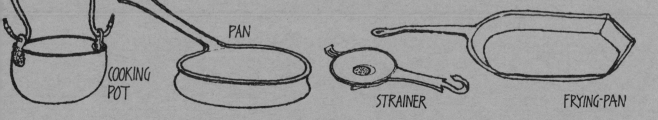

COOKING POT

PAN

STRAINER

FRYING-PAN

ROMAN MERCHANT SHIPS
THE DIAGRAM SHOWS ONE OF THE SHIPS BUILT FOR GRAIN TRAFFIC. IT WAS 175 FT
LONG AND COULD CARRY APPROXIMATELY 1,300 TONS OF GRAIN. THE SHIPS WOULD
BE LOADED WITH GRAIN IN ALEXANDRIA IN APRIL, AND AFTER STRUGGLING
WITH THE PREVAILING WINDS, THEY WOULD ARRIVE IN ROME IN MAY OR JUNE.
THE CARGO WOULD BE QUICKLY UNLOADED AND THE SHIPS WOULD SET
OUT TO RETURN TO ALEXANDRIA

THE SHAPE OF THE BIGGER ROMAN MERCHANT SHIPS REMAINED ALMOST
UNCHANGED DURING THE FIRST THREE CENTURIES A.D.   1. BALCONY WITH TENT
FOR THE CAPTAIN AND DISTINGUISHED PASSENGERS. 2 RUDDER   3 OFFICERS'
AND PASSENGERS' CABINS. 4 SHIPS BOAT. 5/MAIN SAIL 6 TOP SAIL 7 ARTEMON

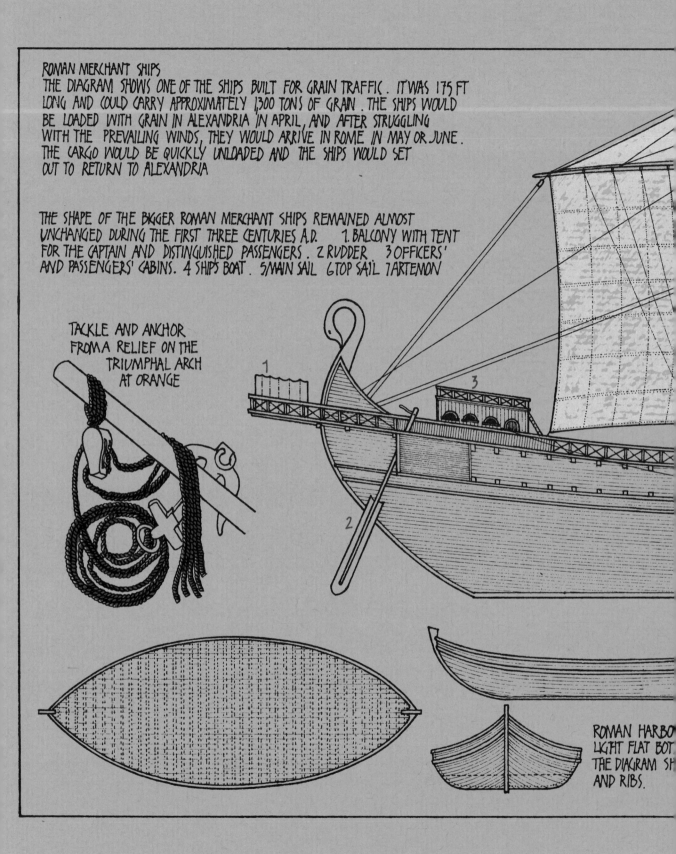

TACKLE AND ANCHOR
FROM A RELIEF ON THE
TRIUMPHAL ARCH
AT ORANGE

ROMAN HARBO
LIGHT FLAT BOT
THE DIAGRAM SH
AND RIBS.

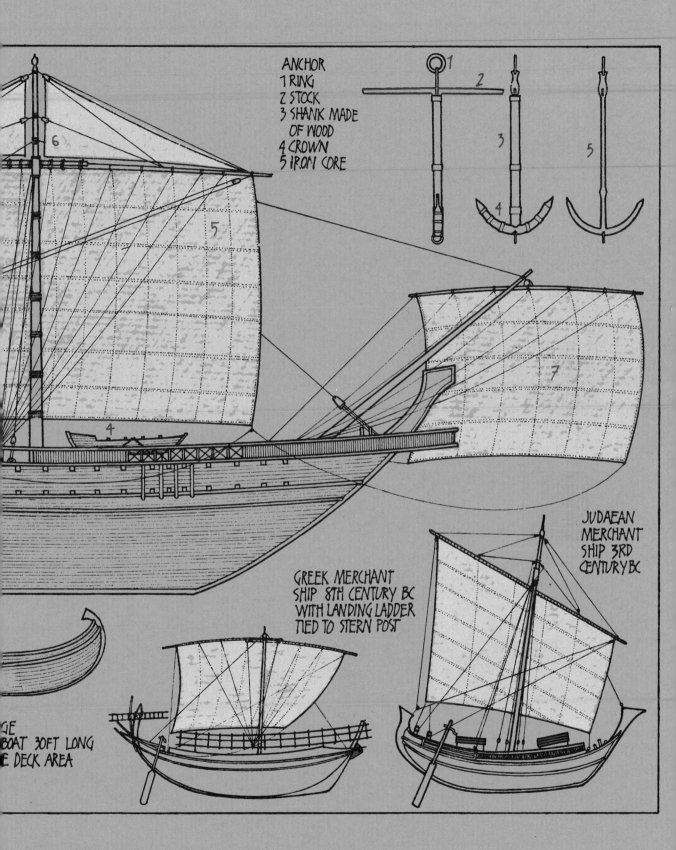

ANCHOR
1 RING
2 STOCK
3 SHANK MADE
  OF WOOD
4 CROWN
5 IRON CORE

JUDAEAN
MERCHANT
SHIP 3RD
CENTURY BC

GREEK MERCHANT
SHIP 8TH CENTURY BC
WITH LANDING LADDER
TIED TO STERN POST

GE
BOAT 30FT LONG
E DECK AREA

MURALIS

VALLARIS

MILITARY AWARDS

THE CROWNS WERE GIVEN TO THE
SOLDIERS FOR OUTSTANDING
SERVICE.
THE CORONA MURALIS WAS AWARD-
ED TO THE FIRST SOLDIER TO
SCALE THE ENEMY WALLS
THE CORONA VALLARIS TO THE
FIRST TO SURMOUNT THE RAM-
PARTS AND FORCE ENTRY INTO
THE ENEMY'S CAMP

THE STANDARDS WERE CARRIED
INTO BATTLE. EACH LEGION HAD
ITS OWN SYMBOLS.

STANDARD TOP
IN THE FORM
OF A HORSE

LEGIONARY
STANDARDS

scanty light glozed them with the glory of day, and, forgetful of pain and thirst and hunger, and of the menace of death, they sank upon the floor and cried, keeping fast hold of each other the while.

And this time they had not long to wait. Gesius, the keeper, told his tale methodically, but finished it at last. The tribune was prompt.

"Within there!" he shouted through the trap.

"Here!" said the mother, rising.

Directly she heard another sound in another place, as of blows on the wall – blows quick, ringing, and delivered with iron tools. She did not speak, nor did Tirzah, but they listened, well knowing the meaning of it all – that a way to liberty was being made for them. So men a long time buried in deep mines hear the coming of rescuers, heralded by thrust of bar and beat of pick, and answer gratefully with heart-throbs, their eyes fixed upon the spot whence the sounds proceed; and they cannot look away, lest the work should cease, and they be returned to despair.

The arms outside were strong, the hands skilful, the will good. Each instant the blows sounded more plainly; now and then a piece fell with a crash; and liberty came nearer and nearer. Presently the workmen could be heard speaking. Then – O happiness! – through a crevice flashed a red ray of torches. Into the darkness it cut incisive as diamond brilliance, beautiful as if from a spear of the morning.

"It is he, mother, it is he! He has found us at last!" cried Tirzah, with the quickened fancy of youth.

But the mother answered meekly, "God is good!"

A block fell inside, and another – then a great mass, and the door was open. A man grimed with mortar and stone-dust stepped in, and stopped, holding a torch over his head. Two or three others followed with torches, and stood aside for the tribune to enter.

Respect for women is not all a conventionality, for it is the best proof of their proper nature. The tribune stopped, because they fled from him – not with fear, be it said, but shame; nor yet, O reader, from shame alone! From the obscurity of their partial hiding he heard these words, the saddest, most dreadful, most utterly despairing of the human tongue:

"Come not near us – unclean, unclean!"

The men flared their torches while they stared at each other.

"Unclean, unclean!" came from the corner again, a slow tremulous wail exceedingly sorrowful.

So the widow and mother performed her duty, and in the moment realized that the freedom she had prayed for and dreamed of, fruit of scarlet and gold seen afar, was but an apple of Sodom in the hand.

She and Tirzah were – lepers!

The torches flashed redly through the dungeon, and liberty was come. "God is good," the widow cried – not for what had been, O reader, but for what was. In thankfulness for present mercy, nothing so becomes us as losing sight of past ills.

The tribune came directly; then in the corner to which she had fled, suddenly a sense of duty smote the elder of the women, and straightway the awful warning:

"Unclean, unclean!"

The tribune heard it with a tremor, but kept his place.

"Who are you?" he asked.

"Two women dying of hunger and thirst. Yet" – the mother did not falter – "come not near us, nor touch the floor or the wall. Unclean, unclean!"

"Give me thy story, woman – thy name, and when thou wert put here, and by whom, and for what."

"There was once in this city of Jerusalem a Prince Ben-Hur, the friend of all generous Romans, and who had Caesar for his friend. I am his widow, and this one with me is his child. How may I tell you for what we were sunk here, when I do not know, unless it was because we were rich? Valerius Gratus can tell you who our enemy was, and when our imprisonment began. I cannot. See to what we have been reduced – oh, see, and have pity!"

The air was heavy with the pest and the smoke of the torches, yet the Roman called one of the torch-bearers to his side, and wrote the answer nearly word for word. It was terse and comprehensive, containing at once a history, an accusation, and a prayer. No common person could have made it, and he could not but pity and believe.

"Thou shalt have relief, woman," he said, closing the tablets. "I will send thee food and drink."

"And raiment, and purifying water, we pray you, O generous Roman!"

"As thou wilt," he replied.

"God is good," said the widow, sobbing. "May His peace abide with you!"

"And, further," he added, "I cannot see thee again. Make preparation, and tonight I will have thee taken to the gate of the Tower, and set free. Thou knowest the law. Farewell."

He spoke to the men, and went out the door.

Very shortly some slaves came to the cell with a large gurglet of water, a basin and napkins, a platter with bread and meat, and some garments of women's wear; and, setting them down within reach of the prisoners, they ran away.

About the middle of the first watch, the two were conducted to the gate, and turned into the street. So the Roman quit himself of them, and in the city of their fathers they were once more free.

BEN HUR RETURNS

It was dark when, parting with the drover inside the gate, Ben-Hur turned into a narrow lane leading to the south. A few of the people whom he met saluted him.

He came, at length, to his father's house.

In the corners the wax used in the sealing-up was still plainly seen, and across the valves was the board with the inscription:

"THIS IS THE PROPERTY OF THE EMPEROR."

Silently, he stole round to the south. There, too, the gate was sealed and inscribed. The mellow splendour of the August moon, pouring over the crest of Olivet, since termed the Mount of Offence, brought the lettering boldly out; and he read, and was filled with rage. As his blood cooled, insensibly he yielded to the fatigue of long travel in the summer heat, and sank down lower, and, at last, slept.

About that time two women came down the street from the direction of the Tower of Antonia, approaching the palace of the Hurs. They advanced stealthily, with timid steps, pausing often to listen. At the corner of the rugged pile, one said to the other, in a low voice:

"This is it, Tirzah!"

And Tirzah, after a look, caught her mother's hand, and leaned upon her heavily, sobbing, but silent.

"Let us go on, my child, because" – the mother hesitated and trembled; then, with an effort to be calm, continued – "because when morning comes they will put us out of the gate of the city to – return no more."

And, creeping in close to the rough wall, they glided on, like two ghosts, till they came to the gate, before which they also paused. Seeing the board, they stepped upon the stone in the scarce cold tracks of Ben-Hur, and read the inscription: "This is the Property of the Emperor."

Tirzah leaned upon her again, and said, whispering, "Let us – let us die!"

"No!" the mother said, firmly. "The Lord has appointed our times, and we are believers in the Lord. We will wait on Him even in this. Come away!"

She caught Tirzah's hand as she spoke, and hastened to the west corner of the house, keeping close to the wall.

"Hist!" said the mother. "There is someone lying upon the step – a man."

They crossed the street hand in hand, ghostly quick, ghostly still. When their shadows fell upon him, they stopped. One of his hands was lying out upon the step palm up. Tirzah fell upon her knees, and and would have kissed it; but the mother drew her back.

"Not for thy life; not for thy life! Unclean, unclean!" she whispered.

Tirzah shrank from him, as if he were the leprous one.

Ben-Hur was handsome as the manly are.

He stirred, and tossed his hand. They moved back, but heard him mutter in his dream:

"Mother! Amrah! Where is——"

He fell off into the deep sleep.

Tirzah stared wistfully. The mother put her face in the dust, struggling to suppress a sob so deep and strong it seemed her heart was bursting. Almost she wished he might waken.

He had asked for her; she was not forgotten; in his sleep he was thinking of her. Was it not enough?

Presently the mother beckoned to Tirzah, and they arose, and, taking one more look, as if to print his image past fading, hand in hand they recrossed the street. Back in the shade of the wall there, they retired and knelt, looking at him, waiting for him to wake – waiting some revelation, they knew not what. Nobody has yet given us a measure for the patience of a love like theirs.

By-and-by, the sleep being yet upon him, another woman appeared at the corner of the palace. The two in the shade saw her plainly in the light; a small figure, much bent, dark-skinned, grey-haired, dressed neatly in servant's garb, and carrying a basket full of vegetables.

At sight of the man upon the step the new-comer stopped; then, as if decided, she walked on – very lightly as she drew near the sleeper. Passing round him, she went to the gate, slid the wicket latch easily to one side, and put her hand in the opening. One of the broad boards in the left valve swung ajar without noise. She put the basket through, and was about to follow, when, yielding to curiosity, she lingered to have one look at the stranger whose face was below her in open view.

The spectators across the street heard a low exclamation, and saw the woman rub her eyes as if to renew their power, bend closer down, clasp her hands, gaze wildly around, look at the sleeper, stoop and raise the outlying hand, and kiss it fondly – that which they wished so mightily to do, but dared not.

Awakened by the action, Ben-Hur instinctively withdrew the hand; as he did so, his eyes met the woman's.

"Amrah! O Amrah, is it thou?" he said.

The good heart made no answer in words, but fell upon his neck, crying for joy.

Gently he put her arms away, and, lifting the dark face wet with tears, kissed it, his joy only a little less than hers. Then those across the way heard him say:

"Mother – Tirzah – O Amrah, tell me of them! Speak, speak, I pray thee!"

Amrah only cried afresh.

"Thou hast seen them, Amrah. Thou knowest where they are; tell me they are at home."

Tirzah moved, but the mother, divining her purpose, caught her and whispered: "Do not go – not for life. Unclean, unclean!"

Her love was in tyrannical mood. Though both their hearts broke, he should not become what they were; and she conquered.

Meanwhile Amrah, so entreated, only wept the more.

"Wert thou going in?" he asked, presently, seeing the board swung back. "Come, then. I will go with thee." He arose as he spoke. "The Romans – be the curse of the Lord upon them! – the Romans lied. The house is mine. Rise, Amrah, and let us go in."

A moment and they were gone, leaving the two in the shade to behold the gate staring blankly at them – the gate which they might not ever enter more. They nestled together in the dust.

They had done their duty.

Their love was proven.

Next morning they were found, and driven out of the city with stones.

"Begone! Ye are of the dead; go to the dead!"

With the doom ringing in their ears, they went forth.

AMRAH'S PROMISE

The second morning after the incidents of the preceding chapter, Amrah drew near the well En-rogel, and seated herself upon a stone.

It was very early, and she was the first to arrive at the well. Soon, however, a man came bringing a rope and a leathern bucket. Saluting the little dark-faced woman, he undid the rope, fixed it to the bucket, and waited customers. Others who chose to do so might draw water for themselves; he was a professional in the business, and would fill the largest jar the stoutest woman could carry for a gerah.

Amrah sat still, and had nothing to say. Seeing a jar, the man asked after awhile if she wished it filled; she answered him civilly, "Not now;" whereupon he gave her no more attention. When the dawn was fairly defined over Olivet, his patrons began to arrive, and he had all he could do to attend to them. All the time she kept her seat, looking intently up at the hill.

The sun made its appearance, yet she sat watching and waiting; and while she thus waits, let us see what her purpose is.

Her custom had been to go to market after nightfall. Stealing out unobserved, she would seek the shops in the Tyropoeon, or those over by the Fish Gate in the east, make her purchases of meat and vegetables, and return and shut herself up again.

The pleasure she derived from the presence of Ben-Hur in the old house once more may be imagined. She had nothing to tell him of her mistress or Tirzah – nothing. He would have had her move to a place not so lonesome; she refused. She would have had him take his own room again, which was just as he had left it; but the danger of discovery was too great, and she wished above all things to avoid inquiry. He would come and see her often as possible. Coming in the night, he would also go away in the night. She was compelled to be satisfied, and at once occupied herself contriving ways to make him happy. That he was a man now did not occur to her; nor did it enter her mind that he might have put by or lost his boyish tastes; to please him, she thought to go on her old round of services. He used to be fond of confections; she remembered the things in that line which delighted him most, and resolved to make them, and have a supply always ready when he came. Could anything be happier? So next night, earlier than usual, she stole out with her basket, and went over to the Fish Gate Market. Wandering about, seeking the best honey, she chanced to hear a man telling a story.

What the story was the reader can arrive at with sufficient certainty when told that the narrator was one of the men who had held torches for the commandant of the Tower of Antonia when, down in cell VI., the Hurs were found. The particulars of the finding were all told, and she heard them, with the names of the prisoners, and the widow's account of herself.

The feelings with which Amrah listened to the recital were such as became the devoted creature she was. She made her purchases, and returned home in a dream. What a happiness she had in store for her boy! She had found his mother!

She put the basket away, now laughing, now crying. Suddenly she stopped and thought. It would kill him to be told that his mother and Tirzah were lepers. He would go through the awful city over on the Hill of Evil Counsel – into each infected tomb he would go without rest, asking for them, and the disease would catch him, and their fate would be his. She wrung her hands. What should she do?

The lepers, she knew, were accustomed of mornings to come down from their sepulchral abodes in the hill, and take a supply of water for the day from the well En-rogel. Bringing their jars, they would set them on the ground and wait, standing afar until they were filled. To that the mistress and Tirzah must come; for the law was inexorable, and admitted no distinction. A rich leper was no better than a poor one.

So Amrah decided not to speak to Ben-Hur of the story she had heard, but go alone to the well and wait. Hunger and thirst would drive the unfortunates thither, and she believed she could recognize them at sight; if not, they might recognize her.

Meantime Ben-Hur came, and they talked much. Tomorrow Malluch would arrive; then the search should be immediately begun. He was impatient to be about it. To amuse himself he would visit the sacred places in the vicinity. The secret, we may be sure, weighed heavily on the woman, but she held her peace.

When he was gone she busied herself in the preparation of things good to eat, applying her utmost skill to the work. At the approach of day, as signalled by the stars, she filled the basket, selected a jar, and took the road to En-rogel, going out by the Fish Gate which was earliest open, and arriving as we have seen.

Shortly after sunrise, when business at the well was most pressing, and the drawer of water most hurried; when, in fact, half a dozen buckets were in use at the same time, everybody making haste to get away before the cool of the morning melted into the heat of the day, the tenantry of the hill began to appear and move about the doors of their tombs. Somewhat later they were discernible in groups, of which not a few were children so young that they suggested the holiest relation. Numbers came momentarily around the turn of the bluff – women with jars upon their shoulders, old and very feeble men hobbling along on staffs and crutches. Some leaned upon the shoulders of others; a few – the utterly helpless – lay, like heaps of rags, upon litters. Even that community of superlative sorrow had its love-light to make life endurable and attractive. Distance softened without entirely veiling the misery of the outcasts.

From her seat by the well Amrah kept watch upon the spectral groups. She scarcely moved. More than once she imagined she saw those she sought. That they were there upon the hill she had no doubt; that they must come down and near she knew; when the people at the well were all served they would come.

Now, quite at the base of the bluff there was a tomb which had more than once attracted Amrah by its wide gaping. A stone of large dimensions stood near its mouth. The sun looked into it through the hottest hours of the day, and altogether it seemed uninhabitable by anything living, unless, perchance, by some wild dogs returning from scavenger duty down in Gehenna. Thence, however, and greatly to her surprise, the patient Egyptian beheld two women come, one half supporting, half leading, the other. They were both white-haired; both looked old; but their garments were not rent, and they gazed about them as if the locality were new. The witness below thought she even saw them shrink terrified at the spectacle offered by the hideous assemblage of which they found themselves part.

The two remained by the stone awhile; then they moved slowly,, painfully, and with much fear towards the well, whereat several voices were raised to stop them; yet they kept on. The drawer of water picked up some pebbles, and made ready to drive them back. The company cursed them. The greater company on the hill shouted shrilly, "Unclean, unclean!"

"Surely," thought Amrah of the two, as they kept coming – "surely, they are strangers to the usage of lepers."

She arose, and went to meet them, taking the basket and jar. The alarm at the well immediately subsided.

"What a fool," said one, laughing, "what a fool to give good bread to the dead in that way!"

"And to think of her coming so far!" said another. "I would at least make them meet me at the gate."

Amrah, with better impulse, proceeded. If she should be mistaken! Her heart arose into her throat. And the farther she went the more doubtful and confused she became. Four or five yards from where they stood waiting for her she stopped.

"These are old women," she said to herself. "I never saw them before. I will go back."

She turned away.

"Amrah!" said one of the lepers.

The Egyptian dropped the jar, and looked back, trembling.

"Who called me?" she asked

"Amrah!"

The servant's wondering eyes settled upon the speaker's face.

"Who are you?" she cried.

"We are they you are seeking."

Amrah fell upon her knees.

"O my mistress, my mistress! As I have made your God my God, be He praised that He has led me to you!"

And upon her knees the poor overwhelmed creature began moving forward.

"Stay, Amrah! Come not nearer!"

The words sufficed. Amrah fell upon her face, sobbing so loud the people at the well heard her. Suddenly she arose upon her knees again.

"O my mistress, where is Tirzah?"

"Here I am, Amrah, here! Will you not bring me a little water?"

The habit of the servant renewed itself. Putting back the coarse hair fallen over her face, Amrah arose and went to the basket and uncovered it.

"See," she said, "here are bread and meat."

She would have spread the napkin upon the ground, but the mistress spoke again:

"Do not so, Amrah. Those yonder may stone you, and refuse us drink. Leave the basket with me. Take up the jar and fill it, and bring it here. We will carry them to the tomb with us. For this day you will then have rendered all the service that is lawful. Haste, Amrah!"

The people under whose eyes all this had passed made way for the servant, and even helped her fill the jar, so piteous was the grief her countenance showed.

"Who are they?" a woman asked.

Amrah meekly answered: "They used to be good to me."

Raising the jar upon her shoulder, she hurried back. In forgetfulness, she would have gone to them, but the cry "Unclean, unclean! Beware!" arrested her. Placing the water by the basket, she stepped back, and stood off a little way.

"Thank you, Amrah," said the mistress, taking the articles into possession. "This is very good of you."

"Is there nothing more I can do?" asked Amrah.

The mother's hand was upon the jar, and she was fevered with thirst; yet she paused, and rising, said firmly: "Yes, I know that Judah has come home. I saw him at the gate the night before last asleep on the step. I saw you wake him."

Amrah clasped her hands.

"O my mistress! You saw it, and did not come!"

"That would have been to kill him. I can never take him in my arms again. I can never kiss him more. O Amrah, Amrah, you love him, I know!"

"Yes," said the true heart, bursting into tears again, and kneeling; "I would die for him."

"Prove to me what you say, Amrah."

"I am ready."

"Then you shall not tell him where we are or that you have seen us – only that, Amrah."

"But he is looking for you. He has come from afar to find you."

"He must not find us. He shall not become what we are. Hear, Amrah. You shall serve us as you have this day. You shall bring us the little we need – not long now – not long. You shall come every morning and evening thus, and – and" – the voice trembled, the strong will almost broke down – "and you shall tell us of him, Amrah; but to him you shall say nothing of us. Hear you?"

"Oh, it will be so hard to hear him speak of you, and see him going about looking for you – to see all his love, and not tell him so much as that you are alive!"

"Can you tell him we are well, Amrah?"

The servant bowed her head in her arms.

"No," the mistress continued; "wherefore be silent altogether. Go now, and come this evening. We will look for you. Till then, farewell."

"The burden will be heavy, O my mistress, and hard to bear," said Amrah, falling upon her face.

"How much harder would it be to see him as we are," the mother answered, as she gave the basket to Tirzah. "Come again this evening," she repeated, taking up the water, and starting for the tomb.

Amrah waited kneeling until they had disappeared; then she took the road sorrowfully home.

In the evening she returned; and thereafter it became her custom to serve them in the morning and evening, so that they wanted for nothing needful. The tomb, though ever so stony and desolate, was less cheerless than the cell in the Tower had been. Daylight gilded its door, and it was in the beautiful world.

ANOTHER FIGHT

The morning of the first day of the seventh month – Tishri in the Hebrew, October in English – Ben-Hur arose from his couch ill satisfied with the whole world.

Little time had been lost in consultation upon the arrival of Malluch. The latter began the search at the Tower of Antonia, and began it boldly, by a direct inquiry of the tribune commanding.

In reply the tribune stated circumstantially the discovery of the women in the Tower, and permitted a reading of the memorandum he had taken of their account of themselves; when leave to copy it was prayed, he even permitted that.

Malluch thereupon hurried to Ben-Hur.

It was useless to attempt description of the effect the terrible story had upon the young man. The pain was not relieved by tears or passionate outcries; it was too deep for any expression. He sat still a long time. Now and then, as if to show the thoughts which were most poignant, he muttered.

"Lepers, lepers! They – my mother and Tirzah – they lepers! How long, how long, O Lord!"

At length he arose.

"I must look for them. They may be dying."

Malluch interposed, and finally prevailed so far as to have the management of the further attempt entrusted to him. Together they went to the gate over on the side opposite the Hill of Evil Counsel, immemorially the lepers' begging-ground. There they stayed all day, giving alms, asking for the two women, and offering rich rewards for their discovery. So they did in repetition day after day through the remainder of the fifth month, and all the sixth. And now, the morning of the first day of the seventh month, the extent of the additional information gained was that not long before two leprous women had been stoned from the Fish Gate by the authorities.

Angry, hopeless, vengeful, he entered the court of the khan, and found it crowded with people come in during the night. While he ate his breakfast, he listened to some of them. To one party he was specially attracted. They were mostly young, stout, active, hardy men, in manner and speech provincial. In their look, the certain indefinable air, the pose of the head, glance of the eye, there was a spirit which did not, as a rule, belong to the outward seeming of the lower orders of Jerusalem; the spirit thought by some to be a peculiarity of life in moun-

HOLY WATER DISPENSER

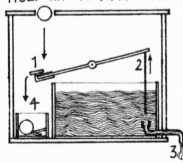

1 COIN FALLS ON DISC

2 LEVER RAISES ROD OUT OF PIPE

3 HOLYWATER IS RELEASED

4 COIN SLIDES OFF INTO COLLECTING BOX AND LEVER RETURNS TO HORIZONTAL, ROD CUTS OFF WATER SUPPLY UNTIL NEXT COIN IS INSERTED

tainous districts, but which may be more surely traced to a life of healthful freedom. In a short time he ascertained they were Galileans.

While observing them, his mind running ahead in thought of achievements possible to a legion of such spirits disciplined after the severe Roman style, a man came into the court, his face much flushed, his eyes bright with excitement.

"Why are you here?" he said to the Galileans. "The rabbis and elders are going from the Temple to see Pilate. Come, make haste, and let us go with them."

They surrounded him in a moment.

"To see Pilate! For what?"

"They have discovered a conspiracy. Pilate's new aqueduct is to be paid for with money of the Temple."

"What, with the sacred treasure?"

They repeated the question to each other with flashing eyes.

"It is Corban – money of God. Let him touch a shekel of it if he dare!"

"Come," cried the messenger. "The procession is by this time across the bridge. The whole city is pouring after. We may be needed. Make haste!"

Then Ben-Hur spoke to them.

"Men of Galilee," he said, "I am a son of Judah. Will you take me in your company?"

"We may have to fight," they replied.

"Oh, then, I will not be first to run away!"

They took the retort in good-humour, and the messenger said: "You seem stout enough. Come along."

Ben-Hur put off his outer garments.

"You think there may be fighting," he asked, quietly, as he tightened his girdle.

"Yes."

"With whom?"

"The guard."

"Legionaries?"

"Whom else can a Roman trust?"

To get to the Praetorium, as the Romans resonantly styled the palace of Herod on Mount Zion, the party had to cross the lowlands north and west of the Temple. When, at length, they reached the gate of the Praetorium, the procession of elders and rabbis had passed in with a great following, leaving a greater crowd clamouring outside.

A centurion kept the entrance with a guard drawn up full armed under the beautiful marble battlements. The sun struck the soldiers fervidly on helm and

shield; but they kept their ranks indifferent alike to its dazzle and to the mouthings of the rabble. Through the open bronze gates a current of citizens poured in, while a much lesser one poured out.

"What is going on?" one of the Galileans asked an out-comer.

"Nothing," was the reply. "The rabbis are before the door of the palace asking to see Pilate. He has refused to come out. They have sent one to tell him they will not go away till he has heard them. They are waiting."

Through the tree-tops shone the outer fronts of the palace. Turning to the right, the party proceeded a short distance to a spacious square, on the west side of which stood the residence of the governor. An excited multitude filled the square. Every face was directed towards a portico built over a broad doorway which was closed. Under the portico there was another array of legionaries.

And at last the end came. In the midst of the assemblage there was heard the sound of blows, succeeded instantly by yells of pain and rage, and a most furious commotion. The venerable men in front of the portico faced about aghast. The common people in the rear at first pushed forward; in the centre, the effort was to get out; and for a short time the pressure of opposing forces was terrible. A thousand voices made inquiry, raised all at once; as no one had time to answer, the surprise speedily became a panic.

Ben-Hur kept his senses.

"You cannot see," he said to one of the Galileans.

"No."

"I will raise you up."

He caught the man about the middle, and lifted him bodily.

"What is it?"

"I see now," said the man. "There are some armed with clubs, and they are beating the people. They are dressed like Jews."

"Who are they?"

"Romans, as the Lord liveth! Romans in disguise. Their clubs fly like flails! There, I saw a rabbi struck down – an old man! They spare nobody!"

Ben-Hur let the man down.

"Men of Galilee," he said, "it is a trick of Pilate's. Now, will you do what I say, we will get even with the club-men."

The Galilean spirit arose.

"Yes, yes!" they answered.

"Let us go back to the trees by the gate, and we may find the planting of Herod, though unlawful, has some good in it after all. Come!"

They ran back all of them fast as they could; and, by throwing their united weight upon the limbs, tore them from the trunks. In a brief time they, too, were armed. Returning, at the corner of the square they met the crowd rushing madly for the gate. Behind, the clamour continued – a medley of shrieks, groans, and execrations.

"To the wall!" Ben-Hur shouted. "To the wall! – and let the herd go by!"

So, clinging to the masonry at their right hand, they escaped the might of the rush, and little by little made headway until, at last, the square was reached.

"Keep together now, and follow me!"

By this time Ben-Hur's leadership was perfect; and as he pushed into the seething mob his party closed after him in a body. And when the Romans, clubbing the people and making merry as they struck them down, came hand to hand with the Galileans, lithe of limb, eager for the fray, and equally armed, they were in turn surprised. Thus surprised and equally matched, the Romans at first retired, but finally turned their backs and fled to the portico. The impetuous Galileans would have pursued them to the steps, but Ben-Hur wisely restrained them.

"Stay, my men," he said. "The centurion yonder is coming with the guard. They have swords and shields; we cannot fight them. We have done well; let us get back and out of the gate while we may."

The party were permitted to pass without challenge by the outer guard. But hardly were they out before the centurion in charge at the portico appeared, and in the gateway called to Ben-Hur:

"Ho, insolent! Art thou a Roman or a Jew?"

Ben-Hur answered: "I am a son of Judah, born here. What wouldst thou with me?"

"Stay and fight."

"Singly?"

"As thou wilt."

Ben-Hur laughed derisively.

"O brave Roman! Worthy son of the bastard Roman Jove! I have no arms."

"Thou shalt have mine," the centurion answered. "I will borrow of the guard here."

The people in hearing of the colloquy became silent; and from them the hush spread afar. But lately Ben-Hur had beaten a Roman under the eyes of Antioch and the Farther East; now, could he beat another one under the eyes of Jerusalem, the honour might be vastly profitable to the cause of the New King. He did not hesitate. Going frankly to the centurion, he said: "I am willing. Lend me thy sword and shield."

"And the helm and breastplate?" asked the Roman.

"Keep them. They might not fit me."

The arms were as frankly delivered, and directly the centurion was ready. All this time the soldiers in rank close by the gate never moved; they simply listened. As to the multitude, only when the combatants advanced to begin the fight the question sped from mouth to mouth, "Who is he?" And no one knew.

Now, the Roman supremacy in arms lay in three things – submission to discipline, the legionary formation of battle, and a peculiar use of the short sword. In combat, they never struck or cut; from first to last they thrust – they advanced thrusting, they retired thrusting; and generally their aim was at the foeman's face. All this was well known to Ben-Hur. As they were about to engage, he said:

"I told thee I was a son of Judah; but I did not tell that I am lanista-taught. Defend thyself!"

At the last word Ben-Hur closed with his antagonist. A moment, standing foot to foot, they glared at each other over the rims of their embossed shields; then the Roman pushed forward and feinted an under-thrust. The Jew laughed at him. A thrust at the face followed. The Jew stepped lightly to the left; quick as the thrust was, the step was quicker. Under the lifted arm of the foe he slid his shield, advancing it until the sword and sword-arm were both caught on its upper surface; another step, this time forward and left, and the man's whole right side was offered to the point. The centurion fell heavily on his breast, clanging the pavement, and Ben-Hur had won. With his foot upon his enemy's back, he raised his shield overhead after a gladiatorial custom, and saluted the imperturbable soldiers by the gate.

When the people realized the victory, they behaved like mad. On the houses far as the Xystus, fast as the word could fly, they waved their shawls and hand-

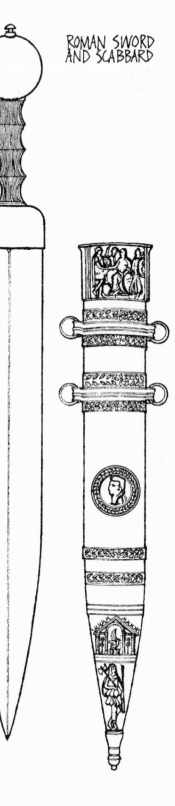

ROMAN SWORD AND SCABBARD

kerchiefs and shouted; and if he had consented, the Galileans would have carried Ben-Hur off upon their shoulders.

To a petty officer who then advanced from the gate he said: "Thy comrade died like a soldier. I leave him undespoiled. Only his sword and shield are mine."

ROMAN DAGGER AND SCABBARD

BOOK SEVEN

BEN HUR JOINS THE GALILEANS

The meeting took place in the khan of Bethany as appointed. Thence Ben-Hur went with the Galileans into their country, where his exploits up in the old market-place gave him fame and influence. Before the winter was gone he raised three legions, and organized them after the Roman pattern.

So with Ben-Hur the winter months rolled by, and spring came, with gladdening showers blown over from the summering sea in the west; and by that time so earnestly and successfully had he toiled that he could say to himself and his followers, "Let the good King come. He has only to tell us where He will have His throne set up. We have the sword-hands to keep it for Him."

*   *   *

One evening, over in Trachonitis, Ben-Hur was sitting with some of his Galileans at the mouth of the cave in which he quartered, when an Arab courier rode to him, and delivered a letter. Breaking the package, he read:

"Jerusalem, Nisan IV.
"A prophet has appeared who men say is Elias. He has been in the wilderness for years, and to our eyes he is a prophet; and such also is his speech, the burden of which is of one much greater than himself, who, he says, is to come presently, and for whom he is now waiting on the eastern shore of the River Jordan. I have been to see and hear him, and the one he is waiting for is certainly the King you are awaiting. Come and judge for yourself.
"All Jerusalem is going out to the prophet, and with many people else the shore on which he abides is like Mount Olivet in the last days of the Passover.
          *"*MALLUCH.*"*

Ben-Hur's face flushed with joy.

"By this word, O my friends," he said – "by this word, our waiting is at end. The herald of the King has appeared and announced Him."

Upon hearing the letter read, they also rejoiced at the promise it held out.

"Get ready now," he added, "and in the morning set your faces homeward; when arrived there, send word to those under you, and bid them be ready to assemble as I may direct. For myself and you, I will go see if the King be indeed at hand, and send you report. Let us, in the meantime,

With that, he walked away. Off a little he spoke to the Galileans:

"Brethren, you have behaved well. Let us now separate, lest we be pursued. Meet me tonight at the khan in Bethany. I have something to propose to you of great interest to Israel."

"Who are you?" they asked him.

"A son of Judah," he answered, simply.

A throng eager to see him surged around the party.

"Will you come to Bethany?" he asked.

"Yes, we will come."

"Then bring with you this sword and shield that I may know you."

Pushing brusquely through the increasing crowd, he speedily disappeared.

87

live in the pleasure of the promise."

Going into the cave, he addressed a letter to Ilderim, and another to Simonides, giving notice of the news received, and of his purpose to go up immediately to Jerusalem. The letters he despatched by swift messengers. When night fell, and the stars of direction came out, he mounted, and with an Arab guide set out for the Jordan, intending to strike the track of the caravans between Rabbath-Ammon and Damascus.

The guide was sure, and Aldebaran swift; so by midnight the two were out of the lava fastness speeding southward.

BALTHASAR RETURNS

It was Ben-Hur's purpose to turn aside at the break of day, and find a safe place in which to rest; but the dawn overtook him while out in the Desert, and he kept on, the guide promising to bring him afterwhile to a vale shut in by great rocks, where there were a spring, some mulberry-trees, and herbage in plenty for the horses.

As he rode thinking of the wondrous events so soon to happen, and of the changes they were to bring about in the affairs of men and nations, the guide, ever on the alert, called attention to an appearance of strangers behind them.

"It is a camel with riders," the guide said, directly.

"Are there others behind?" said Ben-Hur.

"It is alone. No, there is a man on horseback – the driver, probably."

A little later Ben-Hur himself could see the camel was white and unusually large, reminding him of the wonderful animal he had seen bring Balthasar and Iras to the fountain in the Grove of Daphne. But while he debated the question the long swinging stride of the camel brought its riders up to him. The tall brute stopped close by his horse, and Ben-Hur, looking up, lo! Iras herself under the raised curtain looking down at him, her great swimming eyes bright with astonishment and inquiry!

"The blessing of the true God upon you!" said Balthasar, in his tremulous voice.

"And to thee and thine be the peace of the Lord," Ben-Hur replied.

"My eyes are weak with years," said Balthasar; "but they approve you that son of Hur whom lately I knew an honoured guest in the tent of Ilderim the Generous."

"And thou art that Balthasar, the wise Egyptian, whose speech concerning certain holy things in expectation is having so much to do with the finding me in this waste place."

Afterwhile the party came to a shallow wady, down which, turning to the right hand, the guide led them. The bed of the cut was somewhat soft from recent rains, and quite bold in its descent. Momentarily, however, it widened; and ere long the sides became bluffs ribbed with rocks much scarred by floods rushing to lower depths ahead. Finally, from a narrow passage, the travellers entered a spreading vale which was very delightful; but come upon suddenly from the yellow, unrelieved, verdureless plain, it had the effect of a freshly discovered Paradise.

The water started from a crack in the cliff which some loving hand had enlarged into an arched cavity. Graven over it in bold Hebraic letters was the word GOD.

CAMEL WITH HOUDAH

"Bring me a cup," Iras said, with some impatience.

From the houdah the slave brought her a crystal goblet; then she said to Ben-Hur: "I will be your servant at the fountain."

They walked to the pool together. He would have dipped the water for her, but she refused his offer, and kneeling, held the cup to be filled by the stream itself; nor yet content, when it was cooled and overrunning, she tendered him the first draught.

"No," he said, putting the graceful hand aside, and seeing only the large eyes half hidden beneath the arches of the upraised brows, "be the service mine, I pray."

Part of the contents of the cup she returned to the stream, the rest she drank. When she took the crystal from her lips, she laughed at him.

"O son of Hur, is it a fashion of the very brave to be so easily overcome by a woman? Take the cup now, and see if you cannot find a happy word in it for me?"

He took the cup, and stooped to refill it.

"Most fair, were I an Egyptian or a Greek or a Roman, I would say" – he raised the goblet overhead as he spoke – "O ye better gods! I give thanks that there are yet left to the world, despite its wrongs and sufferings, the charm of beauty and the solace of love, and I drink to her who best represents them – to Iras, loveliest of the daughters of the Nile!"

She laid her hand softly upon his shoulder.

"You have offended against the law. The gods you have drunk to are false gods. Why shall I not tell the rabbis on you?"

"Oh!" he replied, laughing, "that is very little to tell for one who knows so much else that is really important."

"I will go further – I will go to the little Jewess who makes the roses grow and the shadows flame in the house of the great merchant over in Antioch. To the rabbis I will accuse you of impenitence; to her——"

"Well, to her?"

He was still a moment, as if waiting for the Egyptian to go on. With quickened fancy he saw Esther at her father's side listening to the despatches he had forwarded – sometimes reading them. In her presence he had told Simonides the story of the affair in the Palace of Idernee. She and Iras were acquainted; this one was shrewd and worldly; the other was simple and affectionate, and therefore easily won. Simonides could not have broken faith – nor Ilderim – for if not held by honour, there was no one, unless it might be himself, to whom the consequences of exposure were more serious and certain. Could Esther have been the Egyptian's informant? He did not accuse her; yet a suspicion was sown with the thought, and suspicions, as we all know, are weeds of the mind which grow of themselves, and most rapidly when least wanted. Before he could answer the allusion to the little Jewess, Balthasar came to the pool.

"We are greatly indebted to you, son of Hur," he said, in his grave manner. "This vale is very beautiful; the grass, the trees, the shade, invite us to stay and rest, and the spring here has the sparkle of diamonds in motion, and sings to me of a loving God. It is not enough to thank you for the enjoyment we find; come sit with us, and taste our bread."

"Suffer me first to serve you."

With that Ben-Hur filled the goblet, and gave it to Balthasar, who lifted his eyes in thanksgiving.

Immediately the slave brought napkins; and after laving their hands and drying them, the three seated themselves in Eastern style under the tent which years before had served the Wise Men at the meeting in the Desert. And they ate heartily of the good things taken from the camel's pack.

A SAVIOUR OR A KING

The tent was cosily pitched beneath a tree where the gurgle of the stream was constantly in ear. The restfulness of the vale, the freshness of the air, the garden beauty, the Sabbath stillness, seemed to have affected the spirits of the elder Egyptian.

"I am impatient," said Balthasar. "Latterly my sleep has been visited by dreams – or rather by the same dream in repetition. A voice – it is nothing more – comes and tells me, 'Haste – arise! He whom thou hast so long awaited is at hand.'"

"You mean He that is to be King of the Jews?" Ben-Hur asked, gazing at the Egyptian in wonder.

"Even so."

"Then you have heard nothing of Him?"

"Nothing, except the words of the voice in the dream."

"Here, then, are tidings to make you glad as they made me."

From his gown Ben-Hur drew the letter received from Malluch. The hand the Egyptian held out trembled violently. He read aloud, and as he read his feelings increased; the limp veins in his neck swelled and throbbed. At the conclusion he raised his suffused eyes in thanksgiving and prayer. He asked no questions, yet had no doubts.

"Thou hast been very good to me, O God," he said. "Give me, I pray thee, to see the Saviour again, and worship Him, and thy servant will be ready to go in peace."

The words, the manner, the singular personality of the simple prayer, touched Ben-Hur with a sensation new and abiding.

The company sat a moment in silence, which was broken by Balthasar.

"Let us rise and set forward again. What I have said has caused a return of impatience to see Him who is ever in my thought; and if I seem to hurry you, O son of Hur – and you, my daughter – be that my excuse."

At his signal the slave brought them wine in a skin bottle; and they poured and drank, and, shaking the lapcloths out, arose.

While the slave restored the tent and wares to the box under the houdah, and the Arab brought up the horses, the three principals laved themselves in the pool.

In a little while they were retracing their steps back through the wady, intending to overtake the caravan if it had passed by them.

THE NIGHTWATCH IN THE DESERT

The caravan, stretched out upon the Desert, was very picturesque; in motion, however, it was like a lazy serpent. By-and-by its stubborn dragging became intolerably irksome to Balthasar, patient as he was; so, at his suggestion, the party determined to go on by themselves.

To be definite as may be, and perfectly confidential, Ben-Hur found a certain charm in Iras's presence. If she looked down upon him from her high place, he made haste to get near her; if she spoke to him, his heart beat out of its usual time. The desire to be agreeable to her was a constant impulse.

And so to them the nooning came, and the evening.

The sun at its going down behind a spur of the old Bashan, left the party halted by a pool of clear water of the rains out in the Abilene Desert. There the tent was pitched, the supper eaten, and preparations made for the night.

The second watch was Ben-Hur's; and he was standing, spear in hand, within arm-reach of the dozing camel, looking awhile at the stars, then over the veiled land. The stillness was intense; only after long spells a warm breath of wind would sough past, but without disturbing him, for yet in thought he entertained the Egyptian, recounting her charms, and sometimes debating how she came by his secrets, the uses she might make of them, and the course he should pursue with her. And through all the debate Love stood off but a little way – a strong temptation, the stronger of a gleam of policy behind. At the very moment he was most inclined to yield to the allurement, a hand very fair even in the moonless gloaming was laid softly upon his shoulder. The touch thrilled him; he started, turned – and she was there.

"I thought you asleep," he said, presently.

"Son of Hur!" – she lowered her voice, and going nearer, spoke so her breath was warm upon his cheek – "son of Hur! He thou art going to find is to be King of the Jews, is He not?"

His heart beat fast and hard.

"A King of the Jews like Herod, only greater," she continued.

He looked away – into the night, up to the stars; then his eyes met hers, and lingered there.

"Since morning," she said, further, "we have been having visions. Now if I tell you mine, will you serve me as well? What! silent still?"

She pushed his hand away, and turned as if to go; but he caught her, and said, eagerly: "Stay – stay and speak!"

She went back, and, with her hand upon his shoulder, leaned against him; and he put his arm around her, and drew her close, very close; and in the caress was the promise she asked.

"Speak, and tell me thy visions, O Egypt, dear Egypt! A prophet – nay, not the Tishbite, not even the Lawgiver – could have refused an asking of thine. I am at thy will. Be merciful – merciful, I pray."

The entreaty passed apparently unheard, for, looking up and nestling in his embrace, she said, slowly: "The vision which followed me was of magnificent war – war on land and sea – with clashing of arms and rush of armies, as if Caesar and Pompey were come again, and Octavius and Antony. A cloud of dust and ashes arose and covered the world, and Rome was not any more; all dominion returned to the East; out of the cloud issued another race of heroes; and there were vaster satrapies and brighter crowns for giving away than were ever known. And, son of Hur, while the vision was passing, and after it was gone, I kept asking myself, 'What shall he not have who served the King earliest and best?'"

Again Ben-Hur recoiled. The question was the very question which had been with him all day. Presently he fancied he had the clue he wanted.

"So," he said, "I have you now. The satrapies and crowns are the things to which you would help me. I see, I see! And there never was such queen as you would be, so shrewd, so beautiful, so royal – never! But, alas, dear Egypt! by the vision as you show it me the prizes are all of war, and you are but a woman, though Isis did kiss you on the heart."

"You will find the King," she said, placing her hand caressingly upon his head. "You will go on and find the King and serve Him. With your sword you will earn His richest gifts; and his best soldier will be my hero."

He turned his face, and saw hers close

above. In all the sky there was that moment nothing so bright to him as her eyes, enshadowed though they were. Presently he put his arms about her, and kissed her passionately, saying, "O Egypt, Egypt! If the King has crowns in gift, one shall be mine; and I will bring it and put it here over the place my lips have marked. You shall be a queen – my queen – no one more beautiful. And we will be ever, ever so happy!"

"And you will tell me everything, and let me help you in all?" she said, kissing him in return.

The question chilled his fervour.

"Is it not enough that I love you?" he asked.

"Perfect love means perfect faith," she replied. "But never mind – you will know me better."

She took her hand from him.

"You are cruel," he said.

Moving away, she stopped by the camel, and touched its front face with her lips.

"O thou noblest of thy kind! – that, because there is no suspicion in thy love."

An instant, and she was gone.

A MAN OUT OF THE WILDERNESS

The third day of the journey the party nooned by the river Jabbok, where there were a hundred or more men, mostly of Peraea, resting themselves and their beasts. Hardly had they dismounted, before a man came to them with a pitcher of water and a bowl, and offered them drink; as they received the attention with much courtesy, he said, looking at the camel, "I am returning from the Jordan, where just now there are many people from distant parts, travelling as you are, illustrious friend; but they had none of them the equal of your servant here. A very noble animal. May I ask of what breed he is sprung?"

Balthasar answered, and sought his rest; but Ben-Hur, more curious, took up the remark.

"At what place on the river are the people?" he asked.

"At Bethabara."

"It used to be a lonesome ford," said Ben-Hur. "I cannot understand how it can have become of such interest."

"I see," the stranger replied; "you, too, are from abroad, and have not heard the good tidings."

"What tidings?"

"Well, a man has appeared out of the wilderness – a very holy man – with his mouth full of strange words, which take hold of all who hear them. He calls himself John the Nazarite, son of Zacharias, and says he is the messenger sent before the Messiah."

Even Iras listened closely while the man continued:

"They say of this John that he has spent his life from childhood in a cave down by En-gedi, praying and living more strictly than the Essenes. Crowds go to hear him preach. I went to hear him with the rest."

"Have all these, your friends, been there?"

"Most of them are going; a few are coming away."

"What does he preach?"

"A new doctrine – one never before taught in Israel, as all say. He calls it repentance and baptism. The rabbis do not know what to make of him; nor do we. Some have asked him if he is the Christ, others if he is Elias; but to them all he has the answer, 'I am the voice of one crying in the wilderness, Make straight the way of the Lord!'"

At this point the man was called away by his friends; as he was going, Balthasar spoke.

"Good stranger!" he said, tremulously, "tell us if we shall find the preacher at the place you left him."

"Yes, at Bethabara."

"Who should this Nazarite be?" said Ben-Hur to Iras, "if not the herald of our King?"

In so short a time he had come to regard the daughter as more interested in the mysterious personage he was looking for than the aged father! Nevertheless, the latter, with a positive glow in his sunken eyes, half arose, and said:

"Let us make haste I am not tired,"

They turned away to help the slave.

There was little conversation between the three at the stopping-place for the night west of Ramoth-Gilead.

"Let us arise early, son of Hur," said the old man. "The Saviour may come, and we not there."

"The King cannot be far behind his herald," Iras whispered, as she prepared to take her place on the camel.

"Tomorrow we will see!" Ben-Hur replied, kissing her hand.

Next day about the third hour, out of the pass through which, skirting the base of Mount Gilead, they had journeyed since leaving Ramoth, the party came upon the barren steppe east of the sacred river. Opposite them they saw the upper limit of the old palm lands of Jericho, stretching off to the hill-country of Judea. Ben-Hur's blood ran quickly, for he knew the ford was close at hand.

"Content you, good Balthasar," he said; "we are almost there."

The driver quickened the camel's pace. Soon they caught sight of booths and tents and tethered animals; and then of the river, and a multitude collected down close by the bank, and yet another multitude on the western shore. Knowing that the preacher was preaching, they made greater haste; yet, as they were drawing near, suddenly there was a commotion in the mass, and it began to break up and disperse.

They were too late!

"Let us stay here," said Ben-Hur to Balthasar, who was wringing his hands. "The Nazarite may come this way."

The people were too intent upon what they had heard, and too busy in discussion, to notice the new-comers. When some hundreds were gone by, and it seemed the opportunity to so much as see the Nazarite was lost to the latter, up the river not far away they beheld a person coming towards them of such singular appearance they forgot all else.

Outwardly the man was rude and uncouth, even savage. Over a thin, gaunt visage of the hue of brown parchment, over his shoulders and down his back below the middle, in witch-like locks, fell a covering of sun-scorched hair. His eyes were burning-bright. All his right side was naked, and of the colour of his face, and quite as meagre; a shirt of the coarsest camel's hair – coarse as Bedouin tent-cloth – clothed the rest of his person to the knees, being gathered at the waist by a broad girdle of untanned leather. His feet were bare. A scrip, also of untanned leather, was fastened to the girdle. He used a knotted staff to help him forward. His movement was quick, decided, and strangely watchful. Every little while he tossed the unruly hair from his eyes, and peered round as if searching for somebody.

The fair Egyptian surveyed the son of the Desert with surprise, not to say disgust. Presently, raising the curtain of the houdah, she spoke to Ben-Hur, who sat his horse near by.

"Is that the herald of thy King?"

"It is the Nazarite," he replied, without looking up.

In this time of such interest to the new-comers, and in which they were so differently moved, another man had been sitting by himself on a stone at the edge of the river, thinking yet, probably, of the sermon he had been hearing. Now, however, he arose, and walked slowly up from the shore, in a course to take him across the line the Nazarite was pursuing and bring him near the camel.

And the two – the preacher and the stranger – kept on until they came, the former within twenty yards of the animal, the latter within ten feet. Then the preacher stopped, and flung the hair from his eyes, looked at the stranger, threw his hands up as a signal to all the people in sight; and they also stopped, each in the pose of a listener; and when the hush was perfect, slowly the staff in the Nazarite's right hand came down pointed at the stranger.

All those who before were but listeners became watchers also.

At the same instant, under the same impulse, Balthasar and Ben-Hur fixed their gaze upon the man pointed out, and both took the same impression, only in different degree. He was moving slowly towards them in a clear space a little to their front, a form slightly above the average in stature, and slender, even delicate. His action was calm and deliberate, like that habitual to men given to serious thought upon grave subjects; and it well became his costume, which was an undergarment full-sleeved and reaching to the ankles, and an outer robe called the talith; on his left arm he carried the usual handkerchief for the head, the red fillet swinging loose down his side.

These points of appearance, however, the three beholders observed briefly, and rather as accessories to the head and face of the man, which – especially the latter – were the real sources of the spell they caught in common with all who stood looking at him.

The head was open to the cloudless light, except as it was draped with hair long and slightly waved, and parted in the middle, and auburn in tint, with a tendency to reddish golden where most strongly touched by the sun. Under a broad, low forehead, under black well-arched brows, beamed eyes dark-blue and large, and softened to exceeding tenderness by lashes of the great length sometimes seen on children, but seldom, if ever, on men. As to the other features, it would have been difficult to decide whether they were Greek or Jewish. The delicacy of the nostrils and mouth was unusual to the latter type; and when it was taken into account with the gentleness of the eyes, the pallor of the complexion, the fine texture of the hair, and the softness of the beard, which fell in waves over his throat to his breast, never a soldier but would have laughed at him in encounter, never a woman who would not have confided in him at sight, never a child that would not, with quick instinct, have given him its hand and whole artless trust; nor might any one have said he was not beautiful.

Slowly he drew near – nearer the three.

Now Ben-Hur, mounted and spear in hand, was an object to claim the glance of a king; yet the eyes of the man approaching were all the time raised above him – and not to Iras, whose loveliness has been so often remarked, but to Balthasar, the old and unserviceable. The hush was profound.

Presently the Nazarite, still pointing with his staff, cried, in a loud voice:

"Behold the Lamb of God, which takest away the sin of the world!"

Balthasar fell upon his knees. For him there was no need of explanation; and as if the Nazarite knew it, he turned to those more immediately about him staring in wonder, and continued:

"This is He of whom I said, After me cometh a Man which is preferred before me. I bare record, that this is the *Son of God!*"

"It is He, it is He!" Balthasar cried, with upraised tearful eyes. Next moment he sank down insensible.

In this time, it should be remembered, Ben-Hur was studying the face of the stranger, though with an interest entirely different. He was not insensible to its purity of feature, and its thoughtfulness; but just then there was room in his mind for but one thought – Who is this man? And what? Messiah or king? Never was apparition more unroyal. Nay, looking at that calm, benignant countenance, the very idea of war and conquest, the lust of dominion, smote him like a profanation. He said, as if speaking to his own heart, Balthasar must be right and Simonides wrong. This man has not come to rebuild the throne of Solomon; He has neither the nature nor the genius of Herod; king He may be, but not of another and greater than Rome.

It should be understood now that this was not a conclusion with Ben-Hur, but an impression merely; and while it was forming, while yet he gazed at the wonderful countenance, his memory began to throe and struggle. "Surely," he said to himself, "I have seen the man; but where and when?" That the look, so calm, so pitiful, so loving, had somewhere in a past time beamed upon him as that moment it was beaming upon Balthasar became an assurance. Faintly at first, at last a clear light, a burst of sunshine, the scene by the well at

Nazareth what time the Roman guard was dragging him to the galleys returned, and all his being thrilled. Those hands had helped him when he was perishing. The face was one of the pictures he had carried in mind ever since. In the effusion of feeling excited, the explanation of the preacher was lost by him, all but the last words – words so marvellous that the world yet rings with them:

"This is the *Son of God!*"

Ben-Hur leaped from his horse to render homage to his benefactor; but Iras cried to him, "Help, son of Hur, help, or my father will die!"

He stopped, looked back, then hurried to her assistance. She gave him a cup; and leaving the slave to bring the camel to its knees, he ran to the river for water. The stranger was gone when he came back.

At last Balthasar was restored to consciousness. Stretching forth his hands, he asked, feebly: "Where is He?"

"Who?" asked Iras.

An intense instant interest shone upon the good man's face, as if a last wish had been gratified, and he answered:

"He – the Redeemer – the Son of God, whom I have seen again."

"Believest thou so?" Iras asked in a low voice of Ben-Hur.

"The time is full of wonders; let us wait," was all he said.

And next day while the three were listening to him, the Nazarite broke off in mid-speech, saying reverently: "Behold the Lamb of God!"

Looking to where he pointed, they beheld the stranger again. As Ben-Hur surveyed the slender figure, and holy beautiful countenance, compassionate to sadness, a new idea broke upon him.

"Balthasar is right – so is Simonides. May not the Redeemer be a king also?"

And he asked one at his side: "Who is the man walking yonder?"

The other laughed, and replied:

"He is the son of a carpenter over in Nazareth."

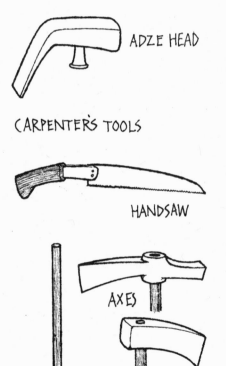

CARPENTER'S TOOLS

ADZE HEAD

HANDSAW

AXES

HAMMER

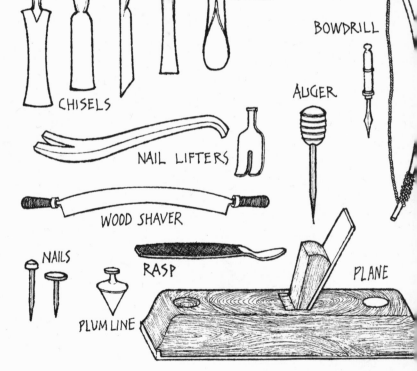

CHISELS

GOUGE

BOWDRILL

AUGER

NAIL LIFTERS

WOOD SHAVER

NAILS

RASP

PLANE

PLUM LINE

BOOK EIGHT

NO MESSAGE FOR ESTHER

"Esther – Esther! Speak to the servant below that he may bring me a cup of water."

"Would you not rather have wine, father?"

"Let him bring both."

This was in the summer-house upon the roof of the old palace of the Hurs, in Jerusalem. From the parapet overlooking the courtyard Esther called to a man-in-waiting there; at the same moment another man-servant came up the steps and saluted respectfully.

"A package for the master," he said, giving her a letter enclosed in linen cloth, tied and sealed.

For the satisfaction of the reader, we stop to say that it is the twenty-first day of March, nearly three years after the annunciation of the Christ at Bethabara.

In the meanwhile, Malluch, acting for Ben-Hur, who could not longer endure the emptiness and decay of his father's house, had bought it from Pontius Pilate; and, had it cleansed and thoroughly restored; not only was there no reminder left of the tragic circumstances so ruinous to the family, but the refurnishment was in a style richer than before. At every point, indeed, a visitor was met by evidences of the higher tastes acquired by the young proprietor during his years of residence in the villa by Misenum and in the Roman capital.

Now it should not be inferred from this explanation that Ben-Hur had publicly assumed ownership of the property. In his opinion, the hour for that was not yet come. Neither had he yet taken his proper name. Passing the time in the labours of preparation in Galilee, he waited patiently the action of the Nazarene, who became daily more and more a mystery to him, and by prodigies done, often before his eyes, kept him in a state of anxious doubt both as to His character and mission. Occasionally he came up to the Holy City, stopping at the paternal house; always, however, as a stranger and a guest.

These visits of Ben-Hur, it should also be observed, were for more than mere rest from labour. Balthasar and Iras made their home in the palace; and the charm of the daughter was still upon him with all its original freshness, while the father, though feebler in body, held him an unflagging listener to speeches of astonishing power, urging the divinity of the wandering miracle-worker of whom they were all so expectant.

As to Simonides and Esther, they had arrived from Antioch only a few days before this their reappearance – a wearisome journey to the merchant, borne, as he had been, in a palanquin swung between two camels, which, in their careening, did not always keep the same step.

As Esther started in return to the summer-house, the sunlight fell softly upon the dustless roof, showing her a woman now – small, graceful in form, of regular features, rosy with youth and health, bright with intelligence, beautiful with the outshining of a devoted nature – a woman to be loved because loving was a habit of life irrepressible with her.

She looked at the package as she turned, paused, looked at it a second time more closely than at first; and the blood rose reddening her cheeks – the seal was Ben-Hur's. With quickened steps she hastened on.

Simonides held the package a moment while he also inspected the seal. Breaking it open, he gave her the roll it contained. "Read," he said.

She began at once, in haste to conclude the distasteful subject.

"*Nisan, 8th day.*
"*On the road from Galilee to Jerusalem.*
"*The Nazarene is on the way also. With him, though without his knowledge, I am bringing a full legion of mine. A second legion follows. The Passover will excuse the multitude. He said upon setting out, 'We will go up to Jerusalem, and all things that are written by the prophets concerning me shall be accomplished.'*
"*Our waiting draws to an end.*
"*In haste.*
"*Peace to thee, Simonides.*

"BEN-HUR."

Esther returned the letter to her father, while a choking sensation gathered in her throat. There was not a word in the missive for her – not even in the salutation had she a share – and it would have been so easy to have written, "and to thine, peace." For the first time in her life she felt the smart of a jealous sting.

"The eighth day," said Simonides, "the

93

eighth day; and this, Esther, this is the——"

"The ninth," she replied.

"Ah, then, they may be in Bethany now."

"And possibly we may see him tonight," she added, pleased into momentary forgetfulness.

"It may be, it may be! Tomorrow is the Feast of Unleavened Bread, and he may wish to celebrate it, so may the Nazarene, and we may see him – we may see both of them, Esther."

At this point the servant appeared with the wine and water. Esther helped her father, and in the midst of the service Iras came upon the roof.

To the Jewess the Egyptian never appeared so very, very beautiful as at that moment.

"Peace to you, Simonides, and to the pretty Esther peace," said Iras, inclining her head to the latter.

They went to the parapet then, stopping at the place where, years before, Ben-Hur loosed the broken tile upon the head of Gratus.

"You have not been to Rome?" Iras began, toying the while with one of her unclasped bracelets.

"No," said Esther, demurely.

"Have you not wished to go?"

"No."

"Ah, how little there has been of your life!"

The sigh that succeeded the exclamation could not have been more piteously expressive had the loss been the Egyptian's own. Next moment her laugh might have been heard in the street below; and she said, "Oh, oh, my pretty simpleton! The half-fledged birds nested in the ear of the great bust out on the Memphian sands know nearly as much as you."

Another laugh, masking excellently the look she turned sharply upon the Jewess, and she said: "The King is coming."

Esther gazed at her in innocent surprise.

"The Nazarene," Iras continued – "He whom our fathers have been talking about so much, whom Ben-Hur has been serving and toiling for so long" – her voice dropped several tones lower – "the Nazarene will be here tomorrow, and Ben-Hur tonight."

Esther struggled to maintain her composure, but failed; her eyes fell, the telltale blood surged to her cheek and fore-head, and she was saved sight of the triumphant smile that passed, like a gleam, over the face of the Egyptian.

"See, here is his promise."

And from her girdle she took a roll.

"Rejoice with me, O my friend! He will be here tonight! On the Tiber there is a house, a royal property, which he has pledged to me; and to be its mistress is to be——"

A sound of someone walking swiftly along the street below interrupted the speech, and she leaned over the parapet to see. Then she drew back, and cried, with hands clasped above her head: "Now blessed be Isis! 'Tis he – Ben-Hur himself! That he should appear while I had such thought of him! There are no gods if it be not a good omen. Put your arms about me, Esther – and a kiss!"

The Jewess looked up. Upon each cheek there was a glow; her eyes sparkled with a light more nearly of anger than ever her nature emitted before. Her gentleness had been too roughly overridden.

"Dost thou love him so much, then, or Rome so much better?"

The Egyptian drew back a step; then she bent her haughty head quite near her questioner.

"What is he to thee, daughter of Simonides?"

Esther, all thrilling, began: "He is my——"

A thought blasting as lightning stayed the words; she paled, trembled, recovered, and answered:

"He is my father's friend."

Her tongue had refused to admit her servile condition.

Iras laughed more lightly than before.

"Not more than that?" she said. "Ah, by the lover-gods of Egypt, thou mayst keep thy kisses – keep them. Thou hast taught me but now that there are others vastly more estimable waiting me here in Judea; and" – she turned away, looking back over her shoulder – "I will go get them. Peace to thee."

Esther saw her disappear down the steps, when, putting her hands over her face, she burst into tears so they ran scalding through her fingers – tears of shame and choking passion.

And all the stars were out, burning low above the city and the dark wall of mountains about it, before she recovered enough to go back to the summer-house, and in silence take her accustomed place at her father's side, humbly waiting his pleasure.

THE MIRACLE WORKER

An hour or thereabouts after the scene upon the roof, Balthasar and Simonides, the latter attended by Esther, met in the great chamber of the palace; and while they were talking, Ben-Hur and Iras came in together.

The young Jew, advancing in front of his companion, walked first to Balthasar, and saluted him, and received his reply; then he turned to Simonides, but paused at sight of Esther.

For an instant he was startled; but recovering, he went to Esther, and said: "Peace to thee, sweet Esther – peace; and thou, Simonides" – he looked to the merchant as he spoke – "the blessing of the Lord be thine, if only because thou hast been a good father to the fatherless."

When seated, after some other conversation, he addressed himself to the men.

"I have come to tell you of the Nazarene."

The two became instantly attentive.

"For many days now I have followed Him with such watchfulness as one may give another upon whom he is waiting so anxiously. I have seen Him under all circumstances said to be trials and tests of men; and while I am certain He is a man as I am, not less certain am I that He is something more."

"What more?" asked Simonides.

"I will tell you——"

Someone coming into the room interrupted him; he turned, and arose with extended hands.

"Amrah! Dear old Amrah!" he cried.

She came forward; and they, seeing the joy in her face, thought not once how wrinkled and tawny it was. She knelt at his feet, clasped his knees, and kissed his hands over and over; and when he could he put the lank grey hair from her cheeks, and kissed them, saying: "Good Amrah, have you nothing, nothing of them – not a word – not one little sign?"

Then she broke into sobbing which

made him answer plainer even than the spoken word.

"God's will has been done," he next said, solemnly, in a tone to make each listener know he had no hope more of finding his people. In his eyes there were tears which he would not have them see, because he was a man.

When he could again, he took seat, and said: "Come, sit by me, Amrah – here. No? then at my feet; for I have much to say to these good friends of a wonderful man come into the world."

But she went off, and, stooping with her back to the wall, joined her hands before her knees, content, they all thought, with seeing him. Then Ben-Hur, bowing to the old men, began again:

"I fear to answer the question asked me about the Nazarene without first telling you some of the things I have seen Him do. He brings twelve men with Him, fishermen, tillers of the soil, one a publican, all of the humbler class; and He and they make their journeys on foot, careless of wind, cold, rain, or sun. Seeing them stop by the wayside at nightfall to break bread or lie down to sleep, I have been reminded of a party of shepherds going back to their flocks from market, not of nobles and kings. Only when He lifts the corners of His handkerchief to look at someone or shake the dust from His head, I am made know He is their teacher as well as their companion – their superior not less than their friend.

"You are shrewd men." Ben-Hur resumed, after a pause. "You know what creatures of certain master motives we are, and that it has become little less than a law of our nature to spend life in eager pursuit of certain objects; now, appealing to that law as something by which we may know ourselves, what would you say of a man who could be rich by making gold of the stones under his feet, yet is poor of choice?"

"The Greeks would call him a philosopher," said Iras.

"Nay, daughter," said Balthasar, "the philosophers had never the power to do such thing."

"How know you this man has?"

"What would you say," said Ben-Hur, with increased earnestness – "what would you say to have seen that I now tell you? A leper came to the Nazarene while I was with Him down in Galilee, and said, 'Lord, if Thou wilt, Thou canst make me clean.' He heard the cry, and touched the

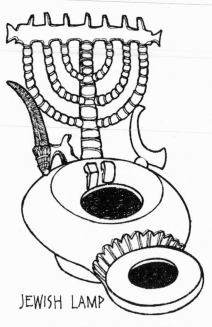

JEWISH LAMP

outcast with His hand, saying, 'Be thou clean;' and forthwith the man was himself again, healthful as any of us who beheld the cure, and we were a multitude."

Here Amrah arose, and with her gaunt fingers held the wiry locks from her eyes. The brain of the poor creature had long since gone to heart, and she was troubled to follow the speech.

"Then, again," said Ben-Hur, without stop, "ten lepers came to Him one day in a body, and falling at His feet, called out – I saw and heard it all – called out, 'Master, Master, have mercy upon us!' He told them, 'Go, show yourselves to the priest, as the law requires; and before you are come there ye shall be healed.'"

"And were they?"

"Yes. On the road going their infirmity left them, so that there was nothing to remind us of it except their polluted clothes."

"Such thing was never heard before – never in all Israel!" said Simonides, in undertone.

And then, while he was speaking, Amrah turned away, and walked noiselessly to the door, and went out; and none of the company saw her go.

"Mark you," Ben-Hur proceeded, "I do but tell you things of which I was a witness, together with a cloud of other men. On the way hither I saw another act still more mighty. In Bethany there was a man named Lazarus, who died and

was buried; and after he had lain four days in a tomb, shut in by a great stone, the Nazarene was shown to the place. Upon rolling the stone away, we beheld the man lying inside bound and rotting. There were many people standing by, and we all heard what the Nazarene said, for He spoke in a loud voice: 'Lazarus, come forth!' I cannot tell you my feelings when in answer, as it were, the man arose and came out to us with all his cerements about him. 'Loose him,' said the Nazarene next, 'loose him, and let him go.' And when the napkin was taken from the face of the resurrected, lo, my friends! the blood ran anew through the wasted body, and he was exactly as he had been in life before the sickness that took him off. He lives yet, and is hourly seen and spoken to. You may go see him tomorrow. And now, as nothing more is needed for the purpose, I ask you that which I came to ask, it being but a repetition of what you asked me, O Simonides, What more than a man is this Nazarene?"

The question was put solemnly, and long after midnight the company sat and debated it; Simonides being yet unwilling to give up his understanding of the sayings of the prophets, and Ben-Hur contending that the elder disputants were both right – that the Nazarene was the Redeemer, as claimed by Balthasar, and also the destined king the merchant would have.

"Tomorrow we will see. Peace to you all."

So saying, Ben-Hur took his leave, intending to return to Bethany.

AMRAH TELLS OF A CURE

The first person to go out of the city upon the opening of the Sheep's Gate next morning was Amrah, basket on arm. No questions were asked her by the keepers, since the morning itself had not been more regular in coming than she; they knew her somebody's faithful servant, and that was enough for them.

When at last she reached the King's Garden she slackened her gait; for then the grim city of the lepers was in view, extending far round the pitted south hill of Hinnom.

As the reader must by this time have surmised, she was going to her mistress, whose tomb, it will be remembered, overlooked the well En-rogel.

Early as it was, the unhappy woman was up and sitting outside, leaving Tirzah asleep within. The course of the malady had been terribly swift in the three years. Conscious of her appearance, with the refined instincts of her nature, she kept her whole person habitually covered. Seldom as possible she permitted even Tirzah to see her.

While she sat there peopling the dusky solitude with thoughts even more cheerless, suddenly a woman came up the hill staggering and spent with exertion.

The widow arose hastily, and covering her head, cried, in a voice unnaturally harsh: "Unclean, unclean!"

In a moment, heedless of the notice, Amrah was at her feet. All the long-pent love of the simple creature burst forth: with tears and passionate exclamations she kissed her mistress's garments, and for awhile the latter strove to escape from her; then, seeing she could not, she waited till the violence of the paroxysm was over.

"What have you done, Amrah?" she said. "Is it by such disobedience you prove your love for us? Wicked woman! You are lost; and he – your master – you can never, never go back to him."

Amrah rose to her knees, and said, brokenly and with clasped hands: "O good mistress! I am not wicked. I bring you good tidings."

"Of Judah?" and as she spoke the widow half withdrew the cloth from her head.

"There is a wonderful man," Amrah continued, "who has power to cure you. He speaks a word, and the sick are made well. I have come to take you to Him."

"Poor Amrah!" said Tirzah, compassionately.

"No" cried Amrah, detecting the doubt underlying the expression – "no, as the Lord lives, even the Lord of Israel, my God as well as yours, I speak the truth. Go with me, I pray, and lose no time. This morning He will pass by on His way to the city. See! the day is at hand. Take the food here – eat, and let us go."

The mother listened eagerly. Not unlikely she had heard of the wonderful man, for by this time His fame had penetrated every nook in the land.

"Who is He?" she asked.

"A Nazarene."

"Who told you about Him?"

"Judah."

"Judah told you? Is he at home?"

"He came last night."

The widow, trying to still the beating of her heart, was silent awhile.

"Did Judah send you to tell us this?" she next asked.

"No. He believes you dead."

"There was a prophet once who cured a leper," the mother said thoughtfully to Tirzah; "but he had his power from God." Then addressing Amrah, she asked: "How does my son know this man so possessed?"

"He was travelling with Him, and heard the lepers call, and saw them go away well. First there was one man; then there were ten; and they were all made whole."

The elder listener was silent again. She did not question the performance, for her own son was the witness testifying through the servant; but she strove to comprehend the power by which work so astonishing could be done by a man. With her, however, the hesitation was brief. To Tirzah she said:

"This must be the Messiah!"

She spoke not coldly, like one reasoning a doubt away, but as a woman of Israel familiar with the promises of God to her race – a woman of understanding, ready to be glad over the least sign of the realization of the promises.

"There was a time when Jerusalem and all Judea were filled with a story that He was born. I remember it. By this time he should be a man. It must be – it is He. Yes," she said to Amrah, "we will go with you. Bring the water which you will find in the tomb in a jar, and set the food for us. We will eat and be gone."

The breakfast, partaken under excitement, was soon despatched, and the three women set out on their extraordinary journey. As Tirzah had caught the confident spirit of the others, there was but one fear that troubled the party. Bethany, Amrah said, was the town the man was coming from; now from that to Jerusalem there were three roads, or rather paths – one over the first summit of Olivet, a second at its base, a third between the second summit and the Mount of Offence. The three were not far apart; far enough, however, to make it possible for the unfortunates to miss the Nazarene if they failed the one He chose to come by.

A little questioning satisfied the mother that Amrah knew nothing of the country beyond the Cedron, and even less of the intentions of the man they were going to see, if they could. She discerned, also, that both Amrah and Tirzah – the one from confirmed habits of servitude, the other from natural dependency – looked to her for guidance; and she accepted the charge.

"We will go first to Bethphage," she said to them. "There, if the Lord favour us, we may learn what else to do."

"I am afraid of the road," the matron said. "Better that we keep to the country among the rocks and trees. This is feast-day, and on the hillsides yonder I see

JEWISH COSTUME

signs of a great multitude in attendance. By going across the Mount of Offence here we may avoid them."

Tirzah had been walking with great difficulty; upon hearing this her heart began to fail her.

"Go on with Amrah, mother, and leave me here," she said, faintly.

"No, no, Tirzah. What would the gain be to me if I were healed and you not? When Judah asks for you, as he will, what would I have to say to him were I to leave you?"

"Tell him I loved him."

The elder leper gazed about her with that sensation of hope perishing which is more nearly like annihilation of the soul than anything else. The supremest joy of the thought of cure was inseparable from Tirzah, who was not too old to forget, in the happiness of healthful life to come, the years of misery by which she had been so reduced in body and broken in spirit. Even as the brave woman was about leaving the venture they were engaged in to the determination of God, she saw a man on foot coming rapidly up the road from the east.

"Courage, Tirzah! Be of cheer," she said. "Yonder I know is one to tell us of the Nazarene."

Amrah helped the girl to a sitting posture, and supported her while the man advanced.

"In your goodness, mother, you forget what we are. The stranger will go around us; his best gift to us will be a curse, if not a stone."

"We will see."

There was no other answer to be given, since the mother was too well and sadly acquainted with the treatment outcasts of the class to which she belonged were accustomed to at the hands of her countrymen.

As has been said, the road at the edge of which the group was posted was little more than a worn path or trail, winding crookedly through tumuli of limestone. If the stranger kept it, he must meet them face to face; and he did so, until near enough to hear the cry she was bound to give. Then, uncovering her head, a further demand of the law, she shouted shrilly:

"Unclean, unclean!"

To her surprise, the man came steadily on.

"What would you have?" he asked, stopping opposite them not four yards off.

"Thou seest us. Have a care," the mother said, with dignity.

"Woman, I am the courier of Him who speaketh but once to such as thou and they are healed. I am not afraid."

"The Nazarene?"

"The Messiah," he said.

"Is it true that He cometh to the city today?"

"He is now at Bethphage."

"On what road, master?"

"This one."

She clasped her hands, and looked up thankfully.

"For whom takest thou Him?" the man asked, with pity.

"The Son of God," she replied.

"Stay thou here then; or, as there is a multitude with Him, take thy stand by the rock yonder, the white one under the tree; and as He goeth by fail not to call to Him; call, and fear not. If thy faith but equal thy knowledge, He will hear thee though all the heavens thunder. I go to tell Israel, assembled in and about the city, that He is at hand, and to make ready to receive Him. Peace to thee and thine, woman."

He went on, and they went slowly to the rock he had pointed out to them, high as their heads, and scarcely thirty yards from the road on the right. Standing in front of it, the mother satisfied herself they could be seen and heard plainly by passers-by whose notice they desired to attract. There they cast themselves under the tree in its shade, and drank of the gourd, and rested refreshed. Ere long Tirzah slept, and, fearing to disturb her, the others held their peace.

A REUNION

During the third hour the road in front of the resting-place of the lepers became gradually more and more frequented by people going in the direction of Bethphage and Bethany; now, however, about the commencement of the fourth hour, a great crowd appeared over the crest of Olivet, and as it defiled down the road thousands in number, the two watchers noticed with wonder that everyone in it carried a palm-branch freshly cut. As they sat absorbed by the novelty, the noise of another multitude approaching from the east drew their eyes that way. Then the mother awoke Tirzah.

"What is the meaning of it all?" the latter asked.

"He is coming," answered the mother. "These we see are from the city going to meet Him; those we hear in the east are His friends bearing him company; and it will not be strange if the processions meet here before us."

Meantime the people in the east came up slowly. When at length the foremost of them were in sight, the gaze of the lepers fixed upon a man riding in the midst of what seemed a chosen company which sang and danced about him in extravagance of joy. The rider was bareheaded and clad all in white. When he was in distance to be more clearly observed, these, looking anxiously, saw an olive-hued face shaded by long chestnut hair slightly sunburned and parted in the middle. He looked neither to the right nor left. There was no need of anyone to tell the lepers that this was He – the wonderful Nazarene!

"He is here, Tirzah," the mother said; "He is here. Come, my child."

As she spoke she glided in front of the white rock and fell upon her knees.

The moment of the meeting of the hosts was come, and with it the opportunity the sufferers were seeking; if not taken, it

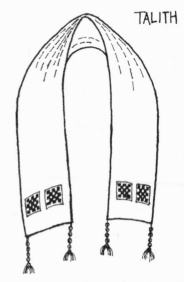

TALITH

would be lost for ever, and they would be lost as well.

"Nearer, my child – let us get nearer. He cannot hear us," said the mother.

She arose, and staggered forward. Her ghastly hands were up, and she screamed with horrible shrillness. The people saw her – saw her hideous face, and stopped awe-struck – an effect for which extreme human misery, visible as in this instance, is as potent as majesty in purple and gold. Tirzah, behind her a little way, fell down too faint and frightened to follow farther.

"The lepers! the lepers!"

"Stone them!"

"The accursed of God! Kill them!"

These, with other yells of like import, broke in upon the hosannas of the part of the multitude too far removed to see and understand the cause of the interruption. Some of them were, however, near by familiar with the nature of the man to whom the unfortunates were appealing – some who, by long intercourse with Him, had caught somewhat of His divine compassion: they gazed at Him, and were silent while, in fair view, He rode up and stopped in front of the woman. She also beheld His face – calm, pitiful, and of exceeding beauty, the large eyes tender with benignant purpose.

And this was the colloquy that ensued:

"O Master, Master! Thou seest our need; Thou canst make us clean. Have mercy upon us – mercy!"

"Believest thou I am able to do this?" He asked.

"Thou art He of whom the prophets spake – Thou art the Messiah!" she replied.

His eyes grew radiant, His manner confident.

"Woman," He said, "great is thy faith; be it unto thee even as thou wilt."

He lingered an instant after, apparently unconscious of the presence of the throng – an instant – then He rode away.

"To God in the highest glory! Blessed, thrice blessed, the Son whom He hath given us!"

Immediately both the hosts, that from the city and that from Bethphage, closed around Him with their joyous demonstrations, with hosannas and waving of palms, and so He passed from the lepers for ever. Covering her head, the elder hastened to Tirzah, and folded her in her arms, crying: "Daughter, look up! I have His promise; He is indeed the Messiah. We are saved – saved!" And

the two remained kneeling while the procession, slowly going, disappeared over the mount. When the noise of its singing afar was a sound scarcely heard the miracle began.

There was first in the hearts of the lepers a freshening of the blood; then it flowed faster and stronger, thrilling their wasted bodies with an infinitely sweet sense of painless healing. Each felt the scourge going from her; their strength revived; they were returning to be themselves.

To this transformation – for such it may be called quite as properly as a cure – there was a witness other than Amrah. The reader will remember the constancy with which Ben-Hur had followed the Nazarene throughout His wanderings; and now, recalling the conversation of the night before, there will be little surprise at learning that the young Jew was present when the leprous woman appeared in the path of the pilgrims. He heard her prayer, and saw her disfigured face; he heard the answer also, and was not so accustomed to incidents of the kind, frequent as they had been, as to have lost interest in them. At the close of the scene, consequently, Ben-Hur had withdrawn from the procession, and seated himself upon a stone to wait its passage.

From his place he nodded recognition to many of the people – Galileans in his league, carrying short swords under their long abbas. After a little a swarthy Arab came up leading two horses; at a sign from Ben-Hur he also drew out.

"Stay here," the young master said, when all were gone by, even the laggards. "I wish to be at the city early, and Aldebaran must do me service."

He stroked the broad forehead of the horse, now in his prime of strength and beauty, then crossed the road towards the two women.

They were to him, it should be borne in mind, strangers in whom he felt interest only as they were subjects of a superhuman experiment, the result of which might possibly help him to solution of the mystery that had so long engaged him. As he proceeded, he glanced casually at the figure of the little woman over by the white rock, standing there her face hidden in her hands.

"As the Lord liveth, it is Amrah!" he said to himself.

He hurried on, and passing by the

mother and daughter, still without recognizing them, he stopped before the servant.

"Amrah," he said to her, "Amrah, what do you here?"

She rushed forward, and fell upon her knees before him, blinded by her tears, nigh speechless with contending joy and fear.

"O master, master! Thy God and mine, how good He is!"

The woman he had seen before the Nazarene was standing with her hands clasped and eyes streaming, looking towards heaven. The mere transformation would have been a sufficient surprise; but it was the least of the causes of her emotion. Could he be mistaken? Never was there in life a stranger so like his mother; and like her as she was the day the Roman snatched her from him. And who was it by her side, if not Tirzah? – fair, beautiful, perfect, more mature, but in all other respects exactly the same in appearance as when she looked with him over the parapet the morning of the accident to Gratus. Scarcely believing his senses, he laid his hand upon the servant's head, and asked, tremulously:

"Amrah, Amrah – my mother! Tirzah! tell me if I see aright."

"Speak to them, O master, speak to them!" she said.

He waited no longer, but ran, with outstretched arms, crying: "Mother! mother! Tirzah! Here I am!"

They heard his call, and with a cry as loving started to meet him. Suddenly the mother stopped, drew back, and uttered the old alarm:

"Stay, Judah, my son; come not nearer. Unclean, unclean!" He had no such thought. They were before him; he had called them, they had answered. Who or what should keep them from him now? Next moment the three, so long separated, were mingling their tears in each other's arms.

The first ecstasy over, the mother said: "In this happiness, O my children, let us not be ungrateful. Let us begin life anew by acknowledgment of Him to whom we are all so indebted."

They fell upon their knees, Amrah with the rest; and the prayer of the elder outspoken was as a psalm.

Naturally, the mother was the first to think of the cares of life.

"What shall we do now, my son? Where shall we go?"

Then Ben-Hur, recalled to duty, observed how completely every trace of scourge had disappeared from his restored people; that each had back her perfection of person; that, as with Naaman when he came up out of the water, their flesh had come again like unto the flesh of a little child; and he took off his cloak, and threw it over Tirzah.

"Take it," he said, smiling; "the eye of the stranger would have shunned you before, now it shall not offend you."

The act exposed a sword belted to his side.

"Is it a time of war?" asked the mother, anxiously.

"No."

"Why, then, are you armed?"

"It may be necessary to defend the Nazarene."

Thus Ben-Hur evaded the whole truth.

"Has He enemies? Who are they?"

"Alas, mother, they are not all Romans!"

"Is He not of Israel, and a man of peace?"

"There was never one more so; but in the opinion of the rabbis and teachers He is guilty of a great crime."

"What crime?"

"In His eyes the uncircumcised Gentile is as worthy favour as a Jew of the strictest habit. He preaches a new dispensation."

The mother was silent, and they moved to the shade of the tree by the rock. Calming his impatience to have them home again and hear their story, he showed them the necessity of obedience to the law governing in cases like theirs, and in conclusion called the Arab, bidding him take the horses to the gate by Bethesda and await him there; whereupon they set out by the way of the Mount of Offence. The return was very different from the coming; they walked rapidly and with ease, and in good time reached a tomb newly made near that of Absalom, overlooking the depths of Cedron. Finding it unoccupied, the women took possession, while he went on hastily to make the preparations required for their new condition.

THE HEALING

Ben-Hur pitched two tents out on the Upper Cedron east a short space of the Tombs of the Kings, and furnished them with every comfort at his command; and thither, without loss of time, he conducted his mother and sister, to remain until the examining priest could certify their perfect cleansing.

In course of the duty, the young man had subjected himself to such serious defilement as to debar him from participation in the ceremonies of the great feast, then near at hand. He could not enter the least sacred of the courts of the Temple. Of necessity, not less than choice, therefore, he stayed at the tents with his beloved people. There was a great deal to hear from them, and a great deal to tell them of himself.

At odd moments the excited schemer found a pleasure in fashioning a speech for the Nazarene:

"Hear, O Israel! I am He, the promised of God, born King of the Jews – come to you with the dominion spoken of by the prophets. Rise now, and lay hold on the world!"

Would the Nazarene but speak these few words, what a tumult would follow! How many mouths performing the office of trumpets would take them up and blow them abroad for the massing of armies!

Would He speak them?

WOUNDED VANITY

Ben-Hur alighted at the gate of the khan from which the three Wise Men more than thirty years before departed, going down to Bethlehem. There, in keeping of his Arab followers, he left the horse, and shortly after was at the wicket of his father's house, and in a yet briefer space in the great chamber. He called for Malluch first; that worthy being out, he sent a salutation to his friends the mer-

chant and the Egyptian. They were being carried abroad to see the celebration. The latter, he was informed, was very feeble, and in a state of deep dejection.

While the servant was answering for the elder, the curtain of the doorway was drawn aside, and the younger Egyptian came in, and walked – or floated, upborne in a white cloud of the gauzy raiment she so loved and lived in – to the centre of the chamber, where the light cast by lamps from the seven-armed brazen stick planted upon the floor was the strongest. With her there was no fear of light.

The servant left the two alone.

Now the influence of the woman revived with all its force the instant Ben-Hur beheld her. He advanced to her eagerly, but stopped and gazed. Such a change he had never seen.

There are few persons who have not a double nature, the real and the acquired; the latter a kind of addendum resulting from education, which in time often perfects it into a part of the being as unquestionable as the first. Leaving the thought to the thoughtful, we proceed to say that now the real nature of the Egyptian made itself manifest.

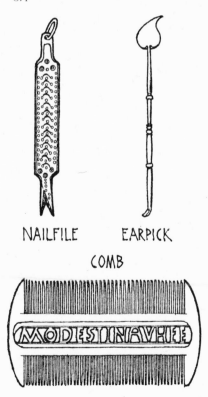

NAILFILE   EARPICK

COMB

It was not possible for her to have received a stranger with repulsion more incisive; yet she was apparently as passionless as a statue, only the small head was a little tilted, the nostrils a little drawn, and the sensuous lower lip pushed the upper the least bit out of its natural curvature.

She was the first to speak.

"Your coming is timely, O son of Hur," she said, in a voice sharply distinct. "I wish to thank you for hospitality; after tomorrow I may not have the opportunity to do so."

Ben-Hur bowed slightly without taking his eyes from her.

Yet very watchful, Ben-Hur answered, lightly: "A man may not balk a woman bent on having her way."

"Tell me," she continued, inclining her head, and permitting the sneer to become positive – "tell me, O prince of Jerusalem, where is He, that son of the carpenter of Nazareth, and son not less of God, from whom so lately such mighty things were expected?"

He waved his hand impatiently, and replied: "I am not His keeper."

The beautiful head sank forward yet lower.

"Has he broken Rome to pieces?"

Again, but with anger, Ben-Hur raised his hand in deprecation.

"I fear you have not entered upon your kingdom – the kingdom I was to share with you."

"The daughter of my wise guest is kinder than she imagines herself; she is teaching me that Isis may kiss a heart without making it better."

Ben-Hur spoke with cold courtesy, and Iras, after playing with the pendant solitaire of her necklet of coins, rejoined: "For a Jew, the son of Hur is clever. I saw your dreaming Caesar make His entry into Jerusalem. You told us He would that day proclaim Himself King of the Jews from the steps of the Temple. I beheld the procession descend the mountain bringing Him. I heard their singing. They were beautiful with palms in motion. I looked everywhere among them for a figure with a promise of royalty – a horseman in purple, a chariot with a driver in shining brass, a stately warrior behind an orbed shield, rivalling his spear in stature. I looked for his guard. It would have been pleasant to have seen a prince of Jerusalem and a cohort of the legions of Galilee."

She flung her listener a glance of provoking disdain, then laughed heartily, as if the ludicrousness of the picture in her mind were too strong for contempt.

"Instead of a Sesostris returning in triumph or a Caesar helmed and sworded – ha, ha, ha! – I saw a man with a woman's face and hair, riding an ass's colt, and in tears. The King! the Son of God! the Redeemer of the world! Ha, ha, ha!"

In spite of himself, Ben-Hur winced.

"Daughter of Balthasar," he said, with dignity, "let us make an end of words. That you have a purpose I am sure. To it, I pray, and I will answer you; then let us go our several ways, and forget we ever met. Say on; I will listen, but not to more of that which you have given me."

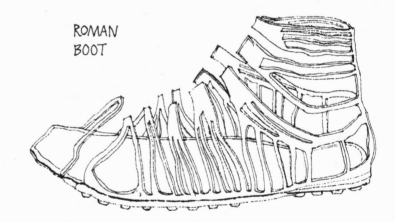

ROMAN
BOOT

She regarded him intently a moment, as if determining what to do – possibly she might have been measuring his will – then she said, coldly: "You have my leave – go."

"Peace to you," he responded, and walked away.

As he was about passing out of the door, she called to him:

"A word."

The pink-stained fingers toyed daintily with the lustrous pendant at the throat, and her voice was exceeding low and soft; only a tapping on the floor with her silken sandal admonished him to have a care.

"There was a Jew, an escaped galley-slave, who killed a man in the Palace of Idernee," she began, slowly.

Ben-Hur was startled.

"The same Jew slew a Roman soldier before the market-place here in Jerusalem; the same Jew has three trained legions from Galilee to seize the Roman governor tonight; the same Jew has alliances perfected for war upon Rome, and Ilderim the Sheik is one of his partners."

Drawing nearer him, she almost whispered:

"You have lived in Rome. Suppose these things repeated in ears we know of. Ah! you change colour."

He drew back from her with somewhat of the look which may be imagined upon the face of a man who, thinking to play with a kitten, has run upon a tiger; and she proceeded:

"You are acquainted in the ante-chamber, and know the Lord Sejanus. Suppose it were told him with the proofs in hand – or without the proofs – that the same Jew is the richest man in the East – nay, in all the empire. The fishes of the Tiber would have fattening other than that they dig out of its ooze, would they not? And while they were feeding – ha! son of Hur! – what splendour there would be on exhibition in the Circus! Keep them amused is another art even finer; and was there ever an artist the equal of the Lord Sejanus?"

Ben-Hur was not too much stirred by the evident baseness of the woman for recollection. The scene at the spring on the way to the Jordan reproduced itself; and he remembered thinking then that Esther had betrayed him, and thinking so now, he said calmly as he could:

"To give you pleasure, daughter of Egypt, I acknowledge your cunning, and that I am at your mercy. It may also please you to hear me acknowledge I have no hope of your favour. I could kill you, but you are a woman. The Desert is open to receive me; and though Rome is a good hunter of men, there she would follow long and far before she caught me, for in its heart there are wildernesses of spears as well as wildernesses of sand, and it is not unlovely to the unconquered Parthian. In the toils as I am – dupe that I have been – yet there is one thing my due: who told you all you know about me? In flight or captivity, dying even, there will be consolation in leaving the traitor the curse of a man who has lived knowing nothing but wretchedness. Who told you all you know about me?"

It might have been a touch of art, or might have been sincere – that as it may – the expression of the Egyptian's face became sympathetic.

She said, presently, "Enough that from this person I gathered a handful of little circumstances, and from that other yet another handful, and that afterwhile I put them together. I had something from Sheik Ilderim as he lay with my father in a grove out in the Desert. The night was still, very still, and the walls of the tent, sooth to say, were poor ward against ears outside listening to – birds and beetles flying through the air."

She smiled at the conceit, but proceeded:

"Some other things – bits of shell for the picture – I had from——"

"Whom?"

"The son of Hur himself."

"Was there no other who contributed?"

"No, not one."

Hur drew a breath of relief, and said, lightly: "Thanks. It were not well to keep the Lord Sejanus waiting for you. The Desert is not so sensitive. Again, O Egypt, peace!"

To this time he had been standing uncovered; now he took the handkerchief from his arm where it had been hanging, and adjusting it upon his head, turned to depart. But she arrested him; in her eagerness, she even reached a hand to him.

"Stay," she said.

He looked back at her, but without taking the hand, though it was very noticeable for its sparkling of jewels; and he knew by her manner that the reserved point of the scene which was so surprising to him was now to come.

She spoke rapidly, and with animation; indeed, she had never appeared to him so fascinating.

"You had once a friend," she continued. "It was in your boyhood. There was a quarrel, and you and he became enemies. He did you wrong. After many year you met him again in the Circus at Antioch."

"Messala!"

"Yes, Messala. You are his creditor. Forgive the past; admit him to friendship again; restore the fortune he lost in the great wager; rescue him. The six talents are as nothing to you; not so much as a bud lost upon a tree already in full leaf; but to him—— Ah, he must go about with a broken body; wherever you meet him he must look up to you from the ground. O Ben-Hur, noble prince! to a Roman descended as he is beggary is the other most odious name for death. Save him from beggary!"

It seemed to him, when at last she paused to have his answer, that he could see Messala himself peering at him over her shoulder; and in its expression the countenance of the Roman was not that of a mendicant or a friend; the sneer was as patrician as ever, and the fine edge of the hauteur as flawless and irritating.

"The appeal has been decided then, and for once a Messala takes nothing. I must go and write it in my book of great occurrences – a judgment by a Roman against a Roman! But did he – did Messala send you to me with this request, O Egypt?"

"He has a noble nature, and judged you by it."

Ben-Hur took the hand upon his arm.

"As you know him in such friendly way, fair Egyptian, tell me, would he do for me, there being a reversal of the conditions, that he asks of me? Answer, by Isis! Answer, for the truth's sake!"

There was insistence in the touch of his hand, and in his look also.

"Oh!" she began, "he is——"

"A Roman, you were about to say; meaning that I, a Jew, must not determine dues from me to him by any measure of dues from him to me; being a Jew, I must forgive him my winnings because he is a Roman.

"If you have more to tell me, daughter of Balthasar, speak quickly, quickly; for by the Lord God of Israel, when this heat of blood, hotter waxing, attains its highest, I may not be able longer to see that you are a woman, and beautiful! I may see but the spy of a master the more hateful because the master is a Roman. Say on, and quickly."

She threw his hand off and stepped back into the full light, with all the evil of her nature collected in her eyes and voice.

"Thou drinker of lees, feeder upon husks! To think I could love thee, having seen Messala! Such as thou were born to serve him. He would have been satisfied with release of the six talents; but I say to the six thou shalt add twenty – twenty, dost thou hear? The merchant here is thy keeper of moneys. If by tomorrow at noon he has not thy order acted upon in favour of my Messala for six-and-twenty talents – mark the sum! – thou shalt settle with the Lord Sejanus. Be wise and – farewell."

As she was going to the door, he put himself in her way.

"The old Egypt lives in you," he said. "Whether you see Messala tomorrow or the next day, here or in Rome, give him this message. Tell him I have back the money, even the six talents, he robbed me of by robbing my father's estate; tell him I survived the galleys to which he had me sent, and in my strength rejoice in his beggary and dishonour; tell him I think the affliction of body which he has from my hand is the curse of our Lord God of Israel upon him more fit than death for his crimes against the helpless; tell him my mother and sister whom he had sent to a cell in Antonia that they might die of leprosy, are alive and well, thanks to the power of the Nazarene whom you so despise; tell him that, to fill my measure of happiness, they are restored to me, and that I will go hence to their love, and find in it more than compensation for the impure passions which you leave me to take to him; tell him – this for your comfort, O cunning incarnate, as much as his – tell him that when the Lord Sejanus comes to despoil me he will find nothing; for the inheritance I had from the duumvir, including the villa by Misenum, has been sold, and the money from the sale is out of reach, afloat in the marts of the world as bills of exchange; and that this house and the goods and merchandise and the ships and caravans with which Simonides plies his commerce with such princely profits are covered by imperial safe-guards; tell him that along with my defiance I do not send him a curse in words, but, as a better expression of my undying hate, I send him one who will prove to him the sum of all curses; and when he looks at you repeating this my message, daughter of Balthasar, his Roman shrewdness will tell him all I mean. Go now – and I will go."

He conducted her to the door, and, with ceremonious politeness, held back the curtain while she passed out.

"Peace to you," he said, as she disappeared.

BETRAYED WITH A KISS

The streets were full of people going and coming, or grouped about the fires roasting meat, and feasting and singing, and happy. The odour of scorching flesh mixed with the odour of cedar-wood aflame and smoking loaded the air; and as this was the occasion when every son of Israel was full brother to every other son of Israel, and hospitality was without bounds, Ben-Hur was saluted at every step, while the groups by the fires insisted, "Stay and partake with us. We are brethren in the love of the Lord." But with thanks to them he hurried on, intending to take horse at the khan and return to the tents on the Cedron.

To make the place, it was necessary for him to cross the thoroughfare so soon to receive sorrowful Christian perpetuation. There also the pious celebration was at its height. Looking up the street, he noticed the flames of torches in motion streaming out like pennons; then he observed that the singing ceased where the torches came. His wonder rose to its highest, however, when he became certain that amidst the smoke and dancing sparks he saw the keener sparkling of burnished spear-tips, arguing the presence of Roman soldiers. What were they, the scoffing legionaries, doing in a Jewish religious procession? The circumstance was unheard of, and he stayed to see the meaning of it.

As the procession began to go by Ben-Hur, his attention was particularly called to three persons walking together. They were well towards the front, and the servants who went before them with lanterns appeared unusually careful in the service. In the person moving on the left of this group he recognized a chief policeman of the Temple; the one on the right was a priest; the middle man was not at first so easily placed, as he walked leaning heavily upon the arms of the others, and carried his head so low upon his breast as to hide his face. His appearance was that of a prisoner not yet recovered from the fright of arrest, or being taken to something dreadful – to torture or death. With great assurance, Ben-Hur fell in on the right of the priest, and walked along with him. Now if the man would lift his head! And presently he did so, letting the light of the lanterns strike full in his face, pale, dazed, pinched with dread; the beard roughed; the eyes filmy, sunken, and despairing. In much going about following the Nazarene, Ben-Hur had come to know his disciples; and now, at sight of the dismal countenance he cried out:

"The 'Scariot!"

Slowly the head of the man turned until his eyes settled upon Ben-Hur, and his lips moved as if he were about to speak; but the priest interfered.

"Who art thou? Begone!" he said to Ben-Hur, pushing him away.

The young man took the push good-naturedly, and waiting an opportunity, fell into the procession again. Thus he was carried passively along down the street, through the crowded lowlands between the hill Bezetha and the Castle of Antonia, and on by the Bethesda reservoir to the Sheep Gate. There were people everywhere, and everywhere the people were engaged in sacred observances.

Down the gorge and over the bridge at the bottom of it. There was a great clatter on the floor as the crowd, now a straggling rabble, passed over beating and pounding with their clubs and staves. A little farther, and they turned off to the left in the direction of an olive orchard enclosed by a stone wall in view from the road. They were all brought to a standstill. Voices called out excitedly in front; a chill sensation ran from man to man; there was a rapid falling back, and a blind stumbling over each other. The soldiers alone kept their order.

It took Ben-Hur but a moment to disengage himself from the mob and run forward. There he found a gateway without a gate admitting to the orchard, and he halted to take in the scene.

A man in white clothes, and bare-headed, was standing outside the entrance, His hands crossed before Him – a slender, stooping figure, with long hair and thin face – in an attitude of resignation and waiting.

It was the Nazarene.

Opposite this most unmartial figure stood the rabble, gaping, silent, awed, cowering – ready at a sign of anger from Him to break and run. And from Him to them – then at Judas, conspicuous in their midst – Ben-Hur looked – one quick glance, and the object of the visit lay open to his understanding. Here was the betrayer, there the betrayed; and these with clubs and staves, and the legionaries, were brought to take Him.

Presently the clear voice of the Christ arose:

"Whom seek ye?"

"Jesus of Nazareth," the priest replied.

"I am He."

At these simplest of words, spoken without passion or alarm, the assailants fell back several steps, the timid among them cowering to the ground; and they might have let Him alone and gone away had not Judas walked over to Him.

"Hail, Master!"

With his friendly speech he kissed Him.

"Judas," said the Nazarene, mildly, "betrayest thou the Son of Man with a kiss? Wherefore art thou come?"

Receiving no reply, the Master spoke to the crowd again.

"Whom seek ye?"

"Jesus of Nazareth."

"I have told you that I am He. If, therefore, you seek Me, let these go their way."

At these words of entreaty the rabbis advanced upon Him; and, seeing their intent, some of the disciples for whom He interceded drew nearer; one of them cut off a man's ear, but without saving the Master from being taken. And yet Ben-Hur stood still. Nay, while the officers were making ready with their ropes the Nazarene was doing His greatest charity – not the greatest in deed, but the very greatest in illustration of His forbearance, so far surpassing that of men.

"Surely He will not allow them to bind Him!"

Thus thought Ben-Hur.

"Put up thy sword into the sheath; the cup which my Father hath given Me, shall I not drink it?" From the offending follower, the Nazarene turned to His captors. "Are you come out as against a thief, with swords and staves to take Me? I was daily with you in the Temple, and you took Me not; but this is your hour, and the power of darkness."

The posse plucked up courage and closed about Him; and when Ben-Hur looked for the faithful they were gone – not one of them remained.

Taking off his long outer garment and the handkerchief from his head, he threw them upon the orchard wall, and started after the posse, which he boldly joined. Through the stragglers he made way, and by littles at length reached the man who carried the ends of the rope with which the prisoner was bound.

The Nazarene was walking slowly, His head down, His hands bound behind Him; the hair fell thickly over His face, and He stooped more than usual; apparently He was oblivious to all going on around Him. In advance a few steps were priests and elders talking and occasionally looking back. When, at length, they were all near the bridge in the gorge, Ben-Hur took the rope from the servant who had it, and stepped past him.

"Master, Master!" he said, hurriedly, speaking close to the Nazarene's ear. "Dost Thou hear, Master? A word – one word. Tell me——"

The fellow from whom he had taken the rope now claimed it.

"Tell me," Ben-Hur continued, "goest Thou with these of Thine own accord?"

The people were come up now, and in his own ears asking angrily, "Who art thou, man?"

"O Master," Ben-Hur made haste to say, his voice sharp with anxiety, "I am Thy friend. Tell me, I pray Thee, if I bring rescue, wilt Thou accept it?"

The Nazarene never so much as looked up or allowed the slightest sign of recognition; yet the something which when we are suffering is always telling it to such as look at us, though they be strangers, failed not now. "Let Him alone," it seemed to say; "He has been abandoned by His friends; the world has denied Him; in bitterness of spirit, He has taken farewell of men; He is going He knows not where, and He cares not. Let Him alone."

And to that Ben-Hur was now driven. A dozen hands were upon him, and from all sides there was shouting, "He is one of them. Bring him along; club him – kill him!"

With a gust of passion which gave him many times his ordinary force, Ben-Hur raised himself, turned once about with his arms outstretched, shook the hands off, and rushed through the circle which was fast hemming him in. The hands snatching at him as he passed tore his garments from his back, so he ran off the road naked; and the gorge, in keeping of the friendly darkness, darker there than elsewhere, received him safe.

Reclaiming his handkerchief and outer garments from the orchard wall, he followed back to the city gate; thence he went to the khan, and on the good horse rode to the tents of his people out by the Tombs of the Kings.

As he rode, he promised himself to see the Nazarene on the morrow – promised it, not knowing that the unfriended man was taken straightway to the house of Hannas to be tried that night.

TIME TO FIGHT

Next morning, about the second hour, two men rode full speed to the doors of Ben-Hur's tents, and dismounting, asked to see him. He was not yet risen, but gave directions for their admission.

"Peace to you, brethren," he said, for they were of his Galileans, and trusted officers. "Will you be seated?"

"Nay," the senior replied, bluntly, "to sit and be at ease is to let the Nazarene die. Rise, son of Judah, and go with us. The judgment has been given. The tree of the cross is already at Golgotha."

Ben-Hur stared at them.

"The cross!" was all he could for the moment say.

His face brightened with resolution, and he clasped his hands.

"The horses – and quickly!" he said to the Arab who answered the signal. "And bid Amrah send me fresh garments, and bring my sword! It is time to die for

Israel, my friends. Tarry without till I come."

He ate a crust, drank a cup of wine, and was soon upon the road.

"Whither would you go first?" asked the Galilean.

"To collect the legions."

"Alas!" the man replied, throwing up his hands.

"Why alas?"

"Master" – the man spoke with shame – "master, I and my friend here are all that are faithful. The rest do follow the priests."

"Seeking what?" and Ben-Hur drew rein.

"To kill Him."

"Not the Nazarene?"

"You have said it."

A dread seized him. It was possible his scheming, and labour, and expenditure of treasure might have been but blasphemous contention with God. When he picked up the reins and said, "Let us go, brethren," all before him was uncertainty. The faculty of resolving quickly, without which one cannot be a hero in the midst of stirring scenes, was numb within him.

"Let us go, brethren; let us to Golgotha."

They passed through excited crowds of people going south, like themselves. All the country north of the city seemed aroused and in motion.

Hearing that the procession with the condemned might be met with somewhere near the great white towers left by

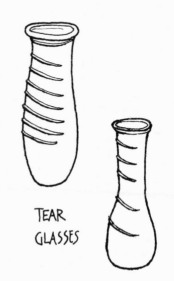

TEAR GLASSES

Herod, the three friends rode thither, passing round south-east of Akra. In the valley below the Pool of Hezekiah, passage-way against the multitude became impossible, and they were compelled to dismount, and take shelter behind the corner of a house and wait.

The waiting was as if they were on a river-bank, watching a flood go by, for such the people seemed.

The going was singularly quiet. A hoof-stroke upon a rock, the glide and rattle of revolving wheels, voices in conversation, and now and then a calling voice, were all the sounds heard above the rustle of the mighty movement.

At length, from the direction of the great towers, Ben-Hur heard, at first faint in the distance, a shouting of many men.

"Hark! they are coming now," said one of his friends.

The people in the street halted to hear; but as the cry rang on over their heads, they looked at each other and in shuddering silence moved along.

The shouting drew nearer each moment; and the air was already full of it and trembling, when Ben-Hur saw the servants of Simonides coming with their master in his chair, and Esther walking by his side; a covered litter was next behind them.

"Peace to you, O Simonides – and to you, Esther," said Ben-Hur, meeting them. "If you are for Golgotha, stay until the procession passes; I will then go with you. There is room to turn in by the house here."

The merchant's large head rested heavily upon his breast; rousing himself, he answered: "Speak to Balthasar; his pleasure will be mine. He is in the litter."

Ben-Hur hastened to draw aside the curtain. The Egyptian was lying within, his wan face so pinched as to appear like a dead man's. The proposal was submitted to him.

"Can we see Him?" he inquired, faintly.

"The Nazarene? yes; He must pass within a few feet of us."

"Dear Lord!" the old man cried, fervently. "Once more, once more! Oh, it is a dreadful day for the world!"

Shortly the whole party were in waiting under shelter of the house. They said but little, afraid, proably, to trust their thoughts to each other; everything was uncertain, and nothing so much so as

opinions. Balthasar drew himself feebly from the litter, and stood supported by a servant; Esther and Ben-Hur kept Simonides company.

Meantime the flood poured along, if anything, more densely than before; and the shouting came nearer, shrill up in the air, hoarse along the earth, and cruel. At last the procession was up.

"See!" said Ben-Hur, bitterly; "that which cometh now is Jerusalem."

A band of legionaries fully armed followed next, marching in sturdy indifference, the glory of burnished brass about them the while.

Then came the Nazarene!

He was nearly dead. Every few steps He staggered as if He would fall. A stained gown badly torn hung from His shoulders over a seamless under-tunic. His bare feet left red splotches upon the stones. An inscription on a board was tied to His neck. A crown of thorns had been crushed hard down upon His head, making cruel wounds from which streams of blood, now dry and blackened, had run over His face and neck. The long hair, tangled in the thorns, was clotted thick. The skin, where it could be seen, was ghastly white. His hands were tied before Him. Back somewhere in the city He had fallen exhausted under the transverse beam of His cross, which, as a condemned person, custom required Him to bear to the place of execution; now a countryman carried the burden in His stead. Four soldiers went with Him as a guard against the mob, who sometimes, nevertheless, broke through, and struck Him with sticks and spat upon Him. Yet no sound escaped Him, neither remonstrance nor groan; nor did He look up until He was nearly in front of the house sheltering Ben-Hur and his friends, all of whom were moved with quick compassion. Esther clung to her father; and he, strong of will as he was, trembled. Balthasar fell down speechless. Even Ben-Hur cried out, "O my God! my God!" Then, as if He divined their feelings or heard the exclamation, the Nazarene turned His wan face towards the party, and looked at them each one, so they carried the look in memory through life. They could see He was thinking of them, not Himself, and the dying eyes gave them the blessing He was not permitted to speak.

"Where are thy legions, son of Hur?" asked Simonides, aroused.

"Hannas can tell thee better than I."

"What, faithless?"

"All but these two."

"Then all is lost, and this good man must die!"

The face of the merchant knit convulsively as he spoke, and his head sank upon his breast. He had borne his part in Ben-Hur's labours well, and he had been inspired by the same hopes, now blown out never to be rekindled.

Two other men succeeded the Nazarene bearing crossbeams.

"Who are these?" Ben-Hur asked of the Galileans.

"Thieves appointed to die with the Nazarene," they replied.

Next in the procession stalked a mitred figure clad all in the golden vestments of the High Priest. Policemen from the Temple curtained him round about; and after him, in order, strode the Sanhedrim, and a long array of priests, the latter in their plain white garments overwrapped by abnets of many folds and gorgeous colours.

"The son-in-law of Hannas," said Ben-Hur, in a low voice.

"Caiaphas! I have seen him," Simonides replied, adding, after a pause during which he thoughtfully watched the haughty pontiff, "And now am I convinced. With such assurance as proceeds from clear enlightenment of the spirit – with absolute assurance – now know I that He who first goes yonder with the inscription about His neck is what the inscription proclaims Him – *King of the Jews*. A common man, an impostor, a felon, was never thus waited upon. For look! Here are the nations – Jerusalem, Israel. Here is the ephod, here the blue robe with its fringe, and purple pomegranates, and golden bells, not seen in the street since the day Jaddua went out to meet the Macedonian – proofs all that this Nazarene is King. Would I could rise and go after Him!"

Ben-Hur listened surprised; and directly, as if himself awakening to his unusual display of feeling, Simonides said, impatiently:

"Speak to Balthasar, I pray you, and let us begone. The vomit of Jerusalem is coming."

Then Esther spoke.

"I see some women there, and they are weeping. Who are they?"

Following the pointing of her hand, the party beheld four women in tears; one of them leaned upon the arm of a man of aspect not unlike the Nazarene's. Presently Ben-Hur answered:

"The man is the disciple whom the Nazarene loves the best of all; she who leans upon his arm is Mary, the Master's mother; the others are friendly women of Galilee."

Esther pursued the mourners with glistening eyes until the multitude received them out of sight.

"Come," said Simonides, when Balthasar was ready to proceed – "come, let us forward."

Ben-Hur did not hear the call. The appearance of the part of the procession then passing, its brutality and hunger for life were reminding him of the Nazarene.

That instant a party of Galileans caught his eye. He rushed through the press and overtook them.

"Follow me," he said. "I would have speech with you."

The men obeyed him, and when they were under shelter of the house, he spoke again:

"You are of those who took my swords, and agreed with me to strike for freedom and the King who was coming. You have the swords now, and now is the time to strike with them. Go, look everywhere, and find our brethren, and tell them to meet me at the tree of the cross making ready for the Nazarene. Haste all of you! Nay, stand not so! The Nazarene is the King, and freedom dies with Him."

They looked at him respectfully, but did not move.

"Hear you?" he asked.

Then one of them replied:

"Son of Judah" – by that name they knew him – "son of Judah, it is you who are deceived, not we or our brethren who have your swords. The Nazarene is not the King; neither has He the spirit of a king. We were with Him when He came into Jerusalem; we saw Him in the Temple; He failed Himself, and us, and Israel; at the Gate Beautiful He turned His back upon God and refused the throne of David. He is not King, and Galilee is not with Him. He shall die the death. But hear you, son of Judah. We have your swords, and we are ready now to draw them and strike for freedom; and so is Galilee. Be it for freedom, O son of Judah, for freedom! and we will meet you at the tree of the cross."

The sovereign moment of his life was upon Ben-Hur. Could he have taken the

offer and said the word, history might have been other than it is; but then it would have been history ordered by men, not God – something that never was, and never will be. A confusion fell upon him; he knew not how, though afterwards he attributed it to the Nazarene; for when the Nazarene was risen, he understood the death was necessary to faith in the resurrection, without which Christianity would be an empty husk. The confusion, as has been said, left him without the faculty of decision; he stood helpless – wordless even. Covering his face with his hand, he shook with the conflict between his wish, which was what he would have ordered, and the power that was upon him.

"Come; we are waiting for you," said Simonides, the fourth time.

Thereupon he walked mechanically after the chair and the litter. Esther walked with him. Like Balthasar and his friends, the Wise Men, the day they went to the meeting in the desert, he was being led along the way.

THE KING OF THE JEWS

When the party – Balthasar, Simonides, Ben-Hur, Esther, and the two faithful Galileans – reached the place of crucifixion, Ben-Hur was in advance leading them.

Ben-Hur came to a stop; those following him also stopped. As a curtain rises before an audience, the spell holding him in its sleep-awake rose, and he saw with a clear understanding.

There was a space upon the top of a low knoll rounded like a skull, and dry, dusty, and without vegetation, except some scrubby hyssop. The boundary of the space was a living wall of men, with men behind struggling, some to look over, other to look through it. An inner wall of Roman soldiery held the dense outer wall rigidly to its place. A centurion kept eye upon the soldiers. Up to the very line so vigilantly guarded Ben-Hur had been led; at the line he now stood, his face to the north-west. The knoll was the old Aramaic Golgotha – in Latin, Calvaria; anglicized, Calvary; translated, The Skull.

All the eyes then looking were fixed upon the Nazarene. It may have been pity with which he was moved; whatever the cause, Ben-Hur was conscious of a change in his feelings. A conception of something better than the best of this life – something so much better that it could serve a weak man with strength to endure agonies of spirit as well as of body; something to make death welcome – perhaps another life purer than this one – perhaps the spirit-life which Balthasar held to so fast, began to dawn upon his mind clearer and clearer, bringing to him a certain sense that, after all, the mission of the Nazarene was that of guide across the boundary for such as loved Him; across the boundary to where His kingdom was set up and waiting for Him. Then, as something borne through

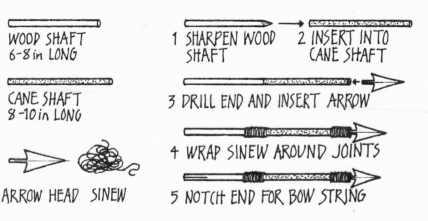

HOW TO MAKE YOUR OWN ARROWS

WOOD SHAFT 6-8 in LONG

CANE SHAFT 8-10 in LONG

ARROW HEAD   SINEW

1 SHARPEN WOOD SHAFT

2 INSERT INTO CANE SHAFT

3 DRILL END AND INSERT ARROW

4 WRAP SINEW AROUND JOINTS

5 NOTCH END FOR BOW STRING

the air out of the almost forgotten, he heard again, or seemed to hear, the saying of the Nazarene:

"I AM THE RESURRECTION AND THE LIFE."

And the words repeated themselves over and over, and took form, and the dawn touched them with its light, and filled them with a new meaning. And as men repeated a question to grasp and fix the meaning, he asked, gazing at the figure on the hill fainting under its crown, Who the Resurrection? and who the Life?

"I AM,"

the figure seemed to say – and say it for him; for instantly he was sensible of a peace such as he had never known – the peace which is the end of doubt and mystery, and the beginning of faith and love and clear understanding.

From this dreamy state Ben-Hur was aroused by the sound of hammering. On the summit of the knoll he observed then what had escaped him before – some soldiers and workmen preparing the crosses. The holes for planting the trees were ready, and now the transverse beams were being fitted to their places.

"Bid the men make haste," said the High Priest to the centurion. "These" – and he pointed to the Nazarene – "must be dead by the going-down of the sun, and buried that the land may not be defiled. Such is the Law."

With a better mind, a soldier went to the Nazarene and offered Him something to drink, but He refused the cup. Then another went to Him and took from his neck the board with the inscription upon it, which he nailed to the tree of the cross – and the preparation was complete.

"The crosses are ready," said the centurion to the pontiff, who received the report with a wave of the hand and the reply:

"Let the blasphemer go first. The Son of God should be able to save Himself. We will see."

The people to whom the preparation in its several stages was visible, and who to this time had assailed the hill with incessant cries of impatience, permitted a lull which directly became a universal hush. The part of the infliction most shocking, at least to the thought, was reached – the men were to be nailed to

their crosses. When for that purpose the soldiers laid their hands upon the Nazarene first, a shudder passed through the great concourse; the most brutalized shrank with dread. Afterwards there were those who said the air suddenly chilled and made them shiver.

"How very still it is!" Esther said, as she put her arm about her father's neck.

And remembering the torture he himself had suffered, he drew her face down upon his breast, and sat trembling.

"Avoid it, Esther, avoid it!" he said. "I know not but all who stand and see it – the innocent as well as the guilty – may be cursed from this hour."

Balthasar sank upon his knees.

"Son of Hur," said Simonides, with increasing excitement – "son of Hur, if Jehovah stretch not forth His hand, and quickly, Israel is lost – and we are lost."

Ben-Hur answered, calmly: "I have been in a dream, Simonides, and heard in it why all this should be, and why it should go on. It is the will of the Nazarene – it is God's will. Let us do as the Egyptian here – let us hold our peace and pray."

As he looked up on the knoll again, the words were wafted to him through the awful stillness:

"I AM THE RESURRECTION AND THE LIFE."

He bowed reverently as to a person speaking.

Up on the summit meantime the work went on. The guard took the Nazarene's clothes from Him; so that He stood before the millions naked. The stripes of the scourging He had received in the early morning were still bloody upon His back; yet He was laid pitilessly down, and stretched upon the cross – first, the arms upon the transverse beam; the spikes were sharp – a few blows, and they were driven through the tender palms; next, they drew His knees up until the soles of the feet rested flat upon the tree; then they placed one foot upon the other, and one spike fixed both of them fast. The dulled sound of the hammering was heard outside the guarded space; and such as could not hear, yet saw the hammer as it fell, shivered with fear. And withal not a groan, or cry, or word of remonstrance from the sufferer: nothing at which an enemy could laugh; nothing a lover could regret.

"Which way wilt thou have Him faced?" asked a soldier, bluntly.

"Towards the Temple," the pontiff replied. "In dying I would have Him see the holy house hath not suffered by Him."

The workmen put their hands to the cross, and carried it, burden and all, to the place of planting. At a word, they dropped the tree into the hole; and the body of the Nazarene also dropped heavily, and hung by the bleeding hands. Still no cry of pain – only the exclamation divinest of all recorded exclamations:

"Father, forgive them, for they know not what they do."

The cross, reared now above all other objects, and standing singly out against the sky, was greeted with a burst of delight; and all who could see and read the writing upon the board over the Nazarene's head made haste to decipher it. Soon as read, the legend was adopted by them and communicated, and presently the whole mighty concourse was ringing the salutation from side to side, and repeating it with laughter and groans:

"King of the Jews! Hail, King of the Jews!"

The pontiff, with a clearer idea of the import of the inscription, protested against it, but in vain; so the titled King, looking from the knoll with dying eyes, must have had the city of His fathers at rest below Him – she who had so ignominiously cast Him out.

The sun was rising rapidly to noon; the hills bared their brown breasts lovingly to it; the more distant mountains rejoiced in the purple with which it so regally dressed them. In the city, the temples, palaces, towers, pinnacles, and all points of beauty and prominence seemed to lift themselves into the unrivalled brilliance, as if they knew the pride they were giving the many who from time to time turned to look at them. Suddenly a dimness began to fill the sky and cover the earth – at first no more than a scarce perceptible fading of the day; a twilight out of time; an evening gliding in upon the splendours of noon. But it deepened, and directly drew attention; whereat the noise of the shouting and laughter fell off, and men, doubting their senses, gazed at each other curiously: then they looked to the sun again; then at the mountains, getting farther away; at the sky and the near landscape, sinking in shadow; at the hill upon which the tragedy was enacting; and from all these they gazed at each other again, and turned pale, and held their peace.

"It is only a mist or passing cloud," Simonides said soothingly to Esther, who was alarmed. "It will brighten presently."

Ben-Hur did not think so.

"It is not a mist or a cloud," he said. "The spirits who live in the air – the prophets and saints – are at work in mercy to themselves and nature. I say to you, O Simonides, truly as God lives, He who hangs yonder is the Son of God."

And leaving Simonides lost in wonder at such a speech from him, he went where Balthasar was kneeling near by, and laid his hand upon the good man's shoulder.

"O wise Egyptian, hearken! Thou alone wert right – the Nazarene is indeed the Son of God."

Balthasar drew him down to him, and replied, feebly: "I saw Him a child in the manger where He was first laid; it is not strange that I knew Him sooner than thou; but O that I should live to see this day! Would I had died with my brethren! Happy Melchior! Happy, happy Gaspar!"

"Comfort thee!" said Ben-Hur. "Doubtless they too are here."

The dimness went on deepening into obscurity, and that into positive darkness, but without deterring the bolder spirits upon the knoll. One after the other the thieves were raised on their crosses, and the crosses planted. The guard was then withdrawn, and the people set free closed in upon the height, and surged up it, like a converging wave. A man might take a look, when a newcomer would push him on, and take his place, to be in turn pushed on – and there were laughter and ribaldry and revilements, all for the Nazarene.

The supernatural night, dropped thus from the heavens, affected Esther as it began to affect thousands of others, braver and stronger.

"Let us go home," she prayed – twice, three times – saying: "It is the frown of God, father. What other dreadful things may happen, who can tell? I am afraid."

Simonides was obstinate. He said little, but was plainly under great excitement. Observing, about the end of the first hour, that the violence of the crowding up on the knoll was somewhat abated, at his suggestion the party advanced to take position nearer the crosses. Ben-Hur gave his arm to Balthasar; yet the

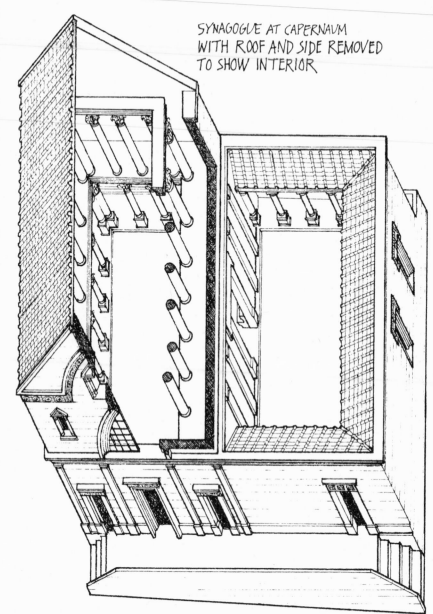

SYNAGOGUE AT CAPERNAUM WITH ROOF AND SIDE REMOVED TO SHOW INTERIOR

Egyptian made the ascent with difficulty. From their new stand, the Nazarene was imperfectly visible, appearing to them not more than a dark suspended figure. They could hear Him, however – hear His sighing, which showed an endurance or exhaustion greater than that of His fellow-sufferers; for they filled every lull in the noises with their groans and entreaties.

The second hour after the suspension passed like the first one. To the Nazarene they were hours of insult, provocation, and slow dying. He spoke but once in the time. Some women came and knelt at the foot of His cross. Among them He recognized His mother with the beloved disciple.

"Woman," He said, raising His voice, "behold they son!" And to the disciple, "Behold thy mother!"

The third hour came, and still the

people surged round the hill, held to it by some strange attraction, with which, in probability, the night in midday had much to do. They were quieter than in the preceding hour; yet at intervals they could be heard off in the darkness shouting to each other, multitude calling unto multitude. It was noticeable, also, that coming now to the Nazarene, they approached His cross in silence, took the look in silence, and so departed. This change extended even to the guard, who so shortly before had cast lots for the clothes of the crucified; they stood with their officers a little apart, more watchful of the one convict than of the throngs coming and going. If He but breathed heavily, or tossed His head in a paroxysm of pain, they were instantly on the alert. Most marvellous of all, however, was the altered behaviour of the High Priest and his following, the wise men who had assisted him in the trial in the night, and, in the victim's face, kept place by him with zealous approval. When the darkness began to fall, they began to lose their confidence. There were among them many learned in astronomy, and familiar with the apparitions so terrible in those days to the masses; much of the knowledge was descended to them from their fathers far back; some of it had been brought away at the end of the Captivity; and the necessities of the Temple service kept it all bright. These closed together when the sun commenced to fade before their eyes, and the mountains and hills to recede; they drew together in a group around their pontiff, and debated what they saw. "The moon is at its full," they said, with truth, "and this cannot be an eclipse." Then, as no one could answer the question common with them all – as no one could account for the darkness, or for its occurrence at that particular time, in their secret hearts they associated it with the Nazarene, and yielded to an alarm which the long continuance of the phenomenon steadily increased. In their place behind the soldiers, they noted every word and motion of the Nazarene, and hung with fear upon His sighs, and talked in whispers. The man might be the Messiah, and then – But they would wait and see!

In the meantime Ben-Hur was not once visited by the old spirit. The perfect peace abode with him. He prayed simply that the end might be hastened. He knew the condition of Simonides' mind – that

he was hesitating on the verge of belief. He could see the massive face weighed down by solemn reflection. He noticed him casting inquiring glances at the sun, as seeking the cause of the darkness. Nor did he fail to notice the solicitude with which Esther clung to him, smothering her fears to accommodate his wishes.

"Be not afraid," he heard him say to her; "but stay and watch with me. Thou mayst live twice the span of my life, and see nothing of human interest equal to this; and there may be revelations more. Let us stay to the close."

When the third hour was about half gone, some men of the rudest class – wretches from the tombs about the city – came and stopped in front of the centre cross.

"This is He, the new King of the Jews," said one of them.

The others cried, with laughter: "Hail, all hail, King of the Jews!"

Receiving no reply, they went closer.

"If Thou be King of the Jews, or Son of God, come down," they said, loudly.

At this, one of the thieves quit groaning, and called to the Nazarene: "Yes, if Thou be Christ, save Thyself and us."

The people laughed and applauded; then, while they were listening for a reply, the other felon was heard to say to the first one: "Dost thou not fear God? We receive the due rewards of our deeds; but this man hath done nothing amiss."

The bystanders were astonished; in the midst of the hush which ensued, the second felon spoke again, but this time to the Nazarene:

"Lord," he said, "remember me when Thou comest into Thy kingdom."

Simonides gave a great start. "When Thou comest into Thy kingdom!" It was the very point of doubt in his mind; the point he had so often debated with Balthasar.

"Didst thou hear?" said Ben-Hur to him. "The kingdom cannot be of this world. Yon witness saith the King is but going to His kingdom; and, in effect, I heard the same in my dream."

"Hush!" said Simonides, more imperiously than ever before in speech to Ben-Hur. "Hush, I pray thee! If the Nazarene should answer——"

And as he spoke the Nazarene did answer, in a clear voice, full of confidence:

"Verily I say unto thee, Today shalt thou be with Me in Paradise!"

Simonides waited to hear if that were all; then he folded his hands and said: "No more, no more, Lord! The darkness is gone; I see with other eyes – even as Balthasar, I see with eyes of perfect faith."

The faithful servant had at last his fitting reward. His broken body might never be restored; nor was there riddance of the recollection of his sufferings, or recall of the years embittered by them; but suddenly a new life was shown him, with assurance that it was for him – a new life lying just beyond this one – and its name was Paradise. There he would find the Kingdom of which he had been dreaming, and the King. A perfect peace fell upon him.

The breathing of the Nazarene grew harder; His sighs became great gasps. Only three hours upon the cross, and He was dying!

The intelligence was carried from man to man, until every one knew it; and then everything hushed; the breeze faltered and died; a stifling vapour loaded the air; heat was superadded to darkness; nor might any one unknowing the fact have thought that off the hill, out under the overhanging pall, there were three millions of people waiting awe-struck what should happen next – they were so still!

Then there went out through the gloom, over the heads of such as were on the hill within hearing of the dying man, a cry of despair, if not reproach:

"My God! my God! why hast Thou forsaken Me?"

The voice startled all who heard it. One it touched uncontrollably.

The soldiers in coming had brought with them a vessel of wine and water, and set it down a little way from Ben-Hur. With a sponge dipped into the liquor, and put on the end of a stick, they could moisten the tongue of a sufferer at their pleasure. Ben-Hur thought of the draught he had had at the well near Nazareth; an impulse seized him; catching up the sponge, he dipped it into the vessel, and started for the cross.

"Let Him be!" the people in the way shouted, angrily. "Let Him be!"

Without minding them, he ran on, and put the sponge to the Nazarene's lips.

Too late, too late!

The face then plainly seen by Ben-Hur, bruised and black with blood and dust as it was, lighted nevertheless with a sudden glow; the eyes opened wide, and fixed upon some one visible to them alone in the far heavens; and there were content and relief, even triumph, in the shout the victim gave.

"It is finished! It is finished!"

So a hero, dying in the doing a great deed, celebrates his success with a last cheer.

The light in the eyes went out; slowly the crowned head sank upon the labouring breast. Ben-Hur thought the struggle over; but the fainting soul recollected itself, so that he and those around him caught the other and last words spoken in a low voice, as if to one listening close by:

"Father, into Thy hands I commend my spirit,"

A tremor shook the tortured body; there was a scream of fiercest anguish, and the mission and the earthly life were over at once. The heart, with all its love, was broken; for of that O reader, the man died!

Ben-Hur went back to his friends, saying simply, "It is over; He is dead."

In a space incredibly short the multitude was informed of the circumstance. No one repeated it aloud; there was a murmur which spread from the knoll in every direction; a murmur that was little more than a whispering, "He is dead! He is dead!" and that was all. The people had their wish; the Nazarene was dead; yet they stared at each other aghast. His blood was upon them! And while they stood staring at each other, the ground commenced to shake; each man took hold of his neighbour to support himself; in a twinkling the darkness disappeared, and the sun came out; and everybody, as with the same glance, beheld the crosses upon the hill all reeling drunken-like in the earthquake. They beheld all three of them; but the one in the centre was arbitrary; it alone would be seen; and for that it seemed to extend itself upwards, and lift its burden, and swing it to and fro higher and higher in the blue of the sky. And every man among them who had jeered at the Nazarene; everyone who had struck Him; everyone who had voted to crucify Him; everyone who had marched in the procession from the city; everyone who had in his heart wished Him dead, and they were as ten to one, felt that he was in some way individually singled out from the many, and that if he would live he must get away quickly as possible from

that menace in the sky. They started to run; they ran with all their might; on horseback, and camels, and in chariots they ran, as well as on foot; but then, as if it were mad at them for what they had done, and had taken up the cause of the unoffending and friendless dead, the earthquake pursued them, and tossed them about, and flung them down, and terrified them yet more by the horrible noise of great rocks grinding and rending beneath them. They beat their breasts and shrieked with fear. His blood was upon them. The home-bred and the foreign, priest and layman, beggar, Sadducee, Pharisee, were overtaken in the race, and tumbled about indiscriminately. If they called on the Lord, the outraged earth answered for Him in fury, and dealt them all alike. It did not even know wherein the High Priest was better than his guilty brethren; overtaking him, it tripped him up also, and smirched the fringing of his robe and filled the golden bells with sand, and his mouth with dust. He and his people were alike in the one thing at least – the blood of the Nazarene was upon them all.

When the sunlight broke upon the crucifixion, the mother of the Nazarene, the disciple, and the faithful women of Galilee, the centurion and his soldiers, and Ben-Hur and his party, were all who remained upon the hill. These had not time to observe the flight of the multitude; they were too loudly called upon to take care of themselves.

"Seat thyself here," said Ben-Hur to Esther, making a place for her at her father's feet. "Now cover thine eyes, and look not up; but put thy trust in God, and the spirit of yon just man so foully slain."

"Nay," said Simonides, reverently, "let us henceforth speak of Him as the Christ."

"Be it so," said Ben-Hur.

Presently a wave of the earthquake struck the hill. The shrieks of the thieves upon the reeling crosses were terrible to hear. Though giddy with the movement of the ground, Ben-Hur had time to look at Balthasar, and beheld him prostrate and still. He ran to him and called – there was no reply. The good man was dead. Then Ben-Hur remembered to have heard a cry in answer, as it were, to the scream of the Nazarene in his last moment; but he had not looked to see from whom it had proceeded; and ever after he believed the spirit of the Egyptian accompanied that of his Master

over the boundary into the kingdom of Paradise. The idea rested not only upon the cry heard, but upon the exceeding fitness of the distinction. If faith were worthy reward in the person of Gaspar, and love in that of Melchior, surely he should have some special meed who through a long life and so excellently illustrated the three virtues in combination – Faith, Love, and Good Works.

The servants of Balthasar had deserted their master; but when all was over, the two Galileans bore the old man in his litter back to the city.

It was a sorrowful procession that entered the south gate of the palace of the Hurs about the set of sun that memorable day. About the same hour the body of Christ was taken down from the cross.

The remains of Balthasar were carried to the guest-chamber. All the servants hastened weeping to see him; for he had the love of every living thing with which he had in anywise to do; but when they beheld his face, and the smile upon it, they dried their tears, saying: "It is well. He is happier this evening than when he went out in the morning."

Ben-Hur would not trust a servant to inform Iras what had befallen her father. He went himself to see her and bring her to the body. He imagined her grief; she would now be alone in the world; it was a time to forgive and pity her. He remembered he had not asked why she was not of the party in the morning, or where she was; he remembered he had not thought of her; and, from shame, he was ready to make any amends, the more so as he was about to plunge her into such acute grief.

He shook the curtains of her door; and though he heard the ringing of the little bells echoing within, he had no response;

he called her name, and again he called –
still no answer. He drew the curtain
aside and went into the room; she was
not there. He ascended hastily to the roof
in search of her; nor was she there. He
questioned the servants; none of them
had seen her during the day. After a
long quest everywhere through the house,
Ben-Hur returned to the guest-chamber,
and took the place by the dead which
should have been hers; and he bethought
him there how merciful the Christ had
been to his aged servant. At the gate of
the kingdom of Paradise happily the
afflictions of his life, even its desertions,
are left behind and forgotten by those
who go in and rest.

When the gloom of the burial was nigh
gone, on the ninth day after the healing,
the law being fulfilled, Ben-Hur brought
his mother and Tirzah home; and from
that day, in that house the most sacred
names possible of utterance by men were
always coupled worshipfully together:

GOD THE FATHER AND CHRIST THE
SON.

FIVE YEARS LATER

MIRROR

About five years after the crucifixion,
Esther, the wife of Ben-Hur, sat in her
room in the beautiful villa by Misenum.
It was noon, with a warm Italian sun
making summer for the roses and vines
outside. Everything in the apartment
was Roman, except that Esther wore the
garments of a Jewish matron. Tirzah and
two children at play upon a lion's skin
on the floor were her companions; and
one had only to observe how carefully
she watched them to know that the little
ones were hers.

Time had treated her generously. She
was more than ever beautiful, and in
becoming mistress of the villa, she had
realized one of her cherished dreams.

In the midst of this simple, home-like
scene, a servant appeared in the doorway, and spoke to her.

"A woman in the atrium to speak with
the mistress."

"Let her come. I will receive her here."

Presently the stranger entered. At
sight of her the Jewess arose, and was
about to speak; then she hesitated,
changed colour, and finally drew back,
saying: "I have known you, good woman.
You are——"

"I was Iras, the daughter of Balthasar."

Esther conquered her surprise, and
bade the servant bring the Egyptian a
seat.

"No," said Iras, coldly. "I will retire
directly."

The two gazed at each other. We know
what Esther presented – a beautiful
woman, a happy mother, a contented
wife. On the other side, it was very plain
that fortune had not dealt so gently with
her former rival. The tall figure remained
with some of its grace; but an evil life
had tainted the whole person. The face
was coarse, the large eyes were red and
pursed beneath the lower lids; there was
no colour in her cheeks. The lips were
cynical and hard and general neglect
was leading rapidly to premature old age.
Her attire was ill chosen and draggled.
The mud of the road clung to her sandals.
Iras broke the painful silence.

"These are thy children?"

Esther looked at them, and smiled.

"Yes. Will you not speak to them?"

"I would scare them," Iras replied.
Then she drew closer to Esther, and seeing her shrink, said: "Be not afraid. Give
thy husband a message for me. Tell him
his enemy is dead, and that for the much
misery he brought me I slew him."

"His enemy!"

"The Messala. Further, tell thy husband that for the harm I sought to do him I have been punished until even he would pity me."

Tears arose in Esther's eyes, and she was about to speak.

"Nay," said Iras, "I do not want pity or tears. Tell him, finally, I have found that to be a Roman is to be a brute. Farewell!"

She moved to go. Esther followed her.

"Stay, and see my husband. He has no feeling against you. He sought for you everywhere. He will be your friend. I will be your friend. We are Christians."

The other was firm.

"No; I am what I am of choice. It will be over shortly."

"But" – Esther hesitated – "have we nothing you would wish; nothing to – to——"

The countenance of the Egyptian softened; something like a smile played about her lips. She looked at the children upon the floor.

"There is something," she said.

Esther followed her eyes, and with quick perception answered, "It is yours."

Iras went to them, and knelt on the lion's skin, and kissed them both. Rising slowly, she looked at them; then passed to the door and out of it without a parting word. She walked rapidly, and was gone before Esther could decide what to do.

Ben-Hur, when he was told of the visit, knew certainly what he had long surmised – that on the day of the crucifixion Iras had deserted her father for Messala. Nevertheless, he set out immediately and hunted for her vainly; they never saw her more, or heard of her. The blue bay, with all its laughing under the sun, has yet its dark secrets. Had it a tongue, it might tell us of the Egyptian.

Simonides lived to be a very old man. In the tenth year of Nero's reign, he gave up the business so long centred in the warehouse at Antioch. To the last he kept a clear head and a good heart, and was successful.

One evening, in the year named, he sat in his armchair on the terrace of the warehouse. Ben-Hur and Esther, and their three children, were with him. The last of the ships swung at mooring in the current of the river; all the rest had been sold. In the long interval between this and the day of the crucifixion but one sorrow had befallen them: that was

when the mother of Ben-Hur died; and then and now their grief would have been greater but for their Christian faith.

The ship spoken of had arrived only the day before, bringing intelligence of the persecution of Christians begun by Nero in Rome, and the party on the terrace were talking of the news when Malluch, who was still in their service, approached and delivered a package to Ben-Hur.

"Who brings this?" the latter asked, after reading.

"An Arab."

"Where is he?"

"He left immediately."

"Listen," said Ben-Hur to Simonides.

He read then the following letter:

"*I, Ilderim, the son of Ilderim the Generous, and sheik of the tribe of Ilderim, to Judah, son of Hur.*

"*Know, O friend of my father's, how my father loved you. Read what is herewith sent, and you will know. His will is my will; therefore what he gave is thine.*

"*All the Parthians took from him in the great battle in which they slew him I have retaken – this writing, with other things, and vengeance, and all the brood of that Mira who in his time was mother of so many stars.*

"*Peace be to you and all yours.*

"*This voice out of the desert is the voice of*
"ILDERIM, *Sheik*."

Ben-Hur next unrolled a scrap of papyrus yellow as a withered mulberry-leaf. Proceeding, he read:

"*Ilderim, surnamed the Generous, sheik of the tribe of Ilderim, to the son who succeeds me.*

"*All I have, O son, shall be thine in the day of thy succession, except that property by Antioch known as the Orchard of Palms; and it shall be to the son of Hur who brought us such glory in the Circus – to him and his for ever.*

"*Dishonour not thy father.*
"ILDERIM THE GENEROUS, *Sheik*."

"What say you?" asked Ben-Hur of Simonides.

Esther took the papers pleased, and read them to herself. Simonides remained silent. His eyes were upon the ship; but he was thinking. At length he spoke.

"Son of Hur," he said, gravely, "the Lord has been good to you in these later

years. You have much to be thankful for. Is it not time to decide finally the meaning of the gift of the great fortune now all in your hand, and growing?"

"I decided that long ago. The fortune was meant for the service of the Giver; not a part, Simonides, but all of it. The question with me has been, how can I make it most useful in His cause? And of that tell me, I pray you."

Simonides answered:

"The great sums you have given to the Church here in Antioch, I am witness to. Now, instantly almost with this gift of the generous sheik's, comes the news of the persecution of the brethren in Rome. It is the opening of a new field. The light must not go out in the capital."

"Tell me how I can keep it alive."

"I will tell you. The Romans, even this Nero, hold two things sacred – I know of no others they so hold – they are the ashes of the dead and all places of burial. If you cannot build temples for the worship of the Lord above ground, then build them below the ground; and to keep them from profanation, carry to them the bodies of all who die in the faith."

Ben-Hur rose excitedly.

"It is a great idea," he said. "I will not wait to begin it. Time forbids waiting. The ship that brought the news of the suffering of our brethren shall take me to Rome. I will sail tomorrow."

He turned to Malluch.

"Get the ship ready, Malluch, and be thou ready to go with me."

"It is well," said Simonides.

"And thou, Esther, what sayest thou?" asked Ben-Hur.

Esther came to his side, and put her hand on his arm, and answered:

"So wilt thou best serve the Christ. O my husband, let me not hinder, but go with thee and help."

If any of my readers, visiting Rome, will make the short journey to the Catacomb of San Calixto, which is more ancient than that of San Sebastiano, he will see what became of the fortune of Ben-Hur, and give him thanks. Out of that vast tomb Christianity issued to supersede the Caesars.

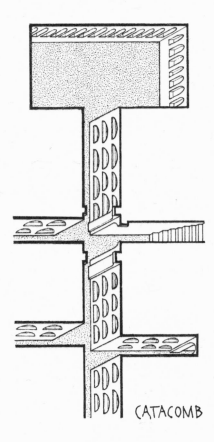

CATACOMB

CHARACTERS IN THE BOOK

Ben-Hur's household

Ben-Hur
: Hero. Jewish, handsome, strong, brave, rich. Also called Judah, son of Ithamar, adopted son of Arrius.

His mother
: A woman of great dignity, miraculously cured of leprosy after a terrible time in prison.

Tirzah
: Beautiful young sister of Ben-Hur. Also miraculously cured of leprosy.

Amrah
: Old nurse of the Hur family. Devoted to them all.

Simonides' household

Simonides
: Former servant of Ithamar, Ben-Hur's father. Shrewd but honest, crippled by torture, he becomes the hero's staunchest adviser.

Esther
: Attractive daughter of Simonides. In love with Ben-Hur.

Malluch
: Faithful attendant of Simonides, loyal companion to Ben-Hur.

The three wise men

Gaspar
: The Greek

Melchior
: The Hindu

Balthasar
: The Egyptian. The Wise Men became in later tradition the Three Kings, but the Gospels say nothing of their names or their numbers. Balthasar survives the other two and dies at the scene of the Crucifixion at the same time as Christ.

Iras
: Daughter of Balthasar. A conniving minx who, too late, repents her sins.

Sheik Ilderim
: Called the Generous. A wily old desert fox, friend to Balthasar, purveyor of chariot, horses and help to Ben-Hur.

Sirius
: Favourite horse of Sheik Ilderim

Sanballat
: A respectable Jew

The Romans

Messala
: Childhood friend, adult sworn-enemy of Ben-Hur. Arrogant, selfish, brave, beautiful, rich.

Valerius Gratus
: Procurator of Judea and Samaria AD14–25. Ben-Hur's accidental "assassination" attempt of V.G. led to the "fall of the House of Hur".

Quintus Arrius
: A good man. Military commander. Adoptive father of Ben-Hur.

Maxentius
: Consul, in whose honour the Games are held, passing through Jerusalem on way to do battle with the Parthians.

Drusus
: Friend of Messala and gambler at the Games.

Gesius
: Keeper of the prisoners in the Tower of Antonia. An honest man.

Herod the Great
: King of the Jews, mistrusted for his Greek ideas. Died 4 BC after ordering the slaughter of all infants in Bethlehem.

There are many others who appear briefly, of whom the most important is *Jesus Christ*. *Joseph of Nazareth, Mary* and *John the Baptist* (the Nazarite) all carry out their Biblical roles. *Thord the Northman* brings a whiff of the gladiatorial ring into the book before he retires to his wineshop near the Circus Maximus. *Rabbi Samuel*, a Zealot, makes a brief appearance; so do the wondering and unnamed *shepherds* who watched their flocks by night.

GLOSSARY

Note: The editor has included only those instances which might cause puzzlement to the reader or which are in themselves of especial interest.

Abaddon – a Hebrew word meaning "destruction."

aplustre – fan-like ornament on the upper part of the stern of a ship.

apple of Sodom – said to turn to ashes when eaten. Compare the poem "The Fire-Worshippers" by Thomas Moore: "Like Dead Sea fruits, that tempt the eye. But turn to ashes on the lips!"

Avernus – a lake in Campania in Italy which filled the crater of an extinct volcano and emitted supposedly poisonous fumes. It was thought to lead to the Underworld.

Bacchae – also called "Maenads", they were in Greek mythology priestesses of Dionysus (Bacchus), the god of wine. At the Dionysiac festivals they worked themselves into a frenzy with wine and religious euphoria.

Bethabara – village to the south of the Sea of Galilee at a ford over the river Jordan.

Bethany – a village to the east of Jerusalem.

Bethphage – a village probably situated just north-west of Bethany.

Brahman – a member of the priestly caste of Hindus. Brahm or Brahma is the Supreme Being or Universal Soul in Hinduism. *See also* Sudra.

bulbul – the eastern song-thrush.

Byzantium – Constantinople (Istanbul).

Catacomb of St. Calixtus – A network of underground tombs of the Christian community in Rome. They lie a little outside the walls of the city to the South, on the Appian Way.

caravan – a company travelling together in the desert for protection.

Chalcedon – a city almost facing Byzantium on the opposite side of the Sea of Marmora.

Chersonese – literally "land-island, peninsula" – in this case the Crimea.

Circus Maximus – the most splendid of the arenas for chariot and horse racing in Rome. The shape of the circus was like a very elongated U, 3 *stadia* long and 1 *stadium* across (i.e. about 606 yds × 202 yds). The Circus Maximus was enormous and is said at various times to have been able to contain 150,000, 260,000 and 385,000 spectators. Other Circuses seem to have been built on very similar lines.
See also the Race.

Consul – At any time in Rome there were two consuls. The Consulship had been the highest office in the state, and the power which went with it was almost boundless, both in the civil and military fields. In the Empire, however, its power and influence waned, largely because the appointment of consuls was used by the emperors merely as a convenient way of rewarding their friends.

Consus – an ancient Roman divinity, sometimes identified with Neptune.

Crucifixion – was not a Jewish form of execution of criminals. It was introduced by the Romans and reserved for the punishment of slaves and the worst malefactors. Scourging was usual as part of the punishment, but in Christ's case it was peculiar, being performed before sentence was pronounced.

Cythera – an island off the extreme southern tip of the Greek Peloponnese.

decurion – a junior officer, in charge of a troop (*decuries*) of 10 horse-soldiers.

denarius – a small Roman silver coin weighing about ⅛ oz. From the initial of its name came the familiar letter for a penny in the old British £sd system.

dowar – A small encampment of Arab tents grouped in a circle round a central enclosure for the cattle.

dragoman – An interpreter and guide in countries where Arabic, Turkish or Persian is spoken.

duumvir – a special magistrate appointed (*duumvir navalis*) for equipping and repairing the fleet. *See also tribune.*

editor – this was a special term used for the person who exhibited a gladiatorial show. In *Ben-Hur* he seems to have been more a Master of Ceremonies.

Edom – *see Idumaeans*

Elias – also called Elijah. *Malachi* iv.5: "Behold, I will send you Elijah the prophet before the coming of the great and dreadful day of the Lord." And, of John the Baptist, *John* i.21: "And they asked him, What then? Art thou Elias? And he saith, I am not. Art thou that prophet? And he answered, No."

Essenes – with the Pharisees and Sadducees the Essenes were one of three philosophical Jewish sects. Some scholars have identified them with Christians; others have said that much of Christ's teaching derived from them; yet others have totally refuted these views. The Essenes, who are not mentioned in the Scriptures, sought after complete purity and freedom from material things. They lived somewhat monastic lives in country districts, embracing a mysticism and a secrecy that has made it hard to discover very much about them.

Ethnarch – A governor of a nation or people; a ruler over a province. (e.g. Caesar appointed a governor over the Jews whom they called Ethnarch; Pompey set up Hyrcanus as high priest and ruler, under the title of Ethnarch.)

Euxine – the Black Sea. Literally it means "friendly to strangers".

frankincense – a fragrant gum, distilled from small trees, called *Boswellia*, which grow in Africa, Arabia and India.

Gamaliel – a Pharisee, a doctor of law, and a great teacher. St Paul says (Acts xxii.3): "I am verily a man which am a Jew, born in Tarsus, a city in Cilicia, yet brought up in this city at the feet of Gamaliel, and taught according to the perfect manner of the law of the fathers . . ."

groves of Athene – Greece or Athens.

Hinnom, valley of – also called Gehenna. This unpleasant spot lay just outside the south-west walls of Jerusalem and was once used for the worship of the Ammonite god Moloch, to whom children were sacrificed. After these horrible rites had been abolished, the Jews, considering the valley desecrated, used it as a dump for all kinds of refuse, including animal carcases and the corpses of executed criminals. Fires were kept burning there continuously to destroy the rubbish. The stench and the undying flames made the valley of Hinnom the symbol of future punishment.

hortator – literally "encourager". Doubtless his "encouragement" of the galley slaves was sometimes painful.

houdah – A litter carried by a camel or an elephant.

Idumaeans – or Edomites. This Semitic race which inhabited the Sinai Peninsula was for long bitterly opposed to the Jews; but in the 1st Century BC, under Antipater and Herod the Great, they became blended into one nation.

Jabbok – a tributary of the river Jordan, running in from the east.

jet – pitch-black, shiny mineral substance, similar in composition to anthracite and formerly much used for decoration.

XII. Kal. Jul – Roman dating for 21 June.

Kedron – "the brook Cedron" ran south between Jerusalem and the Mount of Olives near the Garden of Gethsemane.

lanista-taught – the *lanistae* were the trainers of gladiators. Gladiators were often slaves but, under the Empire freemen and even, amazingly, women fought in the arena.

leben – An Arab drink of coagulated sour milk.

Levites – one of the 12 tribes of Israel. Various minor services of the Temple were allotted to them, but it was to one Levite family, the descendants of Aaron, that the priesthood was confined, normally. Hence Ben-Hur's dilemma.

Maccabees – a family which under Judas Maccabaeus revolted against the Syrian rule of Judea. Under them the country became virtually independent of its oppressors. Judas Maccabaeus was killed in 160 BC.

Messala – this patrician family had for long been distinguished in Roman society. The Messala who fought at Philippi was Marcus Valerius Messala Corvinus. He died about AD 1.

Mizraim – the Hebrew name for Egypt. Traditionally Mizraim was a grandson of Noah and a son of Ham.

Moab – land on the South-East coast of the Dead Sea.

myrrh – an ingredient of the Holy Oil, but also used in perfumes and for embalming. It is a gum resin obtained from a small tree (*Commiphora myrrha*) found in Arabia and Ethiopia.

Myrtilus – the charioteer of Oenomaus, king of Pisa in Elis. The king had been told by an oracle that he would be killed by his son-in-law. Determined not to suffer this fate, he offered the hand of his daughter Hippodamia to whoever could beat him in the chariot race, on the condition that he who lost should die. As he had the swiftest horses in the world he felt assured of victory – and of no sons-in-law. However, after several suitors had failed in the race and been slain, Pelops arrived and bribed Myrtilus to help him conquer Oenomaus, offering him half his kingdom. Myrtilus was persuaded and extracted the linchpins from his king's chariot. In the ensuing race Oenomaus was thrown out and killed. Pelops, however, did not intend to keep his promise to Myrtilus, and one day, driving along a cliff-top, he threw the charioteer into the sea. As Myrtilus sank he cursed Pelops and his race.

nard – a) An aromatic plant. b) An ointment or balsam derived from the plant of the same name.

Nazarene – native of Nazareth.

Nazarite – totally unconnected with Nazarene. A Nazarite was an individual who had consecrated his life to God. He lived a life of extreme asceticism, abstaining from all wine and strong drink, shunning pollution from dead bodies and allowing his hair to grow uncut. Full details of his obligations are set out in *Numbers* vi.

nebel – A Hebrew musical instrument resembling a harp or dulcimer.

Oceanides – nymphs of the ocean, who were lower-ranked female gods.

Padan-aram – the plain of Syria. The "promise of the Lord" was given to Jacob in the vision of the ladder (*Genesis* xxviii. 13–14): "I am the Lord God of Abraham thy father, and the God of Isaac: the land whereon thou liest, to thee will I give it and to thy seed; And thy seed shall be as the dust of the earth, and thou shalt spread abroad to the west, and to the east, and to the north, and to the south: and in thee and in thy seed shall all the families of the earth be blessed."

palaestra – part of a gymnasium, an open area where the art of wrestling was learnt.

Parcae – the three Fates: Clotho, Lachesis and Atropos.

Parthians – people of north-east Persia.

Passover – this great Jewish Festival is in remembrance of the national deliverance from Egyptian bondage. It lasts for a week in April, and its main outward celebration was the selection of a first-year male lamb or kid for each Paschal company (between 10 and 20 persons). The lamb or kid was killed and eaten with unleavened bread, its blood being poured round the Altar of Burnt-Offering. Today the ceremony contents itself with a token offering.

Pharaoh – meaning 'great house' this name was given to the rulers of Ancient Egypt. The accession of the first Pharaoh of the First Dynasty was in 3407 BC. The last Dynasty, the 33rd, from 323–30 BC was that of the Macedonian Ptolemies, and the last of the Ptolemies was the renowned and beautiful Cleopatra.

Pharisees – a Jewish sect which strictly observed the Mosaic Law *and* the additional tradition imposed on it by Rabbinical scholars. They were accused of insincerity and, in several passages of the Gospels, roundly abused by Christ. Though primarily a religious organization, they were politically opposed to the followers of Herod the Great and to the Roman authority in Judea. Despite Christ's censure, it must be remembered that they had good points to be admired and that both St Paul and Gamaliel were Pharisees.

Pilate's new aqueduct – it was intended by the Romans to finance this out of the Corban or Sacred Fund of the Temple.

Pillars – the Pillars of Hercules, the two great rocks of Gibraltar and Ceuta which guard the narrow entrance to the Mediterranean.

Pontius Pilate – succeeded Valerius Gratus as prefect of Judaea in AD 26. His insistent introduction of Roman standards into Jerusalem and his disregard for Jewish property made him extremely unpopular.

Propontis – the Sea of Marmora.

proselyte – a Gentile (i.e. one not of the Jewish race) converted to Judaism. The "sons of Mizraim" (Egyptians) and also Edomites (Idumaeans) could, after three generations as Proselytes of the Gate (a sort of associate membership), become Proselytes of Righteousness, circumcised, baptised, admitted to the full religious privileges and charged with the entire obligations of the Mosaic Law. They were not, however, considered heirs to the promises made to Abraham and his seed.

pugilist – boxing and wrestling, apart from their practice as manly sports, became in professional hands extremely vicious, popular with spectators of the Empire. The boxers wore gloves (*caestus*) on their hands and forearms, which were made of thick ox-hide thongs, and were frequently loaded with lead and iron, making them lethal weapons capable of inflicting appalling injuries – hence the scars on Thord's face.

the Race – At the great chariot race in *Ben-Hur* there were six competing charioteers (*aurigae*). In this story each chariot, except Ben-Hur's, had an accompanying horseman, though they appear to be purely ceremonial. More commonly the horseman was actually used to urge on the horses of his party's chariot and to clear the course in front of the advancing chariot. Normally at the start of the race the gates of the stalls opened, and the chariots surged forward. The chariots in *Ben-Hur* were drawn by four horses (*quadriga*). The two inner and stronger horses were attached to the yoke-pole of the chariot, while the two outer trace-horses were kept in check merely by long reins. The chariot itself was two-wheeled, shaped like a U, open at the back closed at the front, and very light.

Ravenna – city of northern Italy. The emperor Augustus made it one of the two chief stations of the Roman fleet.

rhamnus – today the name *Rhamnus* refers to the buckthorn shrub. But here the author probably means just a thorny hedge.

rivers of Babylon – according to *Psalm* cxxxvii: "By the rivers of Babylon, there we sat down, yea, we wept, when we remembered Zion." This psalm recollects the steadfastness of the Jews in captivity.

Sadducees – Jewish religious sect, opposed to the Pharisees, and believing in moderate and rational views. They took the strict observance of Judaism as their yardstick, refuting its later Rabbinical traditions. But their literal interpretation of the Scriptures and their refusal to countenance the accretions of tradition led to their becoming narrow-minded rationalists. John the Baptist condemned them, together with the Pharisees, as a "generation of vipers", and Christ, even though the Sadducees opposed his teachings less than the Pharisees, could still heap scorn on them.

Sanhedrin – the great "Council" of the Jewish Church, which held chief authority "in all causes and over all persons, ecclesiastical and civil". It was composed of equal numbers (24 each) of priests, scribes and elders – all of whom were married and over 30 years old. The Romans took away from it the power of life and death, but during the period covered by the tale of *Ben-Hur* they respected its other decrees.

Sejanus – favourite and dominating influence throughout most of the reign of the emperor Tiberius (AD 14–37). His ambition was to become emperor, but at last Tiberius realized what his favourite intended, and Sejanus was executed.

Semele, the drunken son of – Dionysus (Bacchus), the god of wine, and the son of Zeus and Semele.

Sesostris – the Pharaoh Khekeure Sesusri (1998–1959 BC). This remarkable man made military expeditions up the Nile to the second cataract to subdue the negroes, who were preparing to invade Egypt. He also voyaged victoriously along the coast of the Indian Ocean, and subsequently led his armies to the frontiers of Syria, successfully defeating Bedouin tribes on his way. His successor, Amenemhet the Third (1959–1910 BC), was the Pharaoh whose dreams Joseph (of the Coat of Many Colours) interpreted.

sestertius – a Roman silver coin worth $\frac{1}{4}$ denarius. (*See denarius*)

Shastras – sacred Hindu writings.

shekel – the shekel was a Jewish weight of about $\frac{1}{2}$ oz. There were 3,000 shekels to one talent. The shekel was also a silver coin of this weight.

Shema – the Jewish confession of faith, "Hear, O Israel".

slavery – the Mosaic Law, by which Jews were bound, recognized the institution of slavery. Surprisingly the New Testament nowhere condemns it, though its condemnation is implicit in Christ's teaching that all men are equal.

solarium – a sundial. Here a navigational instrument.

Sopherim – Hebrew for "scribes", one of the three constituents of the Sanhedrin. Their business was to interpret the Scriptures, but they went far beyond reasonable bounds, adding intolerable interpretations to the Mosaic Law. Jesus roundly and terribly condemns them, together with the Pharisees (*Matthew* xxiii. 33): "Ye serpents, ye generation of vipers, how can ye escape the damnation of hell?"

Sudra – the lowest of the four great Hindu castes. The others, in ascending order are Vaisyas (traders and farmers), Kshatriyas (aristocracy and warriors), and Brahmans (priests, *see above*).

Sylla – the dictator Lucius Sulla Felix (138–78 BC), a cruel and sensual man, with a great love of literature and a magnificent military commander.

Tarquin – probably Lucius Tarquinius Superbus, 7th king of Rome, a part-legendary figure of the 6th century BC. A cruel tyrant, he was banished in 510 BC. After marching against Rome, he was defeated at Lake Regillus, and died after fleeing to Cumae. (On the other hand the author may be referring to Lucius Tarquinius Priscus, the 5th king of Rome, a more enlightened ruler, who among other positive acts built the vast sewer at Rome, the *cloaca maxima*, which can still be seen.)

talent – see shekel

Triad – in Hinduism Brahma, the Supreme Being, works through three gods (the Trimurti or Triad): Brahma the Creator, Vishnu the Preserver, and Siva the Destroyer.

tribune – probably in this reference to Quintus Arrius it means a military tribune. Normally a tribune was one of 10 magistrates in Rome who represented the interests of the people to the Senate. These *tribuni plebis* were extremely powerful and highly honoured. Since to be a duumvir (*see above*) would not have been as great an honour as tribuneship, the author must mean, when he calls Arrius a tribune, some lesser honour, such as military command.

Trachonitis – a mountain area to the east of the Sea of Galilee.

Trumpets, Feast of – the first Jewish feast in October (Tishri): "And in the seventh month, on the first day of the month, ye shall have an holy convocation; ye shall do no servile work: it is a day of blowing the trumpets unto you." *Numbers* xxix.1.

velaria – these were awnings stretched over the more important seats at the Circus to protect their occupants from the weather.

vexillum purpureum – the standard or flag used by smaller divisions of the troops. It was purple (*purpureum*) to show its allegiance to the emperor.

wady – Arab name for the dried and rocky bed of a river which would become filled by a torrent in the wet season.

Xerxes – king of Persia (485–465 BC), called Ahasuerus in the Bible. In 480 BC he invaded Greece and defeated a handful of Spartans under Leonidas at the Pass of Thermopylae. His fleet, however, was defeated by the Greeks at Salamis in the same year, and he retreated with part of his forces.

year of Rome 747 – the traditional foundation of Rome by Romulus was in 753 BC, and the Romans calculated their dates from that time.

Zealots – Jewish nationalists bitterly opposed to Herod the Great and the Roman occupation of Judaea. In several rebellions they were brutally oppressed.

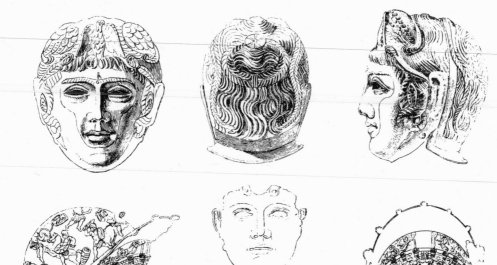

BOOKS FOR FURTHER READING AND SOURCES OF ILLUSTRATIONS

A. Reifenberg, *Ancient Hebrew Arts*. Schocken Books, New York 1950.

C. Blumlein, *Bilder aus dem romisch-germanischen kulturleben*. Verlag Von R. Oldenbourg, Berlin 1918.

M. Wilson, *The Roman toga*. The Johns Hopkins Press, Baltimore.

J. W. Benson, *Time and timetellers*. Robert Hardwicke 1875.

Antiquity and Survival, (the Holy Land) Vol. II no. 2/3. The Hague and Jerusalem 1957.

A. Forestier, *Roman soldier*. A. & C. Black, London 1928.

Edwin R. Goodenough, *Symbolism in the Duva synagogue* (3 vols). Bollinger series xxvii Pantheon Books, New York 1967.

Y. Yadin, *Masada*. Weidenfeld & Nicolson, London 1966.

J. P. V. D. Balsdon, *Life and leisure in ancient Rome*. The Bodley Head, London 1969.

M. Grant, *Gladiators*. Weidenfeld & Nicolson, London 1967.

B. Landström, *The ship*. Allen & Unwin, London 1961.

A. Adams, *Roman antiquities*. Thomas Tegg, London 1836.

L. Casson, *Ships and seamanship in the ancient world*. Princeton Univ. Press 1971.

B. Flower & E. Rosenbaum, *The Roman cookery book*. Harrap, London 1958.

L. Lindenschmit, *Tracht und Bewaffnung des romischen Heeres während der Kaiserzeit*. Brunswick 1882.

H. M. D. Parker, *The Roman legions*. W. Heffer, Cambridge 1961.

G. R. Watson, *The Roman soldier*. Thames & Hudson, London 1969.

W. Ramsay, *Manual of Roman antiquities*. Charles Griffin, London 1898.

W. Smith, *Greek and Roman antiquities*. Taylor and Walton, London 1842.

W. Corswant *A dictionary of life in Bible times* (trans. A. Heathcote). Hodder & Stoughton, London 1960.

Giulio Giannelli (ed.), *The world of ancient Rome*. Putnam, New York 1967.

Webster, *The Roman Imperial army*. A. & C. Black, London 1969.

M. Avi-Yonan, *A history of the Holy Land*. Weidenfeld & Nicolson, London 1969.

V. E. Paoli, *Rome: its people, life and customs*. Longmans, London 1963.

Aegyptisches Museum, Berlin; British Museum, London; Rijksmuseum van Outheiden, Leyden; Israel Maritime Museum, Haifa; Louvre, Paris.

The illustration on this page comes from L. Lindenschmit, Tracht und Bewaffnung des Römischen Heeres während der Kaiserzeit.

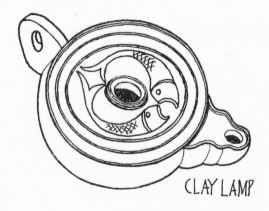

CLAY LAMP

Lew Wallace (1827–1905) wrote *Ben-Hur*, when he was Governor of the
new Union State of New Mexico. The novel was first published in 1880.
This edition has been edited, annotated and abridged by
Robin S. Wright B.A.(Oxon.)

LEW WALLACE

BEN-HUR